PSYCHIC POWER NANAKI™

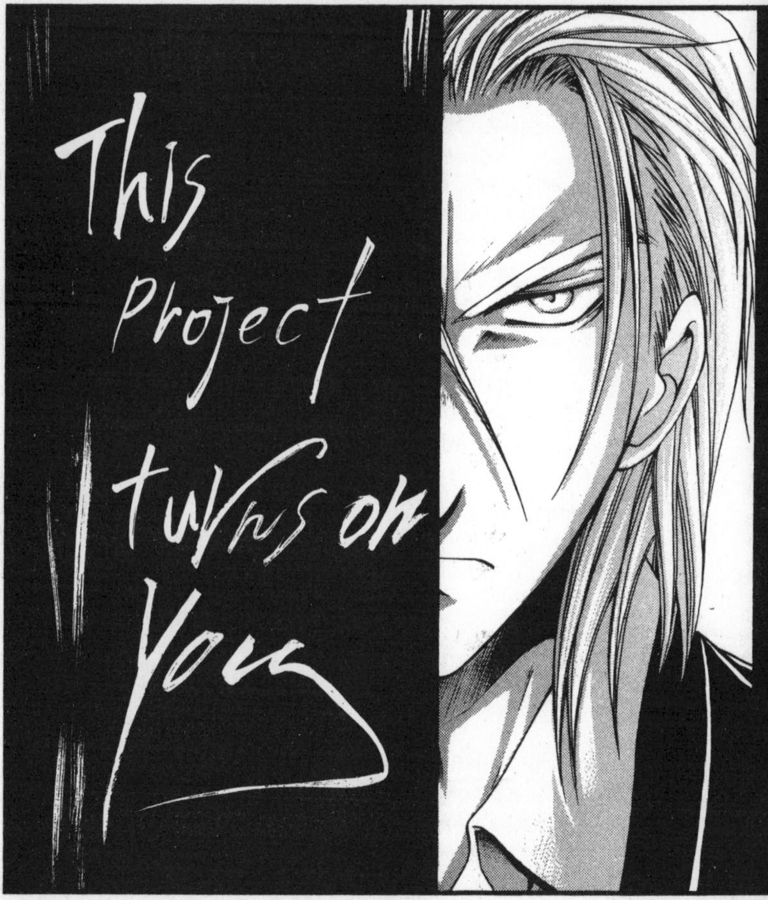
This Project turns on You

Psychic Power Nanaki Volume 3
Created By Ryo Saenagi

Translation - Elina Ishikawa
English Adaptation - Alex de Campi
Retouch and Lettering - Star Print Brokers
Production Artist - Keila N. Ramos
Graphic Designer - James Lee
Copy Editor - Jessica Chavez

Editor - Peter Ahlstrom
Digital Imaging Manager - Chris Buford
Pre-Production Supervisor - Lucas Rivera
Production Manager - Elisabeth Brizzi
Managing Editor - Vy Nguyen
Art Director - Anne Marie Horne
Editor-in-Chief - Rob Tokar
Publisher - Mike Kiley
President and C.O.O. - John Parker
C.E.O. and Chief Creative Officer - Stu Levy

A  Manga

TOKYOPOP and  are trademarks or registered trademarks of TOKYOPOP Inc.

TOKYOPOP Inc.
5900 Wilshire Blvd. Suite 2000
Los Angeles, CA 90036

E-mail: info@TOKYOPOP.com
Come visit us online at www.TOKYOPOP.com

CHOU SHINRIGENSHOU NOURYOKUSHA NANAKI by Ryo Saenagi
© 2002 Ryo Saenagi
All rights reserved.
First published in Japan in 2005 by HAKUSENSHA, INC., Tokyo
English language translation rights in the United States of America
and Canada arranged with HAKUSENSHA, INC., Tokyo through Tuttle-
Mori Agency Inc., Tokyo
English text copyright © 2008 TOKYOPOP Inc.

ISBN: 978-1-4278-0306-1
First TOKYOPOP printing: July 2008
10 9 8 7 6 5 4 3 2 1
Printed in the USA

PSYCHIC POWER NANAKI™

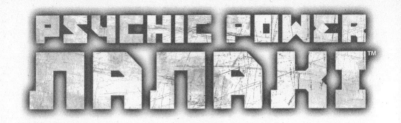

Volume 3

by
Ryo Saenagi

TOKYOPOP®

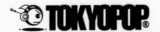

HAMBURG // LONDON // LOS ANGELES // TOKYO

PSYCHIC POWER NANAKI™

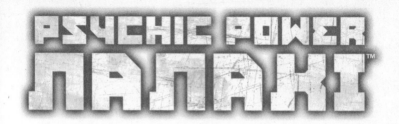

CONTENTS

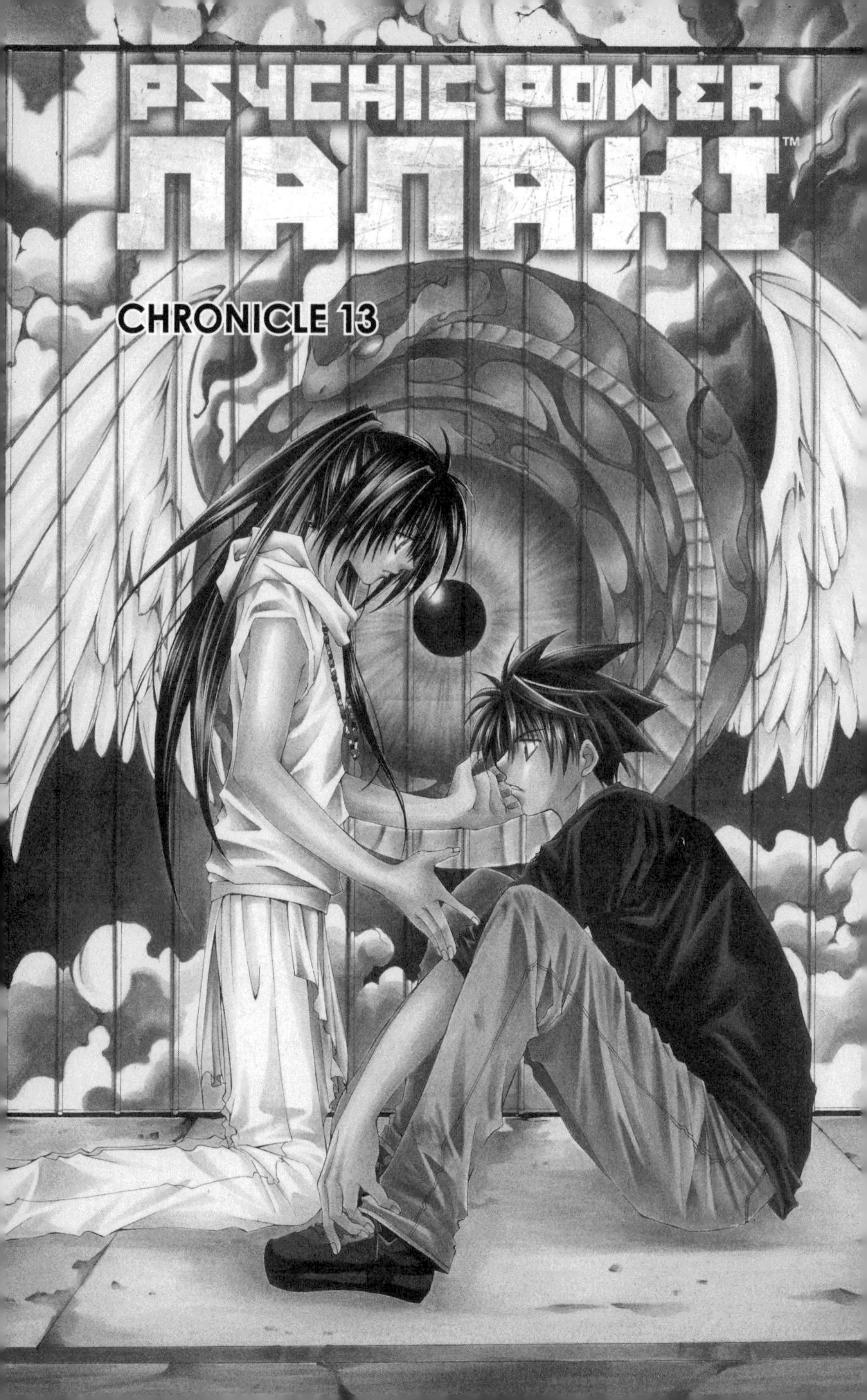
PSYCHIC POWER
NANAKI™
CHRONICLE 13

THE STORY SO FAR...

When an auto accident awakens a mysterious power within high school teen Shunsuke Nanaki, he discovers he's a psychic! The Paranormal Task Force, the LOCK Agency, recruits him to help solve supernatural mysteries and pairs him up with Ao Kudo. Ao is at first reluctant to work with the brash and reckless teenager, but Nanaki's creativity and resourcefulness during a couple tough cases (and his useful teleportation ability) convince Ao he's not so bad. However, Nanaki soon learns of the dangers and temptations facing a psychic—it's all too easy to get drunk on the power and turn into a "freak"...something which apparently happened to Ao's former partner, who has disappeared. In addition, it seems that Ao, along with his possession of healing powers and the ability to morph a rod into any object, also bears one power that's more of a curse than a blessing—although he's already an adult, he will eternally look like a teenager...

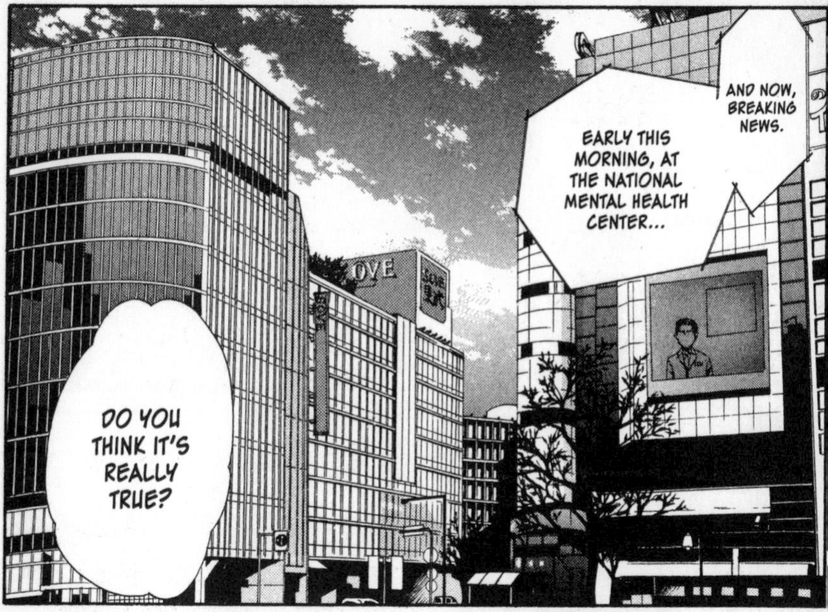
AND NOW, BREAKING NEWS.
EARLY THIS MORNING, AT THE NATIONAL MENTAL HEALTH CENTER...
DO YOU THINK IT'S REALLY TRUE?

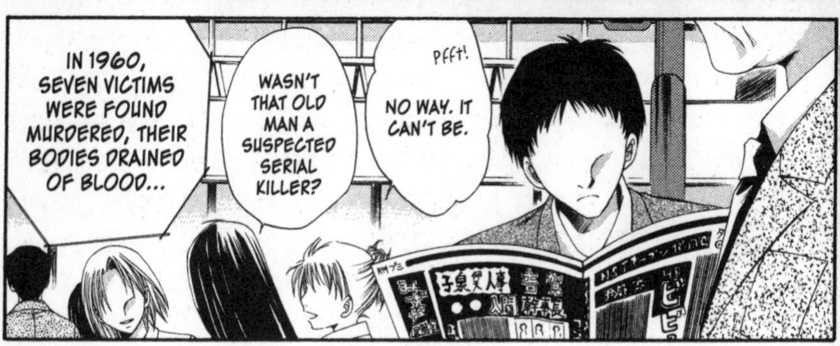
PFFT!
NO WAY. IT CAN'T BE.
WASN'T THAT OLD MAN A SUSPECTED SERIAL KILLER?
IN 1960, SEVEN VICTIMS WERE FOUND MURDERED, THEIR BODIES DRAINED OF BLOOD...

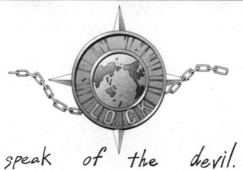

speak of the devil.

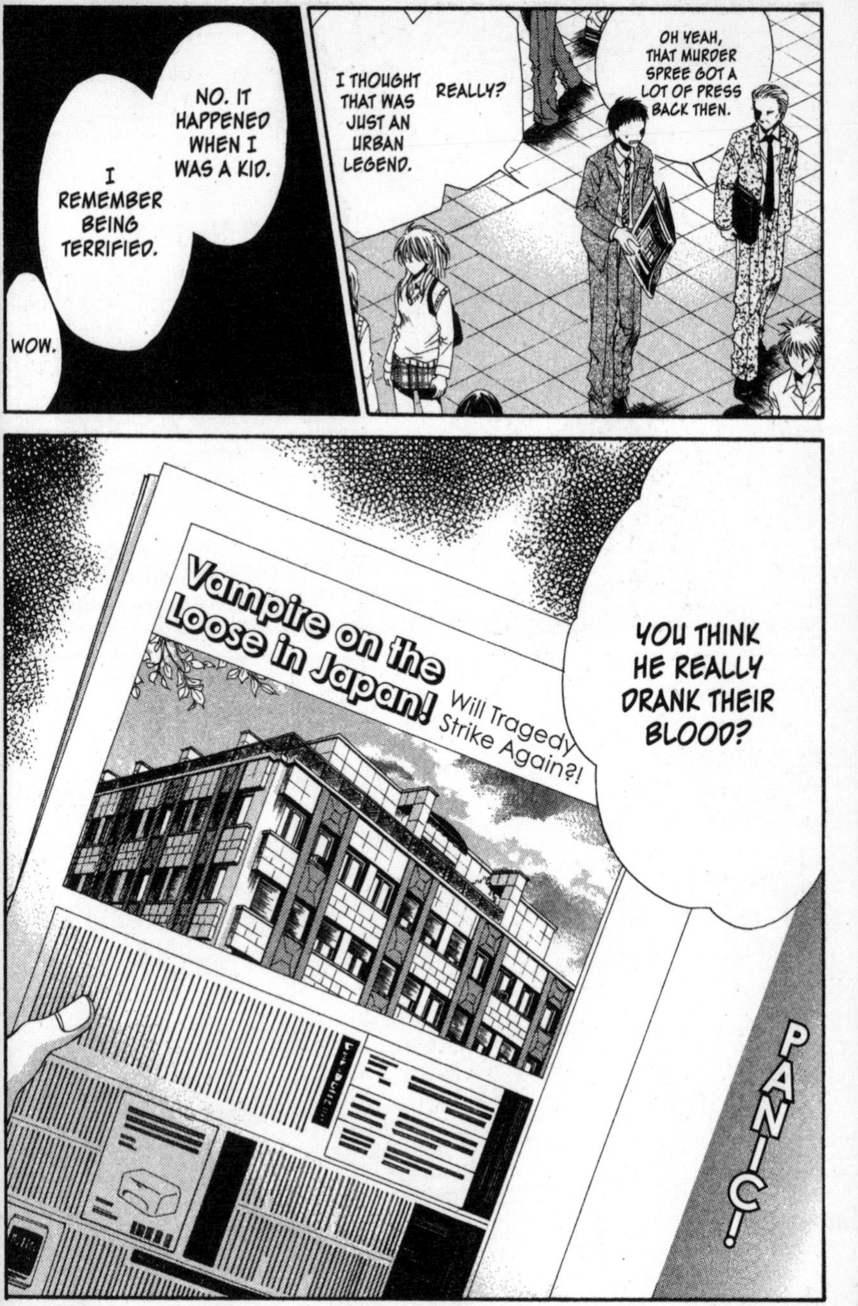
OH YEAH, THAT MURDER SPREE GOT A LOT OF PRESS BACK THEN.
REALLY?
I THOUGHT THAT WAS JUST AN URBAN LEGEND.
NO. IT HAPPENED WHEN I WAS A KID.
I REMEMBER BEING TERRIFIED.
WOW.
YOU THINK HE REALLY DRANK THEIR BLOOD?
Vampire on the Loose in Japan!
Will Tragedy Strike Again?!
PANIC!

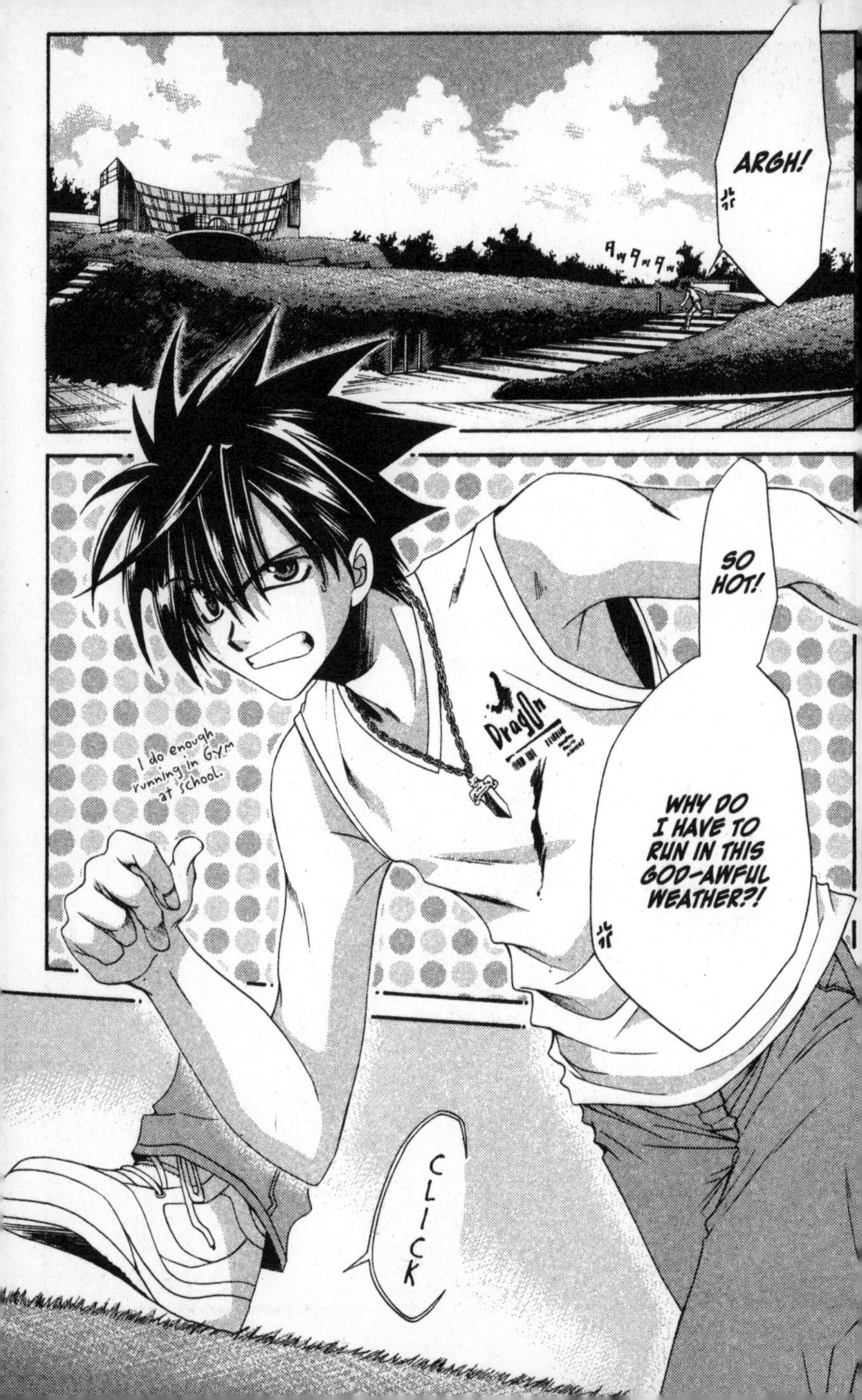
ARGH!
SO HOT!
WHY DO I HAVE TO RUN IN THIS GOD-AWFUL WEATHER?!
I do enough running in GYM at school.
CLICK

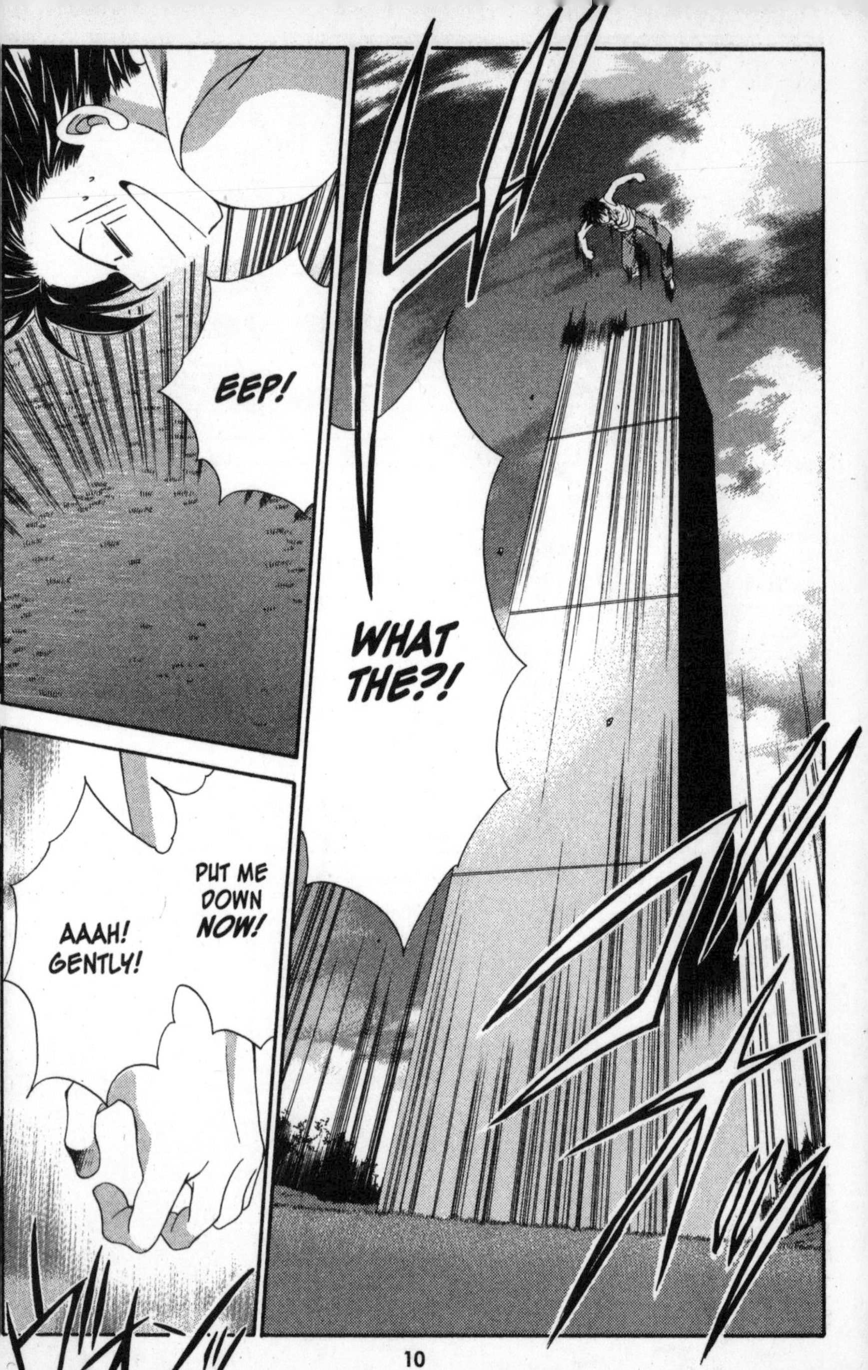
WHAT THE?!
EEP!
PUT ME DOWN NOW!
AAAH! GENTLY!

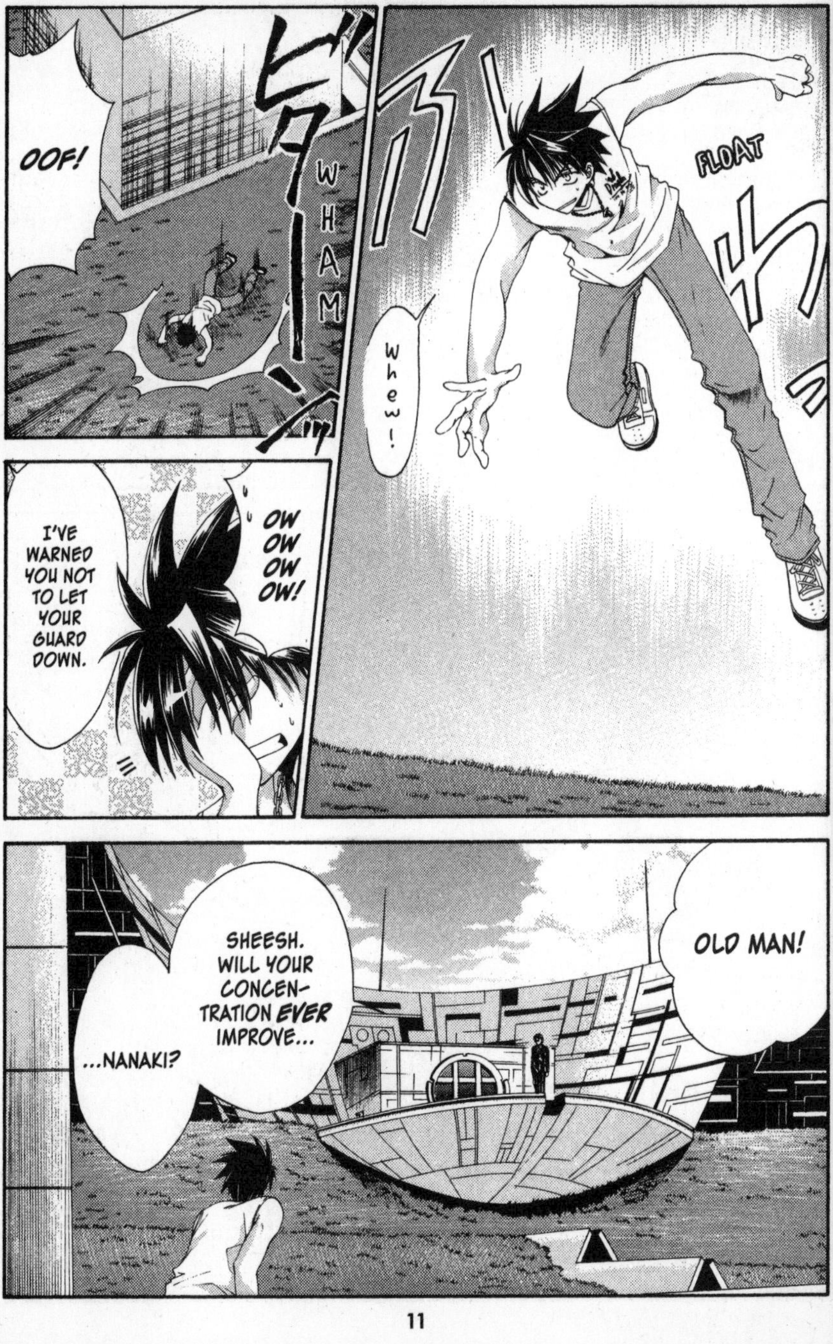
FLOAT
Whew!
WHAM
OOF!
OW OW OW OW!
I'VE WARNED YOU NOT TO LET YOUR GUARD DOWN.
OLD MAN!
SHEESH. WILL YOUR CONCENTRATION EVER IMPROVE...
...NANAKI?

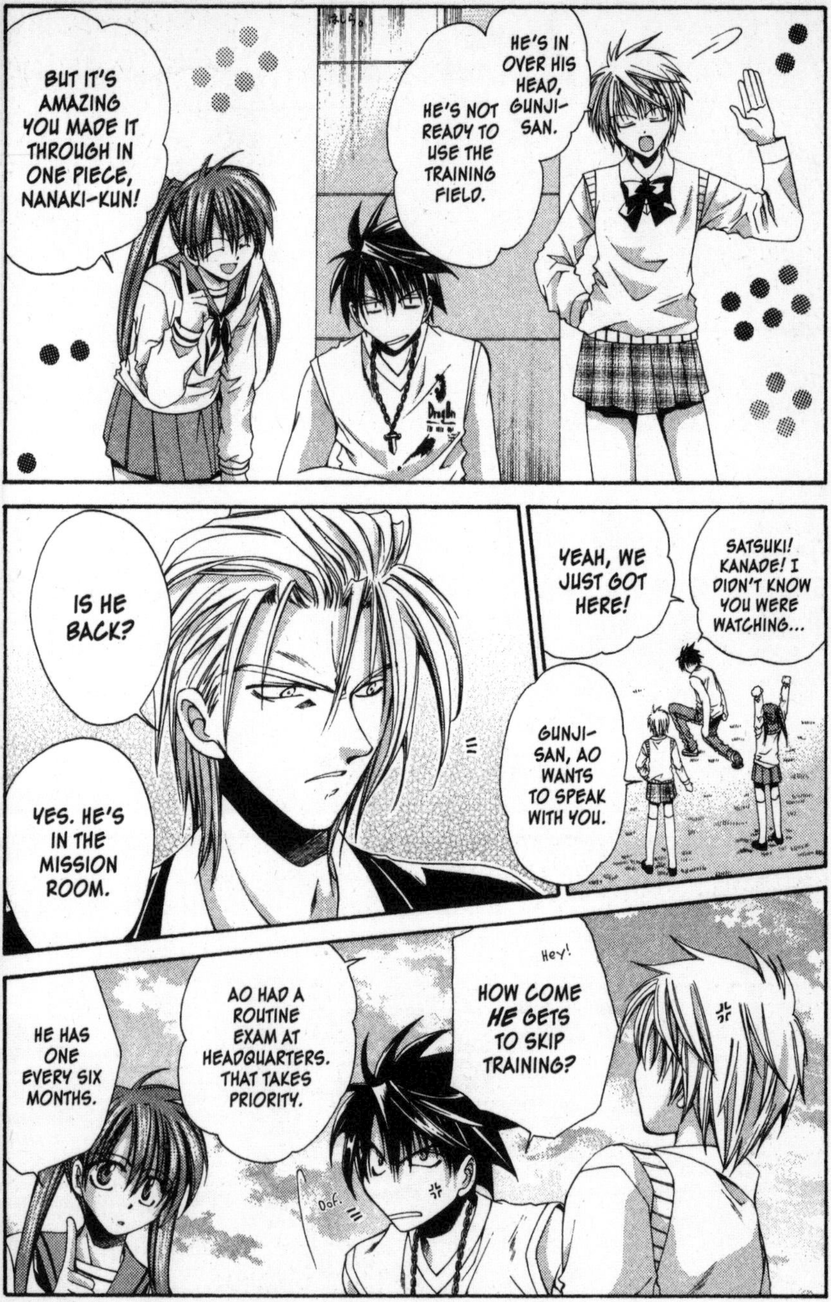
HE'S IN OVER HIS HEAD, GUNJI-SAN.
HE'S NOT READY TO USE THE TRAINING FIELD.
BUT IT'S AMAZING YOU MADE IT THROUGH IN ONE PIECE, NANAKI-KUN!
SATSUKI! KANADE! I DIDN'T KNOW YOU WERE WATCHING...
YEAH, WE JUST GOT HERE!
GUNJI-SAN, AO WANTS TO SPEAK WITH YOU.
IS HE BACK?
YES. HE'S IN THE MISSION ROOM.
Hey!
HOW COME *HE* GETS TO SKIP TRAINING?
AO HAD A ROUTINE EXAM AT HEADQUARTERS. THAT TAKES PRIORITY.
HE HAS ONE EVERY SIX MONTHS.
Oof.

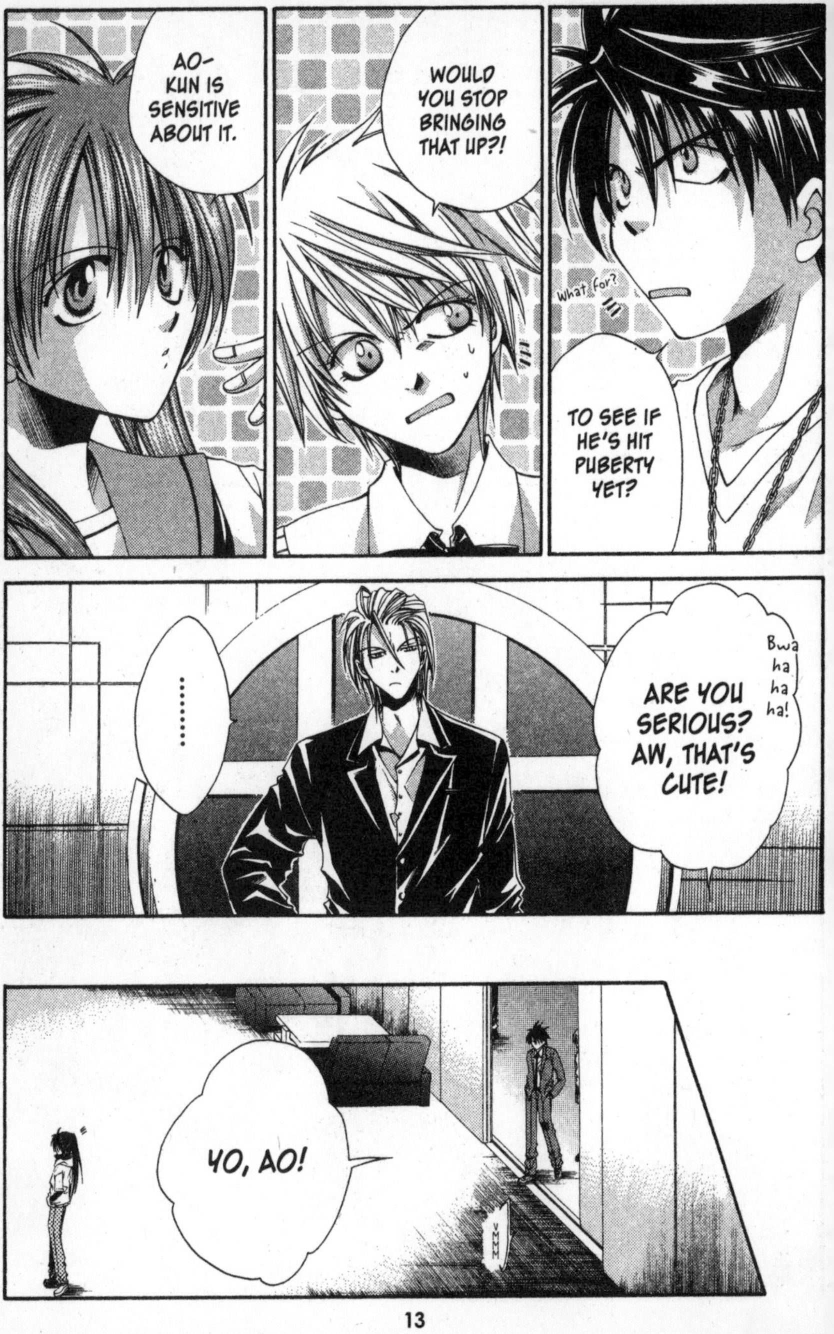
What for?
TO SEE IF HE'S HIT PUBERTY YET?
WOULD YOU STOP BRINGING THAT UP?!
AO-KUN IS SENSITIVE ABOUT IT.
Bwa ha ha ha!
ARE YOU SERIOUS? AW, THAT'S CUTE!
....
YO, AO!

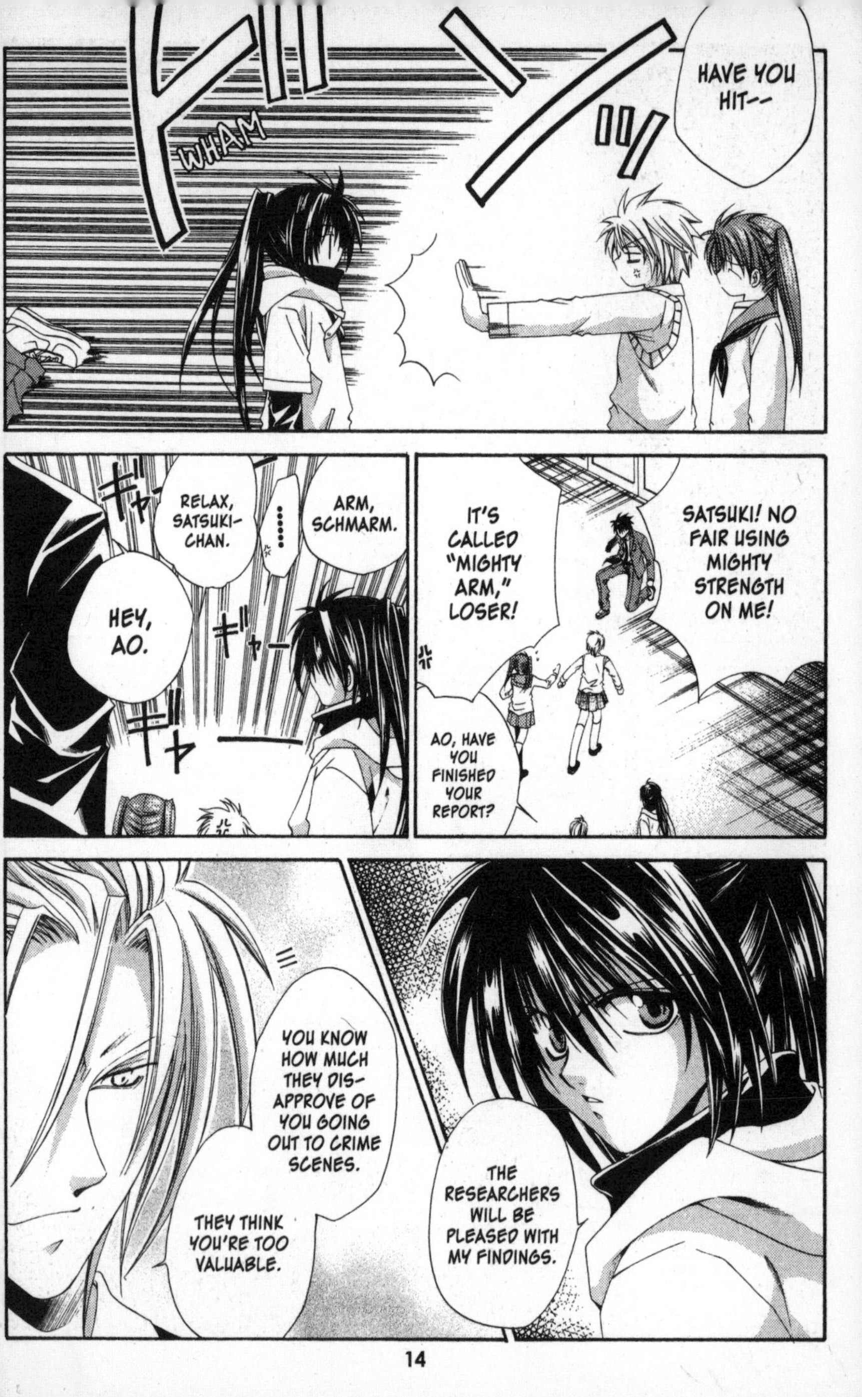
WHAM
HAVE YOU HIT--
SATSUKI! NO FAIR USING MIGHTY STRENGTH ON ME!
IT'S CALLED "MIGHTY ARM," LOSER!
AO, HAVE YOU FINISHED YOUR REPORT?
ARM, SCHMARM.
......
RELAX, SATSUKI-CHAN.
HEY, AO.
THE RESEARCHERS WILL BE PLEASED WITH MY FINDINGS.
YOU KNOW HOW MUCH THEY DIS-APPROVE OF YOU GOING OUT TO CRIME SCENES.
THEY THINK YOU'RE TOO VALUABLE.

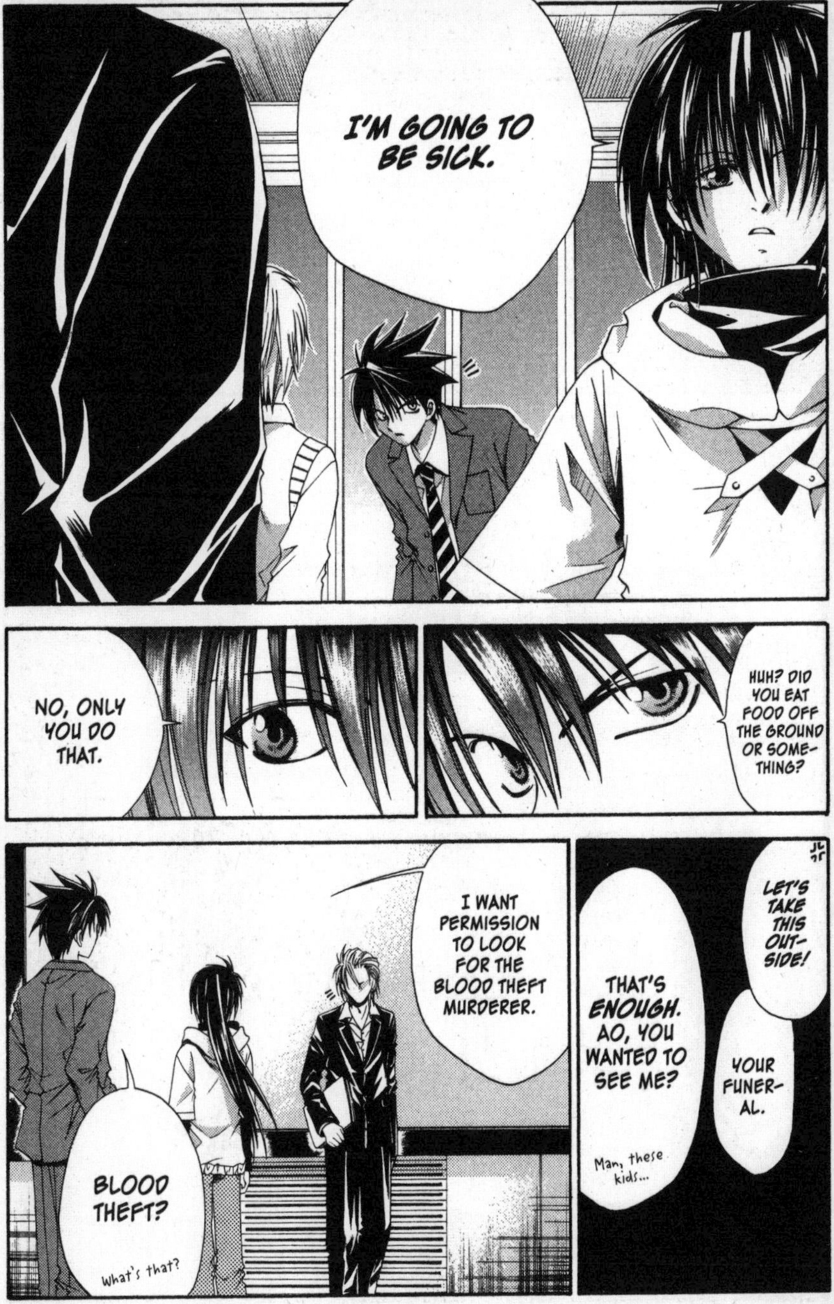
I'M GOING TO BE SICK.
HUH? DID YOU EAT FOOD OFF THE GROUND OR SOMETHING?
NO, ONLY YOU DO THAT.
LET'S TAKE THIS OUTSIDE!
YOUR FUNERAL.
THAT'S ENOUGH. AO, YOU WANTED TO SEE ME?
Man, these kids...
I WANT PERMISSION TO LOOK FOR THE BLOOD THEFT MURDERER.
BLOOD THEFT?
What's that?

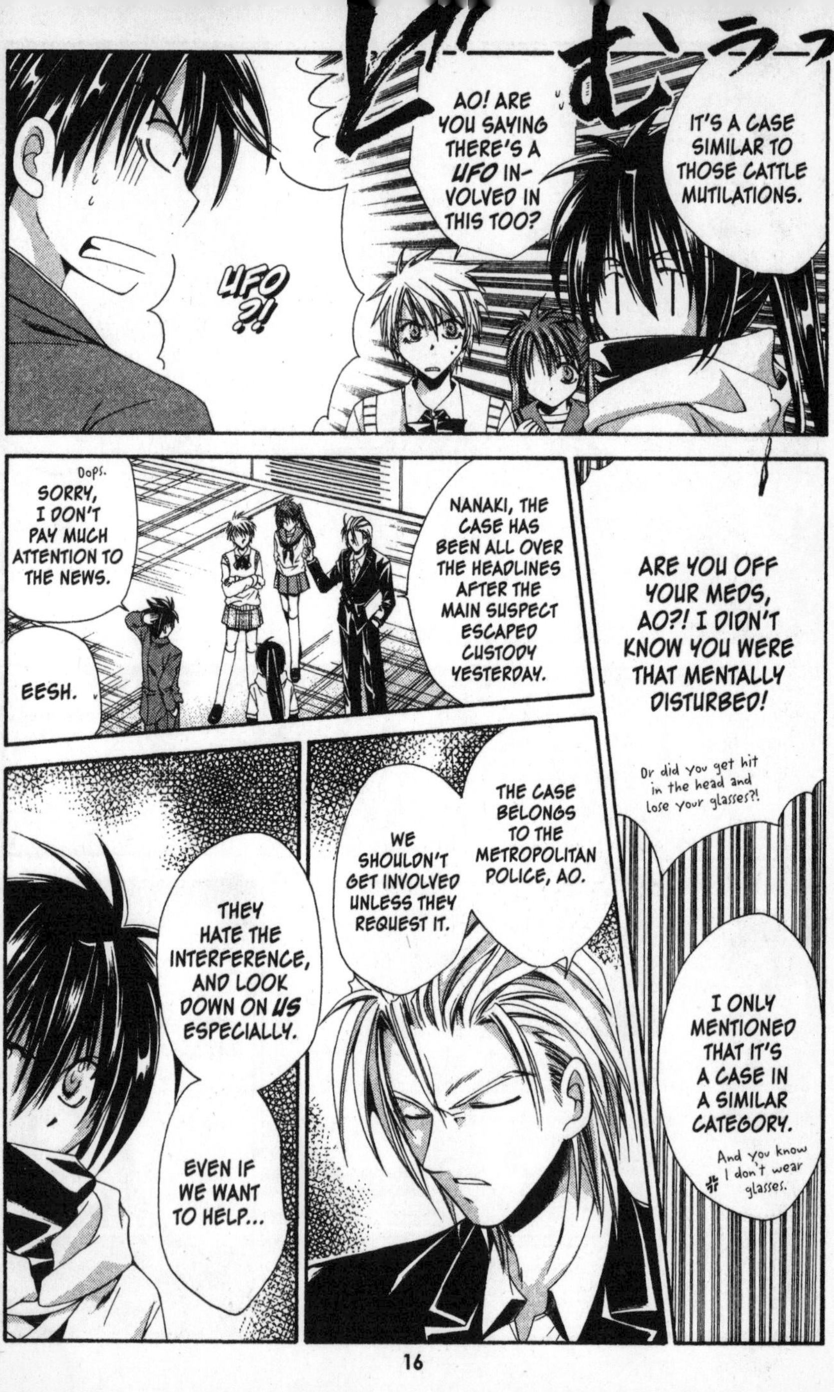
IT'S A CASE SIMILAR TO THOSE CATTLE MUTILATIONS.
AO! ARE YOU SAYING THERE'S A UFO INVOLVED IN THIS TOO?
UFO ?!
ARE YOU OFF YOUR MEDS, AO?! I DIDN'T KNOW YOU WERE THAT MENTALLY DISTURBED!
Or did you get hit in the head and lose your glasses?!
I ONLY MENTIONED THAT IT'S A CASE IN A SIMILAR CATEGORY.
And you know I don't wear glasses.
NANAKI, THE CASE HAS BEEN ALL OVER THE HEADLINES AFTER THE MAIN SUSPECT ESCAPED CUSTODY YESTERDAY.
Dops.
SORRY, I DON'T PAY MUCH ATTENTION TO THE NEWS.
EESH.
THE CASE BELONGS TO THE METROPOLITAN POLICE, AO.
WE SHOULDN'T GET INVOLVED UNLESS THEY REQUEST IT.
THEY HATE THE INTERFERENCE, AND LOOK DOWN ON US ESPECIALLY.
EVEN IF WE WANT TO HELP...

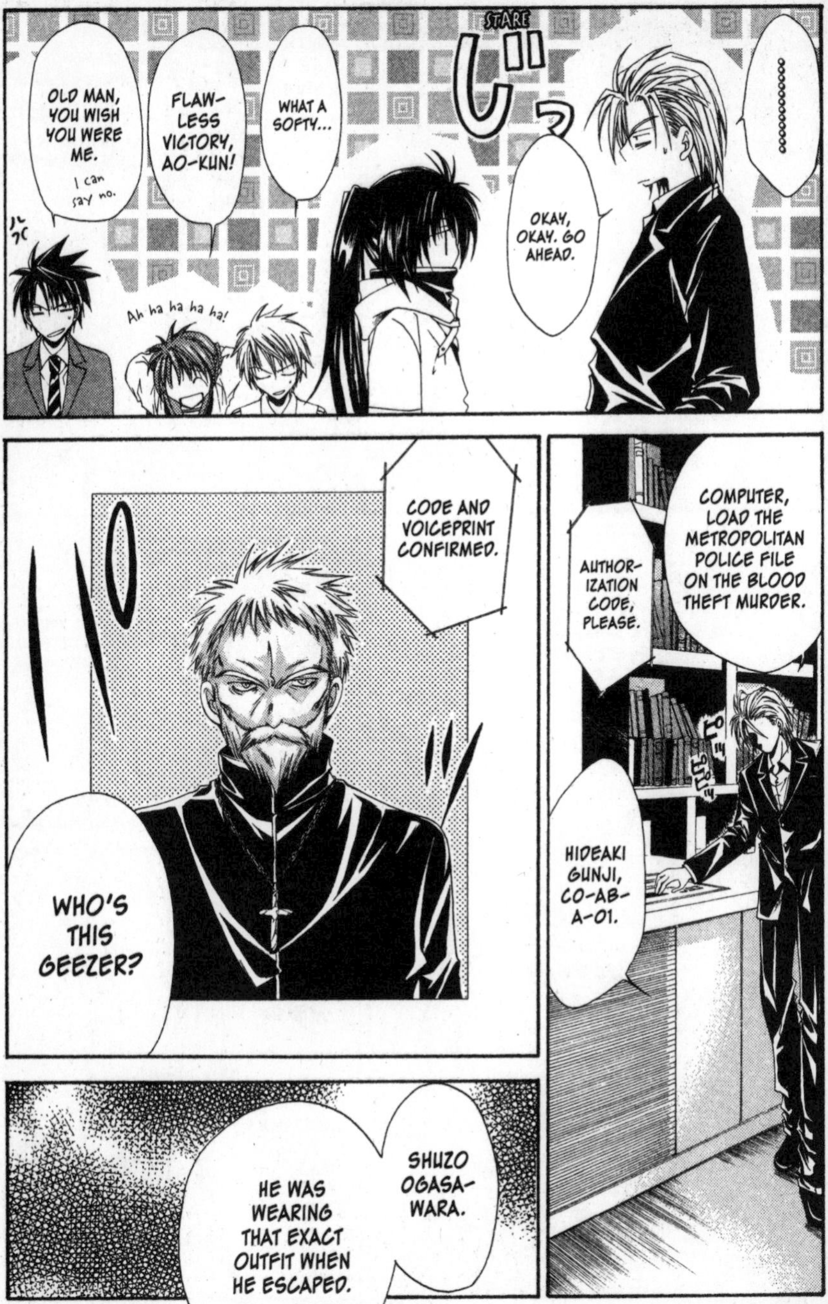
....
STARE
じっ
OKAY, OKAY. GO AHEAD.
WHAT A SOFTY...
FLAWLESS VICTORY, AO-KUN!
OLD MAN, YOU WISH YOU WERE ME.
I can say no.
Ah ha ha ha ha!
COMPUTER, LOAD THE METROPOLITAN POLICE FILE ON THE BLOOD THEFT MURDER.
AUTHORIZATION CODE, PLEASE.
HIDEAKI GUNJI, CO-AB-A-01.
CODE AND VOICEPRINT CONFIRMED.
WHO'S THIS GEEZER?
SHUZO OGASAWARA.
HE WAS WEARING THAT EXACT OUTFIT WHEN HE ESCAPED.

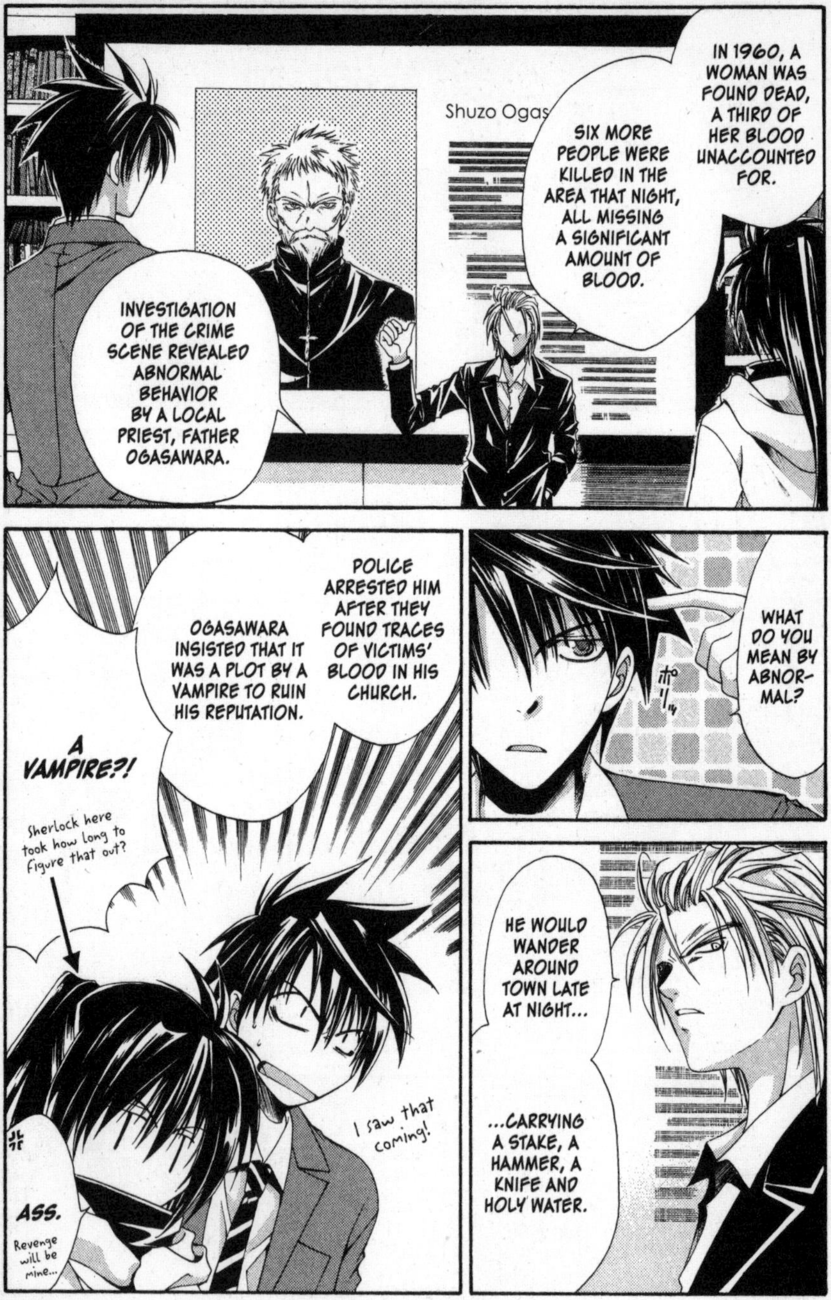
IN 1960, A WOMAN WAS FOUND DEAD, A THIRD OF HER BLOOD UNACCOUNTED FOR.
SIX MORE PEOPLE WERE KILLED IN THE AREA THAT NIGHT, ALL MISSING A SIGNIFICANT AMOUNT OF BLOOD.
Shuzo Ogas
INVESTIGATION OF THE CRIME SCENE REVEALED ABNORMAL BEHAVIOR BY A LOCAL PRIEST, FATHER OGASAWARA.
WHAT DO YOU MEAN BY ABNOR-MAL?
HE WOULD WANDER AROUND TOWN LATE AT NIGHT...
...CARRYING A STAKE, A HAMMER, A KNIFE AND HOLY WATER.
POLICE ARRESTED HIM AFTER THEY FOUND TRACES OF VICTIMS' BLOOD IN HIS CHURCH.
OGASAWARA INSISTED THAT IT WAS A PLOT BY A VAMPIRE TO RUIN HIS REPUTATION.
A VAMPIRE?!
Sherlock here took how long to figure that out?
I saw that coming!
ASS.
Revenge will be mine...

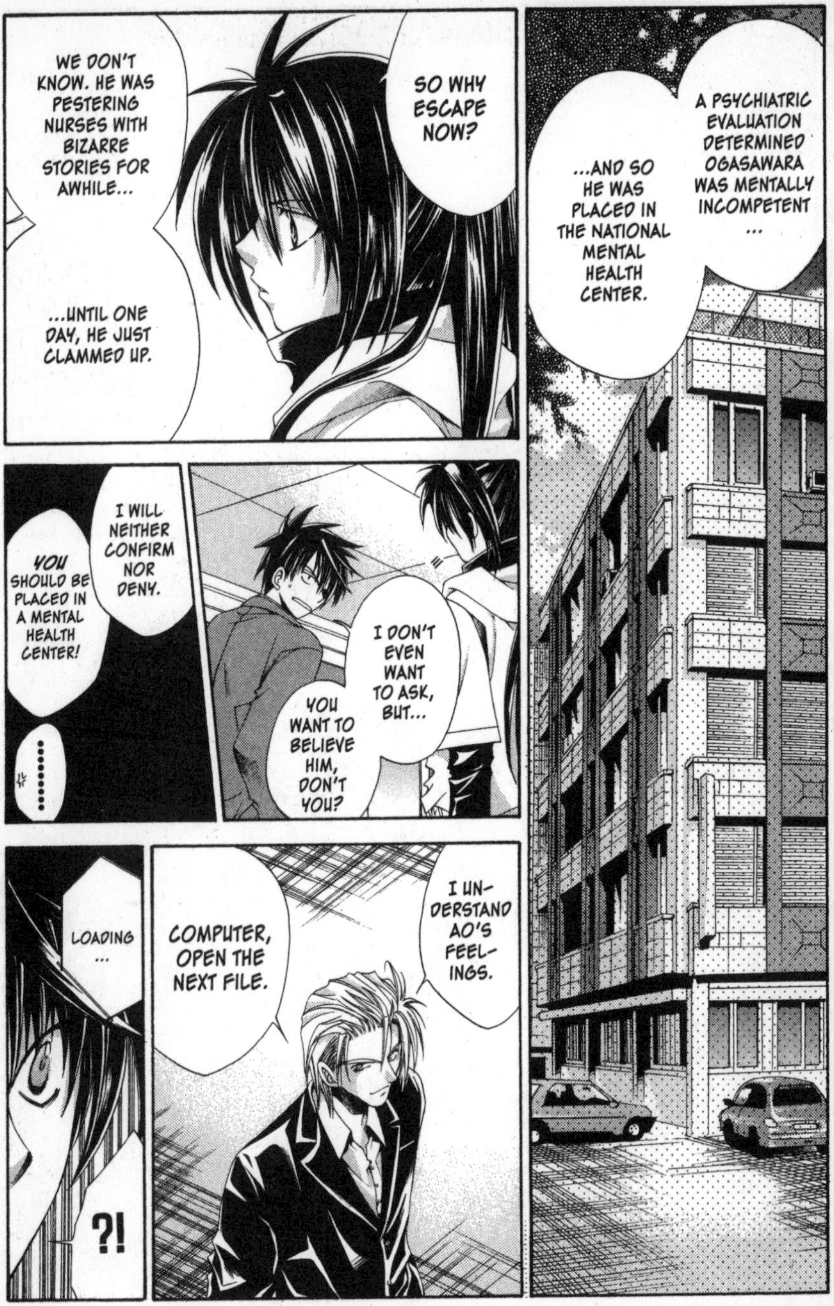
A PSYCHIATRIC EVALUATION DETERMINED OGASAWARA WAS MENTALLY INCOMPETENT ...
...AND SO HE WAS PLACED IN THE NATIONAL MENTAL HEALTH CENTER.
SO WHY ESCAPE NOW?
WE DON'T KNOW. HE WAS PESTERING NURSES WITH BIZARRE STORIES FOR AWHILE...
...UNTIL ONE DAY, HE JUST CLAMMED UP.
I DON'T EVEN WANT TO ASK, BUT...
YOU WANT TO BELIEVE HIM, DON'T YOU?
I WILL NEITHER CONFIRM NOR DENY.
YOU SHOULD BE PLACED IN A MENTAL HEALTH CENTER!
......
I UNDERSTAND AO'S FEELINGS.
COMPUTER, OPEN THE NEXT FILE.
LOADING ...
?!

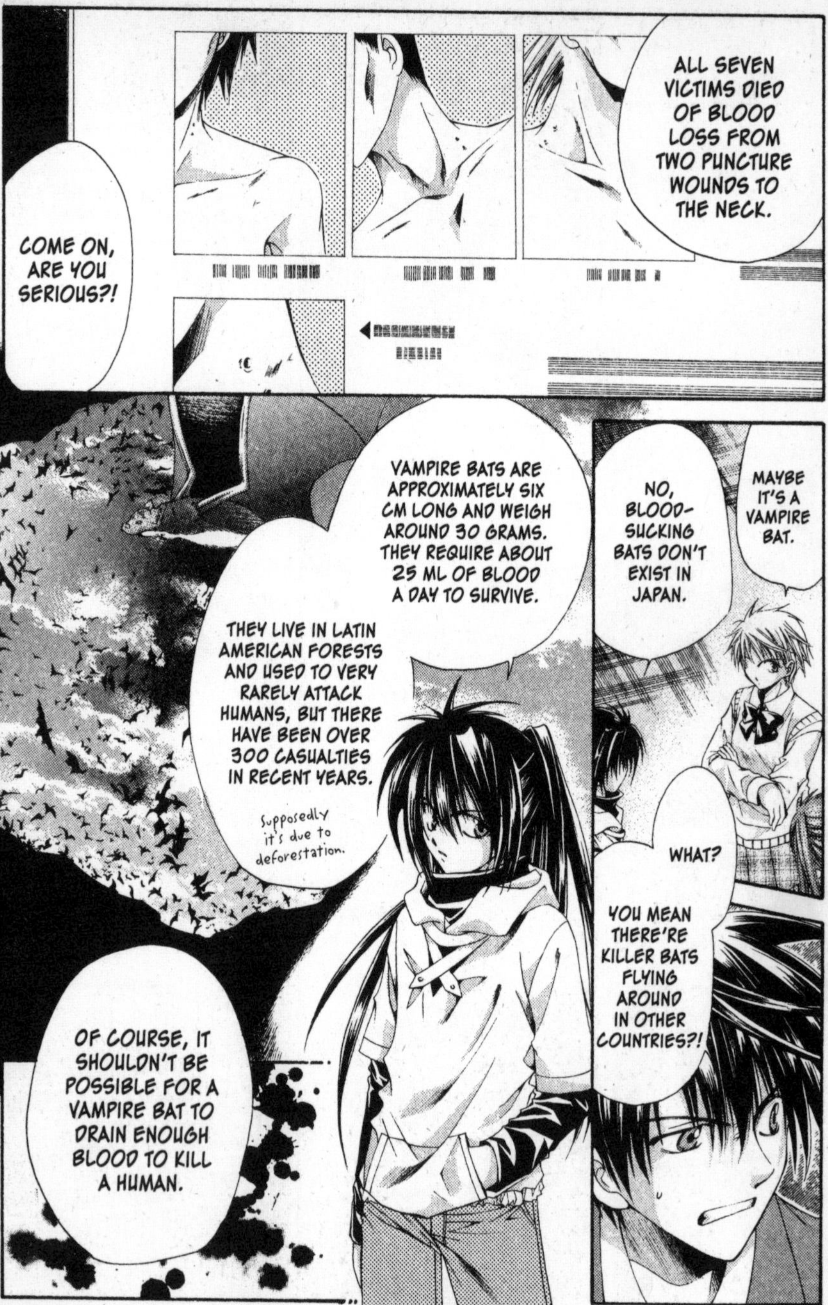
ALL SEVEN VICTIMS DIED OF BLOOD LOSS FROM TWO PUNCTURE WOUNDS TO THE NECK.
COME ON, ARE YOU SERIOUS?!
MAYBE IT'S A VAMPIRE BAT.
NO, BLOOD-SUCKING BATS DON'T EXIST IN JAPAN.
VAMPIRE BATS ARE APPROXIMATELY SIX CM LONG AND WEIGH AROUND 30 GRAMS. THEY REQUIRE ABOUT 25 ML OF BLOOD A DAY TO SURVIVE.
THEY LIVE IN LATIN AMERICAN FORESTS AND USED TO VERY RARELY ATTACK HUMANS, BUT THERE HAVE BEEN OVER 300 CASUALTIES IN RECENT YEARS.
Supposedly it's due to deforestation.
WHAT?
YOU MEAN THERE'RE KILLER BATS FLYING AROUND IN OTHER COUNTRIES?!
OF COURSE, IT SHOULDN'T BE POSSIBLE FOR A VAMPIRE BAT TO DRAIN ENOUGH BLOOD TO KILL A HUMAN.

*Note: 6 cm = 2.4", 30 g = 1 oz., 25 mL = 1.7 tbsp

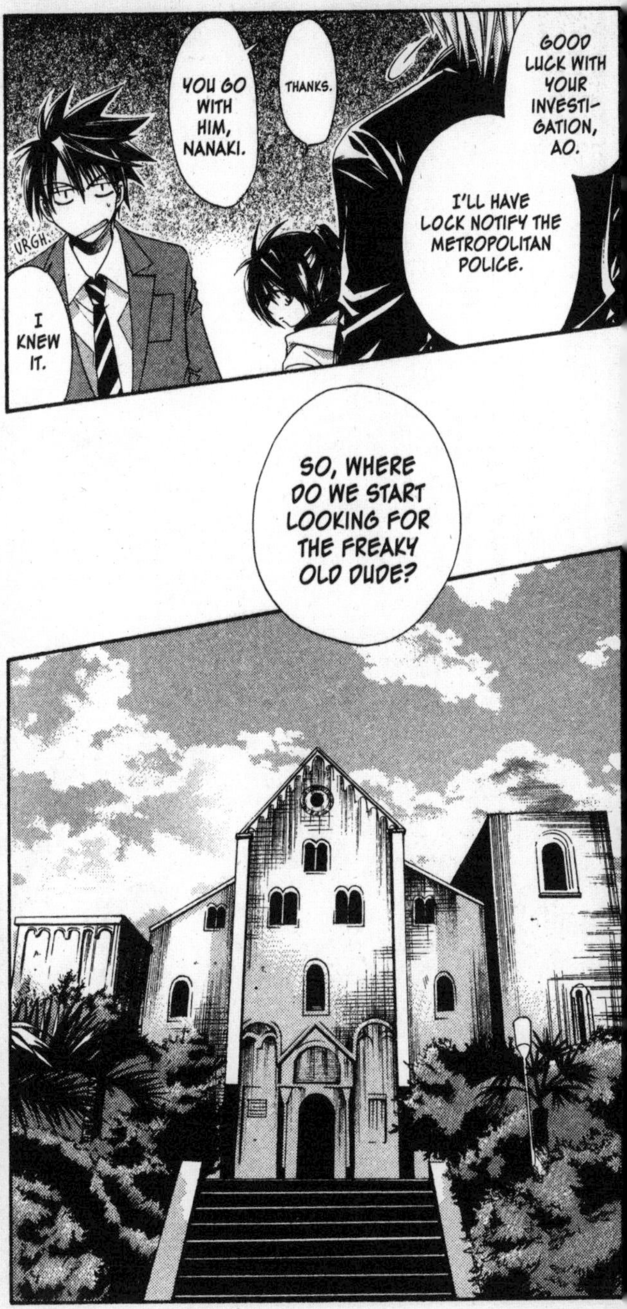
GOOD LUCK WITH YOUR INVESTIGATION, AO.
I'LL HAVE LOCK NOTIFY THE METROPOLITAN POLICE.
THANKS.
YOU GO WITH HIM, NANAKI.
URGH.
I KNEW IT.
SO, WHERE DO WE START LOOKING FOR THE FREAKY OLD DUDE?

WOOHOO!!!...

Saenagi here. ↑ Dumb, huh?

Welcome to the third volume of Nanaki! It's the final one.

I always have trouble coming up with anything to write in this spot (lol).

I'm planning to write some commentary on the manga and the new characters, so stay with me.

Enjoy. ♬

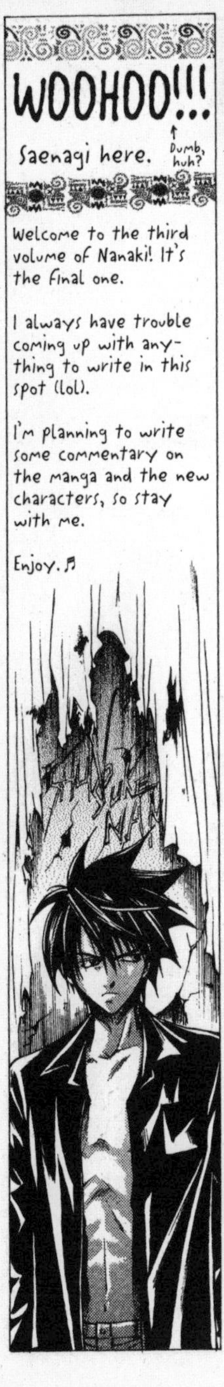

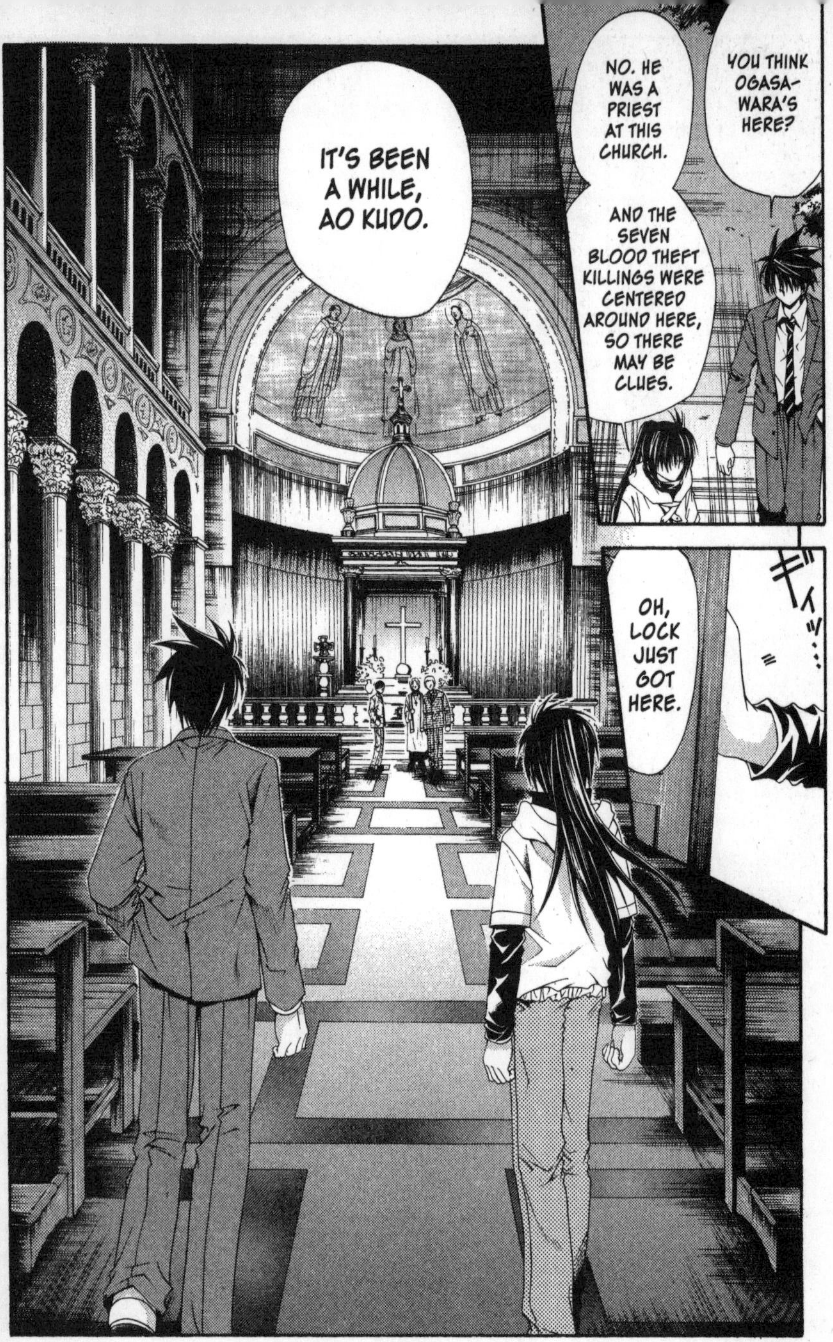
YOU THINK OGASA-WARA'S HERE?
NO. HE WAS A PRIEST AT THIS CHURCH.
AND THE SEVEN BLOOD THEFT KILLINGS WERE CENTERED AROUND HERE, SO THERE MAY BE CLUES.
ギィッ…
OH, LOCK JUST GOT HERE.
IT'S BEEN A WHILE, AO KUDO.

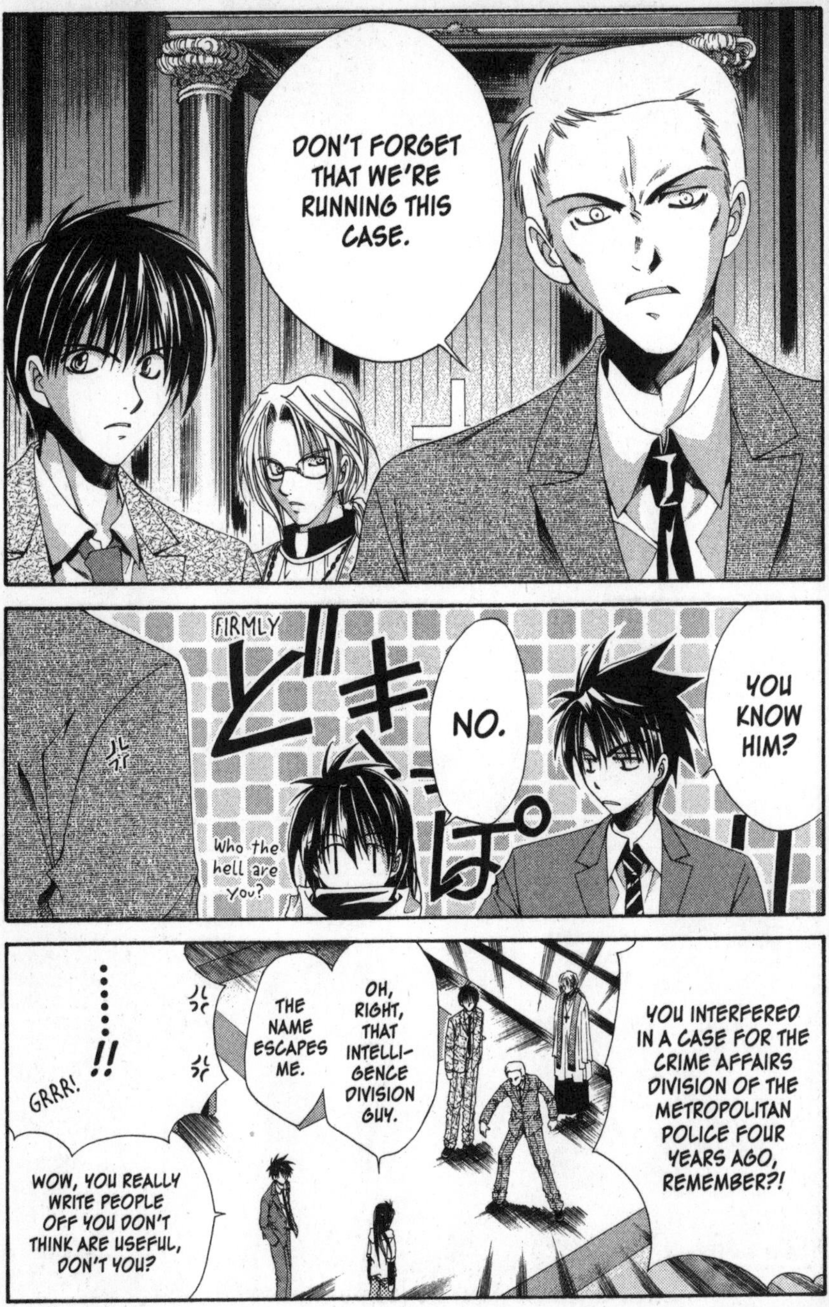
DON'T FORGET THAT WE'RE RUNNING THIS CASE.
YOU KNOW HIM?
NO.
FIRMLY
Who the hell are you?
YOU INTERFERED IN A CASE FOR THE CRIME AFFAIRS DIVISION OF THE METROPOLITAN POLICE FOUR YEARS AGO, REMEMBER?!
OH, RIGHT, THAT INTELLI-GENCE DIVISION GUY.
THE NAME ESCAPES ME.
......!!
GRRR!
WOW, YOU REALLY WRITE PEOPLE OFF YOU DON'T THINK ARE USEFUL, DON'T YOU?

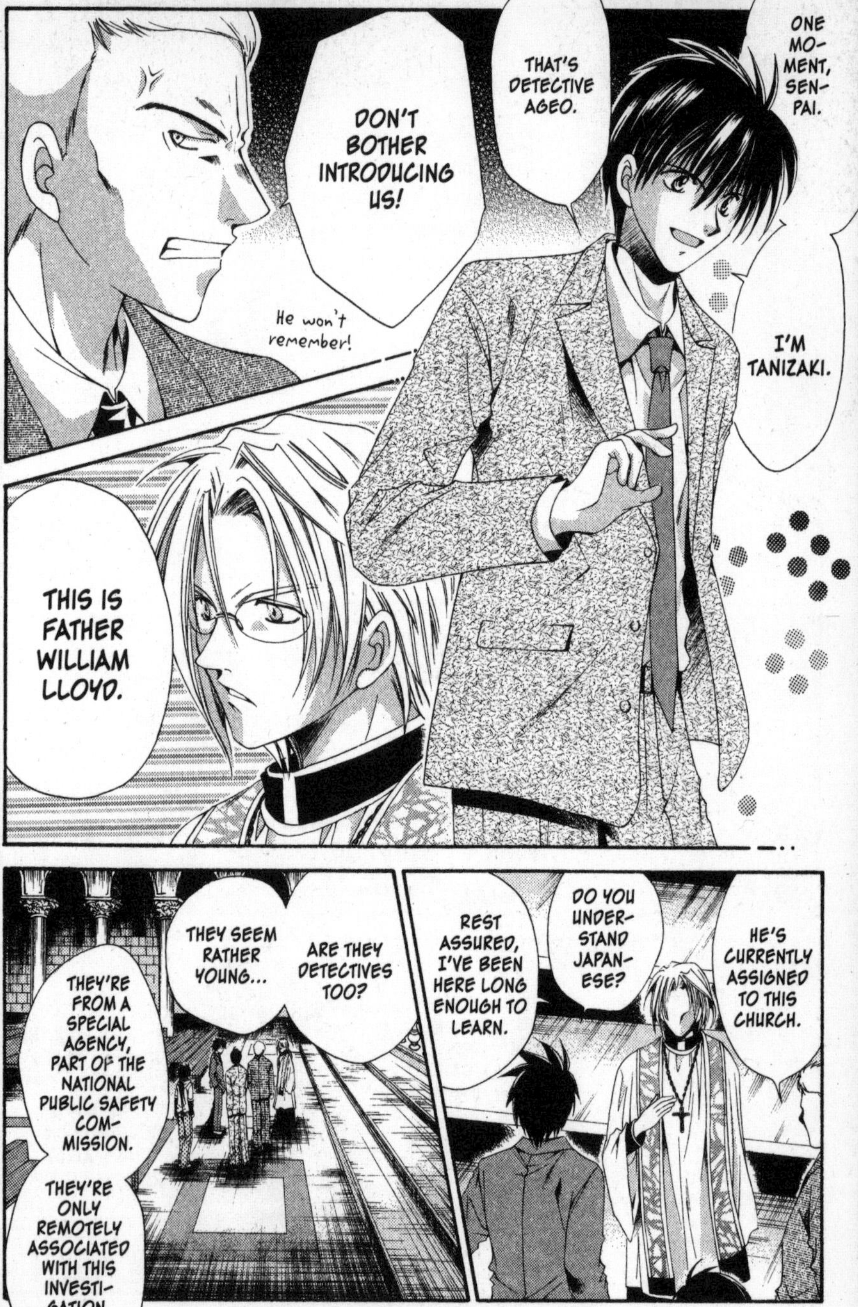
ONE MOMENT, SENPAI.
I'M TANIZAKI.
THAT'S DETECTIVE AGEO.
DON'T BOTHER INTRODUCING US!
He won't remember!
THIS IS FATHER WILLIAM LLOYD.
HE'S CURRENTLY ASSIGNED TO THIS CHURCH.
DO YOU UNDERSTAND JAPANESE?
REST ASSURED, I'VE BEEN HERE LONG ENOUGH TO LEARN.
ARE THEY DETECTIVES TOO?
THEY SEEM RATHER YOUNG...
THEY'RE FROM A SPECIAL AGENCY, PART OF THE NATIONAL PUBLIC SAFETY COMMISSION.
THEY'RE ONLY REMOTELY ASSOCIATED WITH THIS INVESTIGATION.

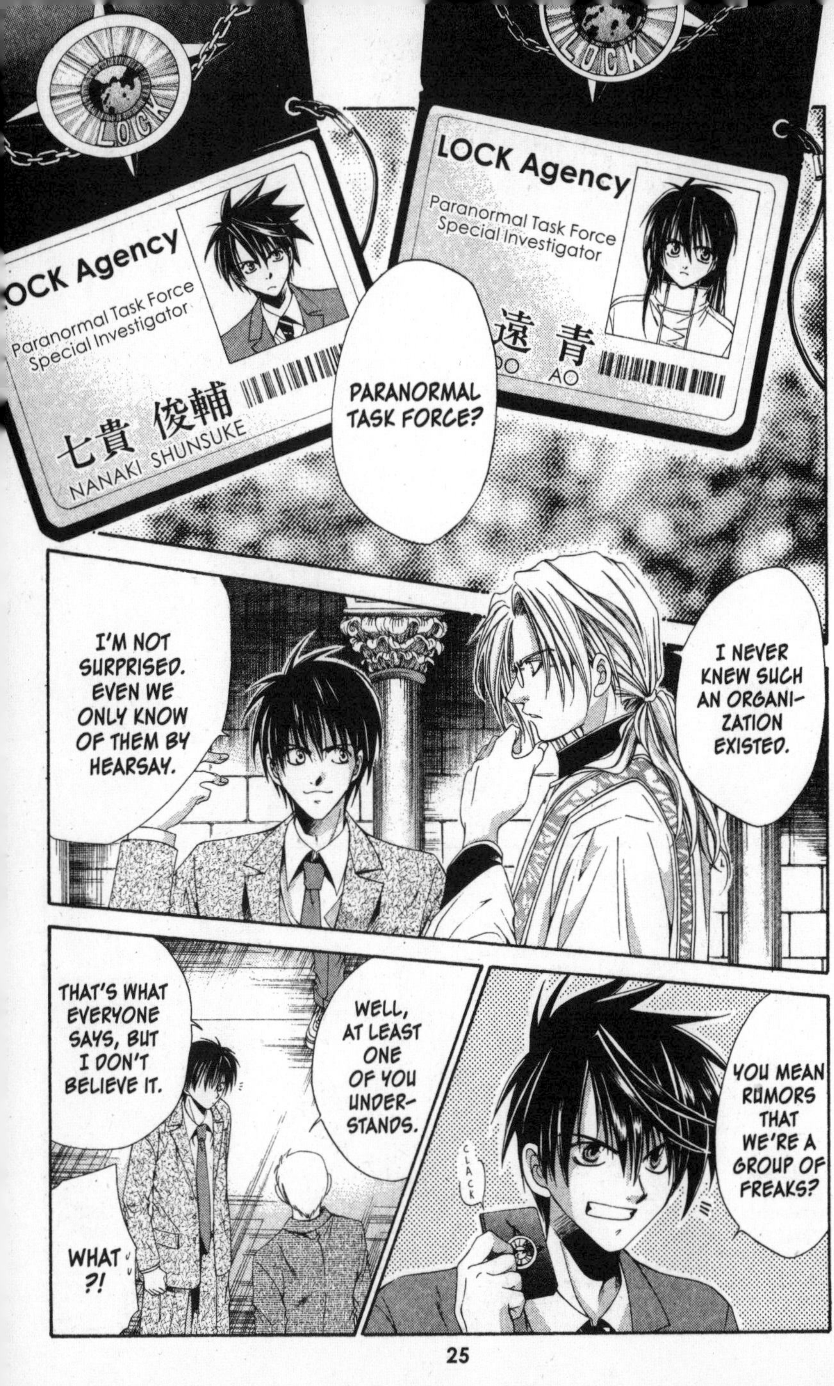
LOCK Agency
Paranormal Task Force
Special Investigator
遠 青
OO AO
PARANORMAL TASK FORCE?
OCK Agency
Paranormal Task Force
Special Investigator
七貴 俊輔
NANAKI SHUNSUKE
I NEVER KNEW SUCH AN ORGANI-ZATION EXISTED.
I'M NOT SURPRISED. EVEN WE ONLY KNOW OF THEM BY HEARSAY.
YOU MEAN RUMORS THAT WE'RE A GROUP OF FREAKS?
CLACK
WELL, AT LEAST ONE OF YOU UNDER-STANDS.
THAT'S WHAT EVERYONE SAYS, BUT I DON'T BELIEVE IT.
WHAT ?!

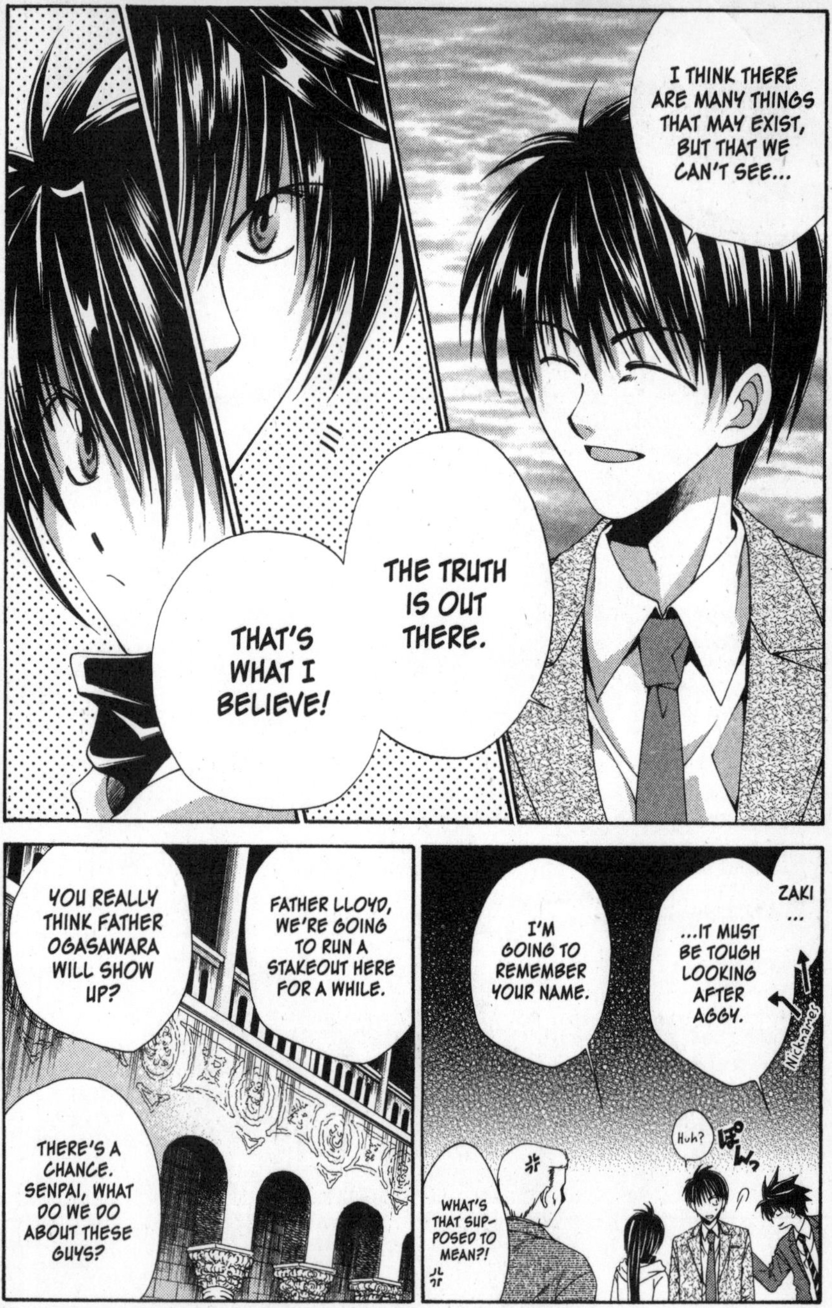
I THINK THERE ARE MANY THINGS THAT MAY EXIST, BUT THAT WE CAN'T SEE...
THE TRUTH IS OUT THERE.
THAT'S WHAT I BELIEVE!
ZAKI ...
...IT MUST BE TOUGH LOOKING AFTER AGGY.
Nicknames
I'M GOING TO REMEMBER YOUR NAME.
Huh?
ぽんっ
WHAT'S THAT SUP-POSED TO MEAN?!
FATHER LLOYD, WE'RE GOING TO RUN A STAKEOUT HERE FOR A WHILE.
YOU REALLY THINK FATHER OGASAWARA WILL SHOW UP?
THERE'S A CHANCE. SENPAI, WHAT DO WE DO ABOUT THESE GUYS?

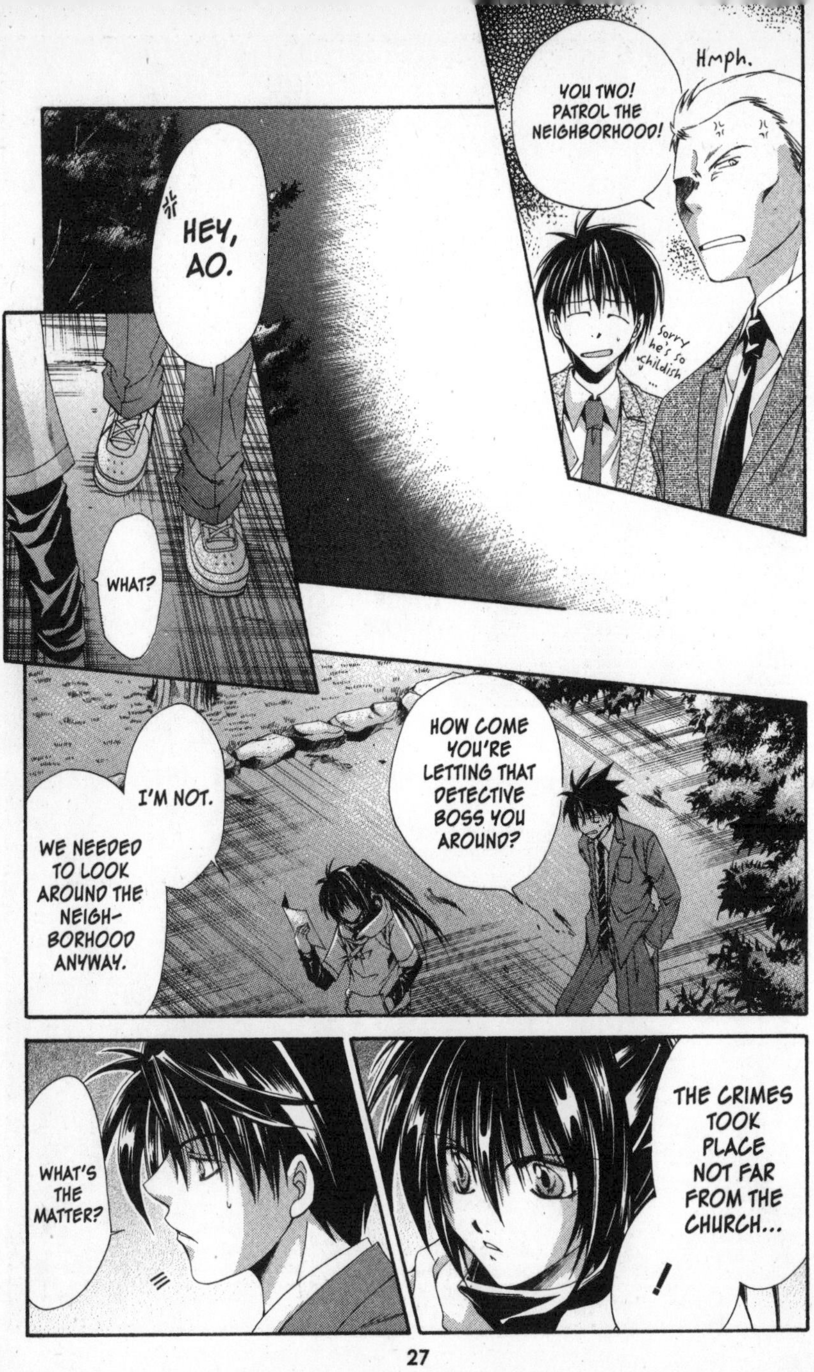
Hmph.
YOU TWO! PATROL THE NEIGHBORHOOD!
Sorry he's so childish ...
HEY, AO.
WHAT?
HOW COME YOU'RE LETTING THAT DETECTIVE BOSS YOU AROUND?
I'M NOT.
WE NEEDED TO LOOK AROUND THE NEIGH-BORHOOD ANYWAY.
THE CRIMES TOOK PLACE NOT FAR FROM THE CHURCH...
WHAT'S THE MATTER?

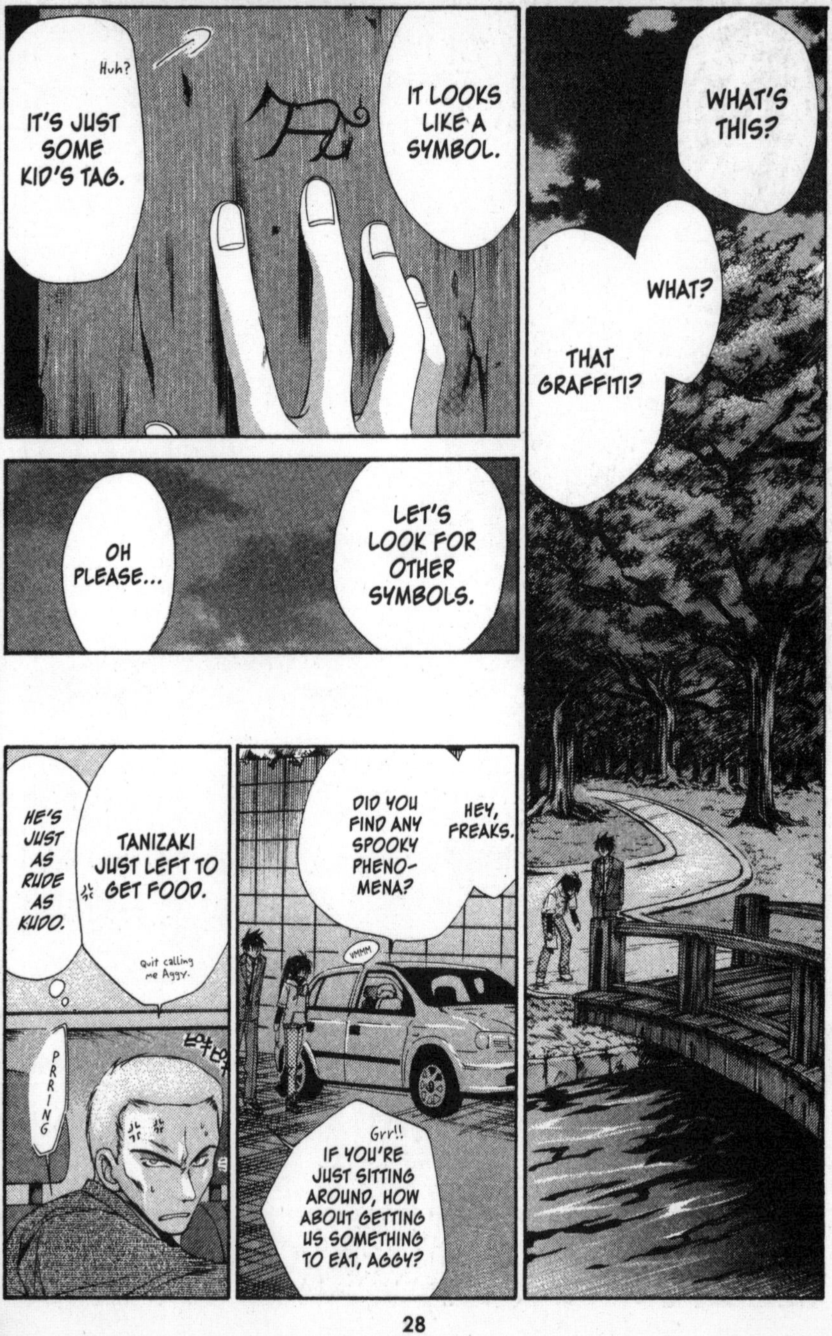
WHAT'S THIS?
WHAT?
THAT GRAFFITI?
IT LOOKS LIKE A SYMBOL.
Huh?
IT'S JUST SOME KID'S TAG.
LET'S LOOK FOR OTHER SYMBOLS.
OH PLEASE...
HEY, FREAKS.
DID YOU FIND ANY SPOOKY PHENO-MENA?
VMMM
Grr!!
IF YOU'RE JUST SITTING AROUND, HOW ABOUT GETTING US SOMETHING TO EAT, AGGY?
TANIZAKI JUST LEFT TO GET FOOD.
Quit calling me Aggy.
HE'S JUST AS RUDE AS KUDO.
PRRING

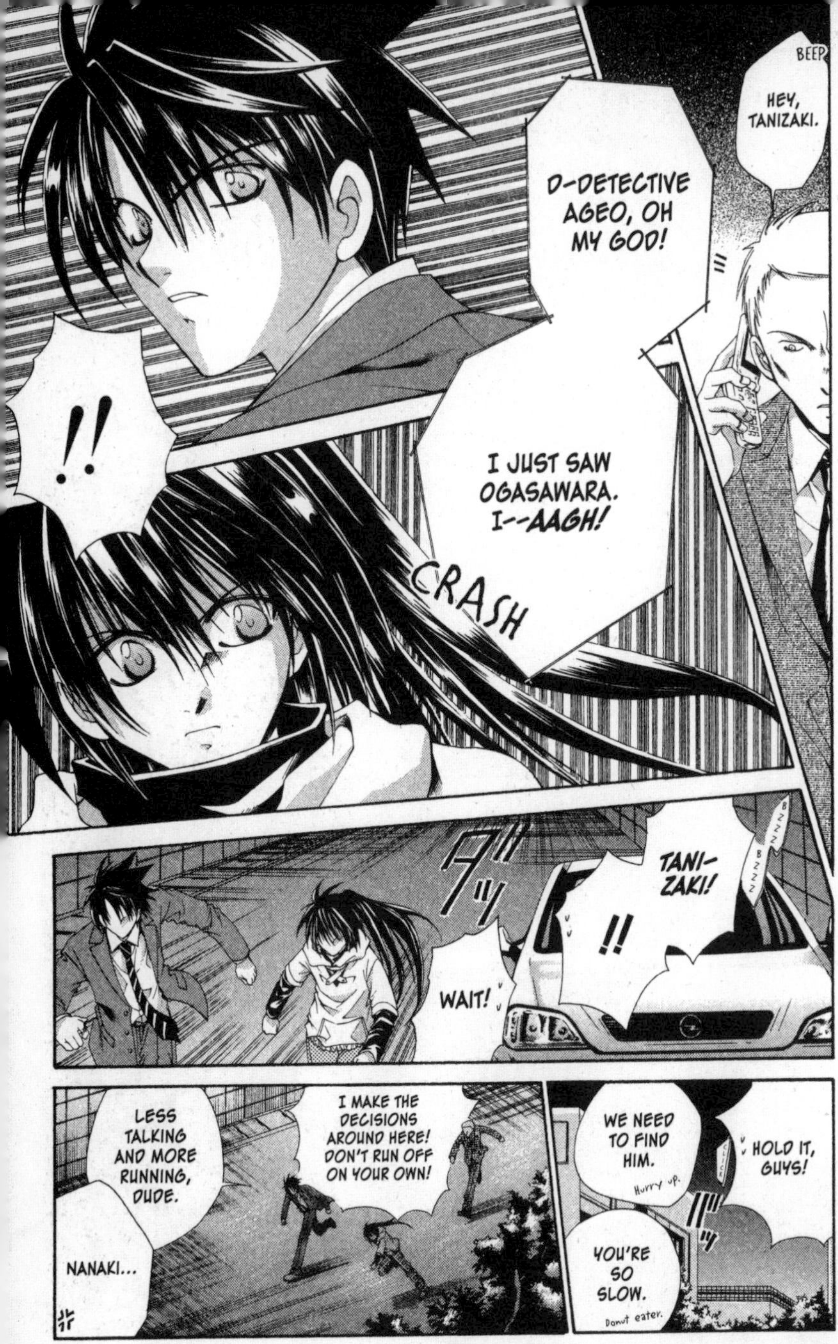
BEEP
HEY, TANIZAKI.
D-DETECTIVE AGEO, OH MY GOD!
I JUST SAW OGASAWARA. I--AAGH!
CRASH
!!
BZZZ BZZZ
TANI-ZAKI!
!!
WAIT!
HOLD IT, GUYS!
WE NEED TO FIND HIM.
Hurry up.
YOU'RE SO SLOW.
Donut eater.
I MAKE THE DECISIONS AROUND HERE! DON'T RUN OFF ON YOUR OWN!
LESS TALKING AND MORE RUNNING, DUDE.
NANAKI...

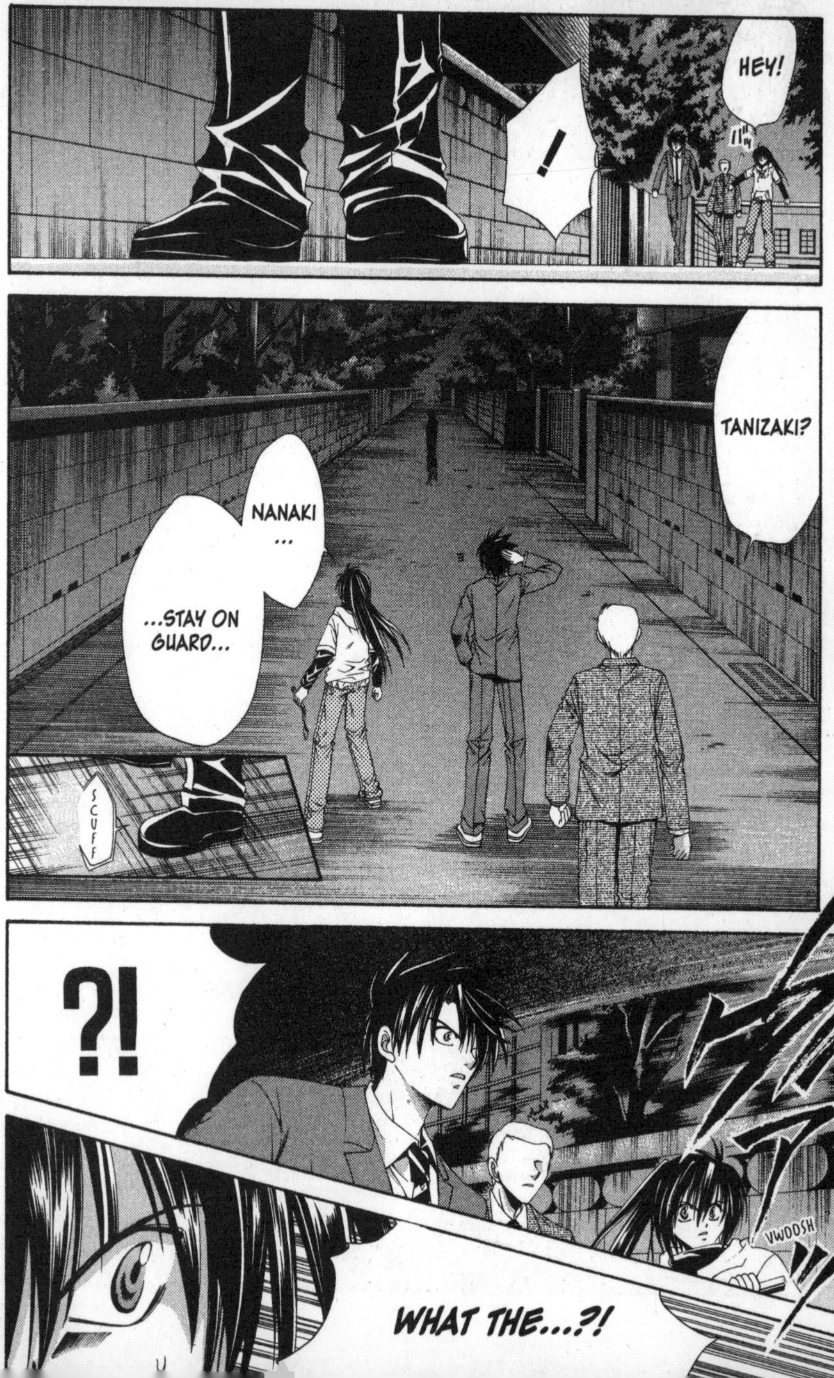
HEY!
!
TANIZAKI?
NANAKI ...
...STAY ON GUARD...
SCUFF
VWOOSH
?!
WHAT THE...?!

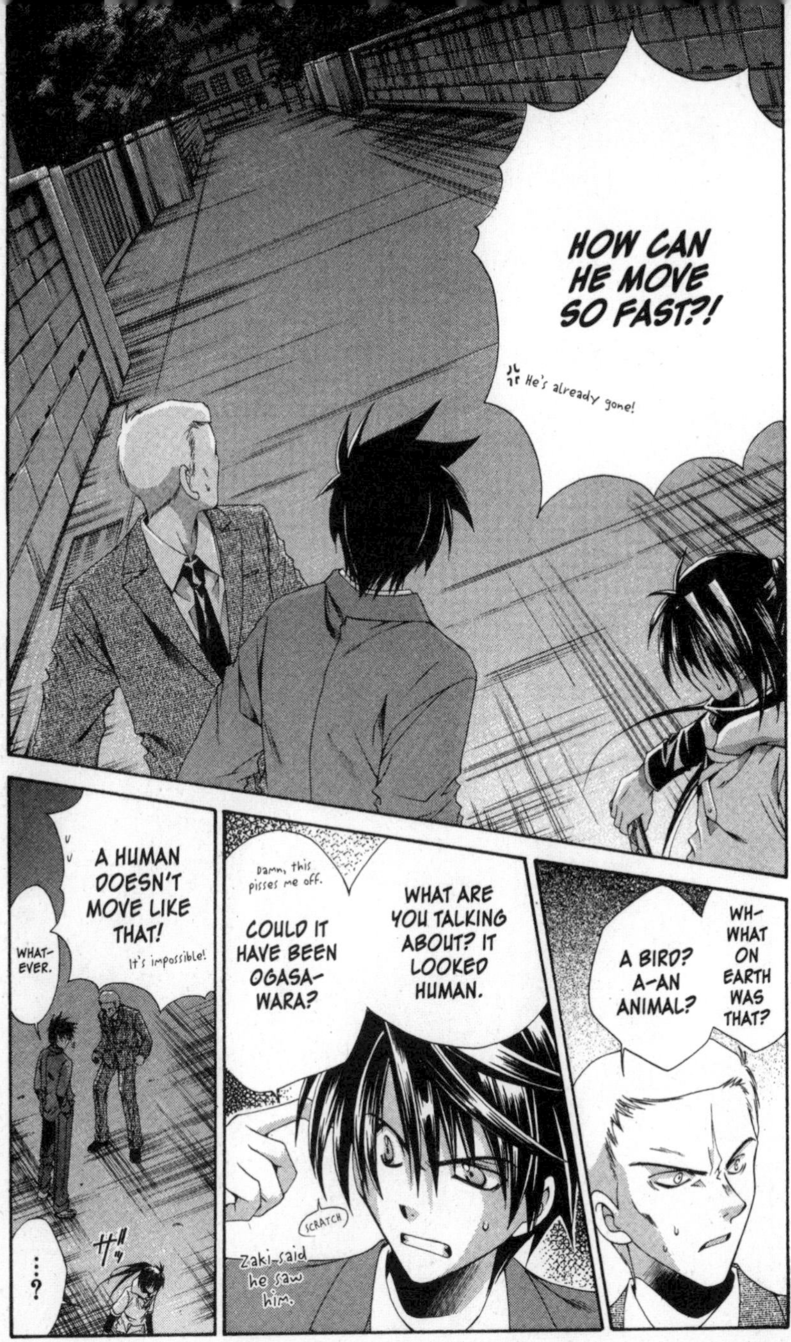
HOW CAN HE MOVE SO FAST?!
He's already gone!
WH-WHAT ON EARTH WAS THAT?
A BIRD? A-AN ANIMAL?
WHAT ARE YOU TALKING ABOUT? IT LOOKED HUMAN.
Damn, this pisses me off.
COULD IT HAVE BEEN OGASAWARA?
SCRATCH
Zaki said he saw him.
A HUMAN DOESN'T MOVE LIKE THAT!
It's impossible!
WHAT-EVER.
...?

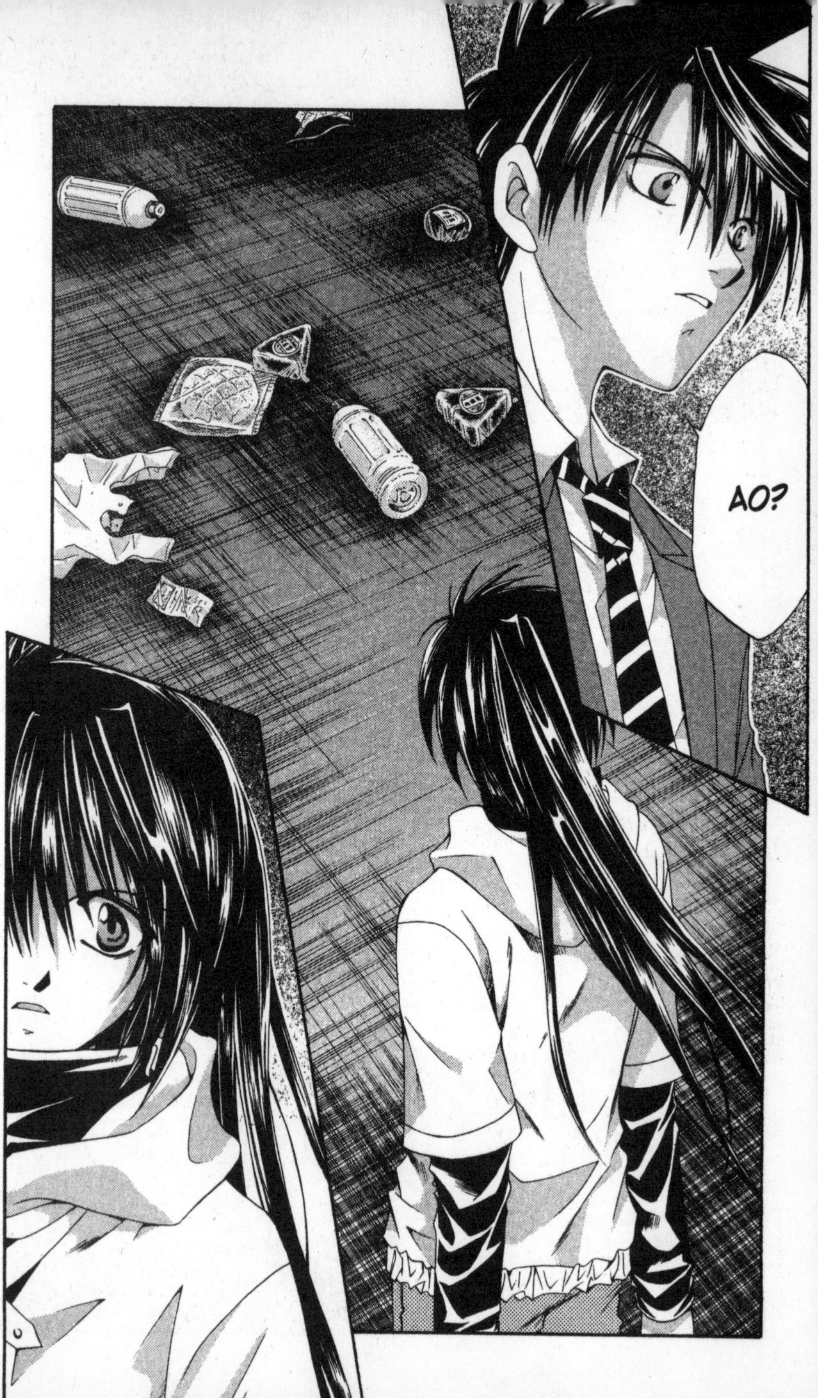
AO?

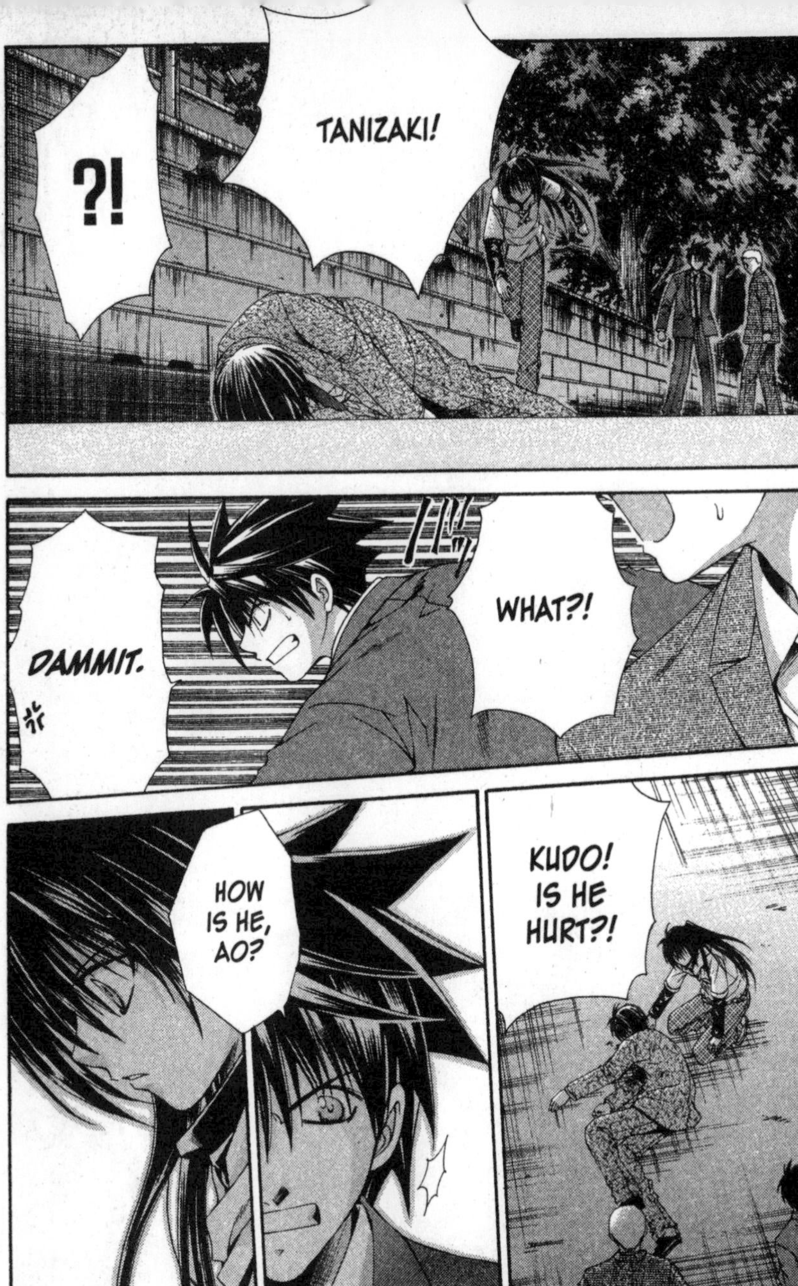
TANIZAKI!
?!
WHAT?!
DAMMIT.
KUDO! IS HE HURT?!
HOW IS HE, AO?

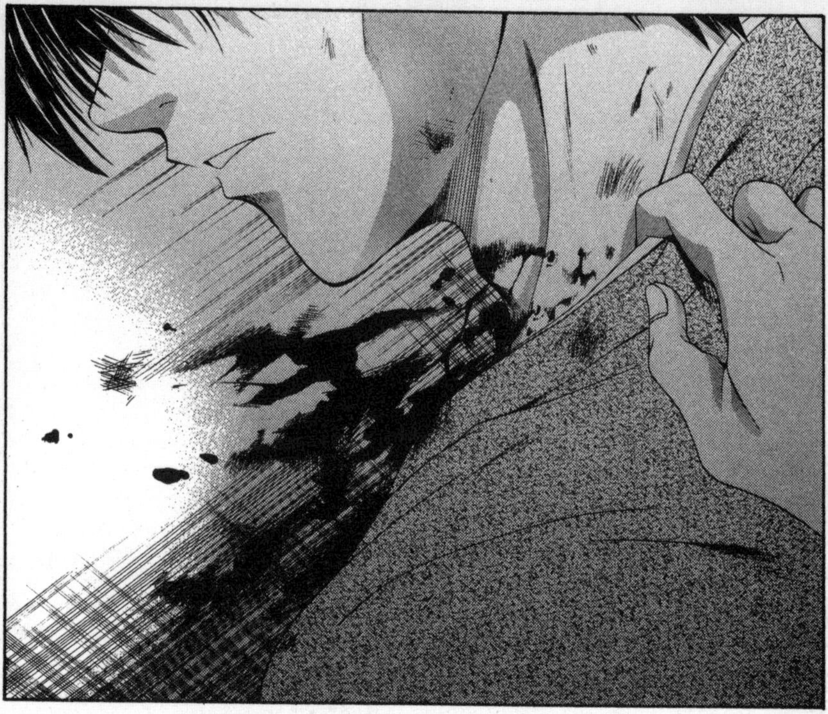
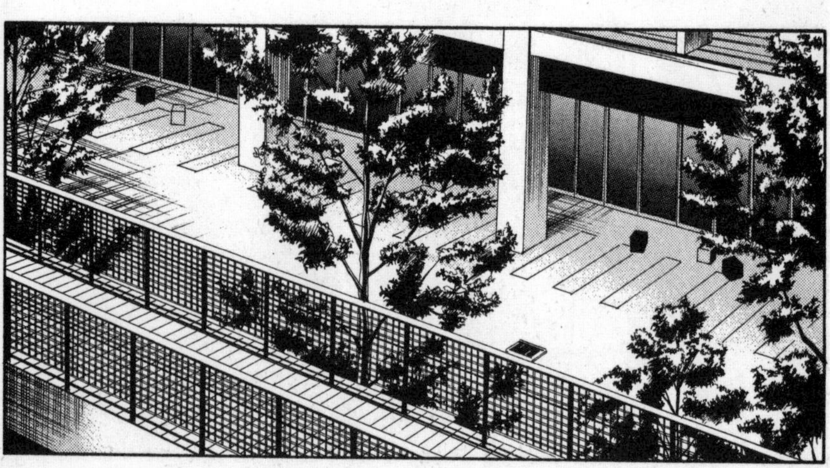

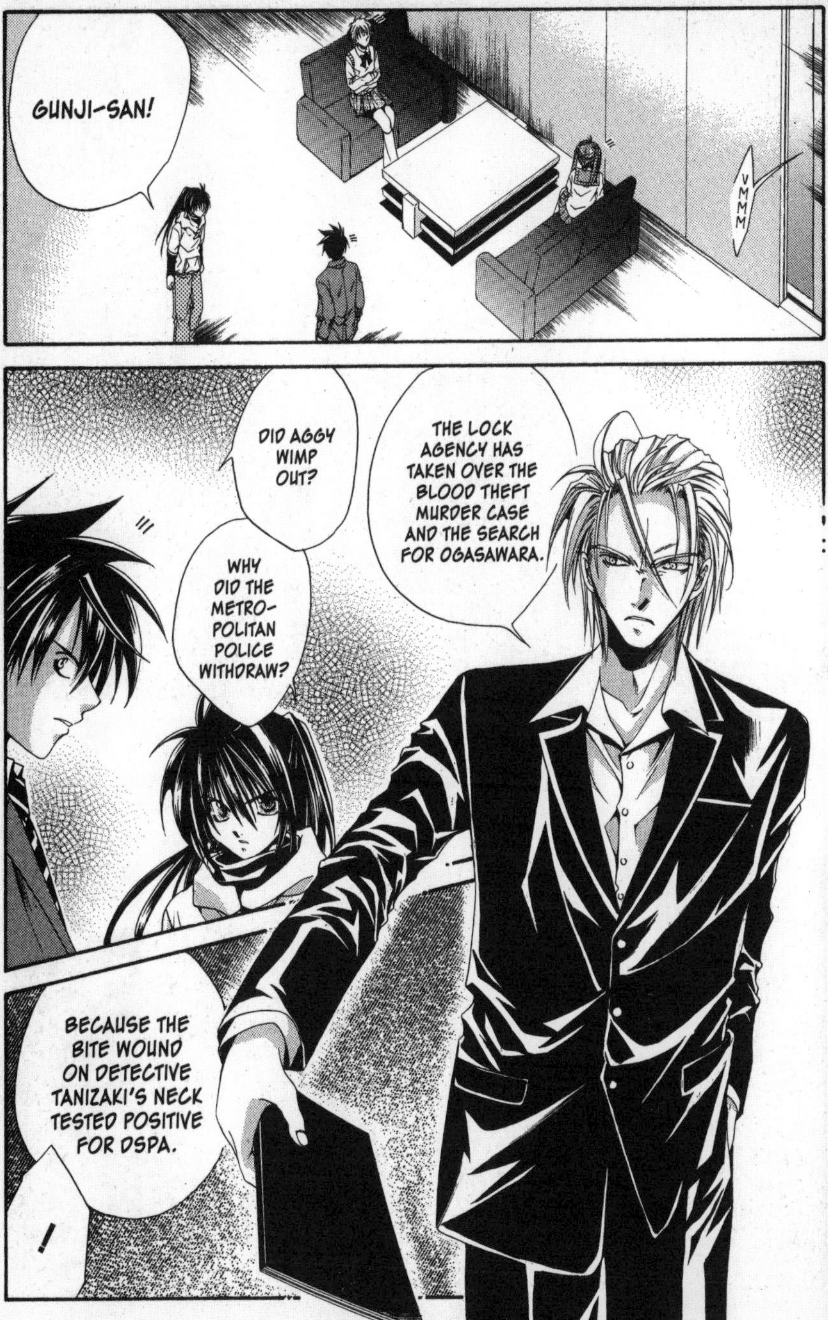
VMMM
GUNJI-SAN!
THE LOCK AGENCY HAS TAKEN OVER THE BLOOD THEFT MURDER CASE AND THE SEARCH FOR OGASAWARA.
DID AGGY WIMP OUT?
WHY DID THE METRO-POLITAN POLICE WITHDRAW?
BECAUSE THE BITE WOUND ON DETECTIVE TANIZAKI'S NECK TESTED POSITIVE FOR DSPA.
!

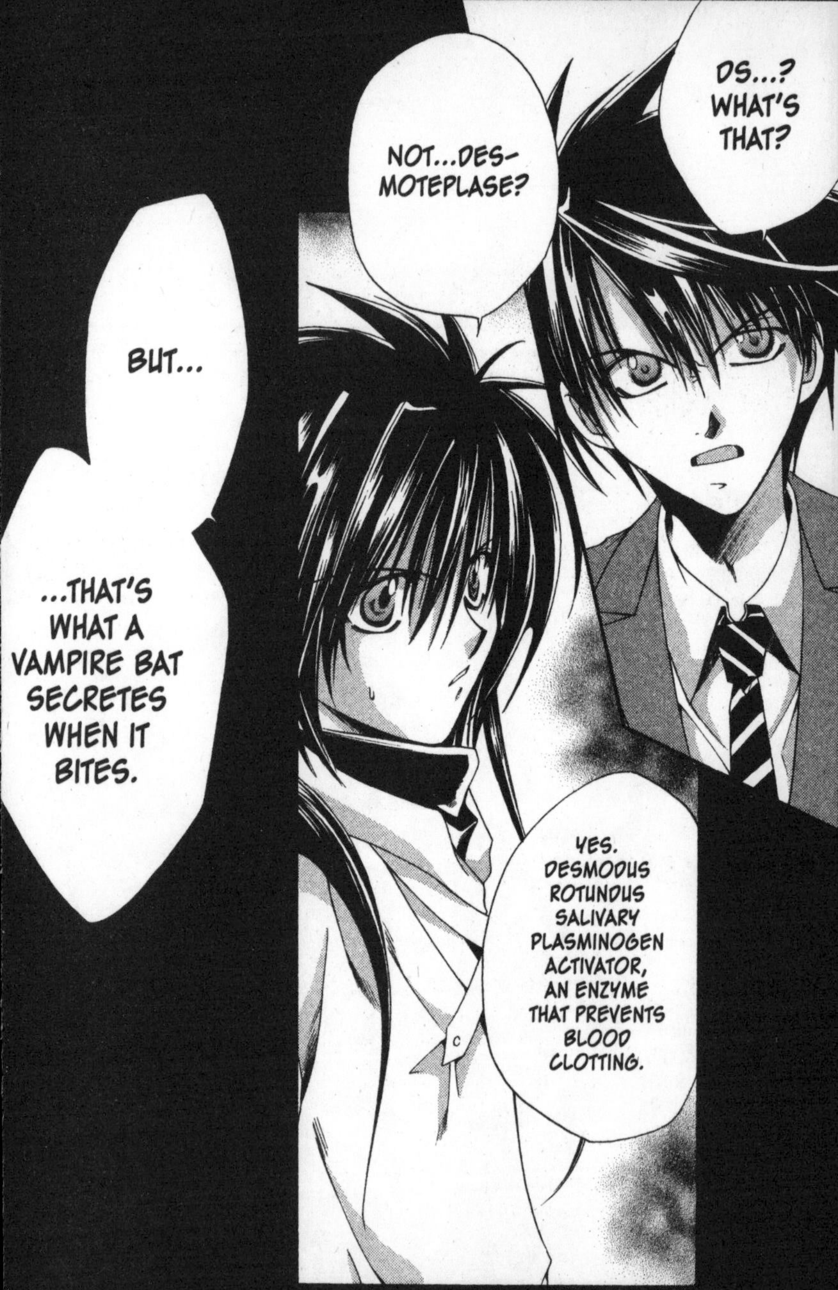
DS...? WHAT'S THAT?
NOT...DES-MOTEPLASE?
YES. DESMODUS ROTUNDUS SALIVARY PLASMINOGEN ACTIVATOR, AN ENZYME THAT PREVENTS BLOOD CLOTTING.
BUT...
...THAT'S WHAT A VAMPIRE BAT SECRETES WHEN IT BITES.

CHRONICLE 14

PSYCHIC POWER NANAKI™

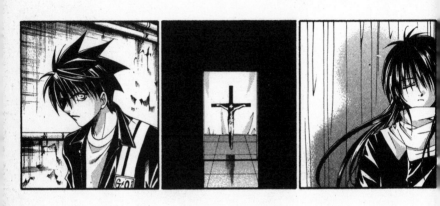

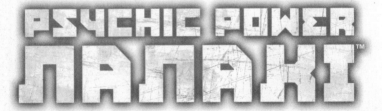

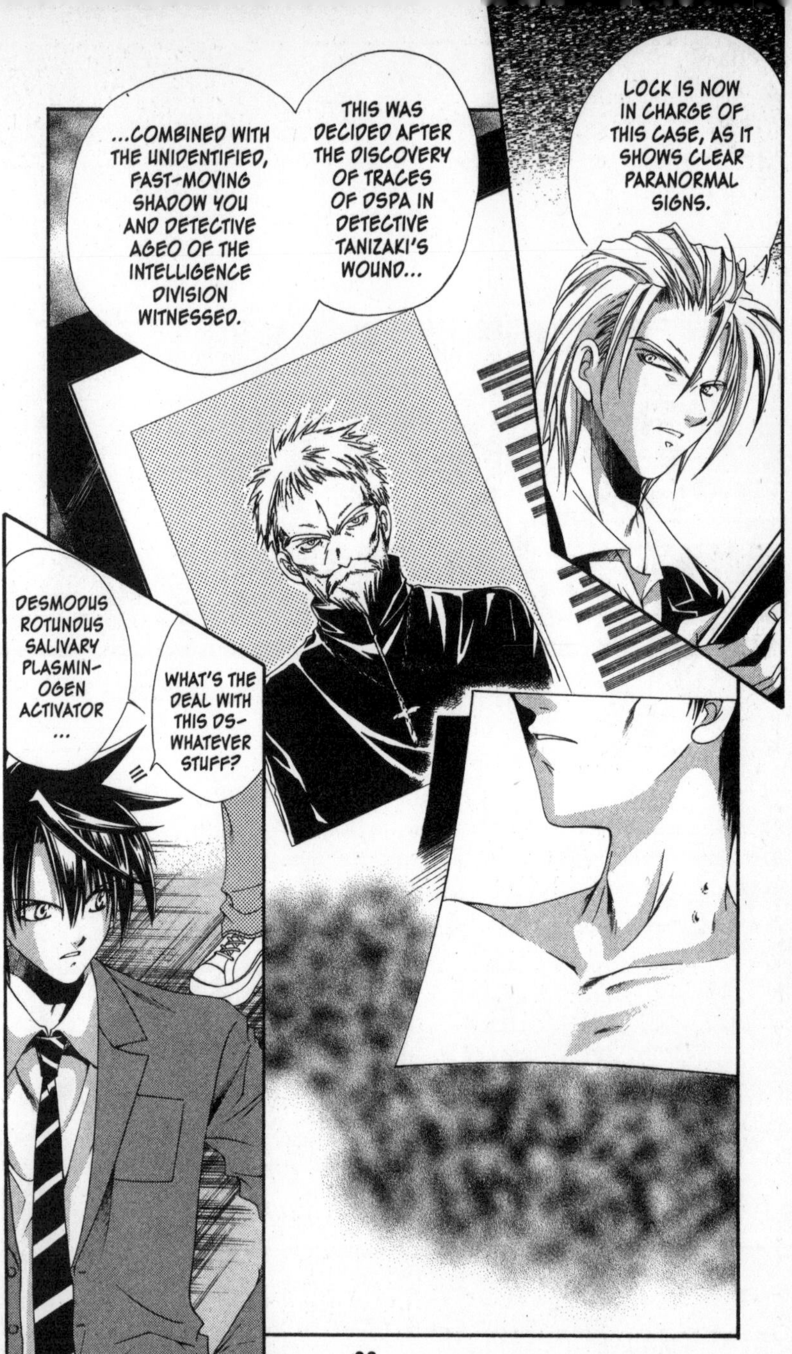
LOCK IS NOW IN CHARGE OF THIS CASE, AS IT SHOWS CLEAR PARANORMAL SIGNS.
THIS WAS DECIDED AFTER THE DISCOVERY OF TRACES OF DSPA IN DETECTIVE TANIZAKI'S WOUND...
...COMBINED WITH THE UNIDENTIFIED, FAST-MOVING SHADOW YOU AND DETECTIVE AGEO OF THE INTELLIGENCE DIVISION WITNESSED.
WHAT'S THE DEAL WITH THIS DS-WHATEVER STUFF?
DESMODUS ROTUNDUS SALIVARY PLASMIN-OGEN ACTIVATOR ...

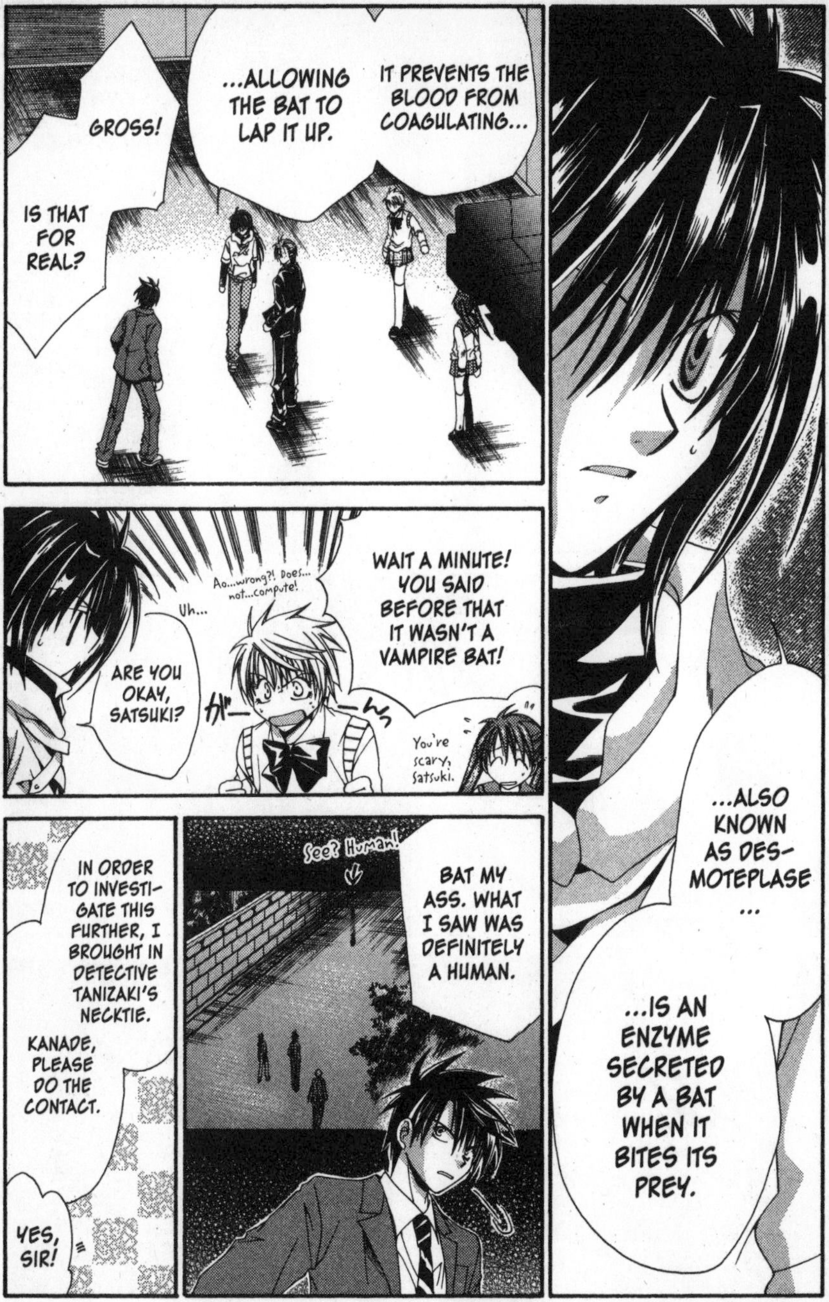
...ALSO KNOWN AS DES-MOTEPLASE ...
...IS AN ENZYME SECRETED BY A BAT WHEN IT BITES ITS PREY.
IT PREVENTS THE BLOOD FROM COAGULATING...
...ALLOWING THE BAT TO LAP IT UP.
GROSS!
IS THAT FOR REAL?
WAIT A MINUTE! YOU SAID BEFORE THAT IT WASN'T A VAMPIRE BAT!
You're scary, Satsuki.
Ao...wrong?! Does... not...compute!
Uh...
ARE YOU OKAY, SATSUKI?
See? Human!
BAT MY ASS. WHAT I SAW WAS DEFINITELY A HUMAN.
IN ORDER TO INVESTIGATE THIS FURTHER, I BROUGHT IN DETECTIVE TANIZAKI'S NECKTIE.
KANADE, PLEASE DO THE CONTACT.
YES, SIR!

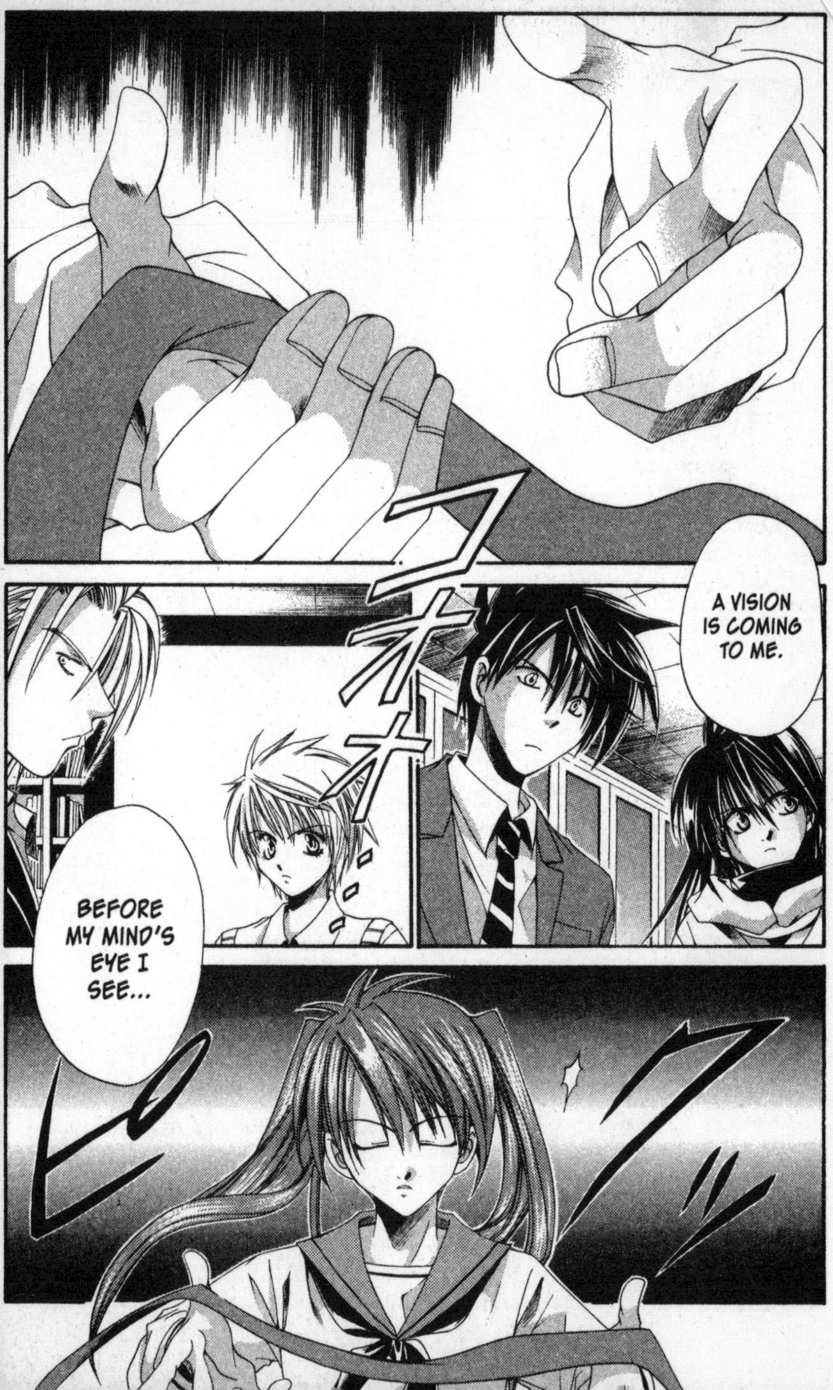
A VISION IS COMING TO ME.
BEFORE MY MIND'S EYE I SEE...

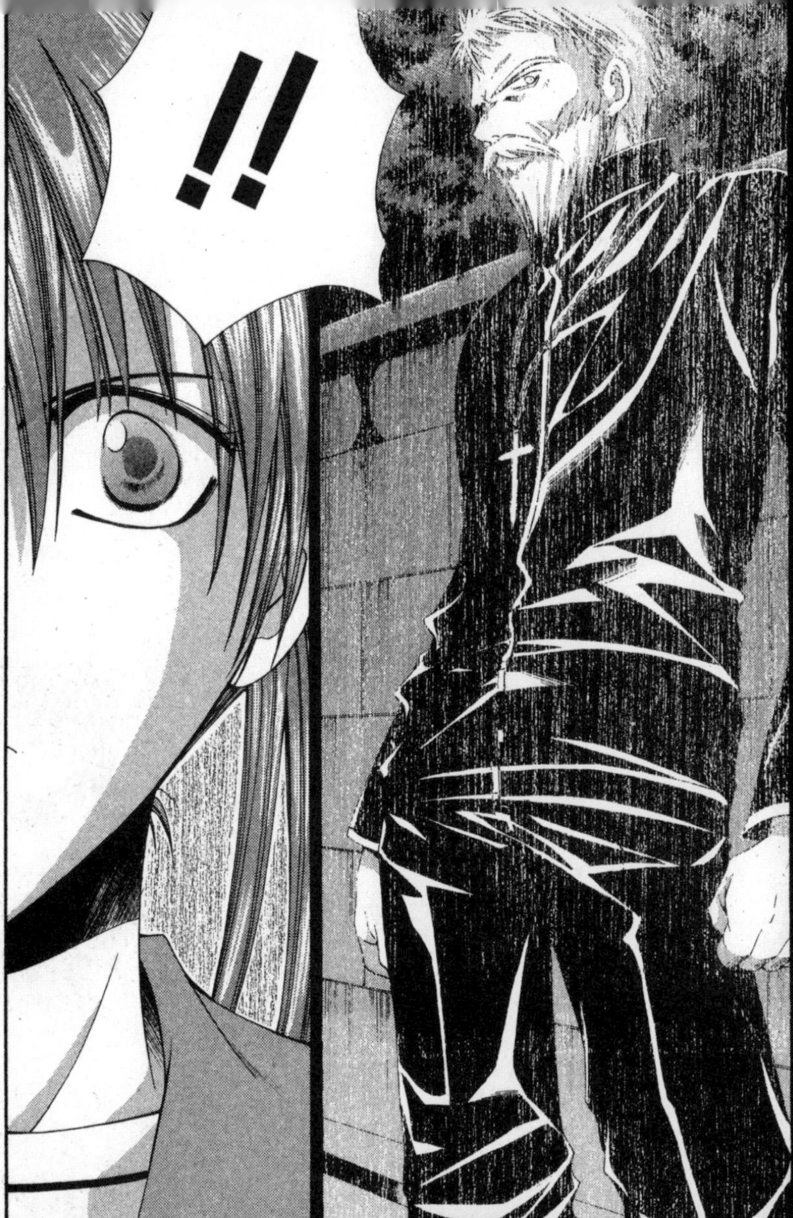
!!

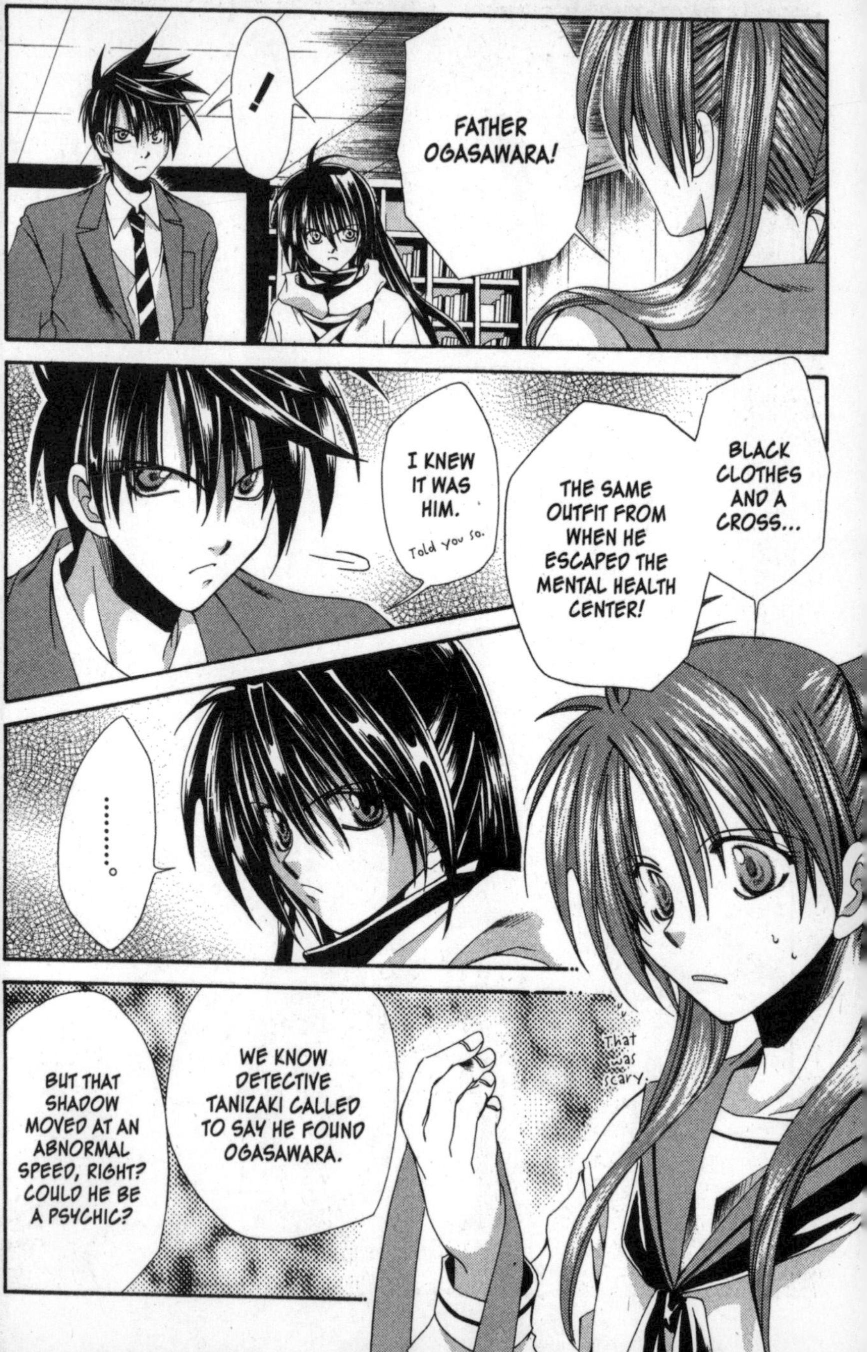
FATHER OGASAWARA!
!
BLACK CLOTHES AND A CROSS...
THE SAME OUTFIT FROM WHEN HE ESCAPED THE MENTAL HEALTH CENTER!
I KNEW IT WAS HIM.
Told you so.
....
That was scary.
WE KNOW DETECTIVE TANIZAKI CALLED TO SAY HE FOUND OGASAWARA.
BUT THAT SHADOW MOVED AT AN ABNORMAL SPEED, RIGHT? COULD HE BE A PSYCHIC?

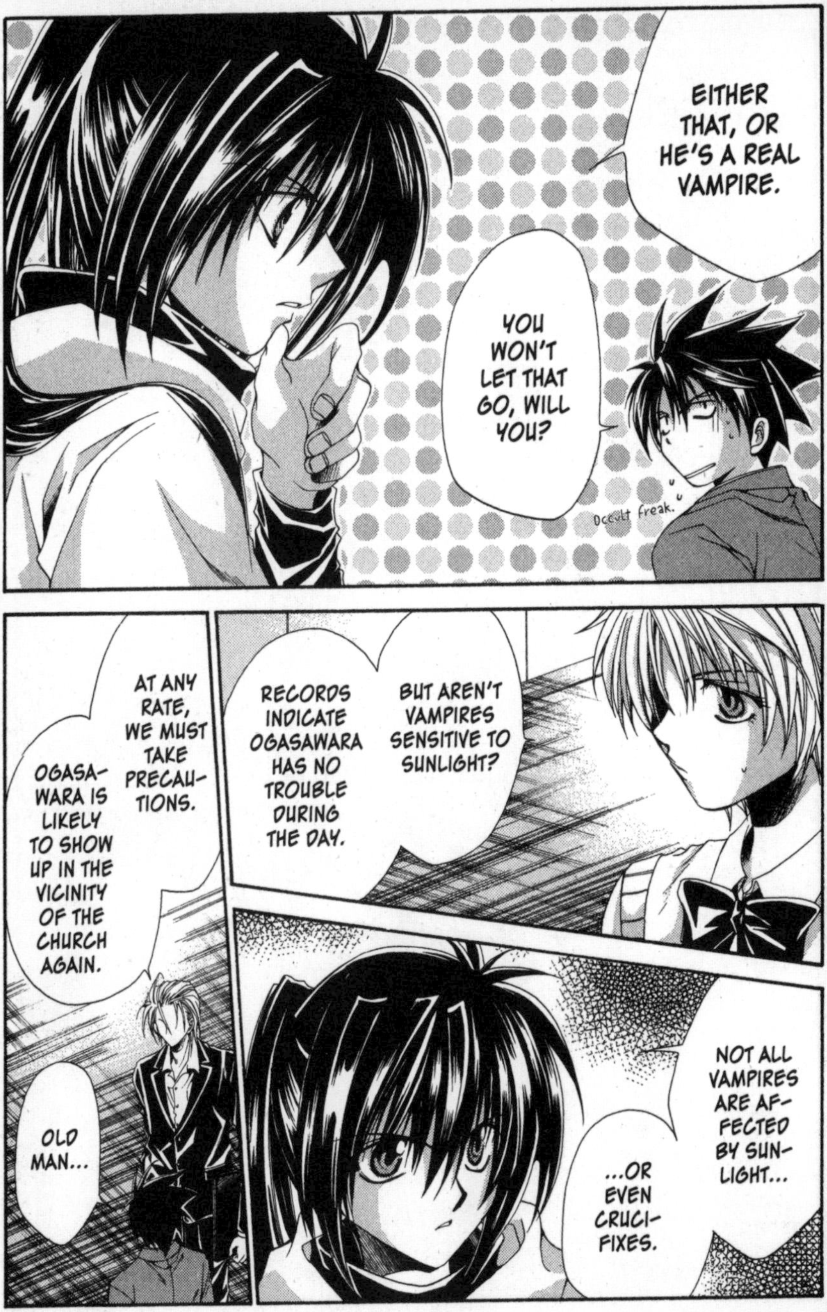
EITHER THAT, OR HE'S A REAL VAMPIRE.
YOU WON'T LET THAT GO, WILL YOU?
Occult freak.
BUT AREN'T VAMPIRES SENSITIVE TO SUNLIGHT?
RECORDS INDICATE OGASAWARA HAS NO TROUBLE DURING THE DAY.
NOT ALL VAMPIRES ARE AF-FECTED BY SUN-LIGHT...
...OR EVEN CRUCI-FIXES.
AT ANY RATE, WE MUST TAKE PRECAU-TIONS.
OGASA-WARA IS LIKELY TO SHOW UP IN THE VICINITY OF THE CHURCH AGAIN.
OLD MAN...

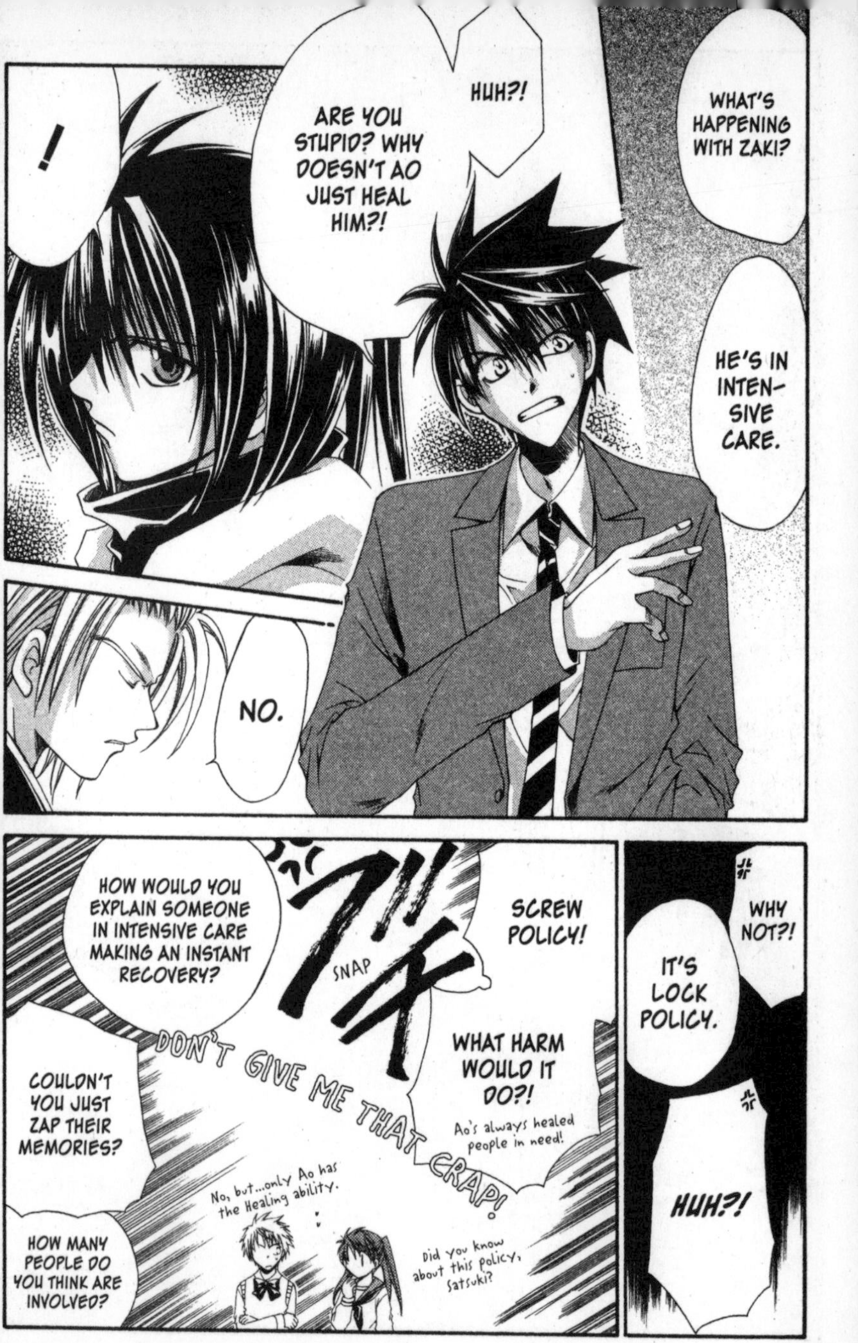
WHAT'S HAPPENING WITH ZAKI?
HE'S IN INTEN-SIVE CARE.
HUH?!
ARE YOU STUPID? WHY DOESN'T AO JUST HEAL HIM?!
!
NO.
WHY NOT?!
IT'S LOCK POLICY.
HUH?!
SCREW POLICY!
WHAT HARM WOULD IT DO?!
Ao's always healed people in need!
SNAP
DON'T GIVE ME THAT CRAP!
HOW WOULD YOU EXPLAIN SOMEONE IN INTENSIVE CARE MAKING AN INSTANT RECOVERY?
COULDN'T YOU JUST ZAP THEIR MEMORIES?
HOW MANY PEOPLE DO YOU THINK ARE INVOLVED?
Did you know about this policy, Satsuki?
No, but...only Ao has the Healing ability.

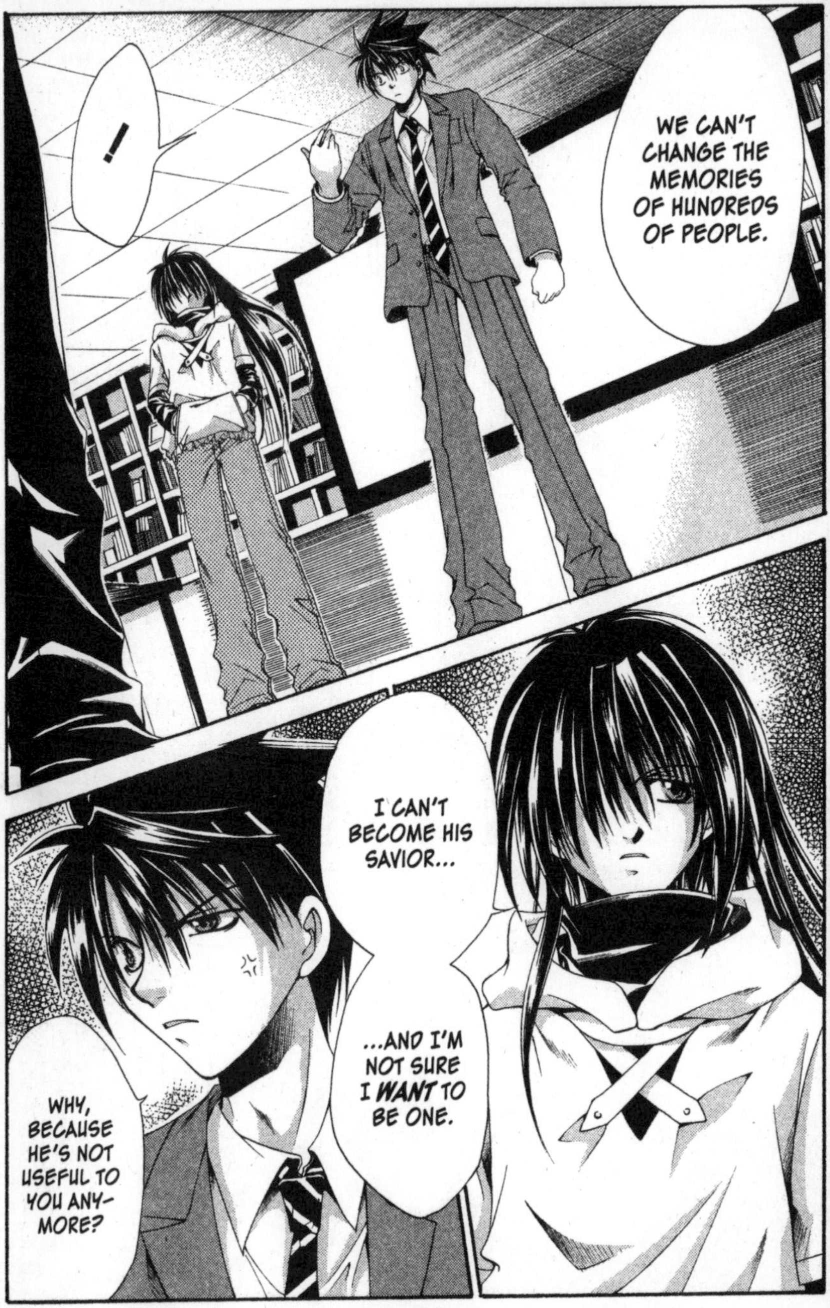
WE CAN'T CHANGE THE MEMORIES OF HUNDREDS OF PEOPLE.
!
I CAN'T BECOME HIS SAVIOR...
...AND I'M NOT SURE I *WANT* TO BE ONE.
WHY, BECAUSE HE'S NOT USEFUL TO YOU ANY-MORE?

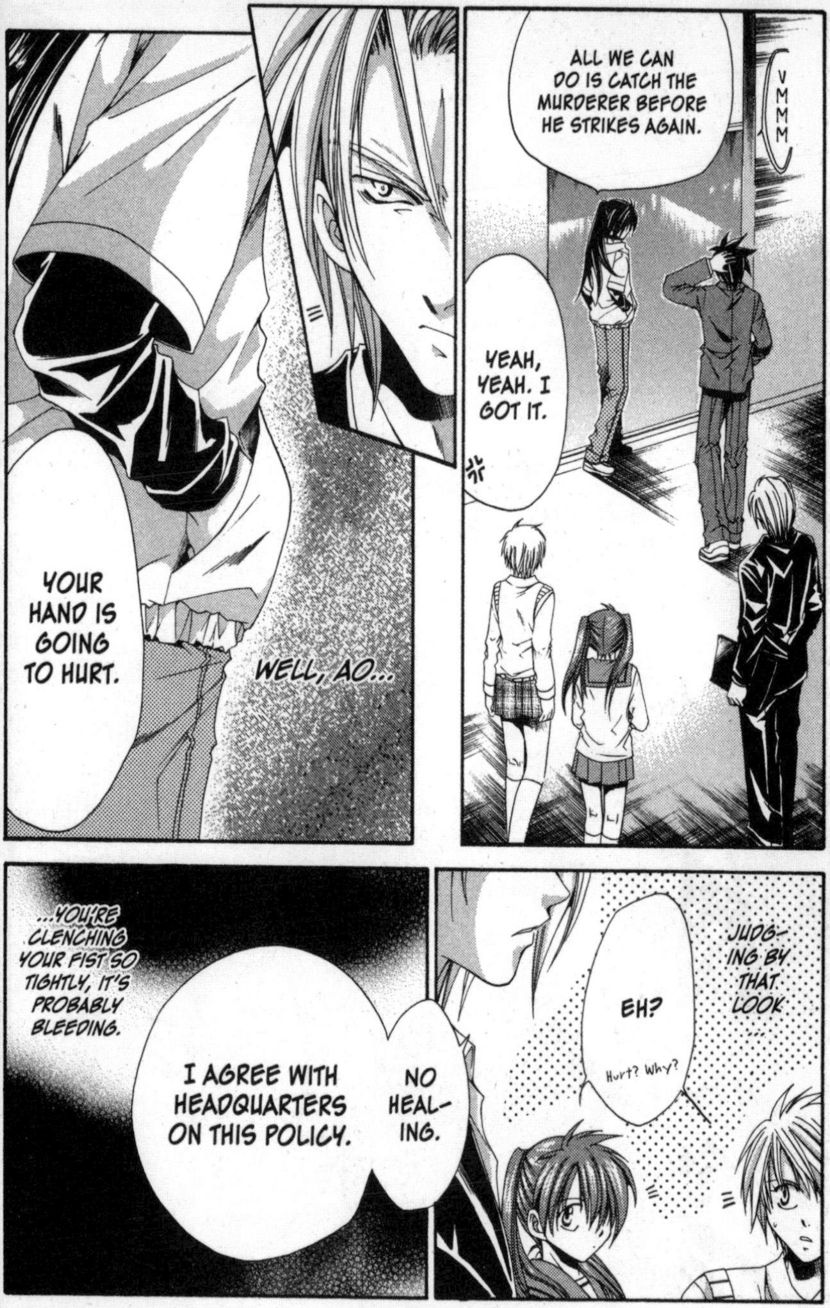
ALL WE CAN DO IS CATCH THE MURDERER BEFORE HE STRIKES AGAIN.
VMMM
YEAH, YEAH. I GOT IT.
WELL, AO...
YOUR HAND IS GOING TO HURT.
JUDGING BY THAT LOOK
EH?
Hurt? Why?
...YOU'RE CLENCHING YOUR FIST SO TIGHTLY, IT'S PROBABLY BLEEDING.
NO HEALING.
I AGREE WITH HEADQUARTERS ON THIS POLICY.

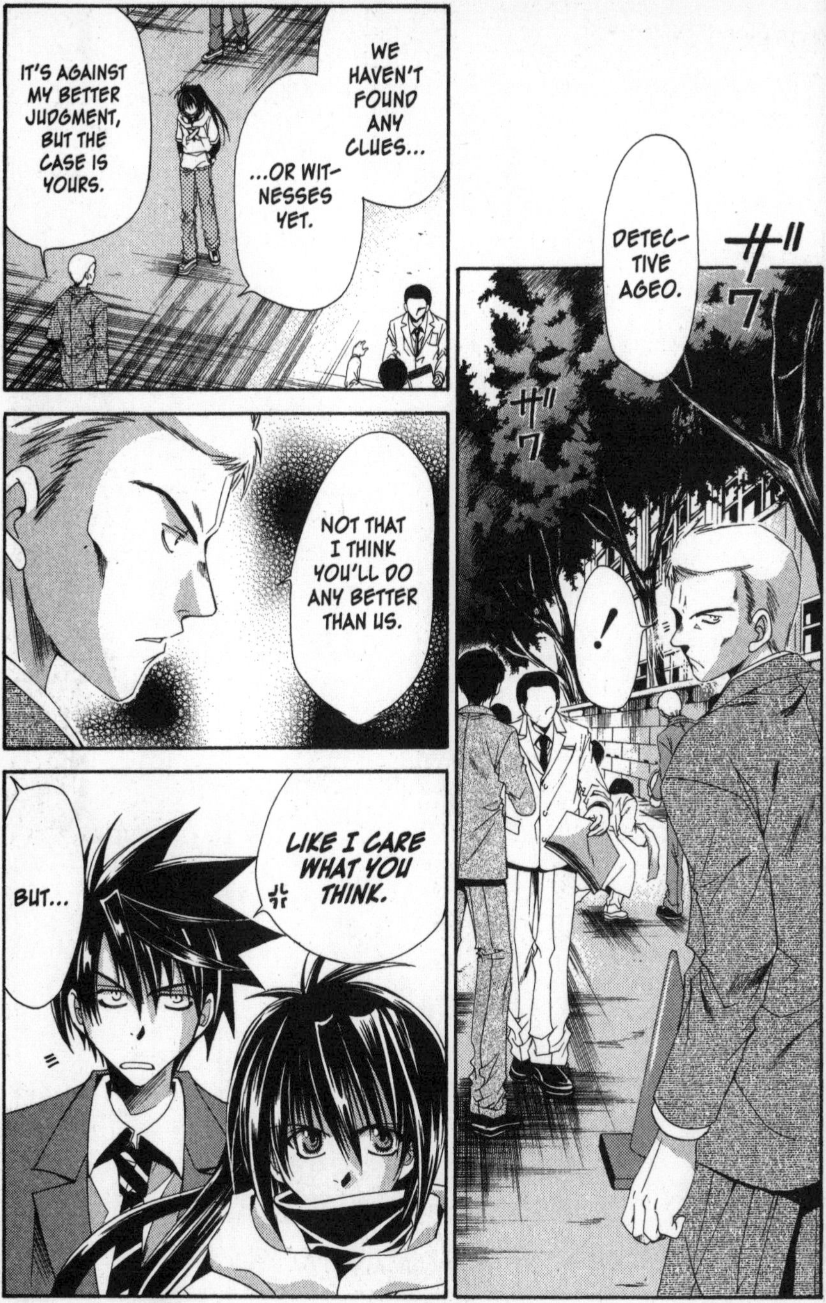
DETECTIVE AGEO.
ザワ
ザワ
!
WE HAVEN'T FOUND ANY CLUES...
...OR WITNESSES YET.
IT'S AGAINST MY BETTER JUDGMENT, BUT THE CASE IS YOURS.
NOT THAT I THINK YOU'LL DO ANY BETTER THAN US.
LIKE I CARE WHAT YOU THINK.
BUT...

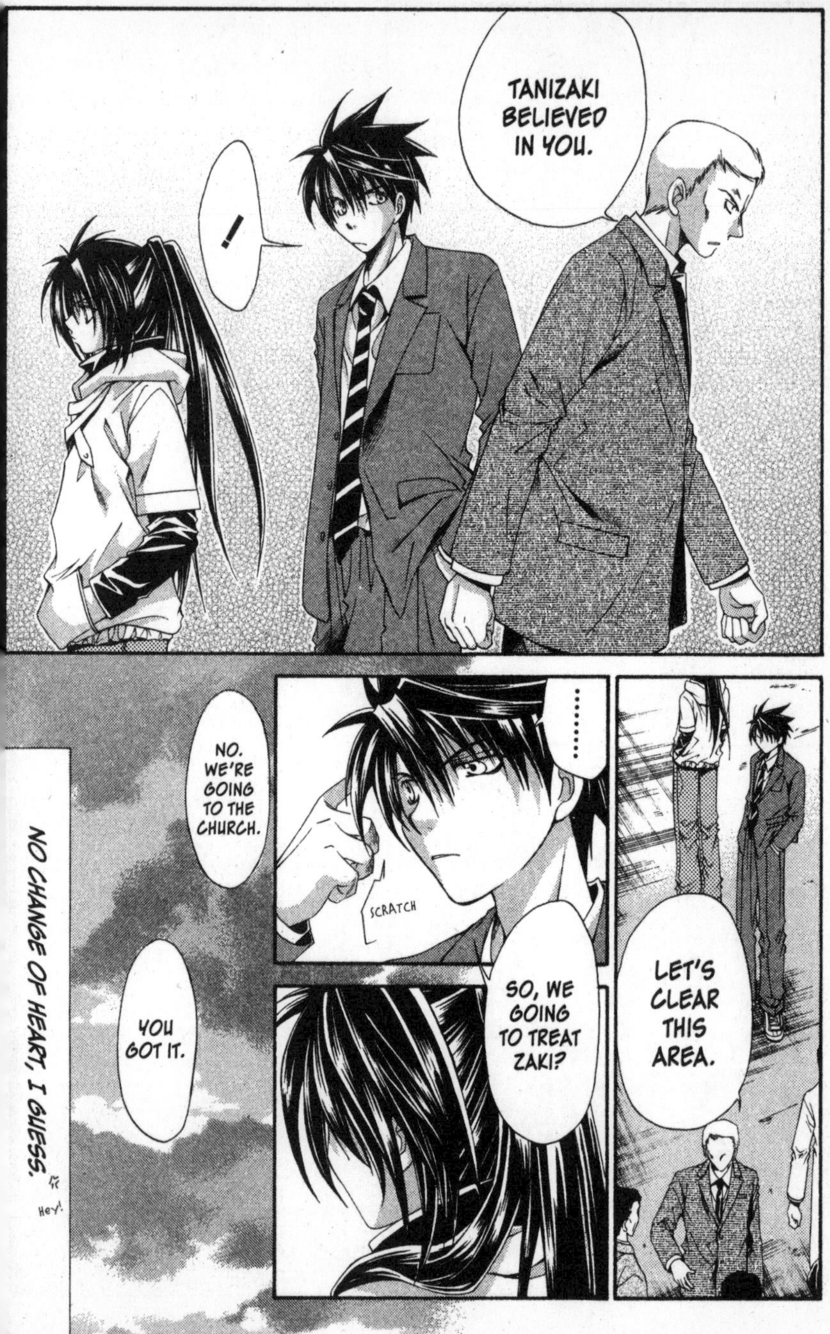
TANIZAKI BELIEVED IN YOU.
!
LET'S CLEAR THIS AREA.
SO, WE GOING TO TREAT ZAKI?
......
SCRATCH
NO. WE'RE GOING TO THE CHURCH.
YOU GOT IT.
NO CHANGE OF HEART, I GUESS.
Hey!

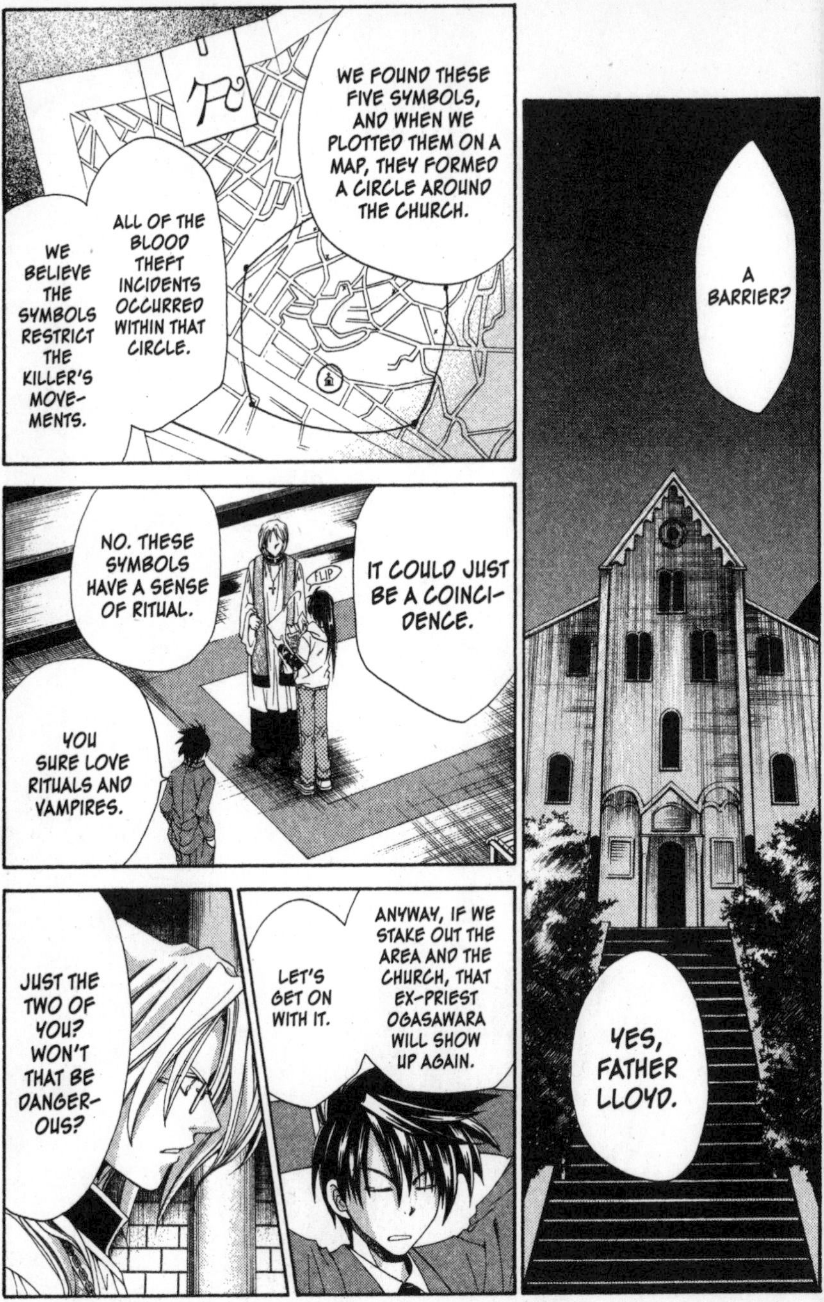
A BARRIER?
YES, FATHER LLOYD.
WE FOUND THESE FIVE SYMBOLS, AND WHEN WE PLOTTED THEM ON A MAP, THEY FORMED A CIRCLE AROUND THE CHURCH.
ALL OF THE BLOOD THEFT INCIDENTS OCCURRED WITHIN THAT CIRCLE.
WE BELIEVE THE SYMBOLS RESTRICT THE KILLER'S MOVE-MENTS.
IT COULD JUST BE A COINCI-DENCE.
FLIP
NO. THESE SYMBOLS HAVE A SENSE OF RITUAL.
YOU SURE LOVE RITUALS AND VAMPIRES.
ANYWAY, IF WE STAKE OUT THE AREA AND THE CHURCH, THAT EX-PRIEST OGASAWARA WILL SHOW UP AGAIN.
LET'S GET ON WITH IT.
JUST THE TWO OF YOU? WON'T THAT BE DANGER-OUS?

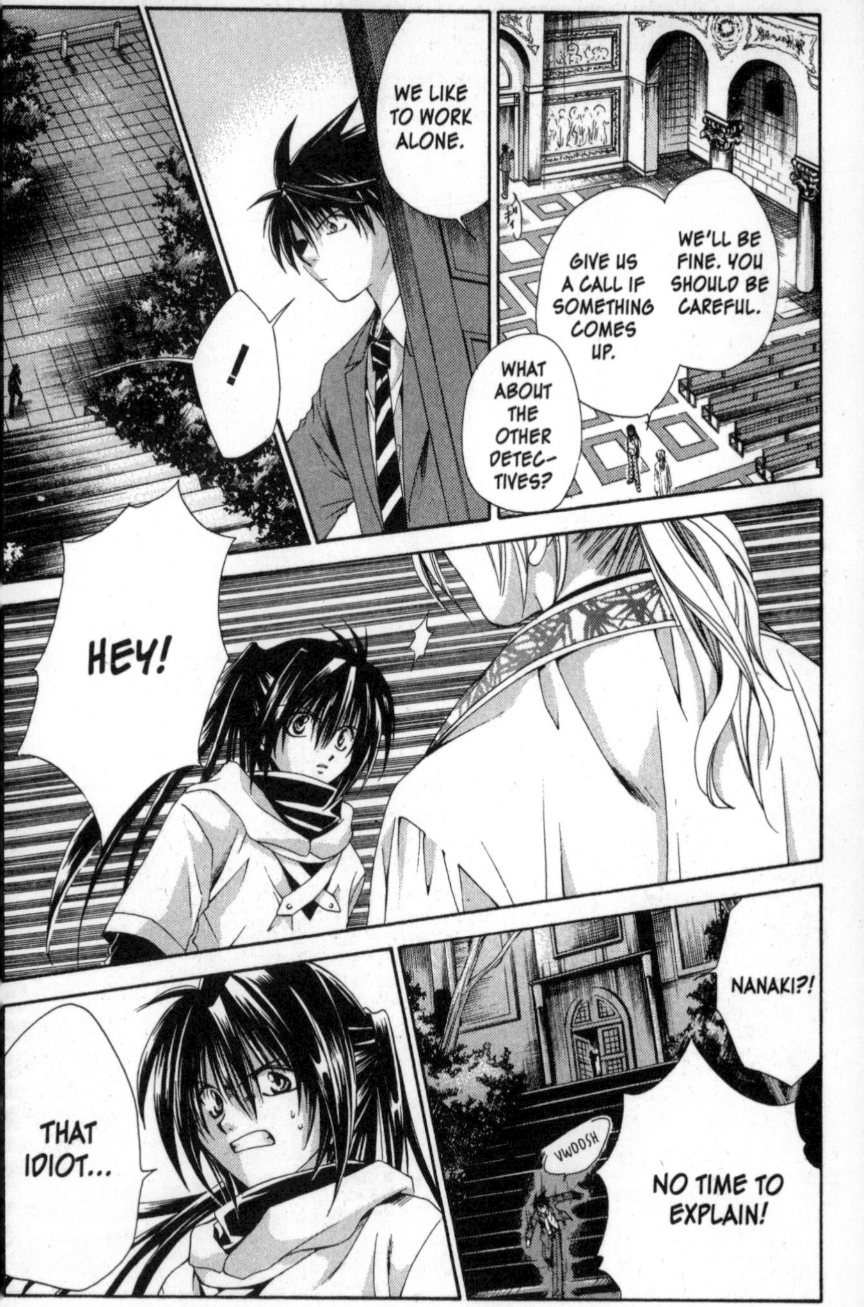
WE'LL BE FINE. YOU SHOULD BE CAREFUL.
GIVE US A CALL IF SOMETHING COMES UP.
WHAT ABOUT THE OTHER DETECTIVES?
WE LIKE TO WORK ALONE.
!
HEY!
NANAKI?!
NO TIME TO EXPLAIN!
VWOOSH
THAT IDIOT...

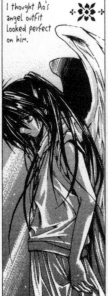

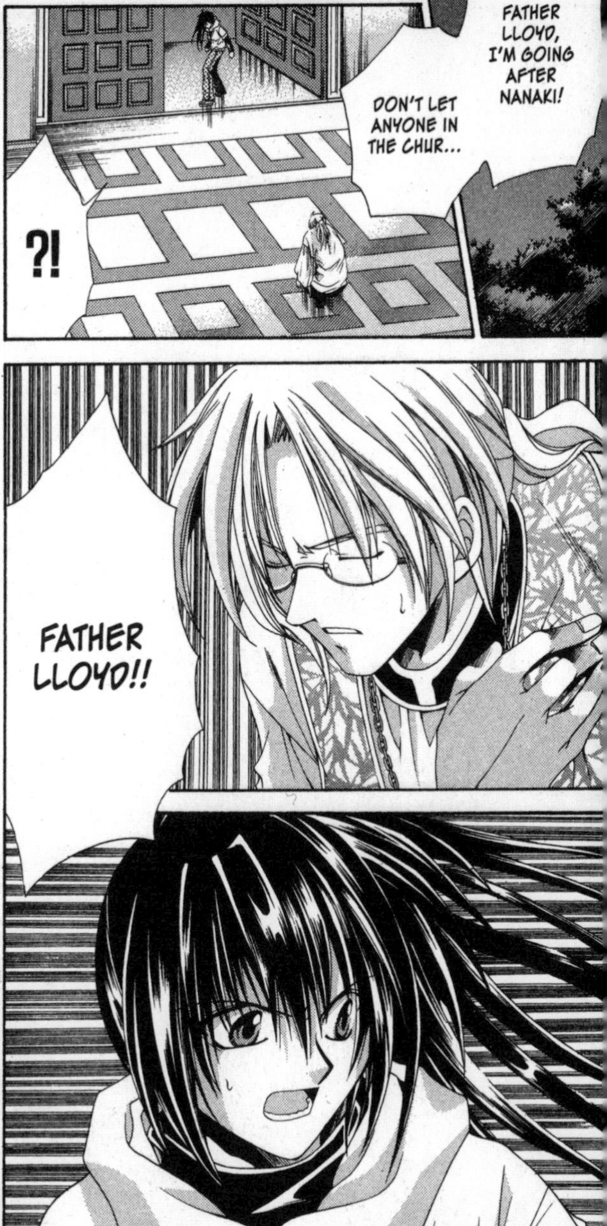
FATHER LLOYD, I'M GOING AFTER NANAKI!
DON'T LET ANYONE IN THE CHUR...
?!
FATHER LLOYD!!

The last four installments of the Blood Theft Murder Case are actually an entire volume compressed. I had planned to do it in two or three installments. I was reluctant to have it four chapters long but it just grew (lol)!

By the way, I really enjoyed drawing the title page of Chronicle 13, especially the snake and the eye in the mural (wry smile). I really love that kind of stuff.

I tried to make the wings in the mural appear to be attached to Ao's back, but what do you think? Is it too difficult to tell? (smile)

I did a similar illustration for fun a long time ago and I thought I should give that layout a try again. Ha ha... ;

I thought Ao's angel outfit looked perfect on him.

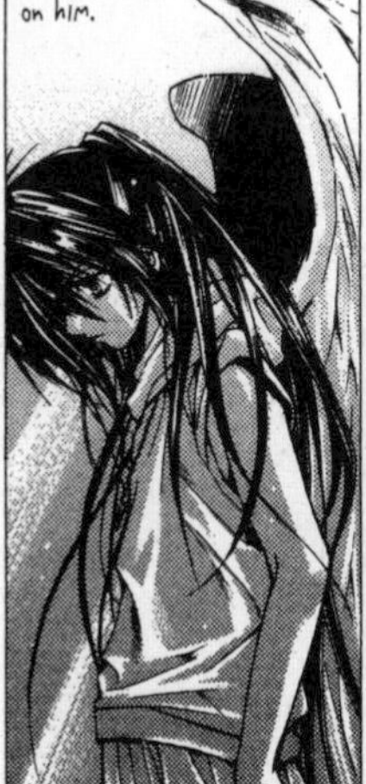

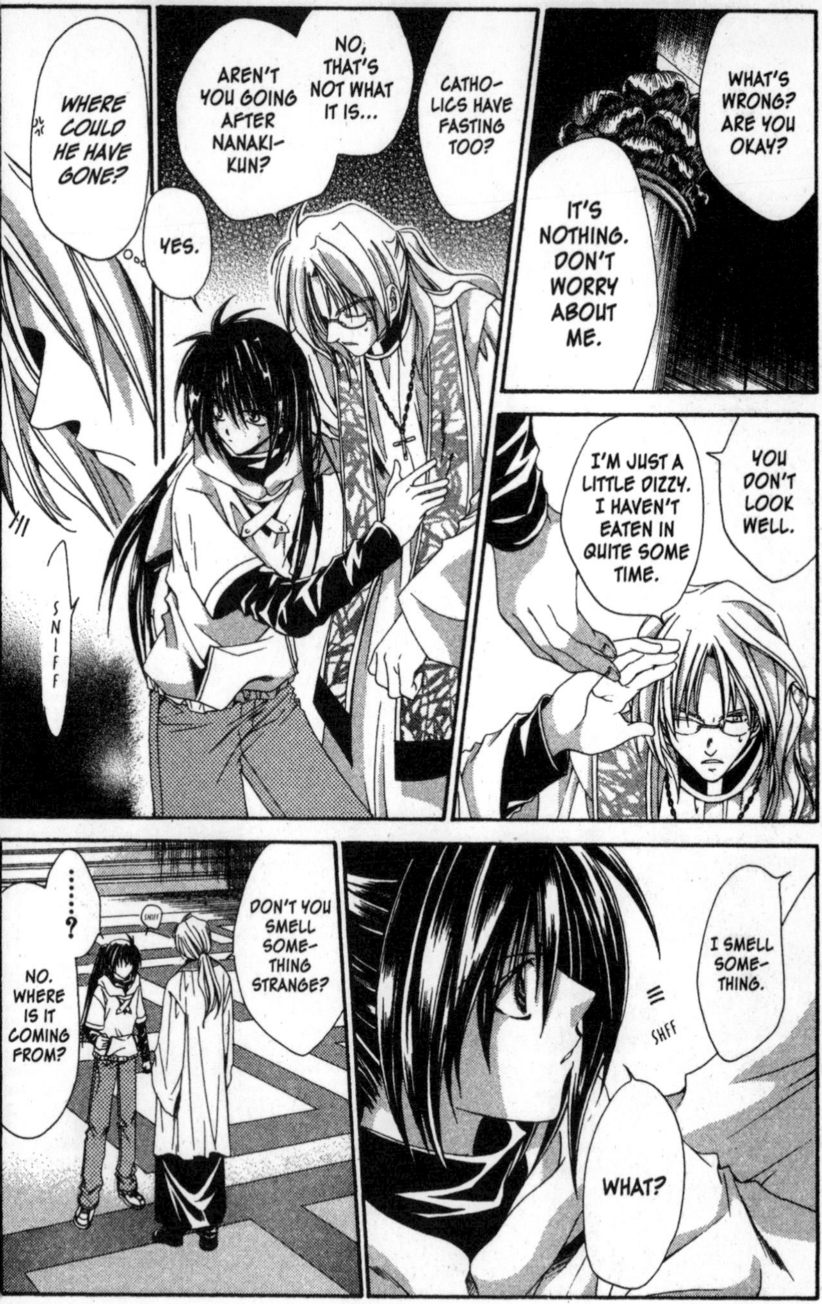
WHAT'S WRONG? ARE YOU OKAY?
IT'S NOTHING. DON'T WORRY ABOUT ME.
YOU DON'T LOOK WELL.
I'M JUST A LITTLE DIZZY. I HAVEN'T EATEN IN QUITE SOME TIME.
CATHOLICS HAVE FASTING TOO?
NO, THAT'S NOT WHAT IT IS...
AREN'T YOU GOING AFTER NANAKI-KUN?
YES.
WHERE COULD HE HAVE GONE?
SNIFF
I SMELL SOMETHING.
SHFF
WHAT?
DON'T YOU SMELL SOMETHING STRANGE?
SNIFF
......?
NO. WHERE IS IT COMING FROM?

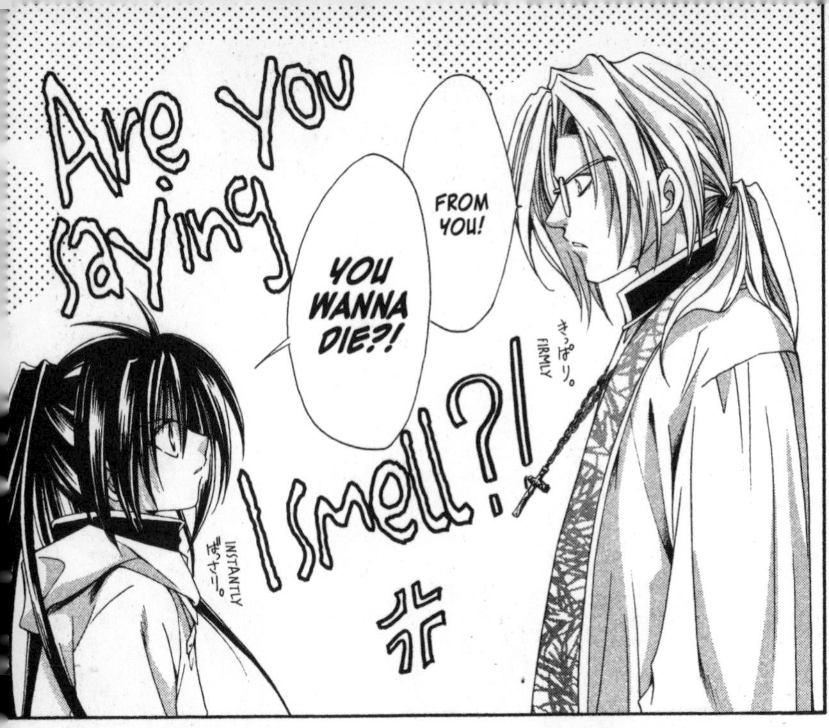
FROM YOU!
きっぱり。 FIRMLY
Are you saying I smell?!
YOU WANNA DIE?!
ばっさり。 INSTANTLY

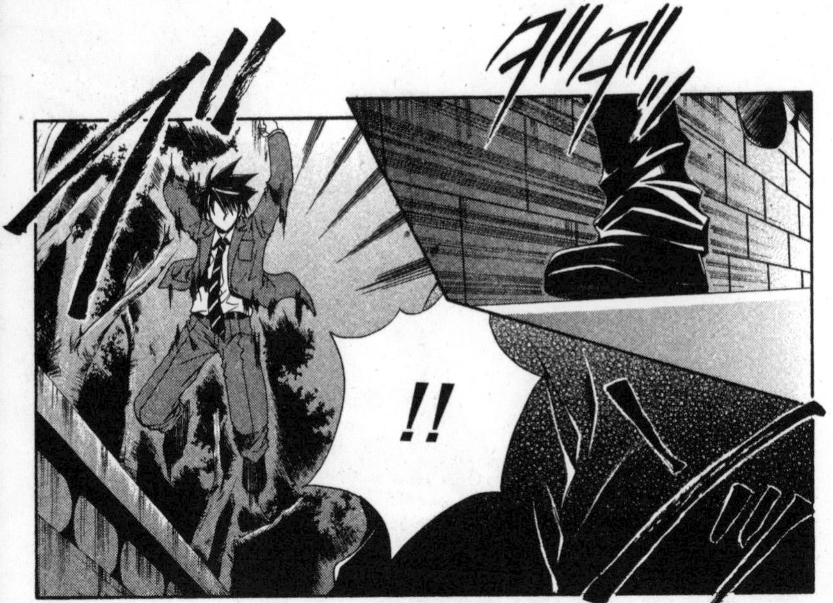
!!

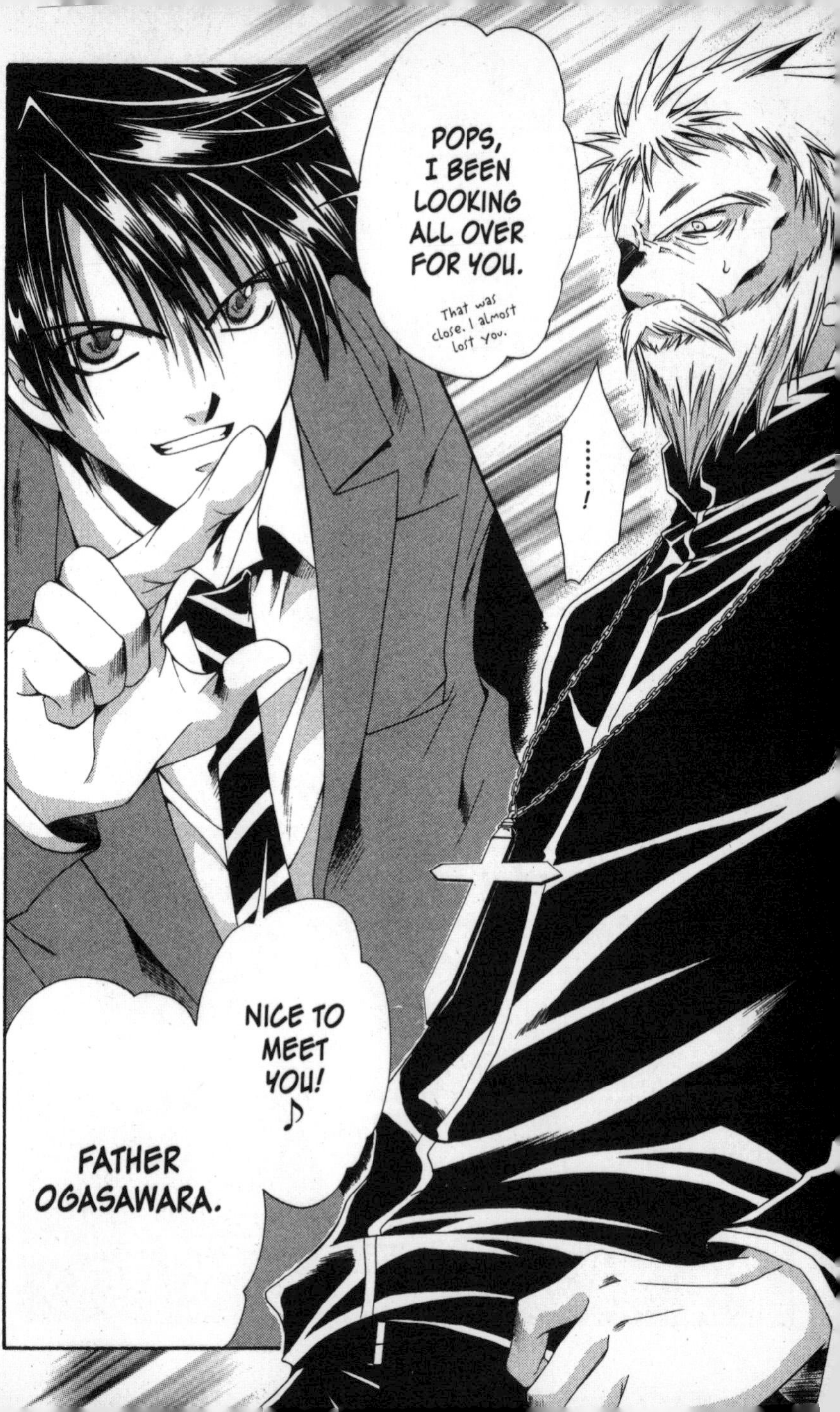
POPS, I BEEN LOOKING ALL OVER FOR YOU.
That was close. I almost lost you.
......!
NICE TO MEET YOU! ♪
FATHER OGASAWARA.

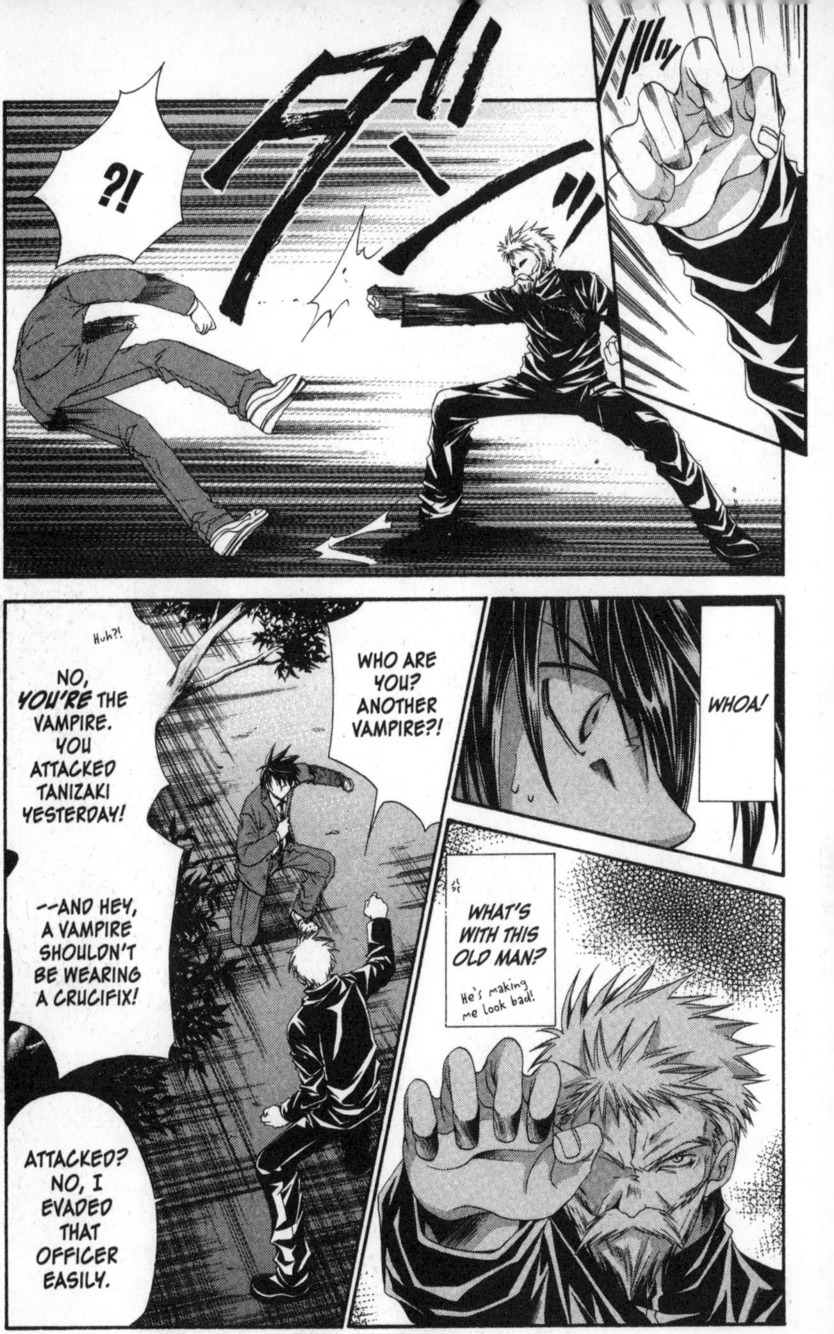
?!
WHOA!
WHAT'S WITH THIS OLD MAN?
He's making me look bad!
WHO ARE YOU? ANOTHER VAMPIRE?!
Huh?!
NO, *YOU'RE* THE VAMPIRE. YOU ATTACKED TANIZAKI YESTERDAY!
--AND HEY, A VAMPIRE SHOULDN'T BE WEARING A CRUCIFIX!
ATTACKED? NO, I EVADED THAT OFFICER EASILY.

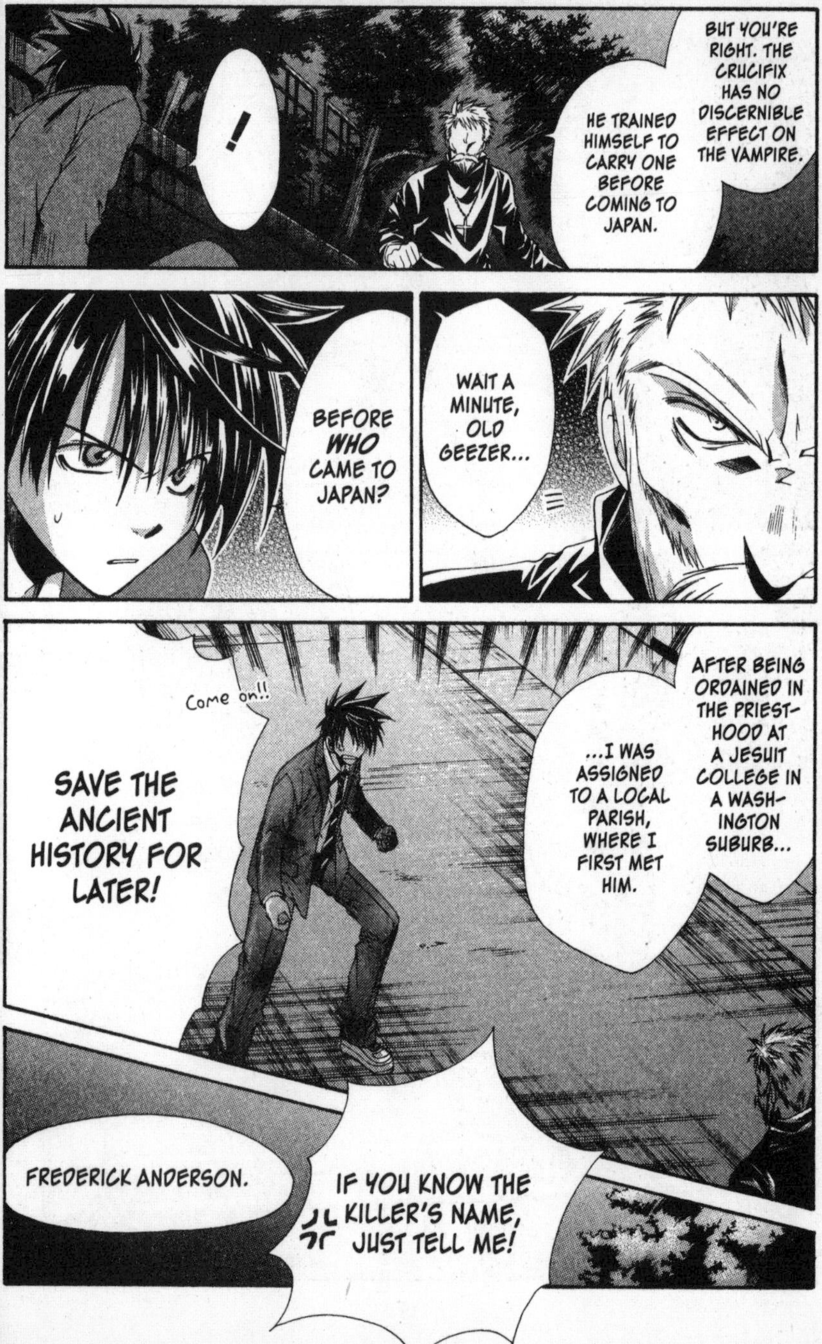
BUT YOU'RE RIGHT. THE CRUCIFIX HAS NO DISCERNIBLE EFFECT ON THE VAMPIRE.
HE TRAINED HIMSELF TO CARRY ONE BEFORE COMING TO JAPAN.
!
WAIT A MINUTE, OLD GEEZER...
BEFORE *WHO* CAME TO JAPAN?
AFTER BEING ORDAINED IN THE PRIEST-HOOD AT A JESUIT COLLEGE IN A WASH-INGTON SUBURB...
...I WAS ASSIGNED TO A LOCAL PARISH, WHERE I FIRST MET HIM.
Come on!!
SAVE THE ANCIENT HISTORY FOR LATER!
IF YOU KNOW THE KILLER'S NAME, JUST TELL ME!
FREDERICK ANDERSON.

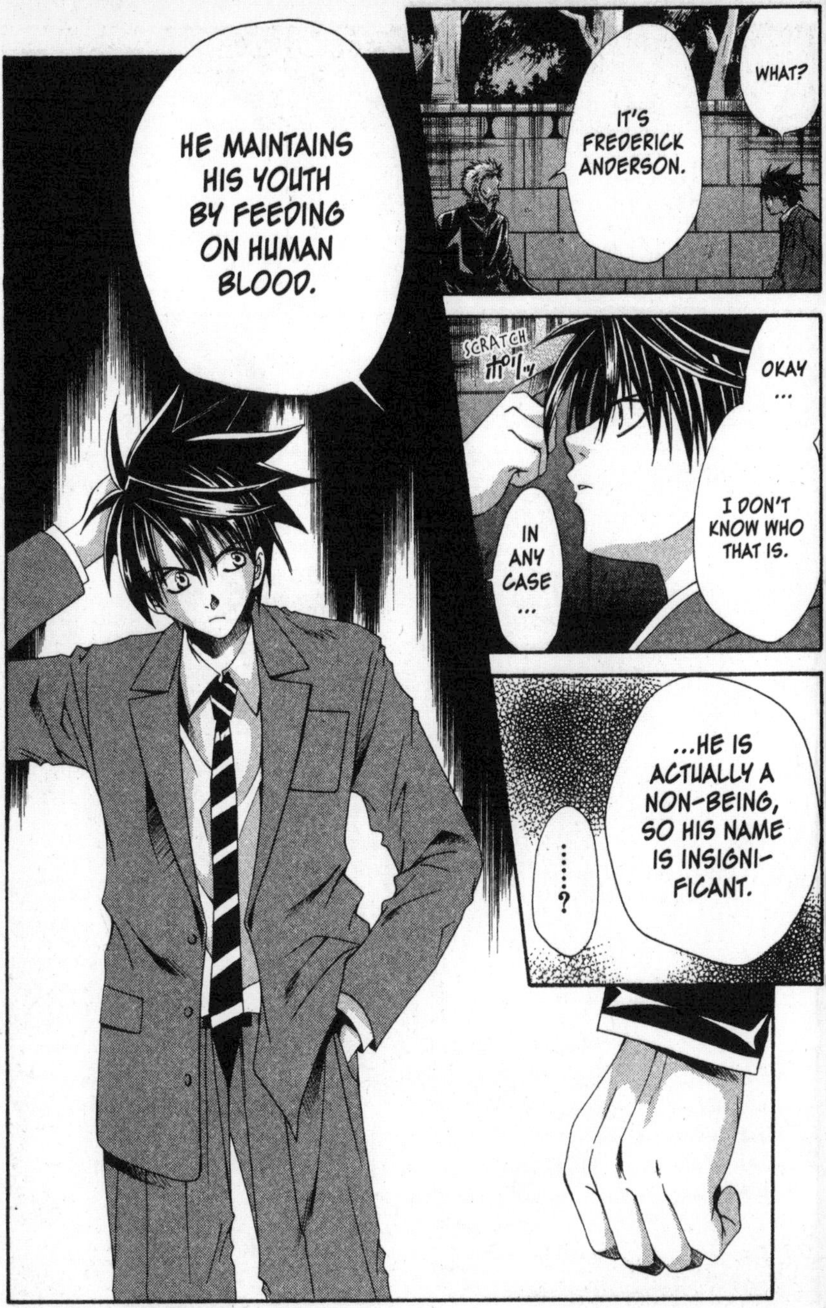
WHAT?
IT'S FREDERICK ANDERSON.
SCRATCH ポリッ
OKAY ...
I DON'T KNOW WHO THAT IS.
IN ANY CASE ...
...HE IS ACTUALLY A NON-BEING, SO HIS NAME IS INSIGNI-FICANT.
......?
HE MAINTAINS HIS YOUTH BY FEEDING ON HUMAN BLOOD.

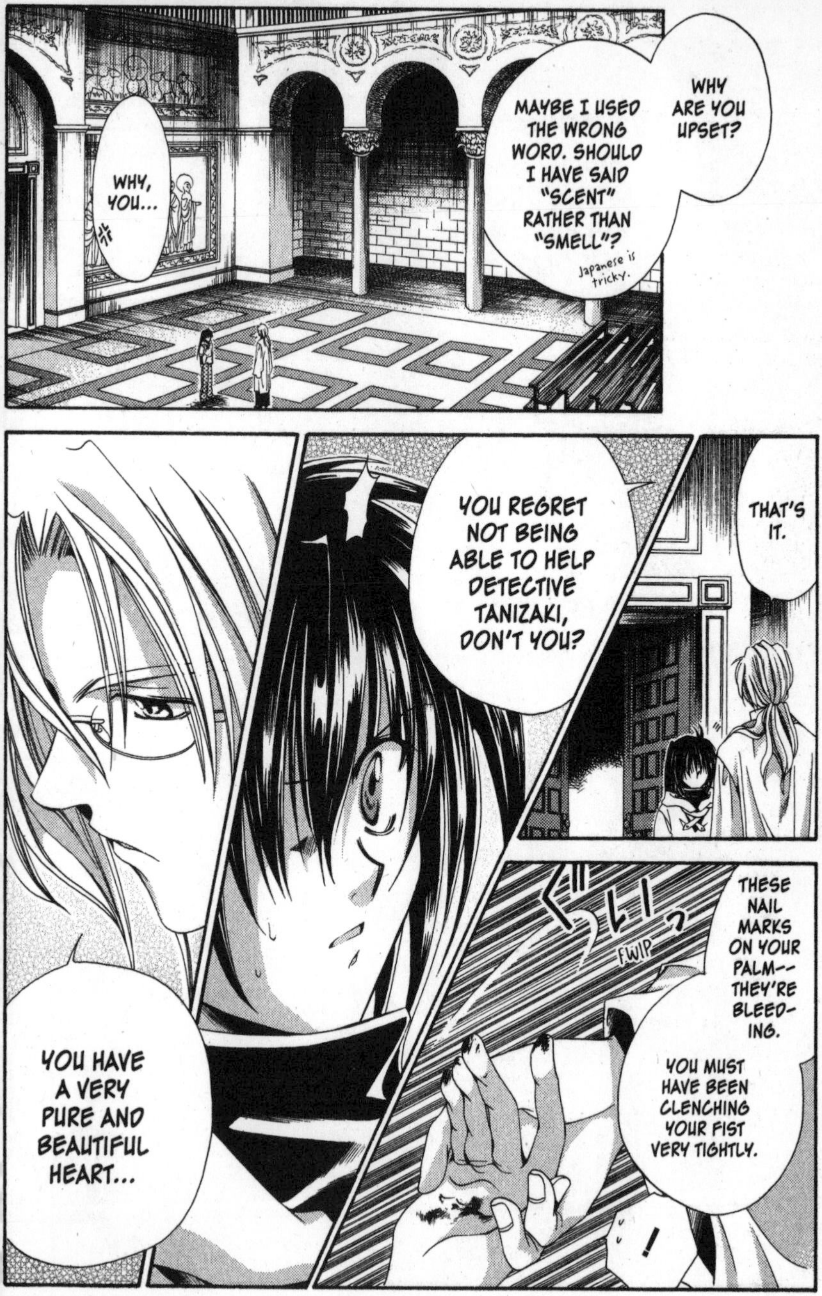
WHY ARE YOU UPSET?
MAYBE I USED THE WRONG WORD. SHOULD I HAVE SAID "SCENT" RATHER THAN "SMELL"?
Japanese is tricky.
WHY, YOU...
THAT'S IT.
THESE NAIL MARKS ON YOUR PALM-- THEY'RE BLEED-ING.
YOU MUST HAVE BEEN CLENCHING YOUR FIST VERY TIGHTLY.
FWIP
!
YOU REGRET NOT BEING ABLE TO HELP DETECTIVE TANIZAKI, DON'T YOU?
YOU HAVE A VERY PURE AND BEAUTIFUL HEART...

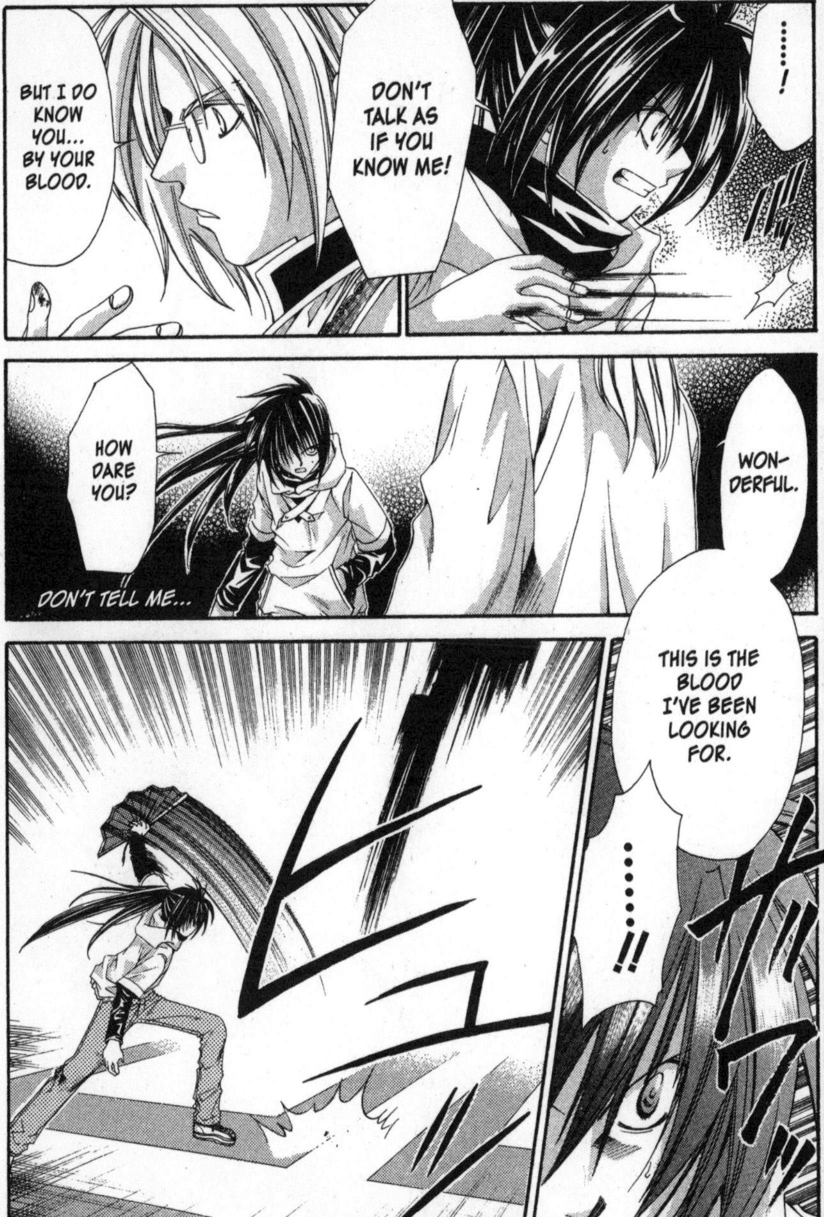
......!
DON'T TALK AS IF YOU KNOW ME!
BUT I DO KNOW YOU... BY YOUR BLOOD.
WON-DERFUL.
HOW DARE YOU?
DON'T TELL ME...
THIS IS THE BLOOD I'VE BEEN LOOKING FOR.
......!!

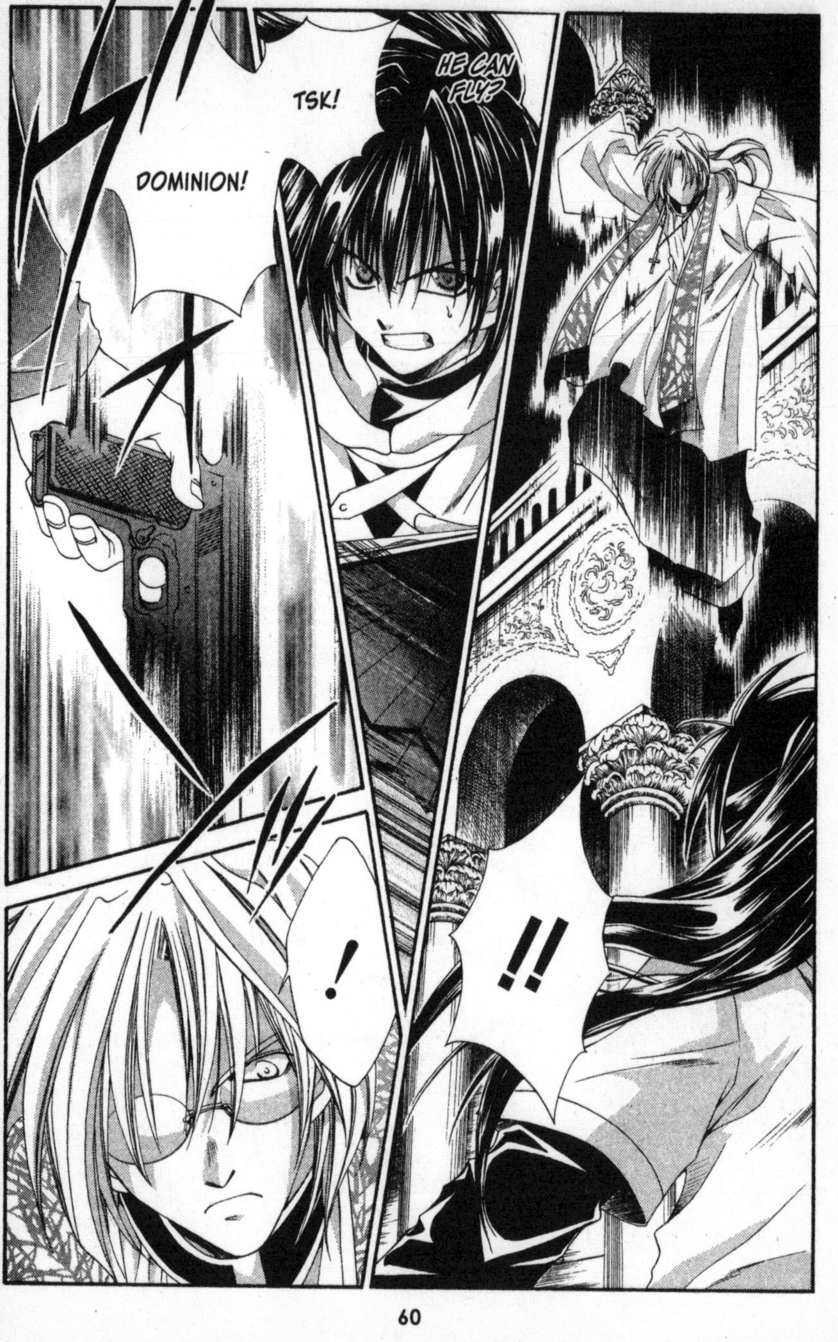
HE CAN FLY?
TSK!
DOMINION!
!!
!

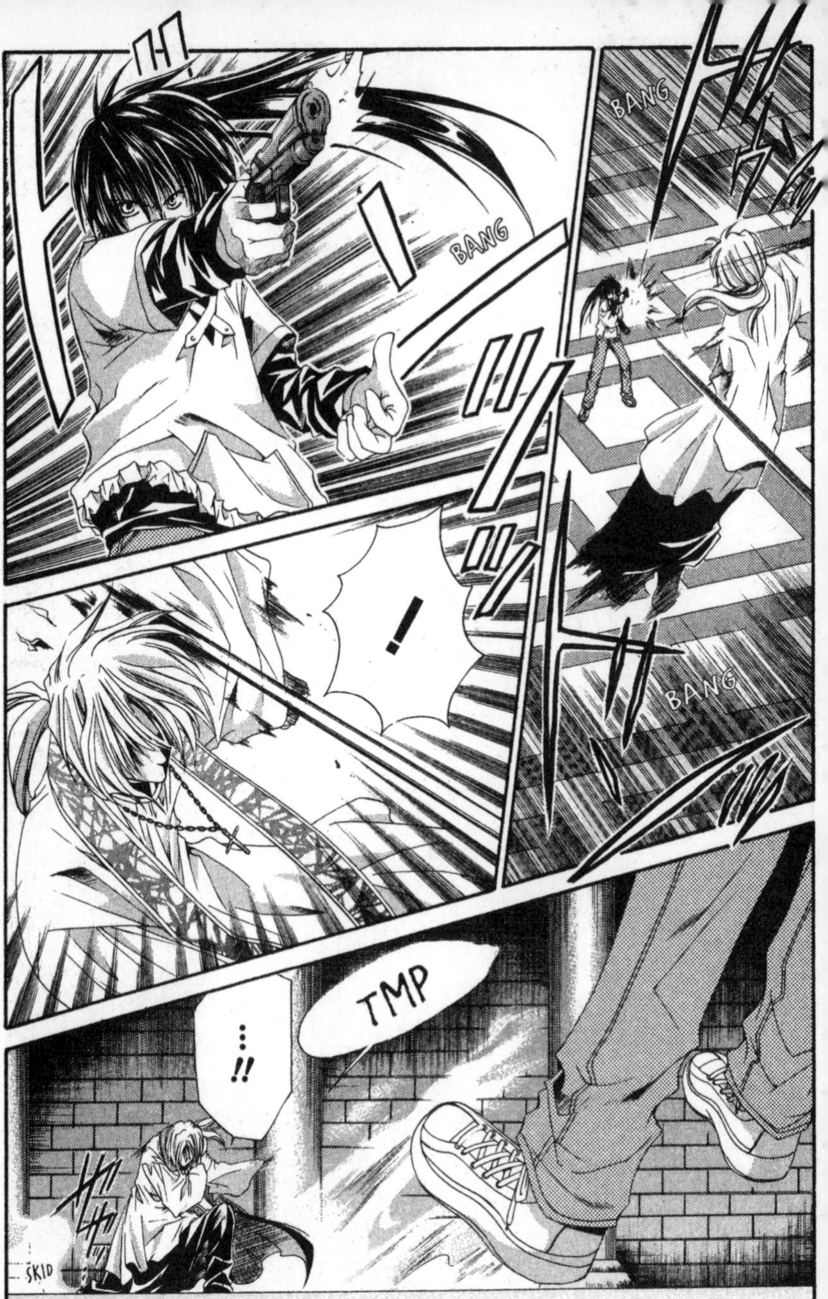
BANG
BANG
BANG
!
TMP
...!!
SKID

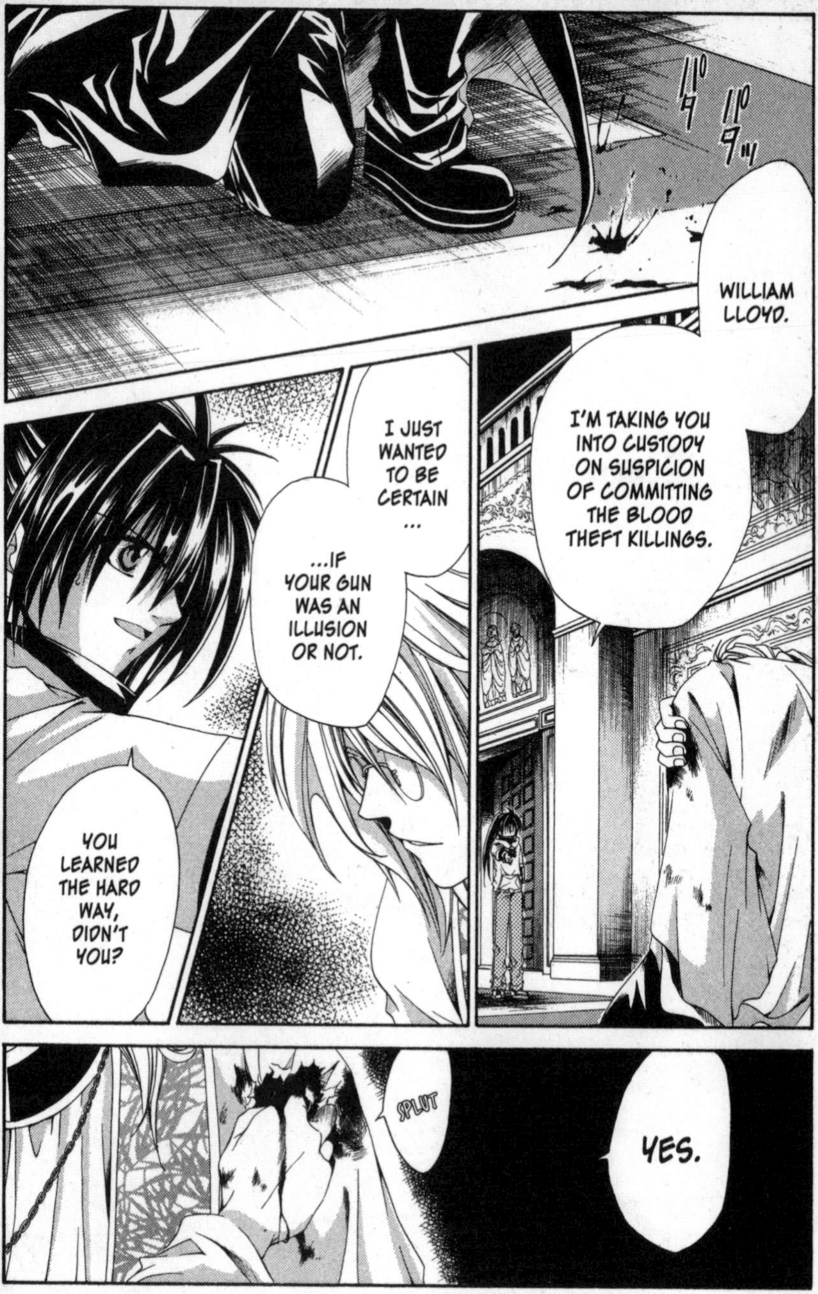
パタ パタッ
WILLIAM LLOYD.
I'M TAKING YOU INTO CUSTODY ON SUSPICION OF COMMITTING THE BLOOD THEFT KILLINGS.
I JUST WANTED TO BE CERTAIN ...
...IF YOUR GUN WAS AN ILLUSION OR NOT.
YOU LEARNED THE HARD WAY, DIDN'T YOU?
YES.
SPLUT

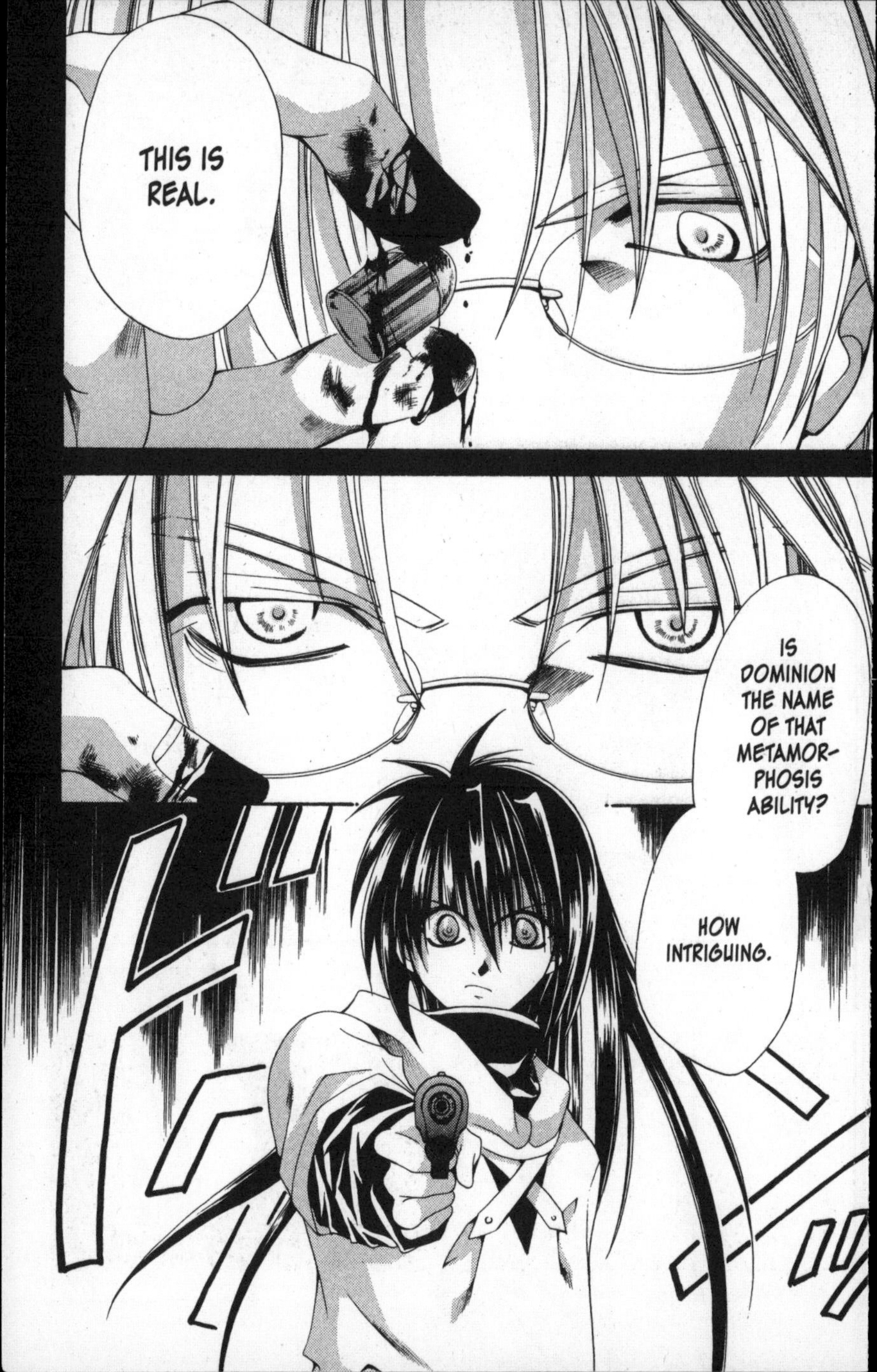
THIS IS REAL.
IS DOMINION THE NAME OF THAT METAMOR-PHOSIS ABILITY?
HOW INTRIGUING.

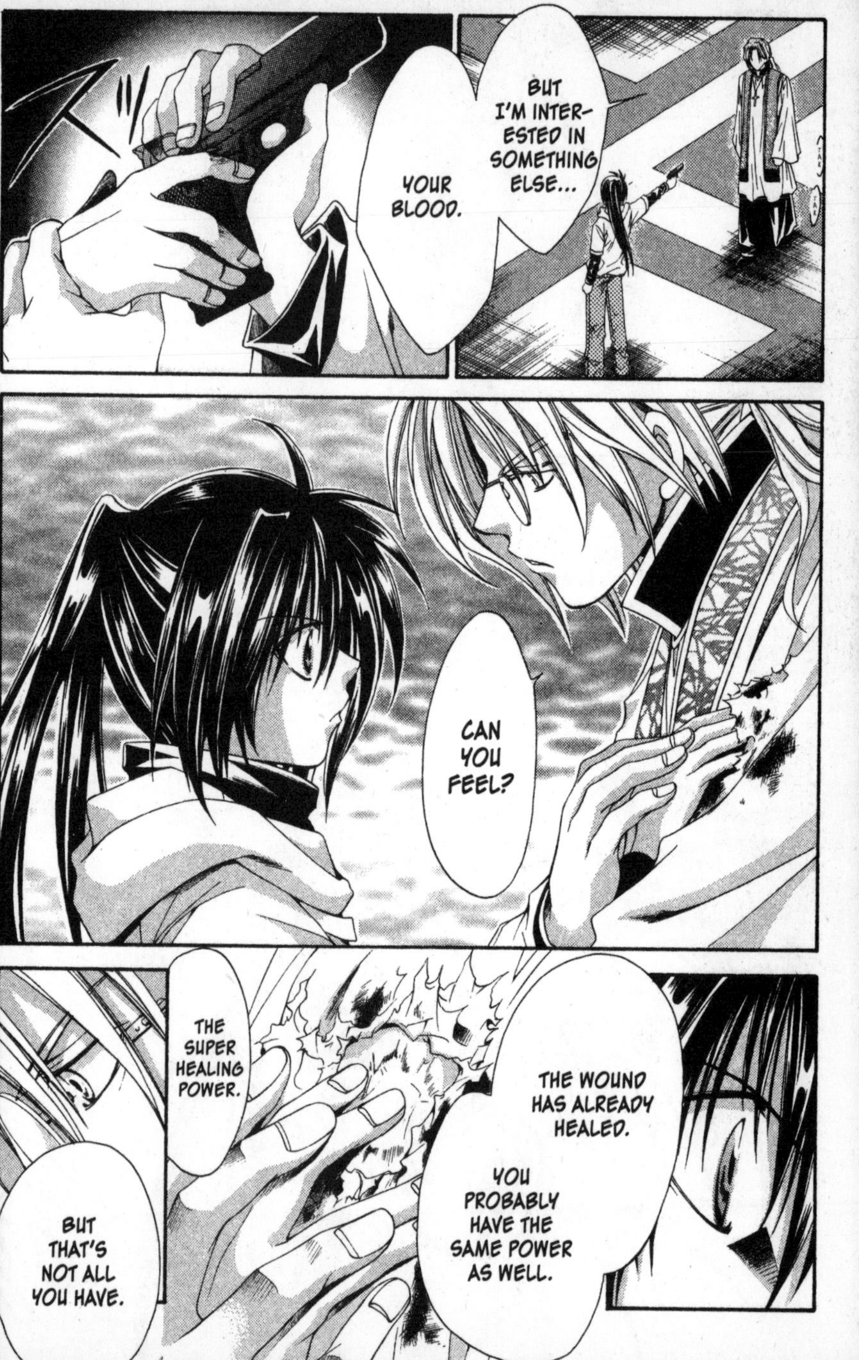
TAK
TAK
BUT I'M INTER-ESTED IN SOMETHING ELSE...
YOUR BLOOD.
CAN YOU FEEL?
THE WOUND HAS ALREADY HEALED.
YOU PROBABLY HAVE THE SAME POWER AS WELL.
THE SUPER HEALING POWER.
BUT THAT'S NOT ALL YOU HAVE.

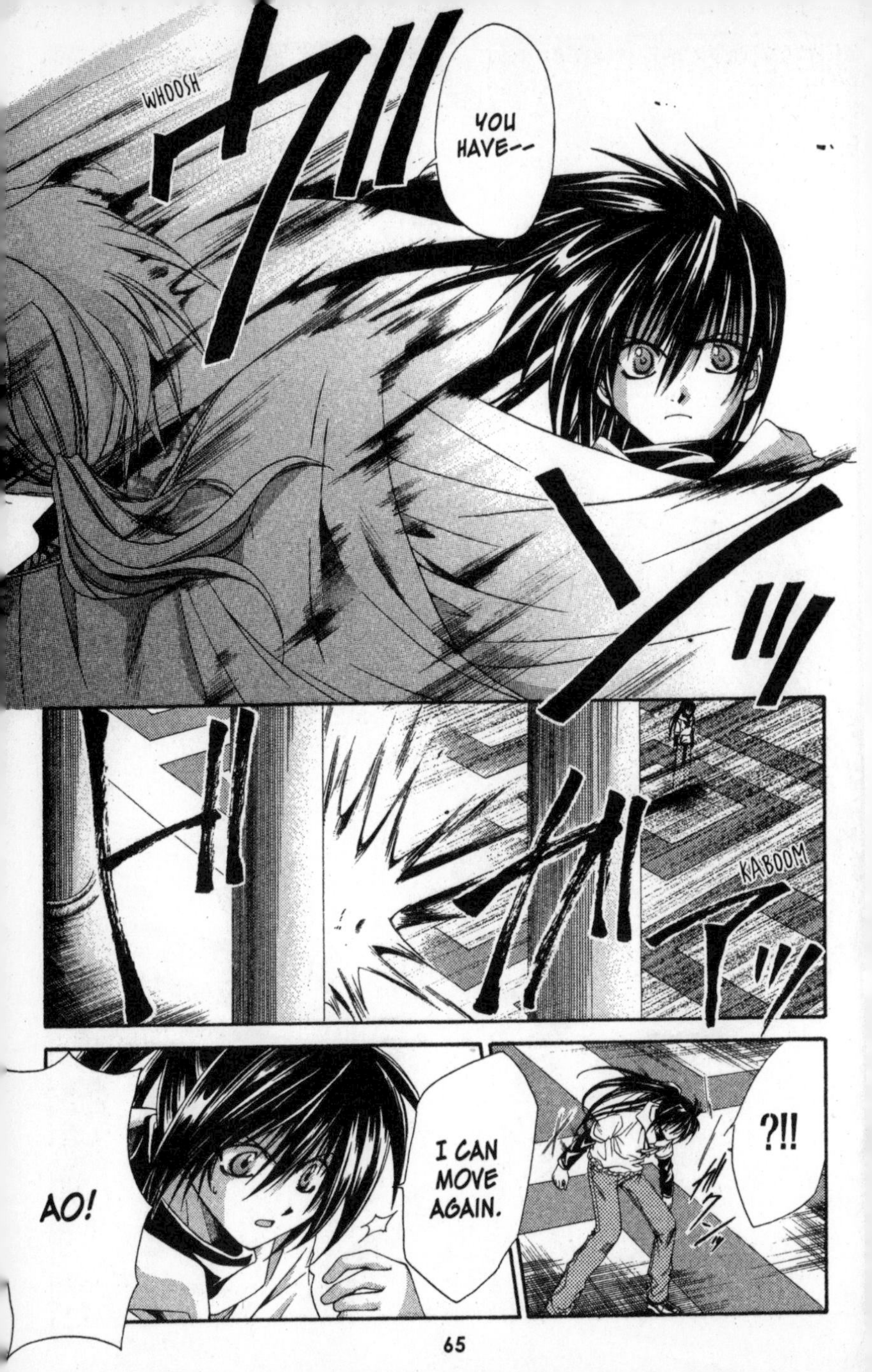
YOU HAVE--
WHOOSH
KABOOM
?!!
I CAN MOVE AGAIN.
AO!

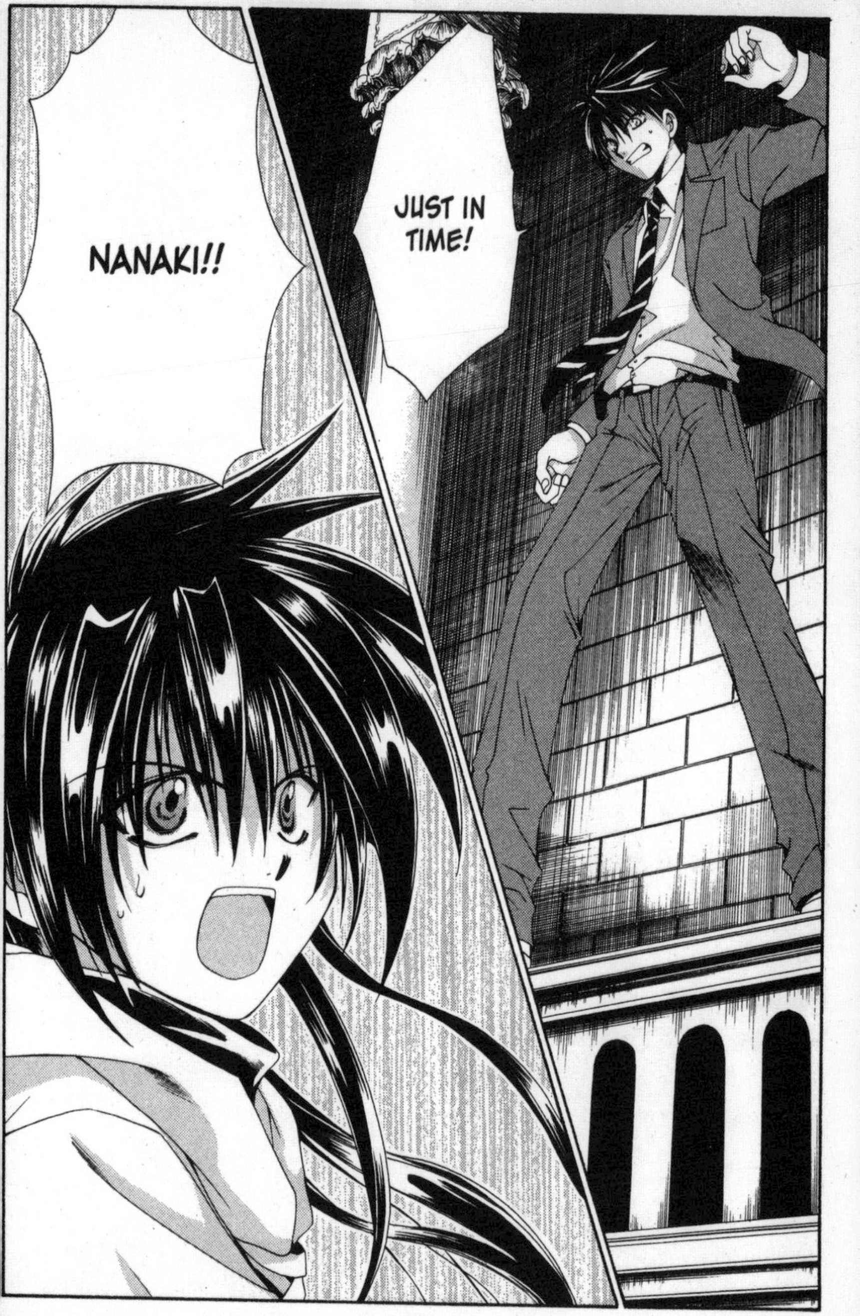
JUST IN TIME!
NANAKI!!

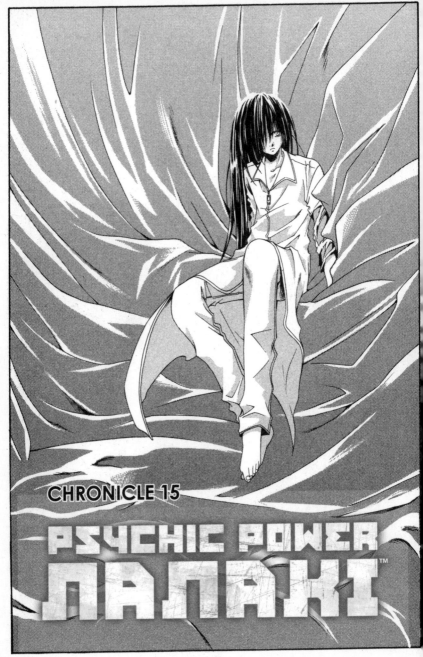

CHRONICLE 15

PSYCHIC POWER
NANAKI™

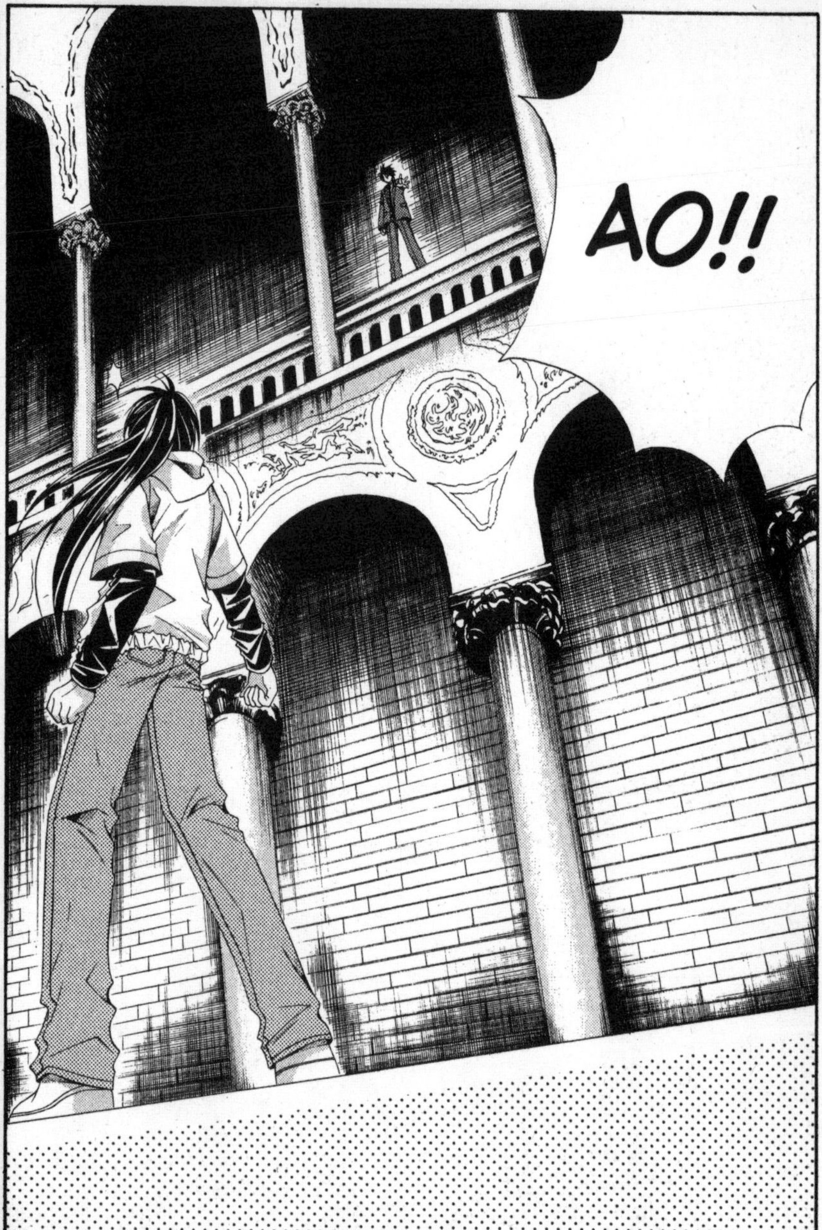
AO!!

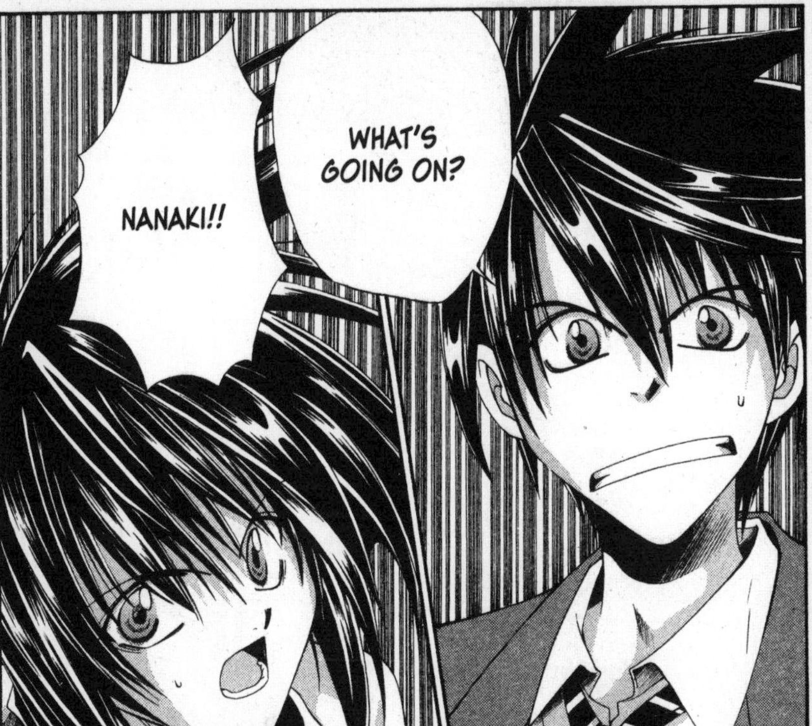
WHAT'S GOING ON?
NANAKI!!

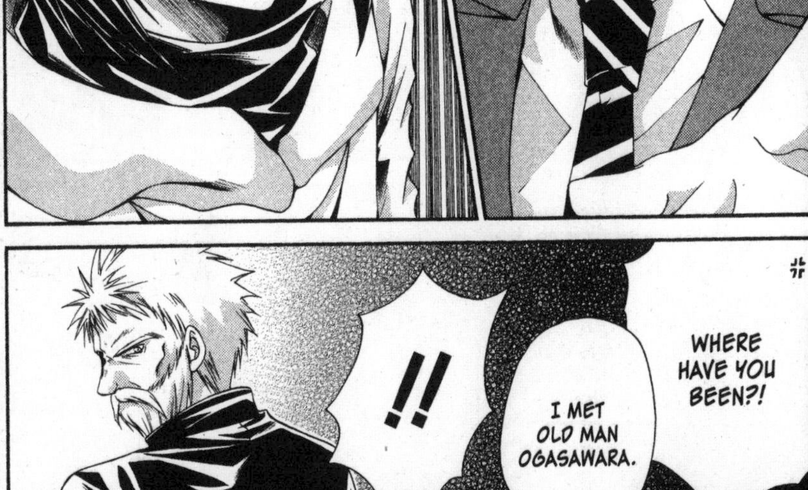
WHERE HAVE YOU BEEN?!
I MET OLD MAN OGASAWARA.
!!

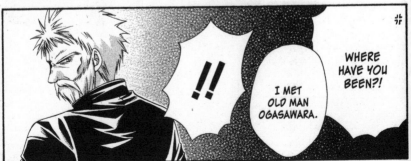

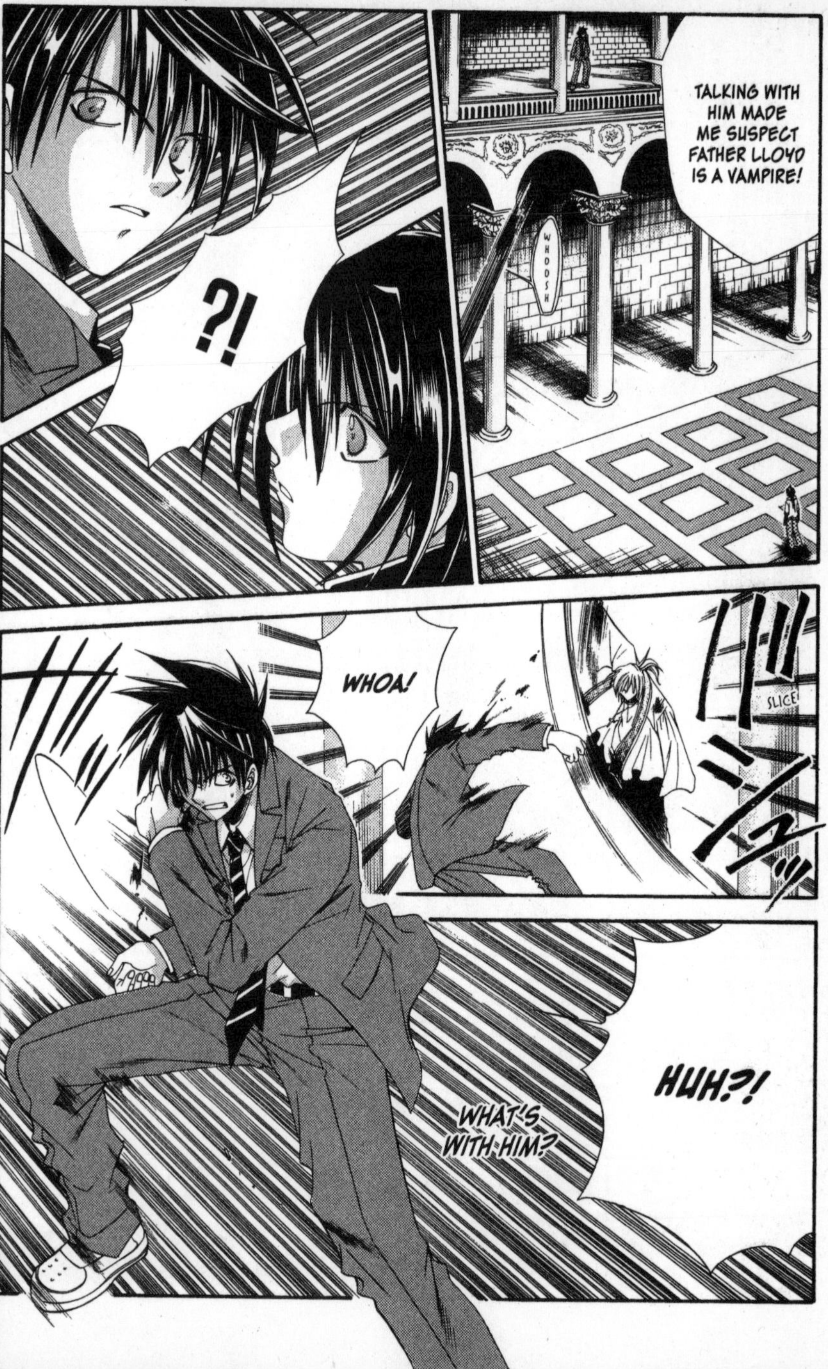
TALKING WITH HIM MADE ME SUSPECT FATHER LLOYD IS A VAMPIRE!
WHOOSH
?!
SLICE
WHOA!
HUH?!
WHAT'S WITH HIM?

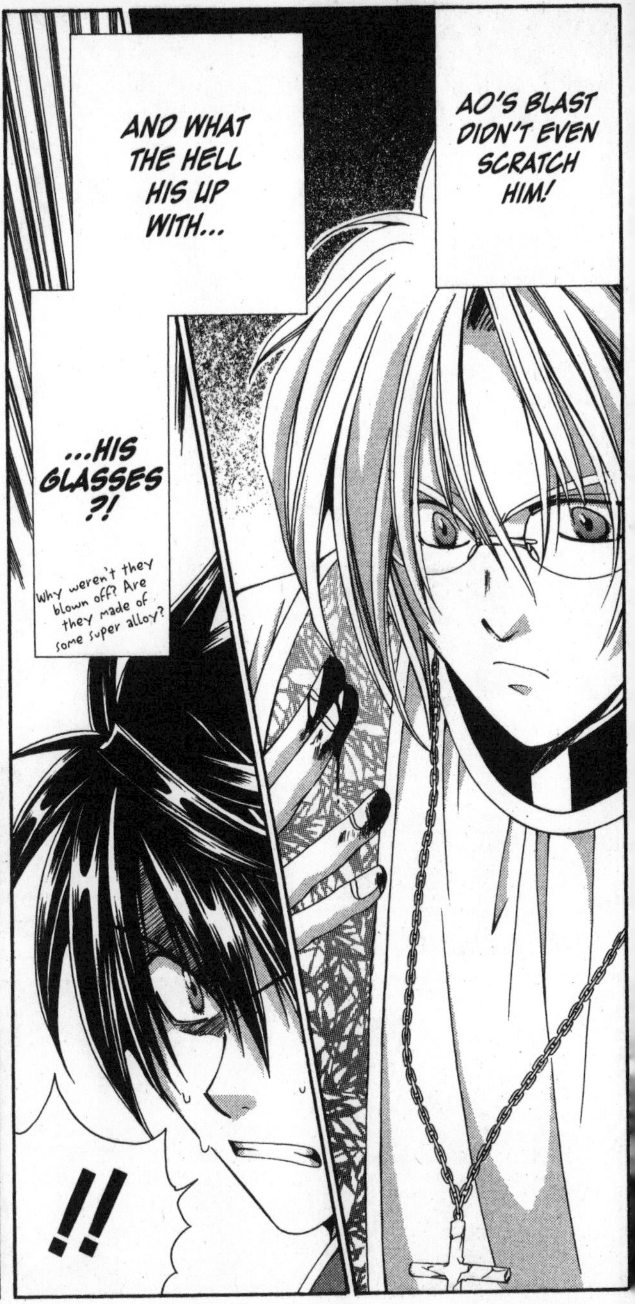
AO'S BLAST DIDN'T EVEN SCRATCH HIM!
AND WHAT THE HELL HIS UP WITH...
...HIS GLASSES?!
Why weren't they blown off? Are they made of some super alloy?
!!

Some of you may have noticed that Detective Ageo is the character from a certain manga that I love (lol). His alias is Agepan (wry smile). He only appeared in two or three panels of that manga--such a small part that you'd hardly remember him.

Though Detective Ageo and Ao have worked together in the past, they are on bad terms (wry smile). Since LOCK is known as an oddball group, Detective Ageo probably thinks they're as suspicious as the criminals!

Detective Tanizaki is a character who's much more understanding, and Nanaki and Ao like him. It's especially rare for Ao to like someone (lol).

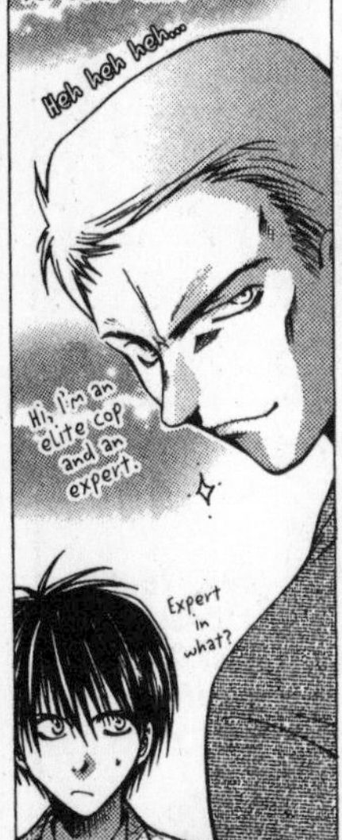
Heh heh heh...
Hi, I'm an elite cop and an expert.
Expert in what?

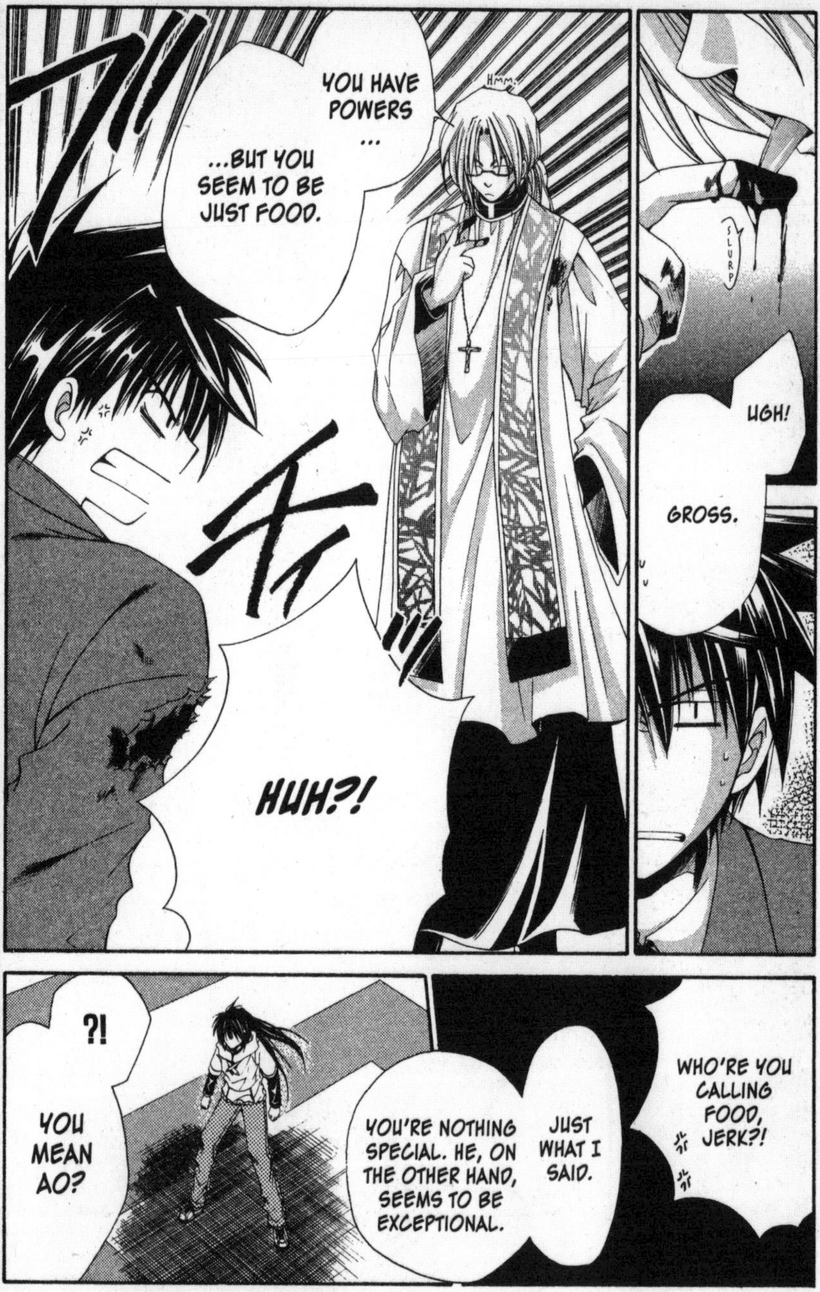
SLURP
UGH!
GROSS.
HMM.
YOU HAVE POWERS ...
...BUT YOU SEEM TO BE JUST FOOD.
HUH?!
WHO'RE YOU CALLING FOOD, JERK?!
JUST WHAT I SAID.
YOU'RE NOTHING SPECIAL. HE, ON THE OTHER HAND, SEEMS TO BE EXCEPTIONAL.
?!
YOU MEAN AO?

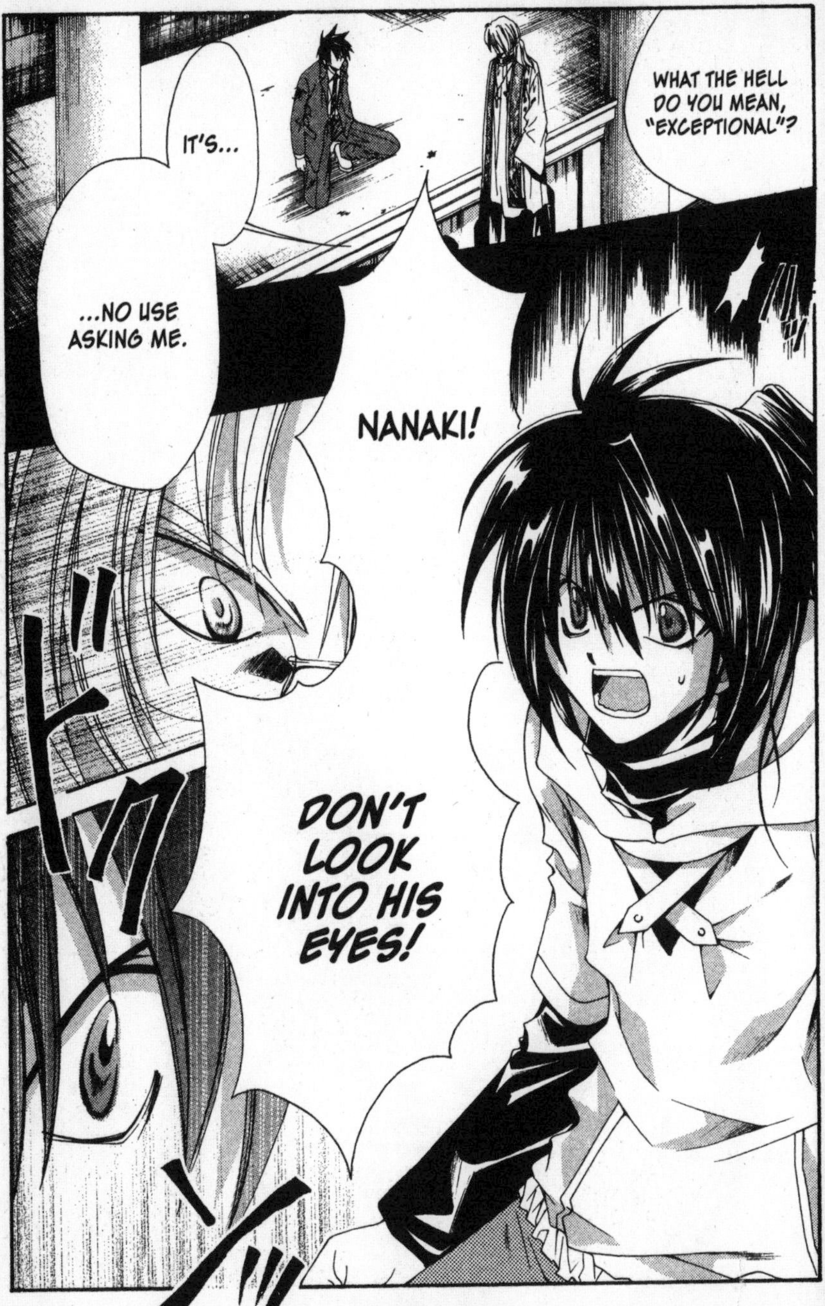
WHAT THE HELL DO YOU MEAN, "EXCEPTIONAL"?
IT'S...
...NO USE ASKING ME.
NANAKI!
DON'T LOOK INTO HIS EYES!

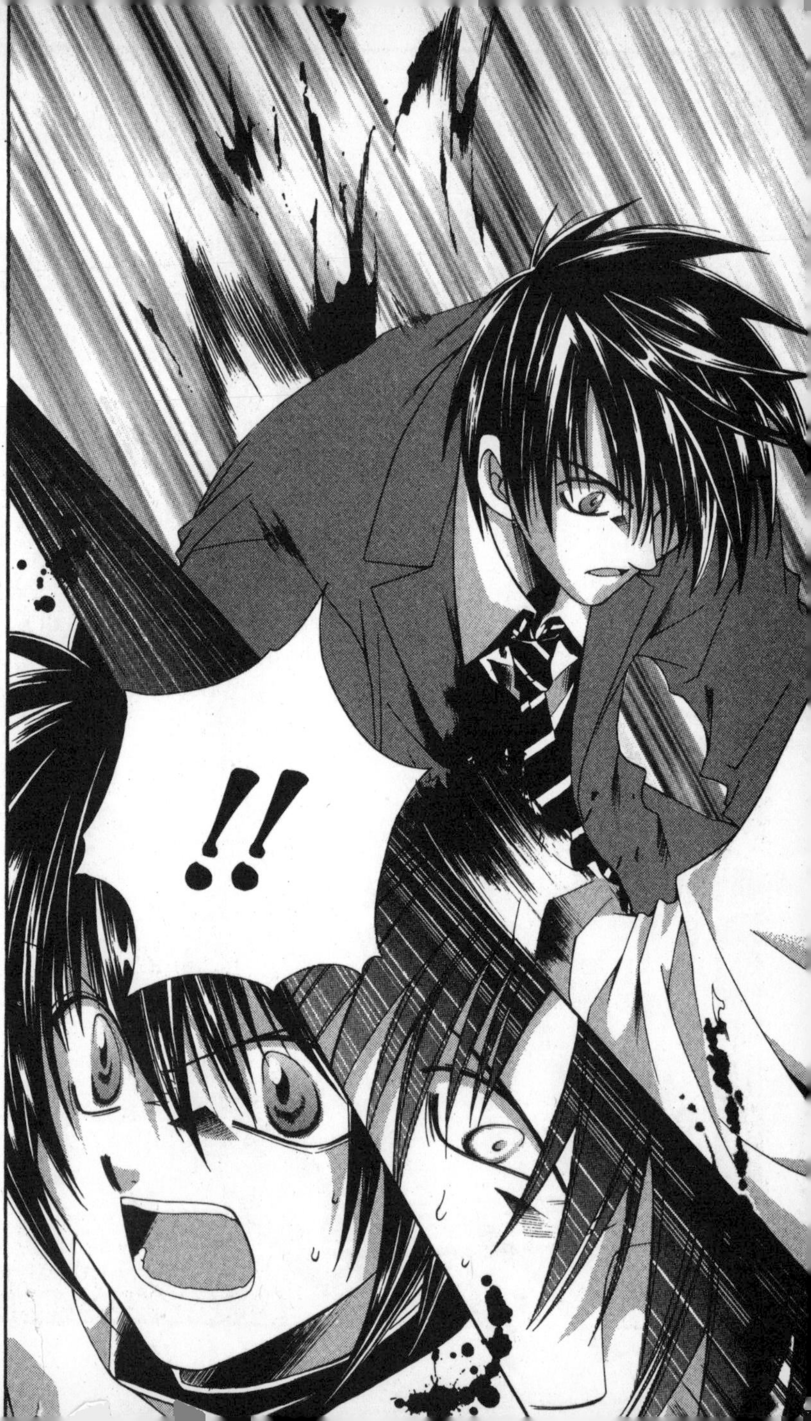
!!

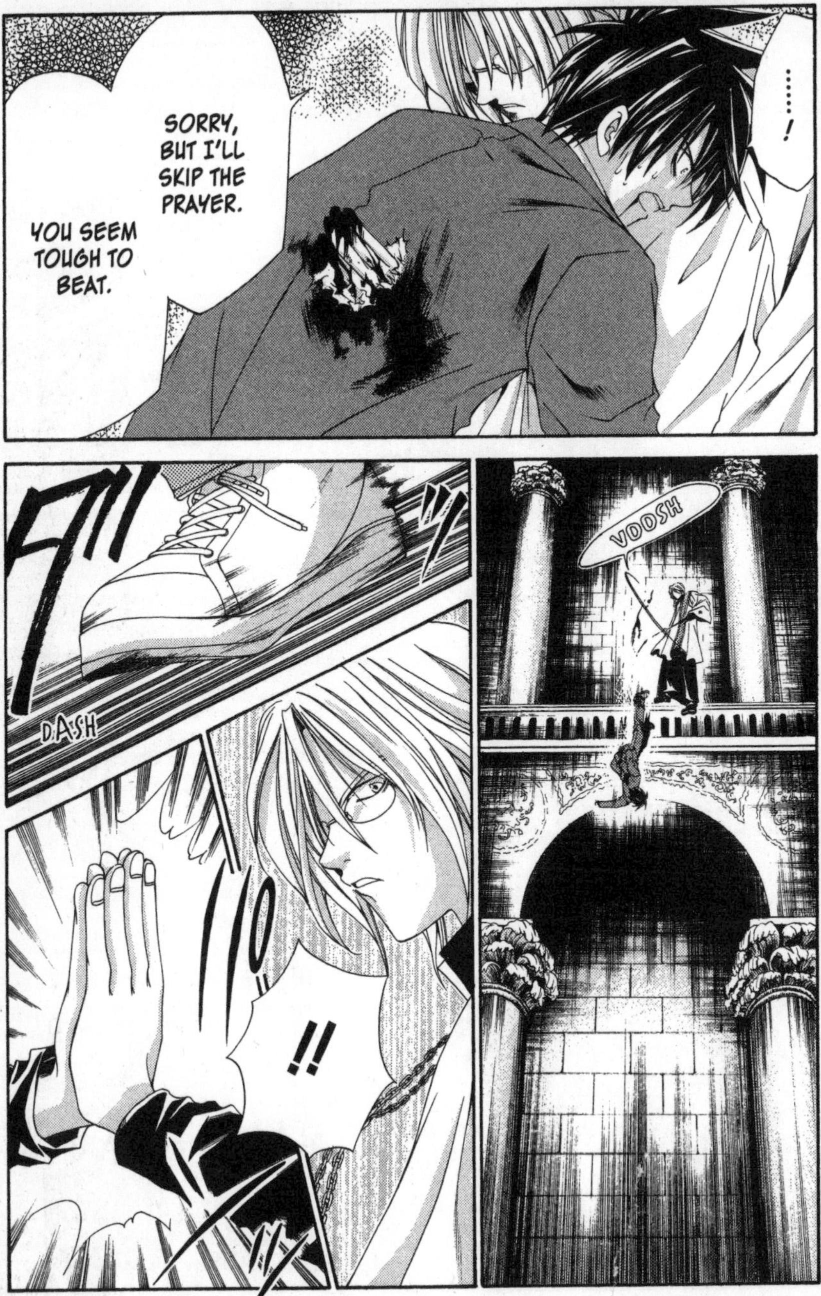
......!
SORRY, BUT I'LL SKIP THE PRAYER.
YOU SEEM TOUGH TO BEAT.
VOOSH
DASH
!!

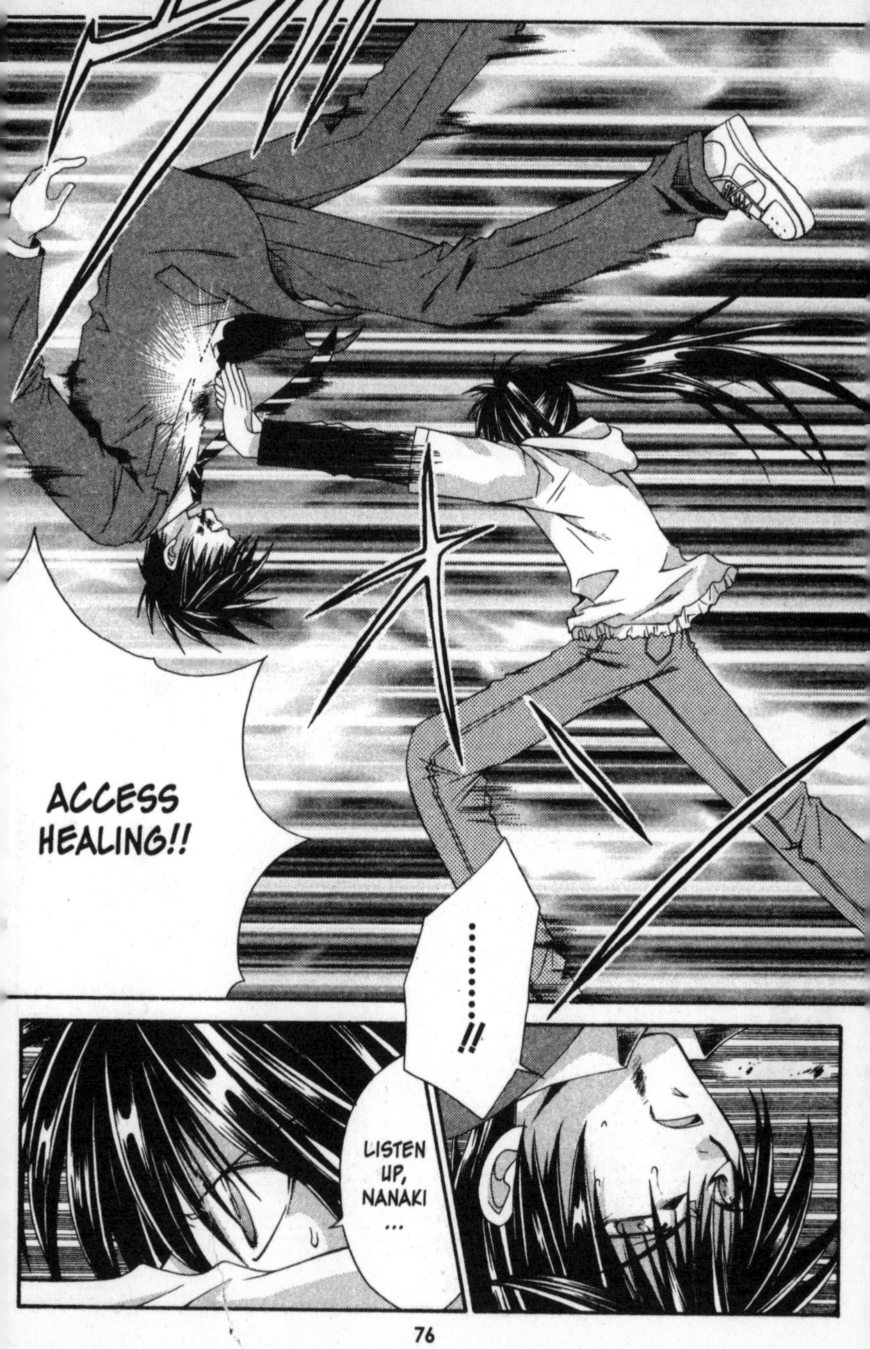
ACCESS HEALING!!
.........!!
LISTEN UP, NANAKI ...

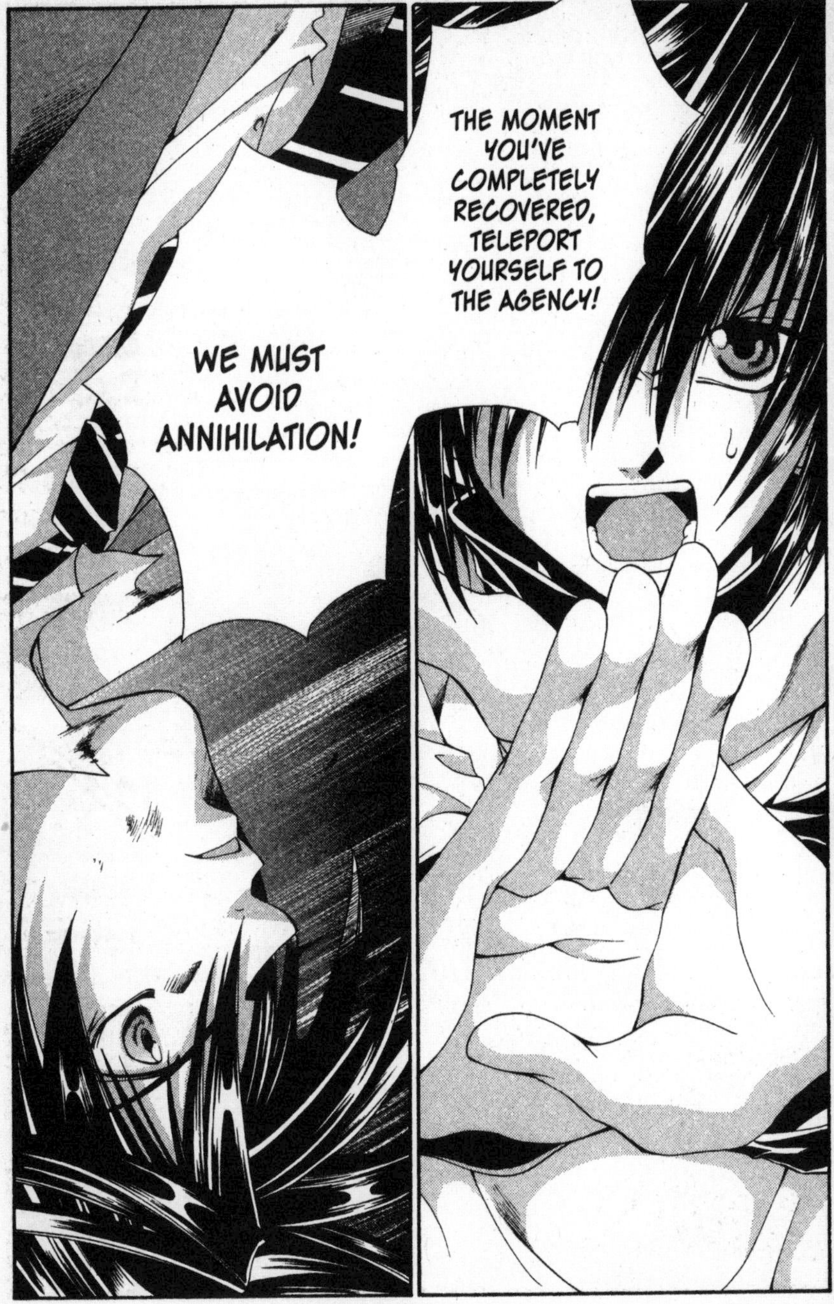
THE MOMENT YOU'VE COMPLETELY RECOVERED, TELEPORT YOURSELF TO THE AGENCY!
WE MUST AVOID ANNIHILATION!

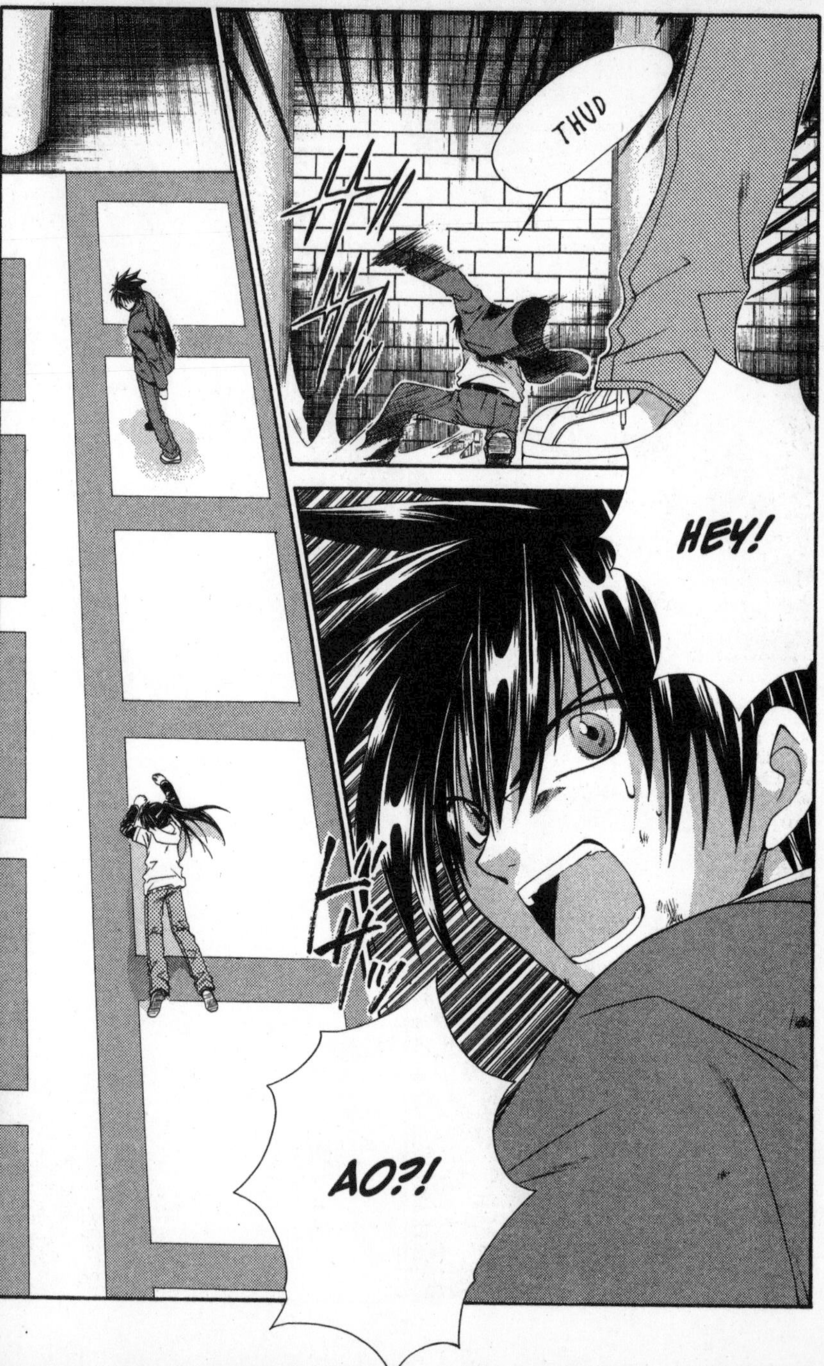
THUD
HEY!
AO?!

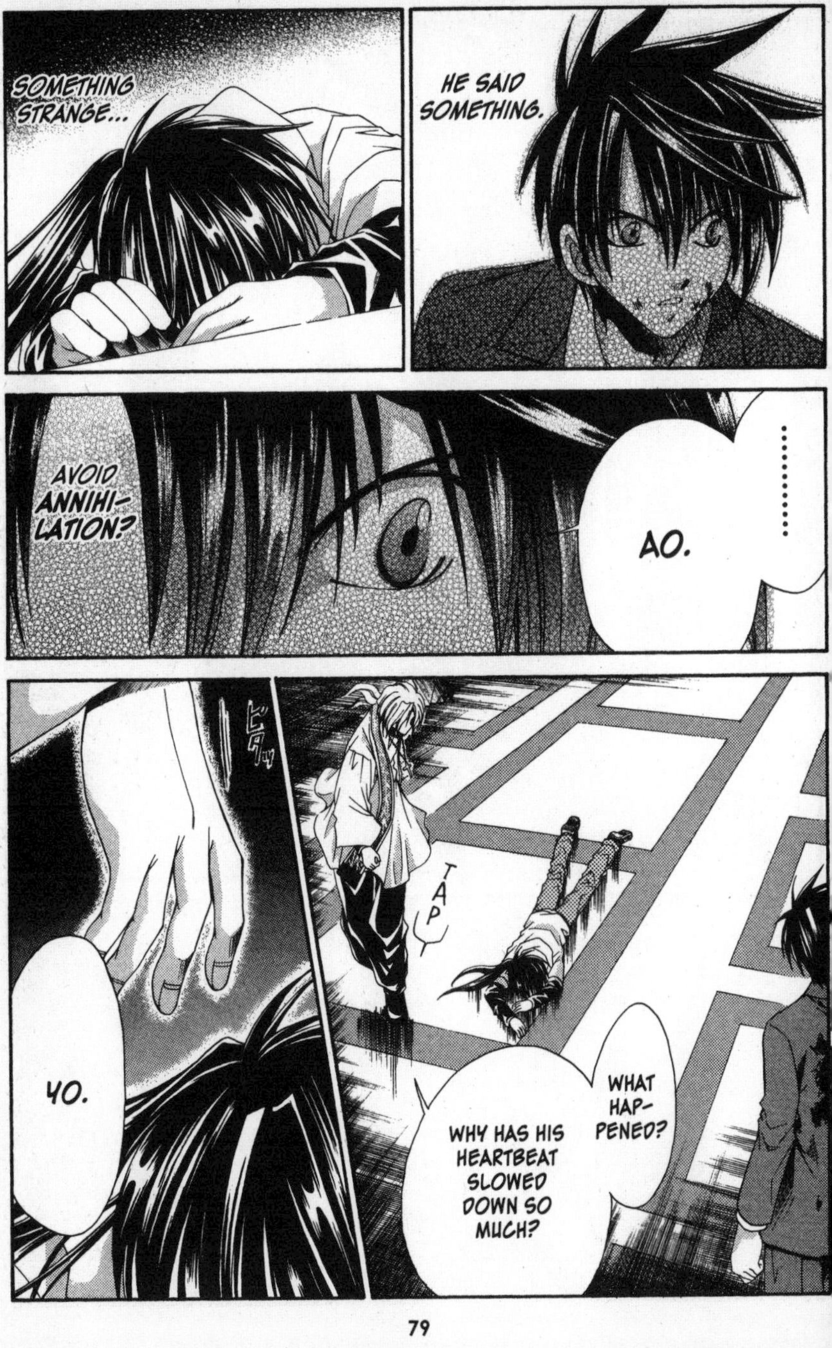
HE SAID SOMETHING.
SOMETHING STRANGE...
......
AO.
AVOID ANNIHILATION?
WHAT HAPPENED?
WHY HAS HIS HEARTBEAT SLOWED DOWN SO MUCH?
TAP
ピクッ
YO.

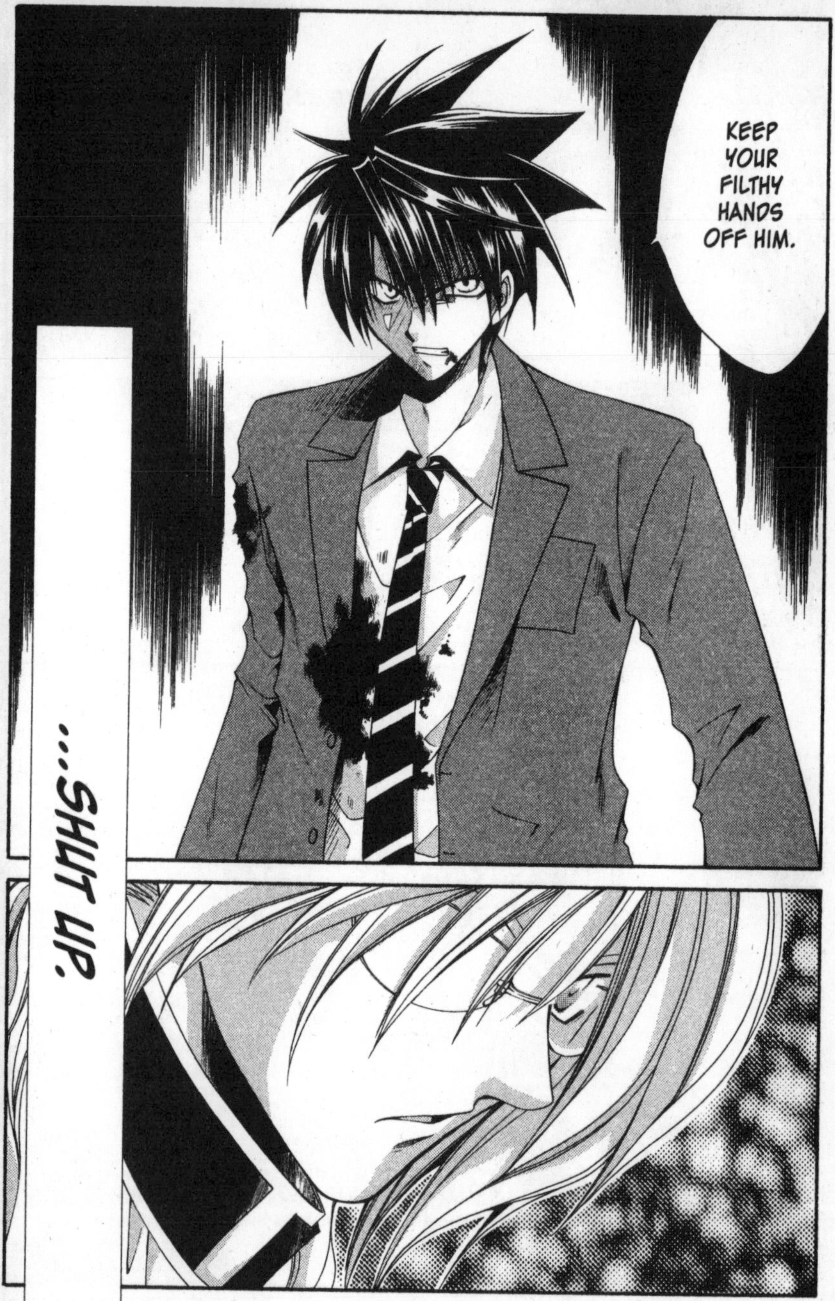
KEEP YOUR FILTHY HANDS OFF HIM.
...SHUT UP.

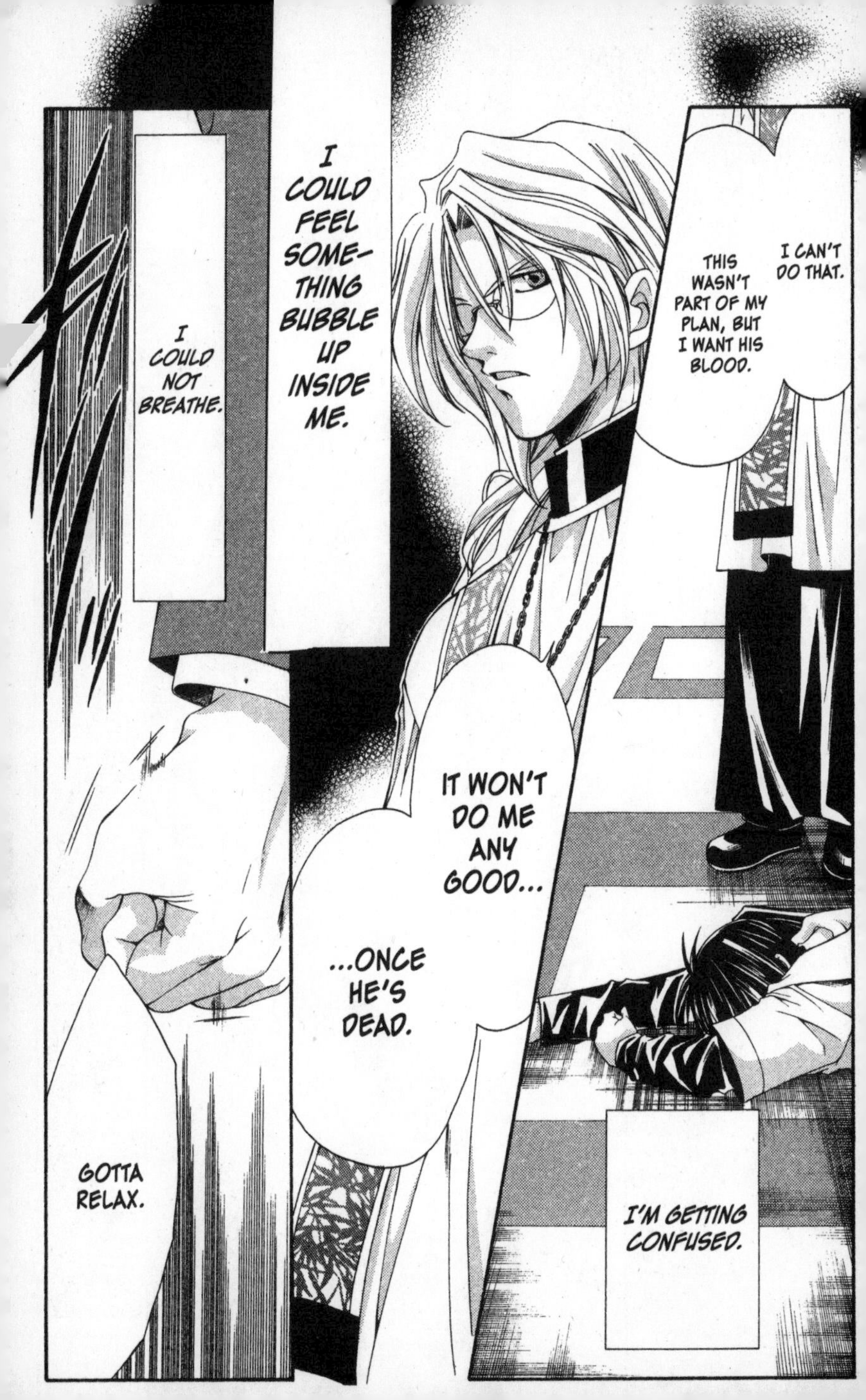
I CAN'T DO THAT.
THIS WASN'T PART OF MY PLAN, BUT I WANT HIS BLOOD.
IT WON'T DO ME ANY GOOD...
...ONCE HE'S DEAD.
I'M GETTING CONFUSED.
I COULD FEEL SOME-THING BUBBLE UP INSIDE ME.
I COULD NOT BREATHE.
GOTTA RELAX.

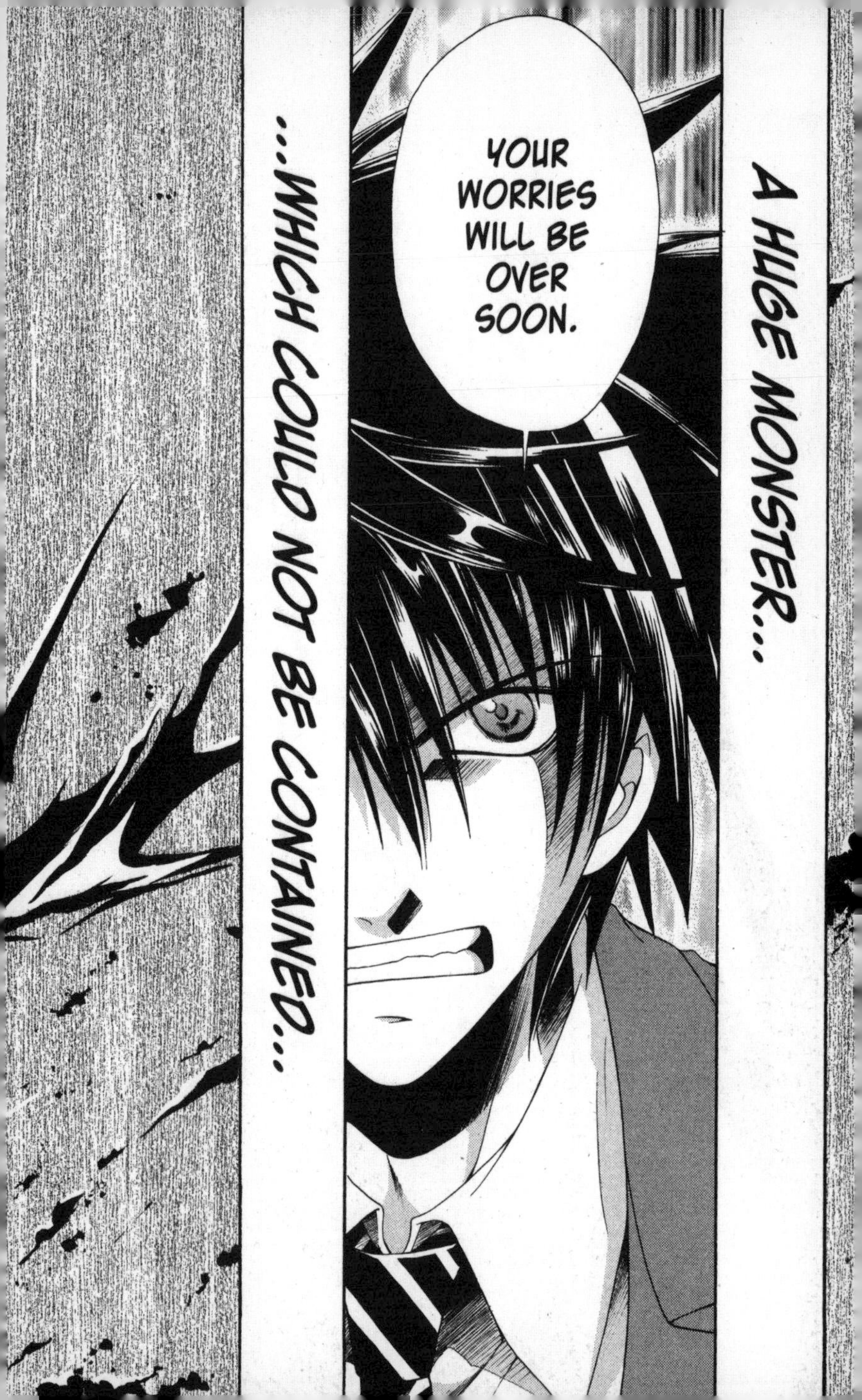
A HUGE MONSTER...
YOUR WORRIES WILL BE OVER SOON.
...WHICH COULD NOT BE CONTAINED...

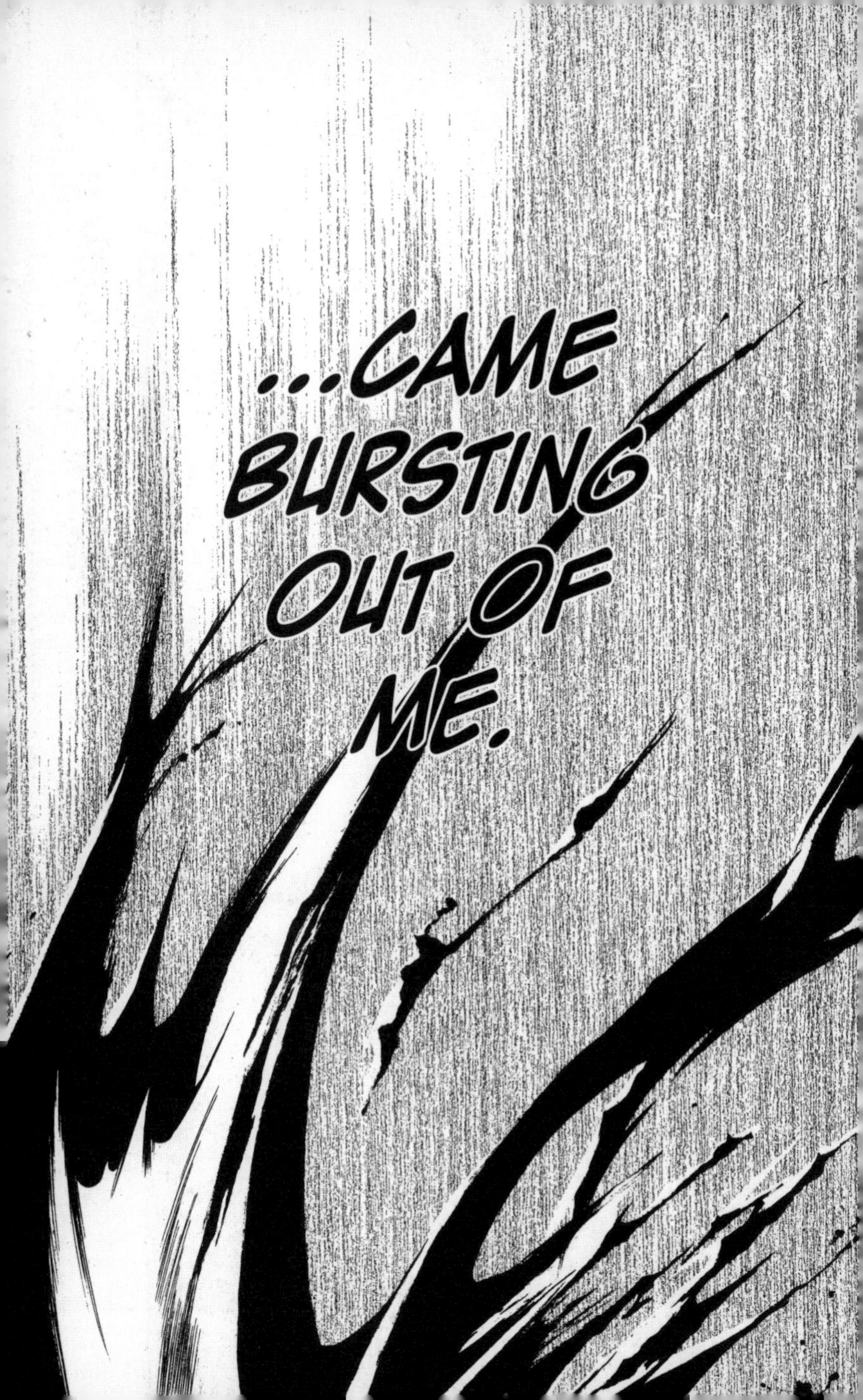
...CAME BURSTING OUT OF ME.

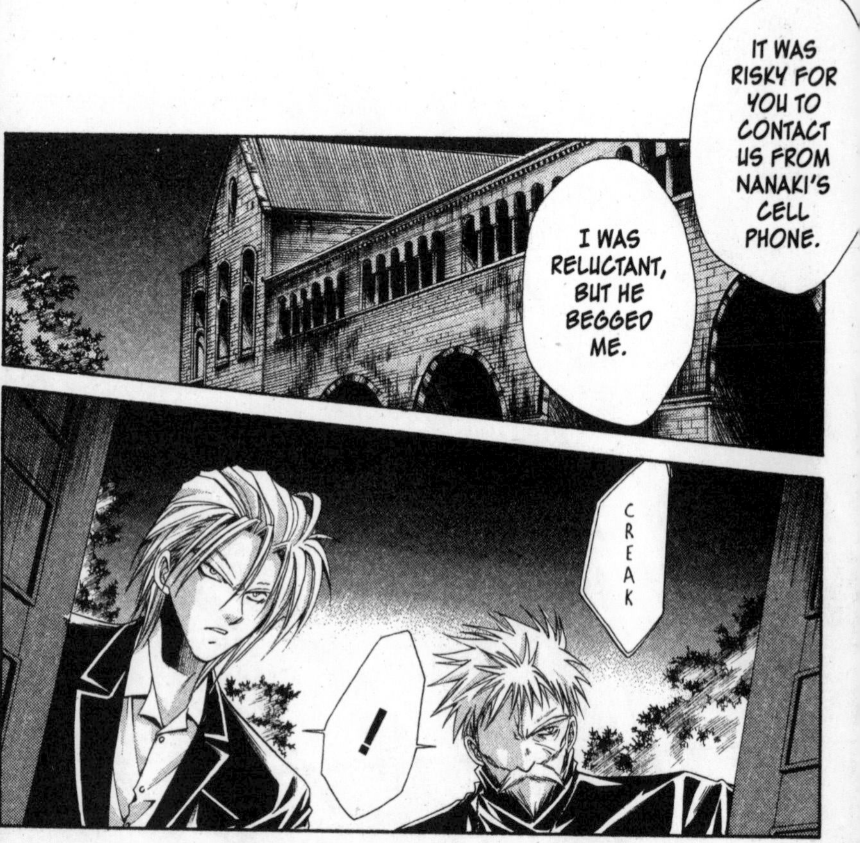
IT WAS RISKY FOR YOU TO CONTACT US FROM NANAKI'S CELL PHONE.
I WAS RELUCTANT, BUT HE BEGGED ME.
CREAK
!

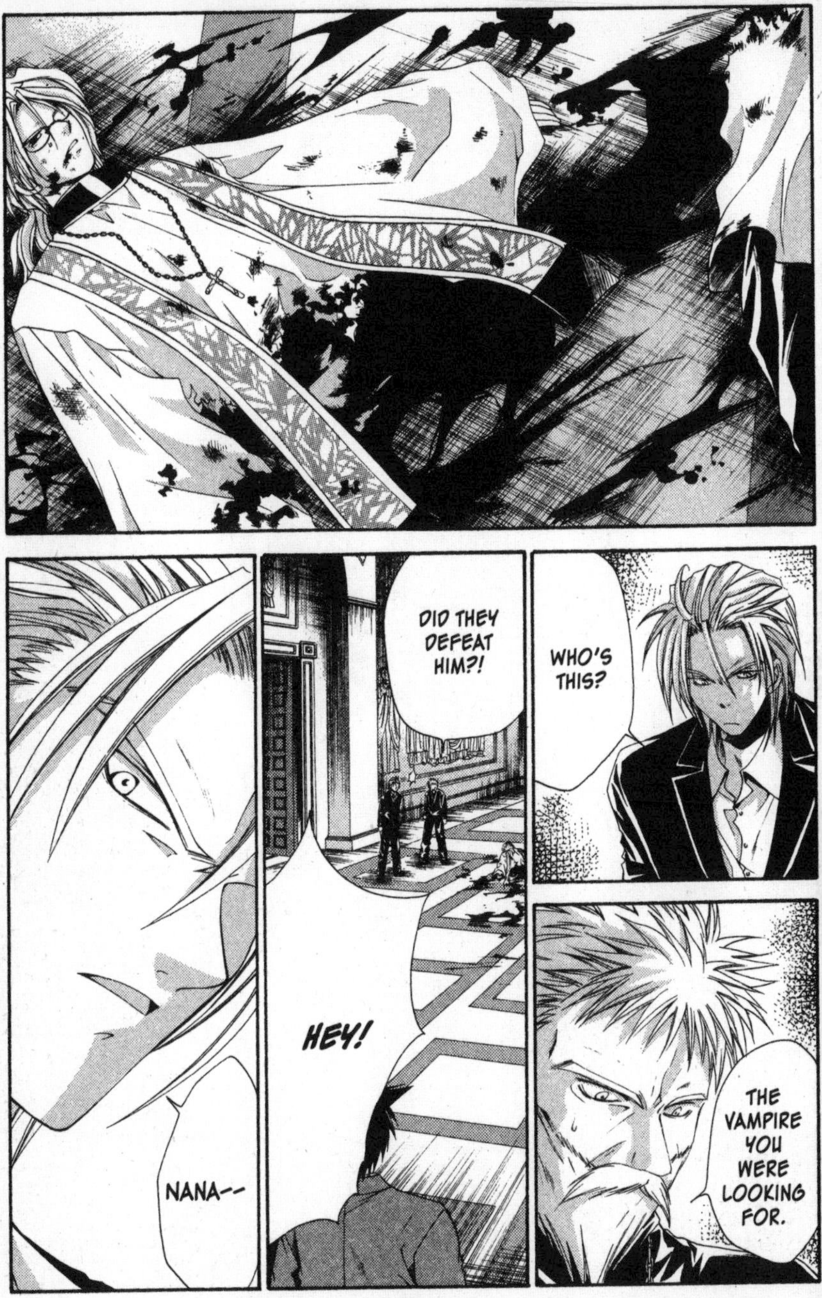
WHO'S THIS?
THE VAMPIRE YOU WERE LOOKING FOR.
DID THEY DEFEAT HIM?!
HEY!
NANA--

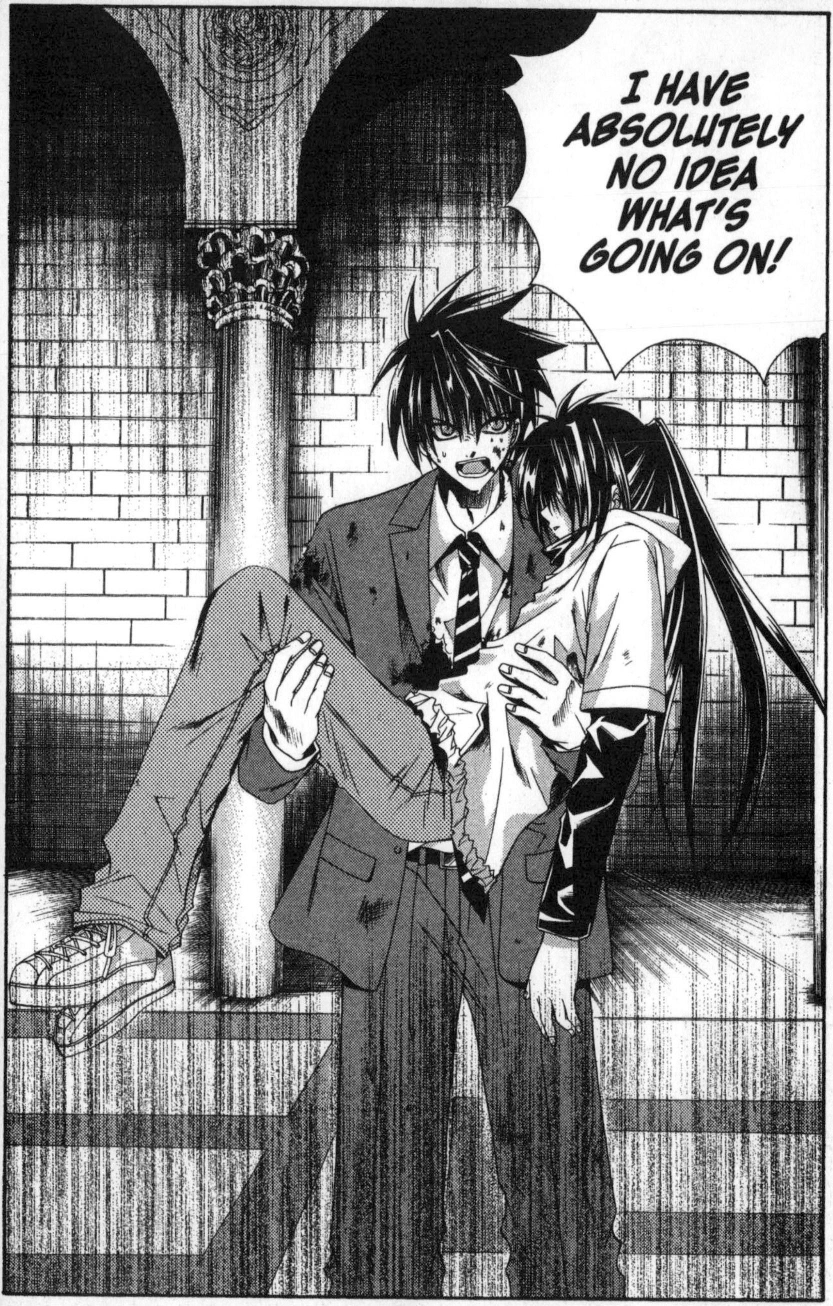
I HAVE ABSOLUTELY NO IDEA WHAT'S GOING ON!

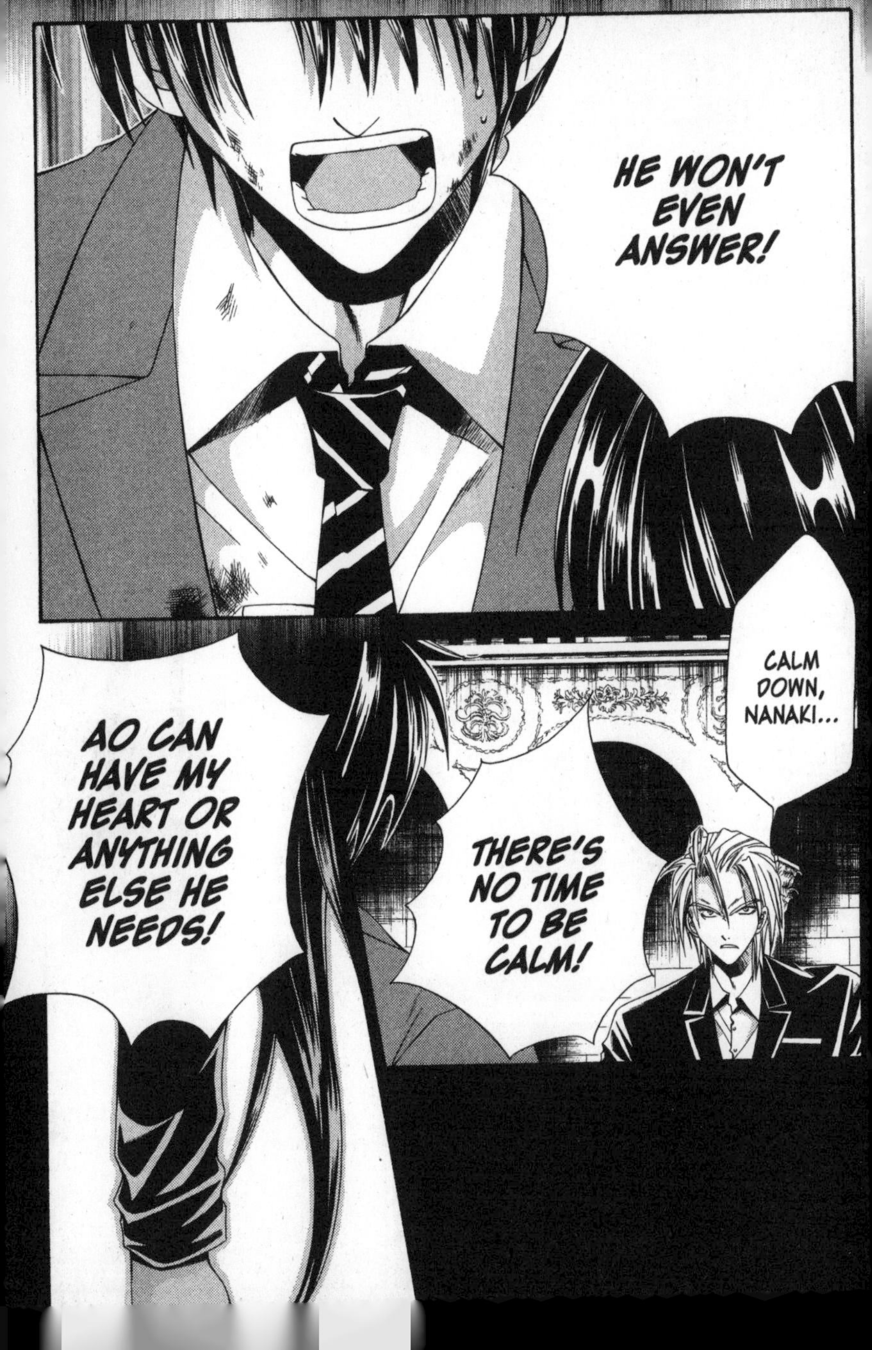
HE WON'T EVEN ANSWER!
CALM DOWN, NANAKI...
THERE'S NO TIME TO BE CALM!
AO CAN HAVE MY HEART OR ANYTHING ELSE HE NEEDS!

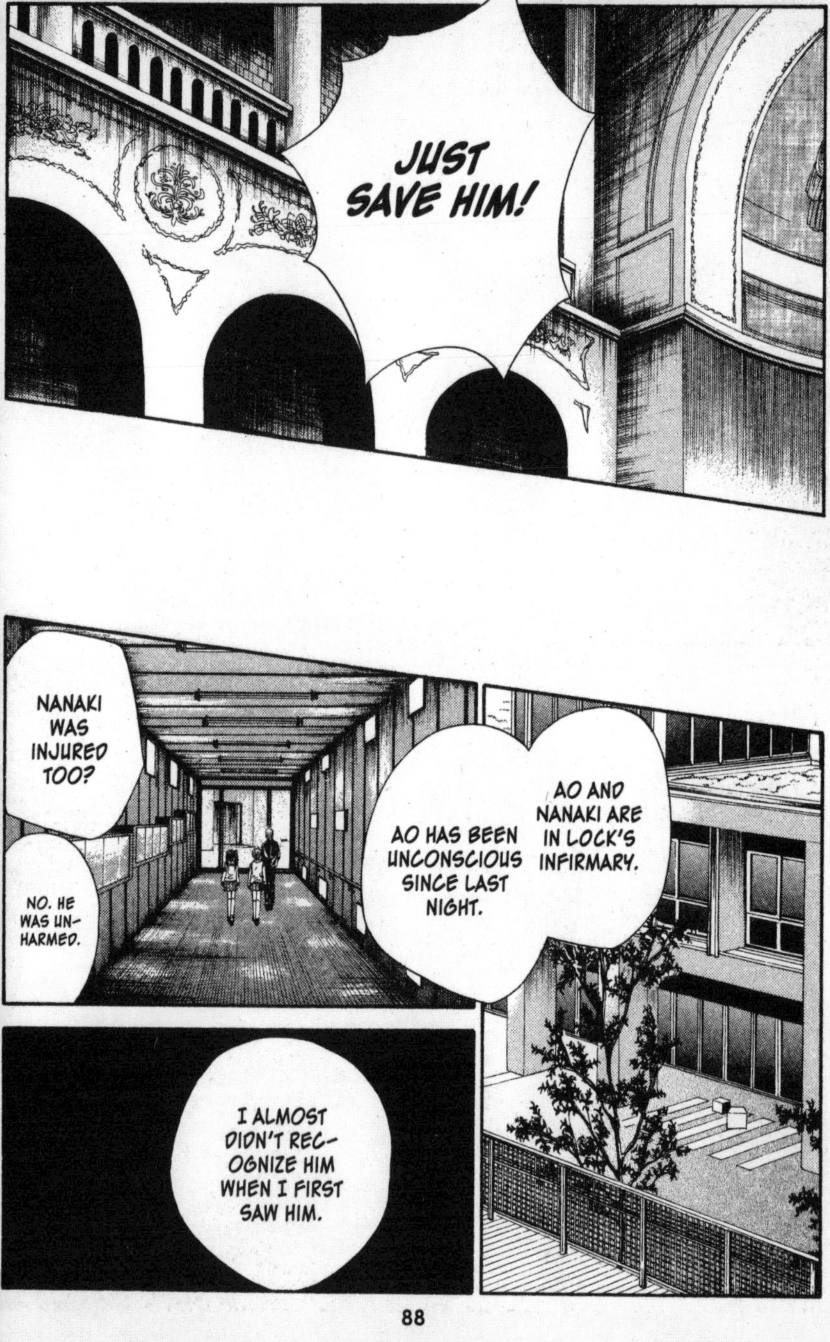
JUST SAVE HIM!
AO AND NANAKI ARE IN LOCK'S INFIRMARY.
AO HAS BEEN UNCONSCIOUS SINCE LAST NIGHT.
NANAKI WAS INJURED TOO?
NO. HE WAS UN-HARMED.
I ALMOST DIDN'T REC-OGNIZE HIM WHEN I FIRST SAW HIM.

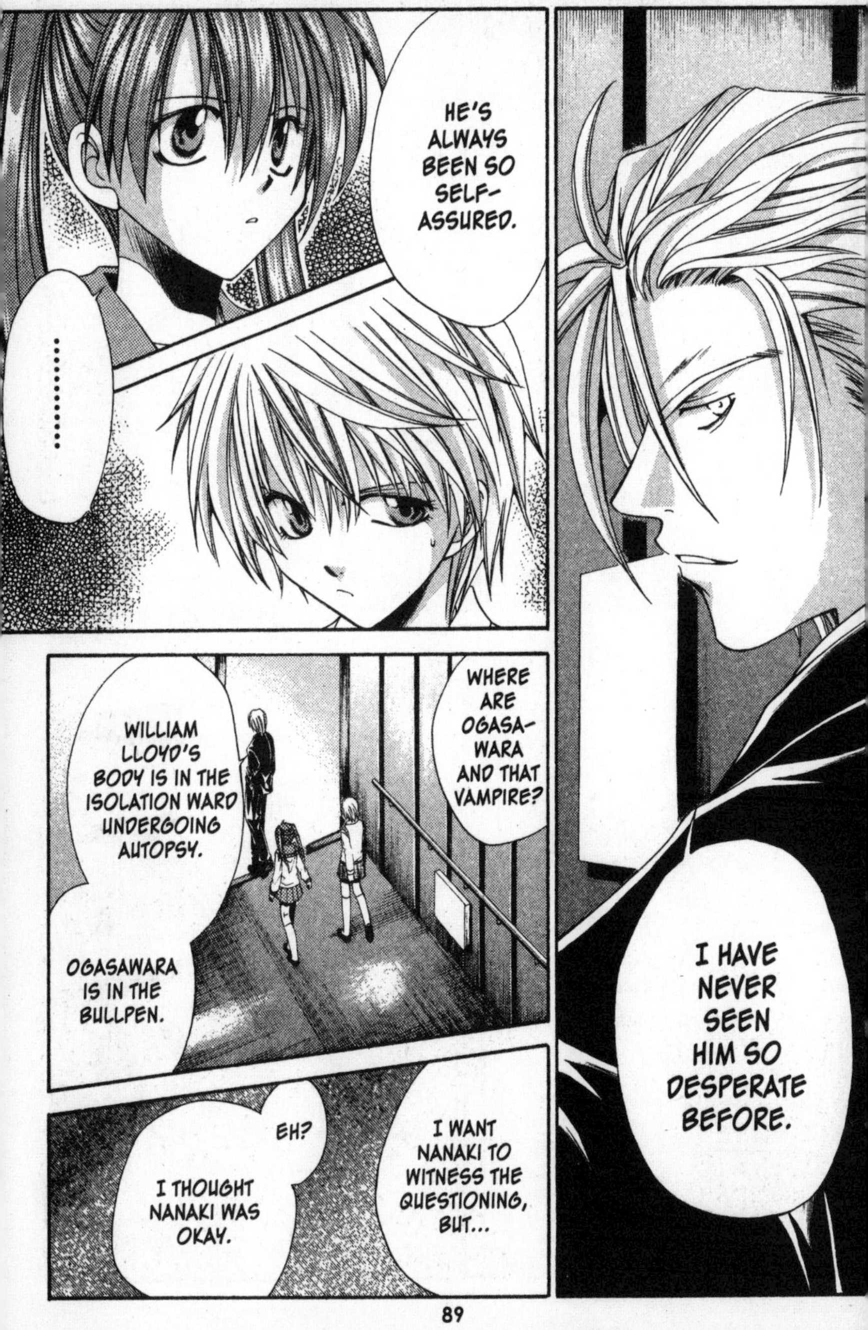
I HAVE NEVER SEEN HIM SO DESPERATE BEFORE.
HE'S ALWAYS BEEN SO SELF-ASSURED.
......
WHERE ARE OGASAWARA AND THAT VAMPIRE?
WILLIAM LLOYD'S BODY IS IN THE ISOLATION WARD UNDERGOING AUTOPSY.
OGASAWARA IS IN THE BULLPEN.
I WANT NANAKI TO WITNESS THE QUESTIONING, BUT...
EH?
I THOUGHT NANAKI WAS OKAY.

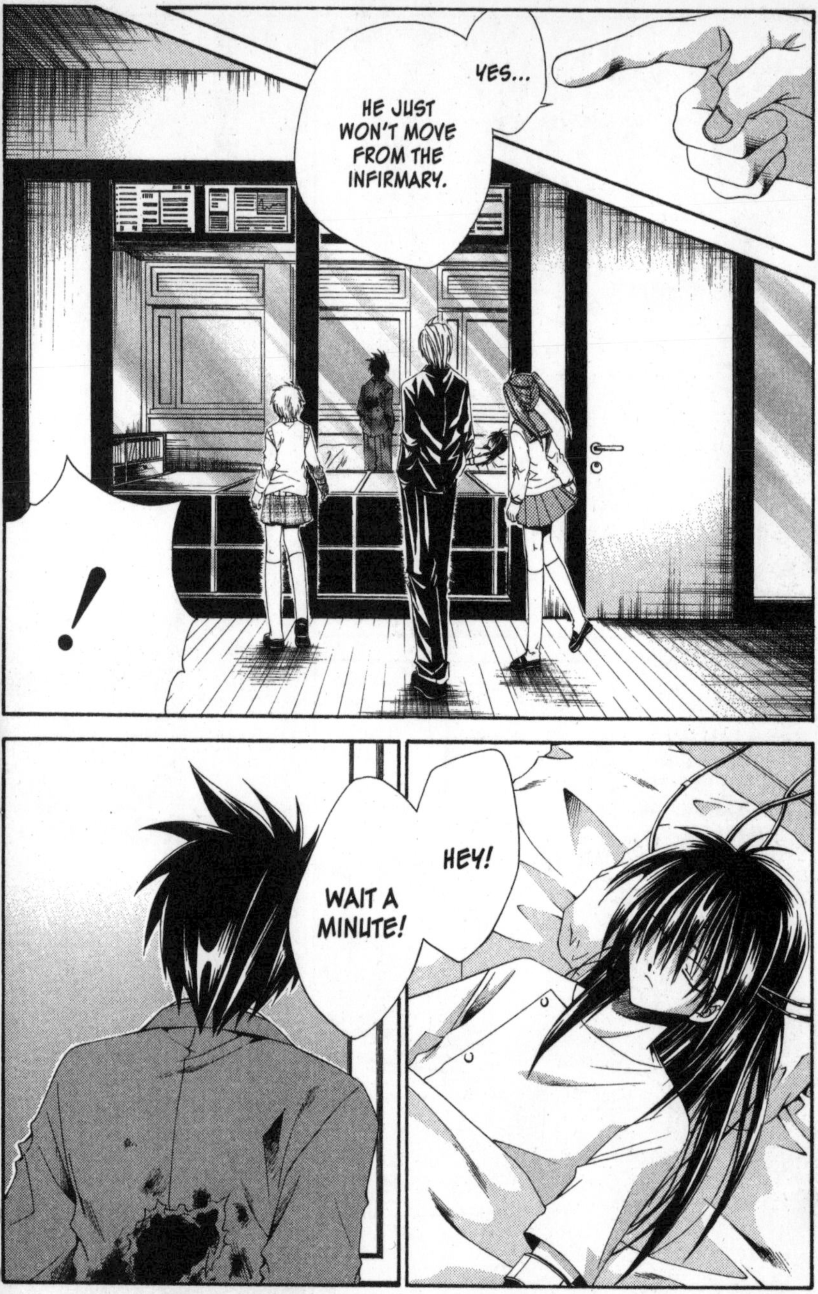
YES...
HE JUST WON'T MOVE FROM THE INFIRMARY.
!
HEY!
WAIT A MINUTE!

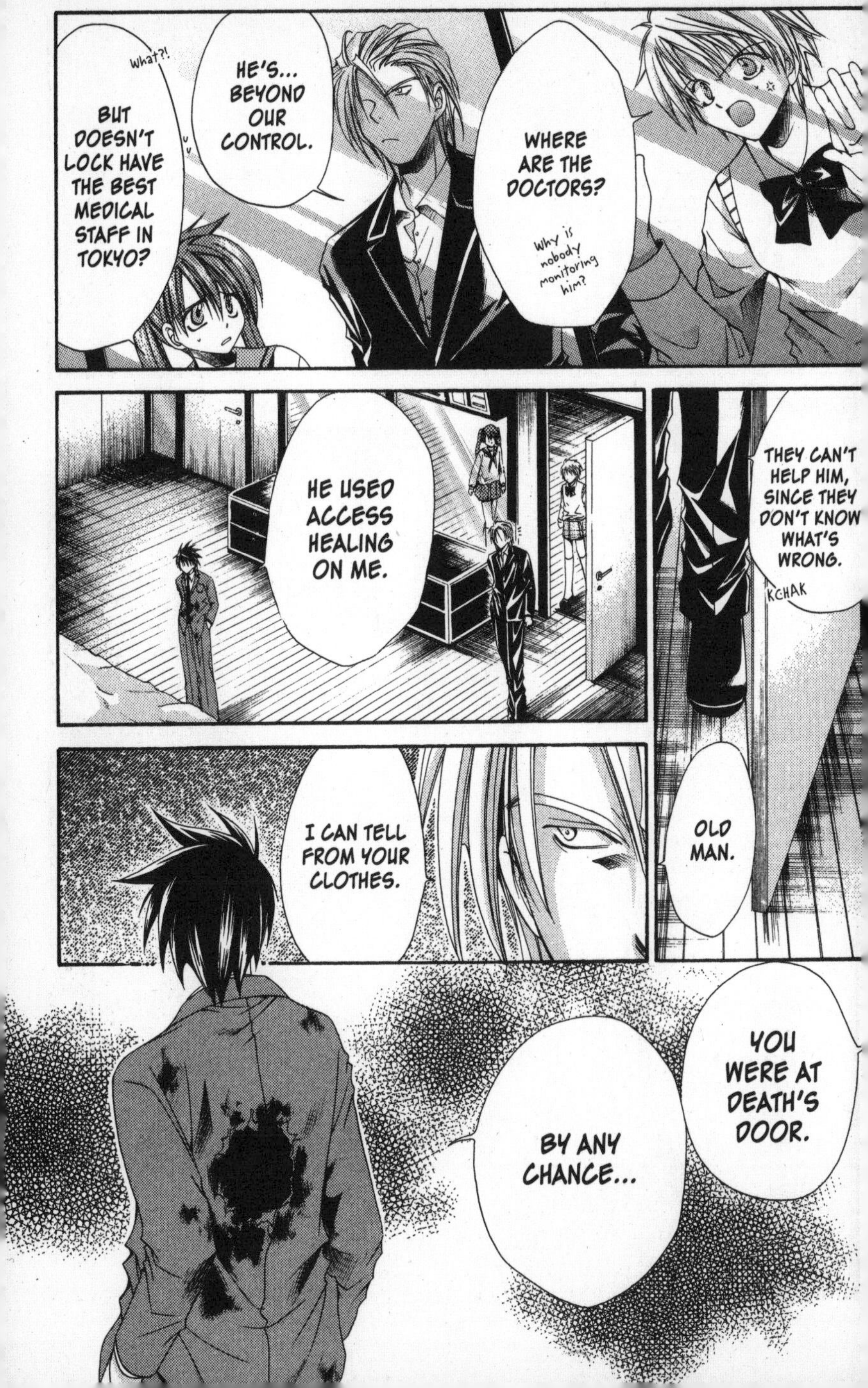
WHERE ARE THE DOCTORS?
Why is nobody monitoring him?
HE'S... BEYOND OUR CONTROL.
What?!
BUT DOESN'T LOCK HAVE THE BEST MEDICAL STAFF IN TOKYO?
THEY CAN'T HELP HIM, SINCE THEY DON'T KNOW WHAT'S WRONG.
KCHAK
OLD MAN.
HE USED ACCESS HEALING ON ME.
I CAN TELL FROM YOUR CLOTHES.
YOU WERE AT DEATH'S DOOR.
BY ANY CHANCE...

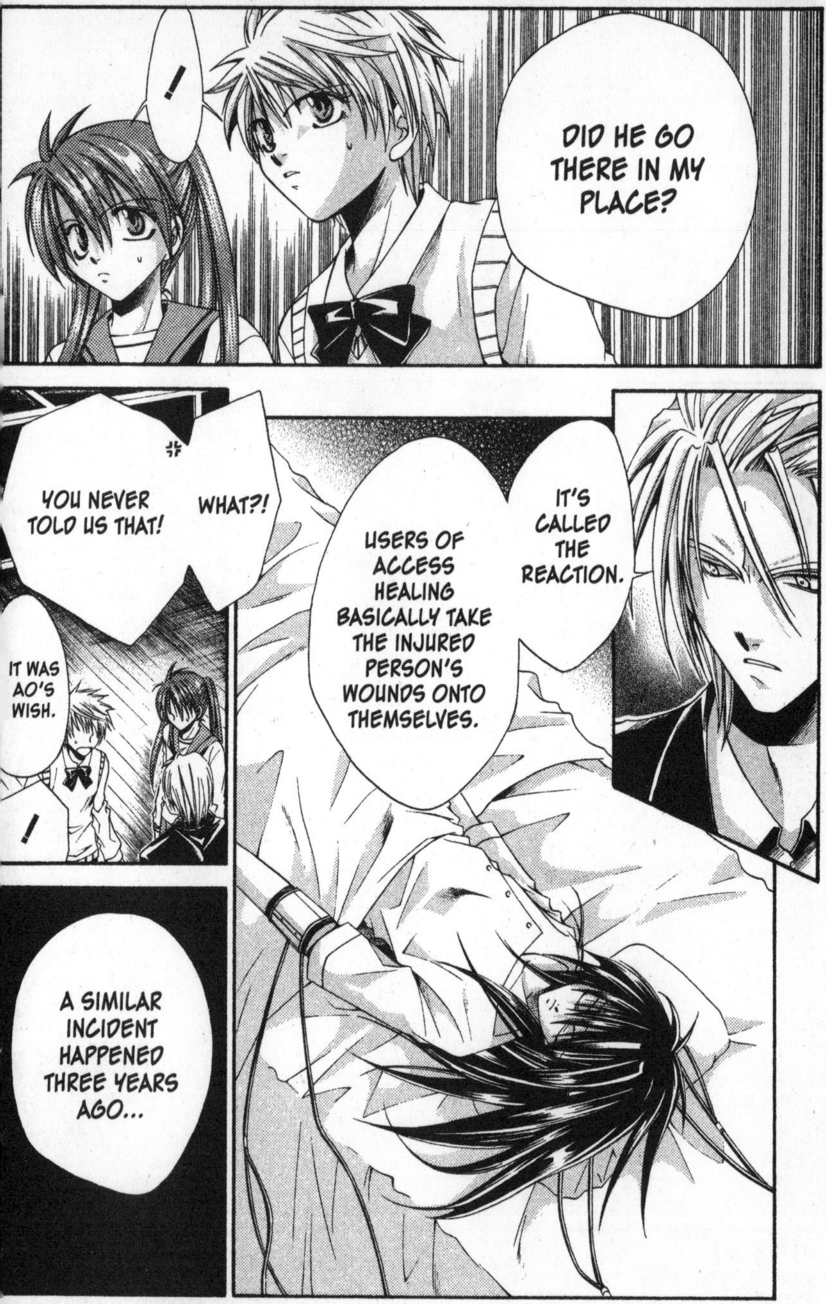
DID HE GO THERE IN MY PLACE?
!
IT'S CALLED THE REACTION.
USERS OF ACCESS HEALING BASICALLY TAKE THE INJURED PERSON'S WOUNDS ONTO THEMSELVES.
WHAT?!
YOU NEVER TOLD US THAT!
IT WAS AO'S WISH.
!
A SIMILAR INCIDENT HAPPENED THREE YEARS AGO...

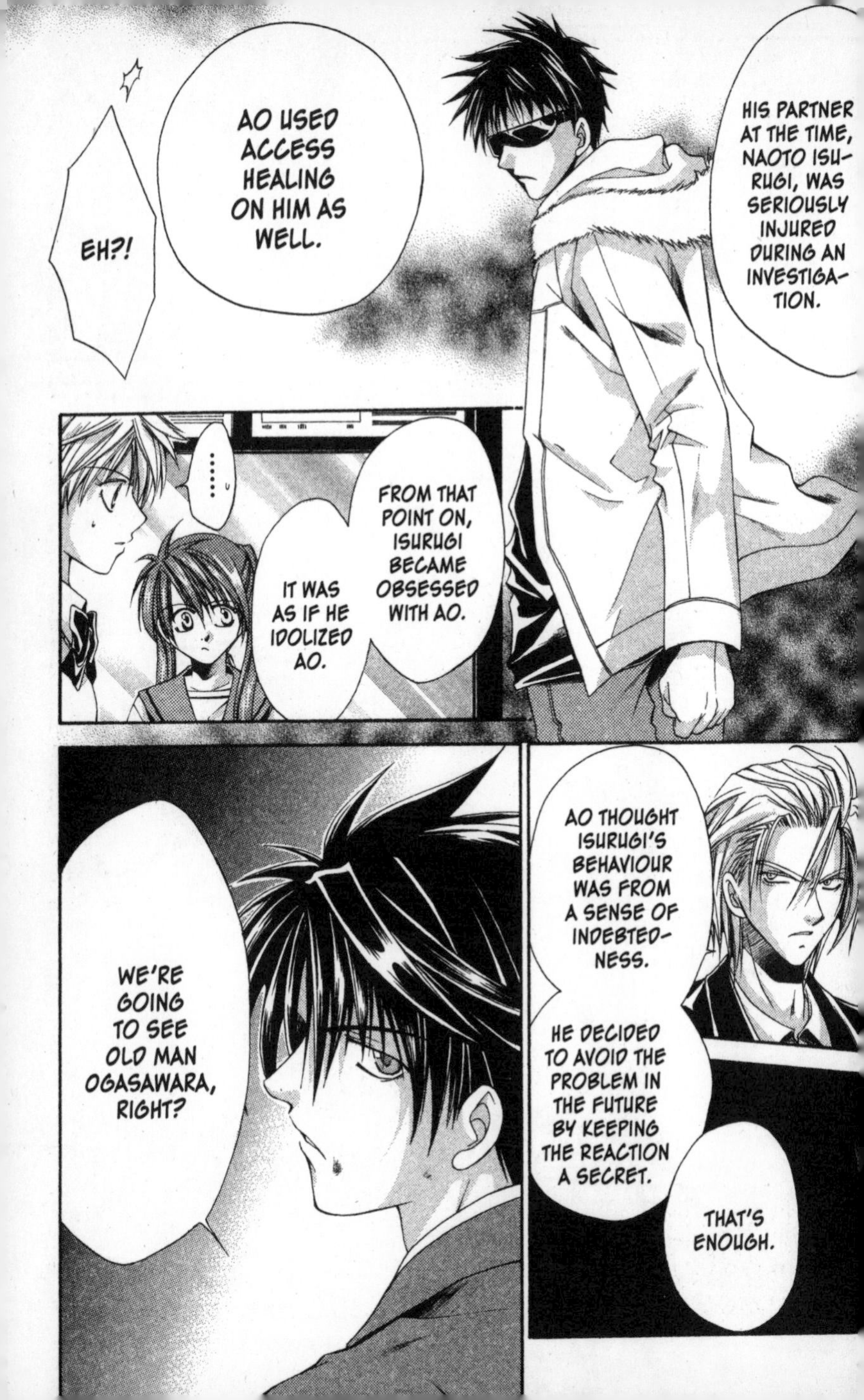
HIS PARTNER AT THE TIME, NAOTO ISURUGI, WAS SERIOUSLY INJURED DURING AN INVESTIGATION.
AO USED ACCESS HEALING ON HIM AS WELL.
EH?!
FROM THAT POINT ON, ISURUGI BECAME OBSESSED WITH AO.
IT WAS AS IF HE IDOLIZED AO.
......
AO THOUGHT ISURUGI'S BEHAVIOUR WAS FROM A SENSE OF INDEBTEDNESS.
HE DECIDED TO AVOID THE PROBLEM IN THE FUTURE BY KEEPING THE REACTION A SECRET.
THAT'S ENOUGH.
WE'RE GOING TO SEE OLD MAN OGASAWARA, RIGHT?

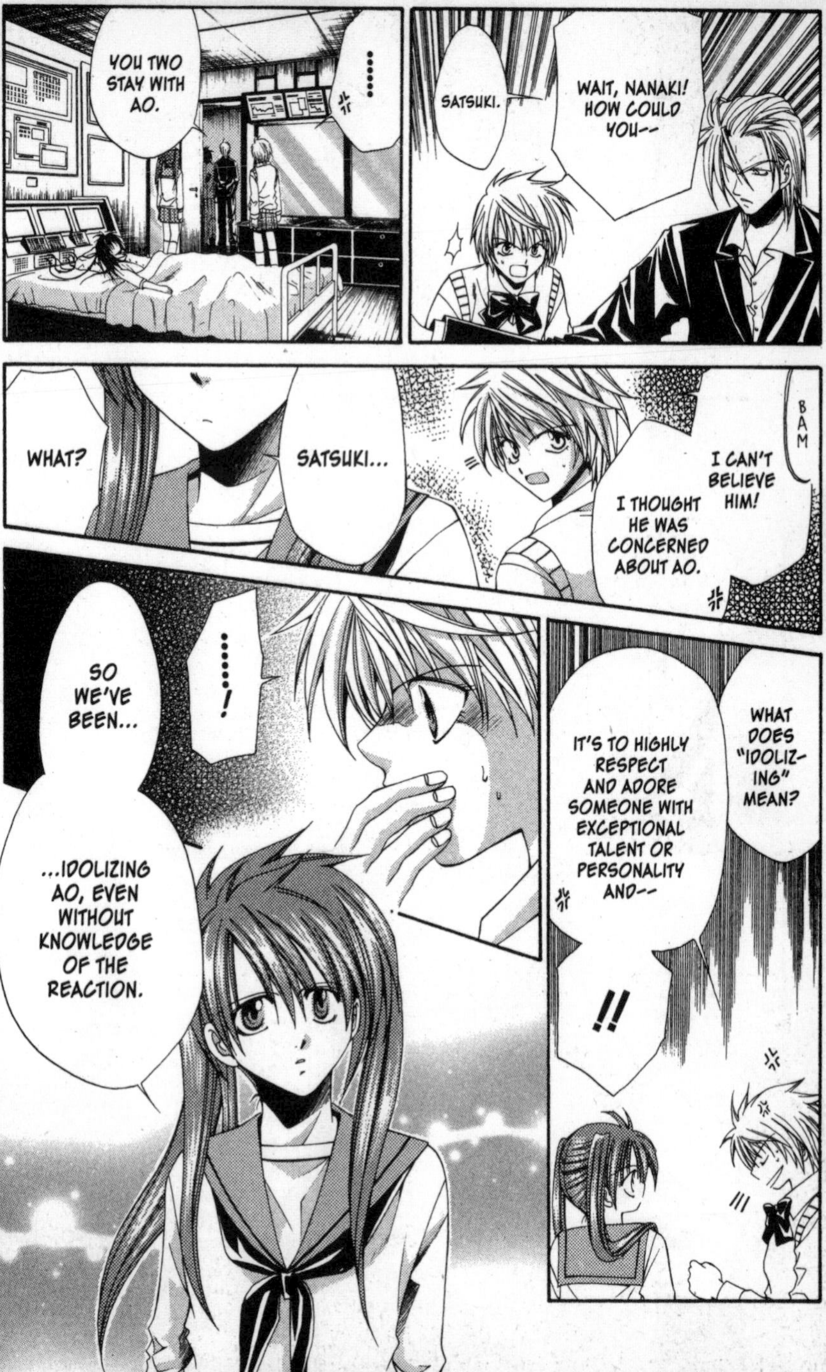
WAIT, NANAKI! HOW COULD YOU--
SATSUKI.
......
YOU TWO STAY WITH AO.
BAM
I CAN'T BELIEVE HIM!
I THOUGHT HE WAS CONCERNED ABOUT AO.
SATSUKI...
WHAT?
WHAT DOES "IDOLIZING" MEAN?
IT'S TO HIGHLY RESPECT AND ADORE SOMEONE WITH EXCEPTIONAL TALENT OR PERSONALITY AND--
!!
......!
SO WE'VE BEEN...
...IDOLIZING AO, EVEN WITHOUT KNOWLEDGE OF THE REACTION.

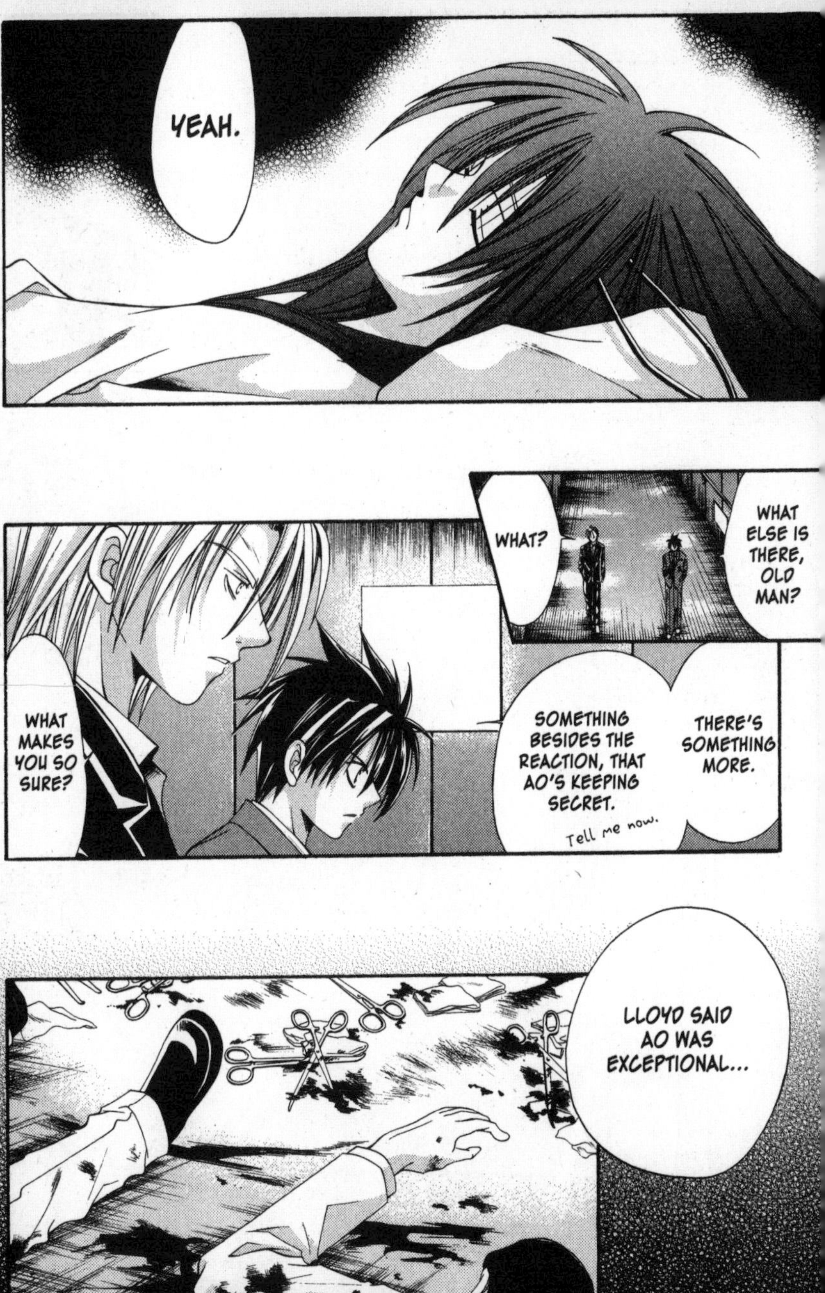
YEAH.
WHAT ELSE IS THERE, OLD MAN?
WHAT?
THERE'S SOMETHING MORE.
SOMETHING BESIDES THE REACTION, THAT AO'S KEEPING SECRET.
Tell me now.
WHAT MAKES YOU SO SURE?
LLOYD SAID AO WAS EXCEPTIONAL...

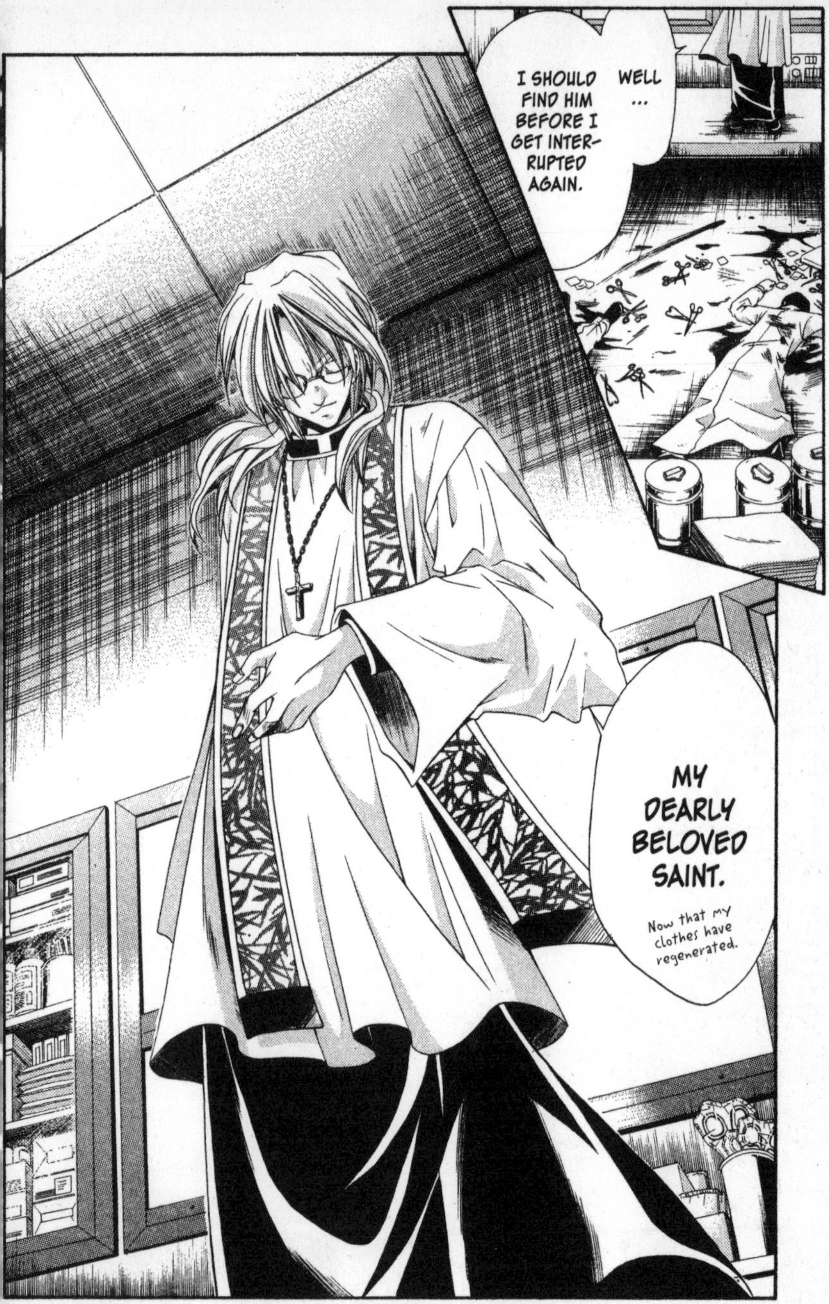
WELL ...
I SHOULD FIND HIM BEFORE I GET INTER-RUPTED AGAIN.
MY DEARLY BELOVED SAINT.
Now that my clothes have regenerated.

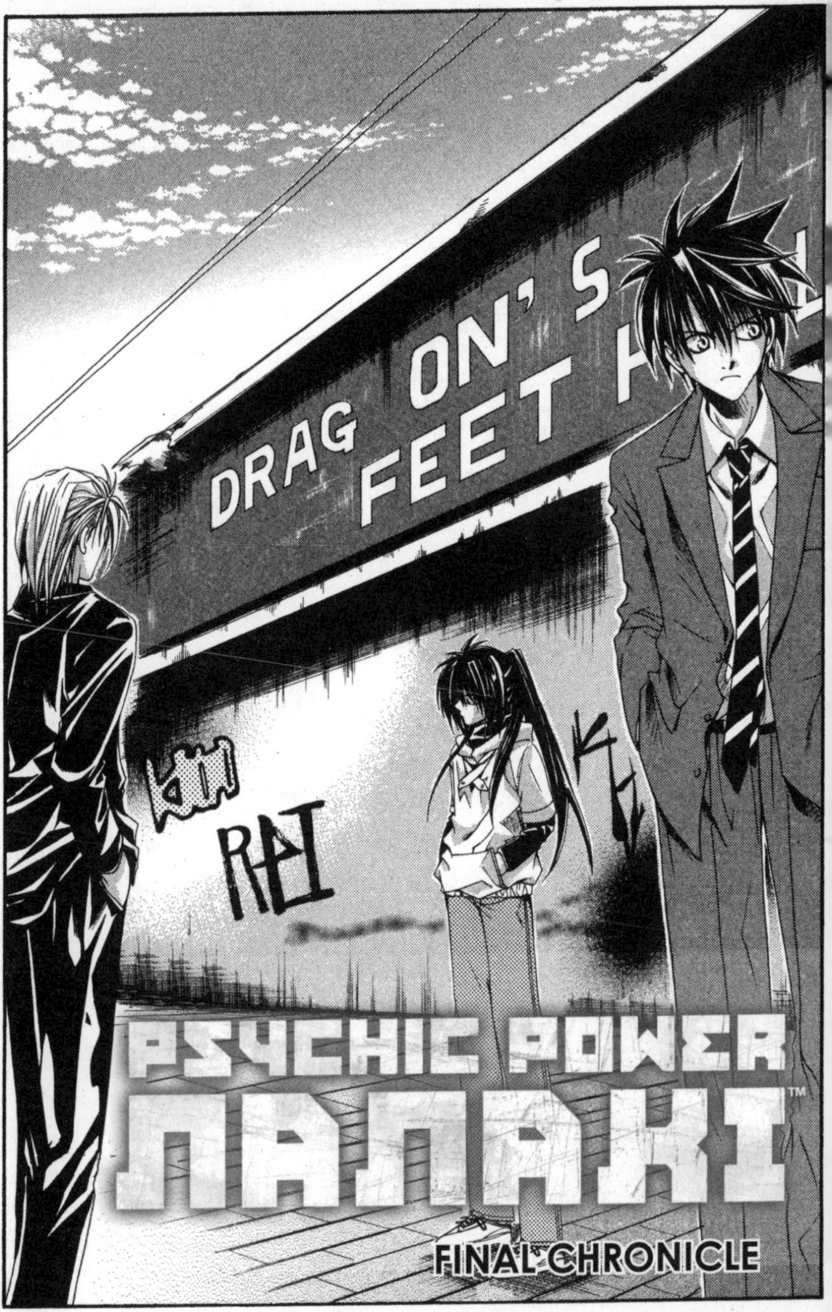
DRAG ON' S
FEET H
PSYCHIC POWER
NANAKI™
FINAL CHRONICLE

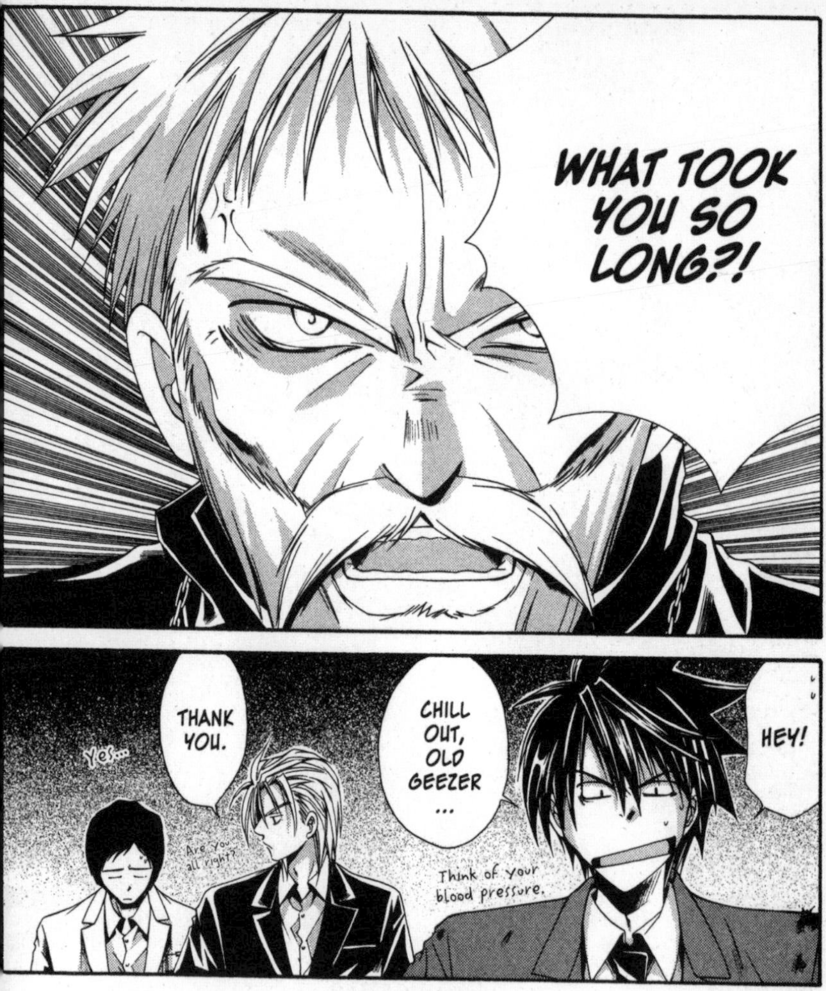
WHAT TOOK YOU SO LONG?!
HEY!
CHILL OUT, OLD GEEZER...
Think of your blood pressure.
THANK YOU.
Yes...
Are you all right?

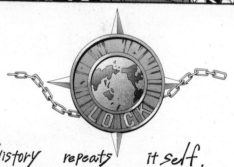

history repeats itself.

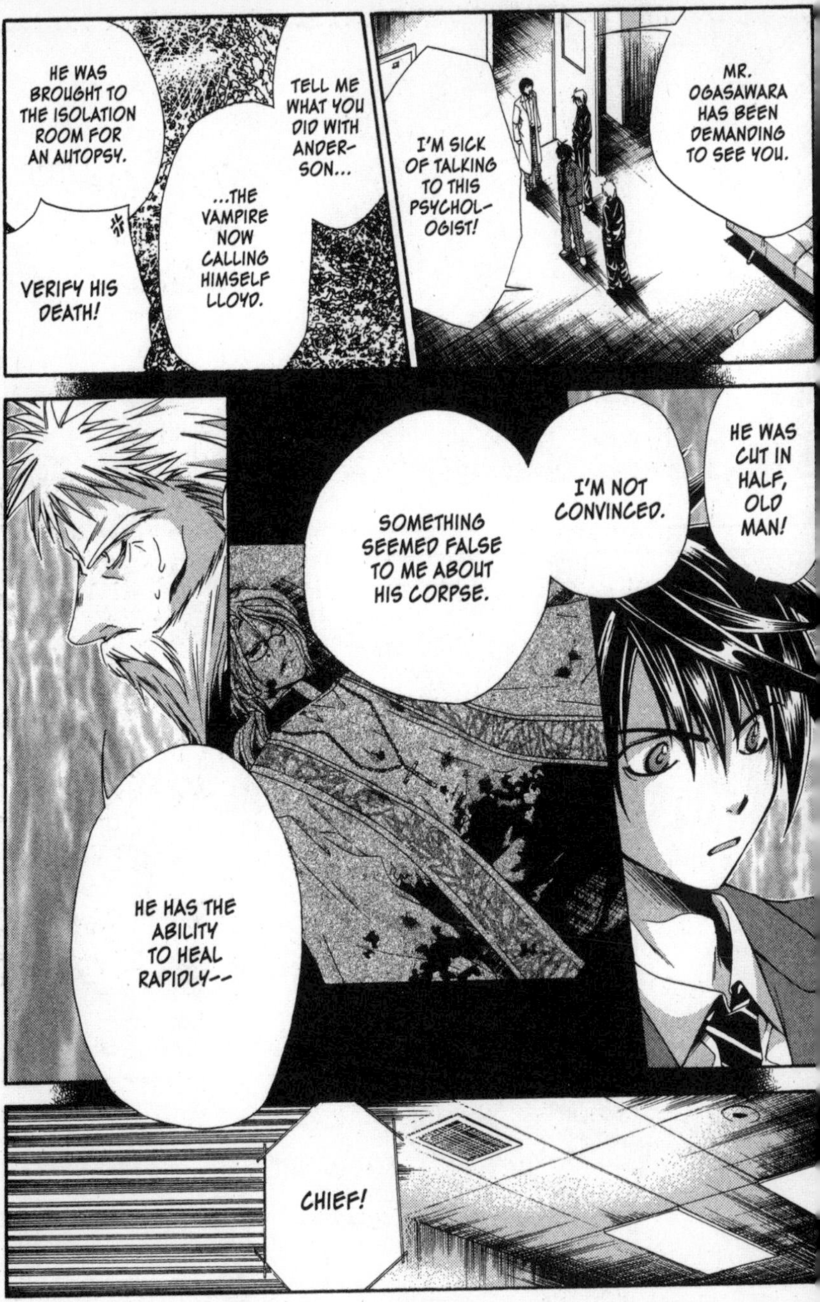
MR. OGASAWARA HAS BEEN DEMANDING TO SEE YOU.
I'M SICK OF TALKING TO THIS PSYCHOLOGIST!
TELL ME WHAT YOU DID WITH ANDERSON...
...THE VAMPIRE NOW CALLING HIMSELF LLOYD.
HE WAS BROUGHT TO THE ISOLATION ROOM FOR AN AUTOPSY.
VERIFY HIS DEATH!
HE WAS CUT IN HALF, OLD MAN!
I'M NOT CONVINCED.
SOMETHING SEEMED FALSE TO ME ABOUT HIS CORPSE.
HE HAS THE ABILITY TO HEAL RAPIDLY--
CHIEF!

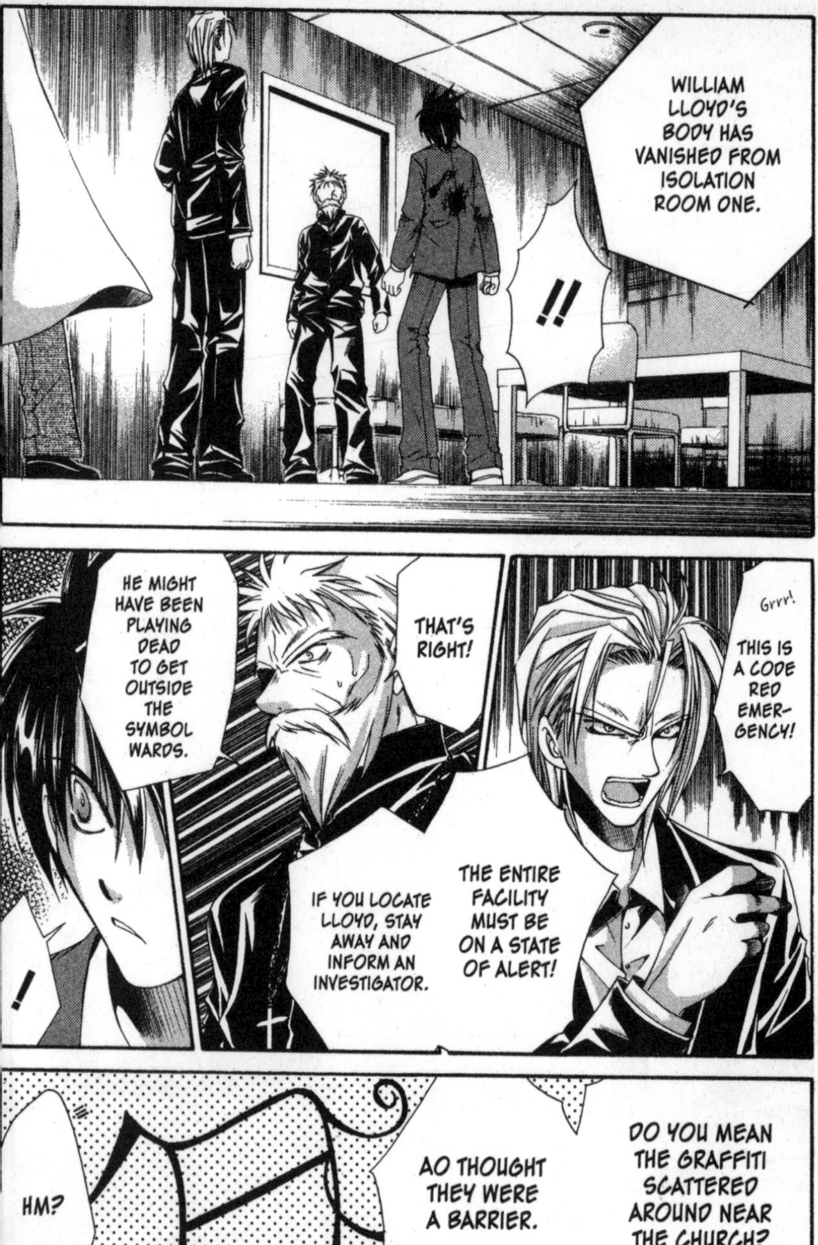
WILLIAM LLOYD'S BODY HAS VANISHED FROM ISOLATION ROOM ONE.
!!
Grrr!
THIS IS A CODE RED EMERGENCY!
THE ENTIRE FACILITY MUST BE ON A STATE OF ALERT!
IF YOU LOCATE LLOYD, STAY AWAY AND INFORM AN INVESTIGATOR.
THAT'S RIGHT!
HE MIGHT HAVE BEEN PLAYING DEAD TO GET OUTSIDE THE SYMBOL WARDS.
!
DO YOU MEAN THE GRAFFITI SCATTERED AROUND NEAR THE CHURCH?
AO THOUGHT THEY WERE A BARRIER.
HM?

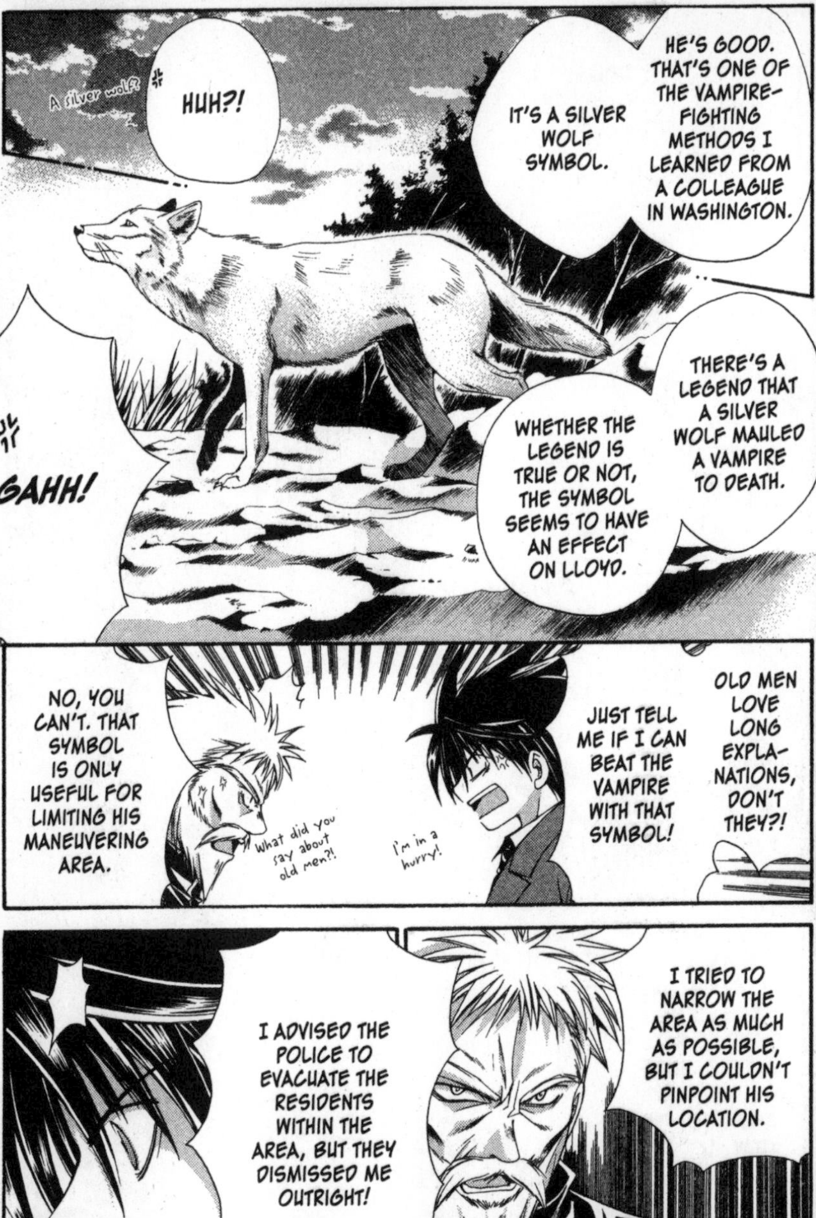
HE'S GOOD. THAT'S ONE OF THE VAMPIRE-FIGHTING METHODS I LEARNED FROM A COLLEAGUE IN WASHINGTON.
IT'S A SILVER WOLF SYMBOL.
HUH?!
A silver wolf?
THERE'S A LEGEND THAT A SILVER WOLF MAULED A VAMPIRE TO DEATH.
WHETHER THE LEGEND IS TRUE OR NOT, THE SYMBOL SEEMS TO HAVE AN EFFECT ON LLOYD.
GAHH!
OLD MEN LOVE LONG EXPLANATIONS, DON'T THEY?!
JUST TELL ME IF I CAN BEAT THE VAMPIRE WITH THAT SYMBOL!
I'm in a hurry!
What did you say about old men?!
NO, YOU CAN'T. THAT SYMBOL IS ONLY USEFUL FOR LIMITING HIS MANEUVERING AREA.
I TRIED TO NARROW THE AREA AS MUCH AS POSSIBLE, BUT I COULDN'T PINPOINT HIS LOCATION.
I ADVISED THE POLICE TO EVACUATE THE RESIDENTS WITHIN THE AREA, BUT THEY DISMISSED ME OUTRIGHT!

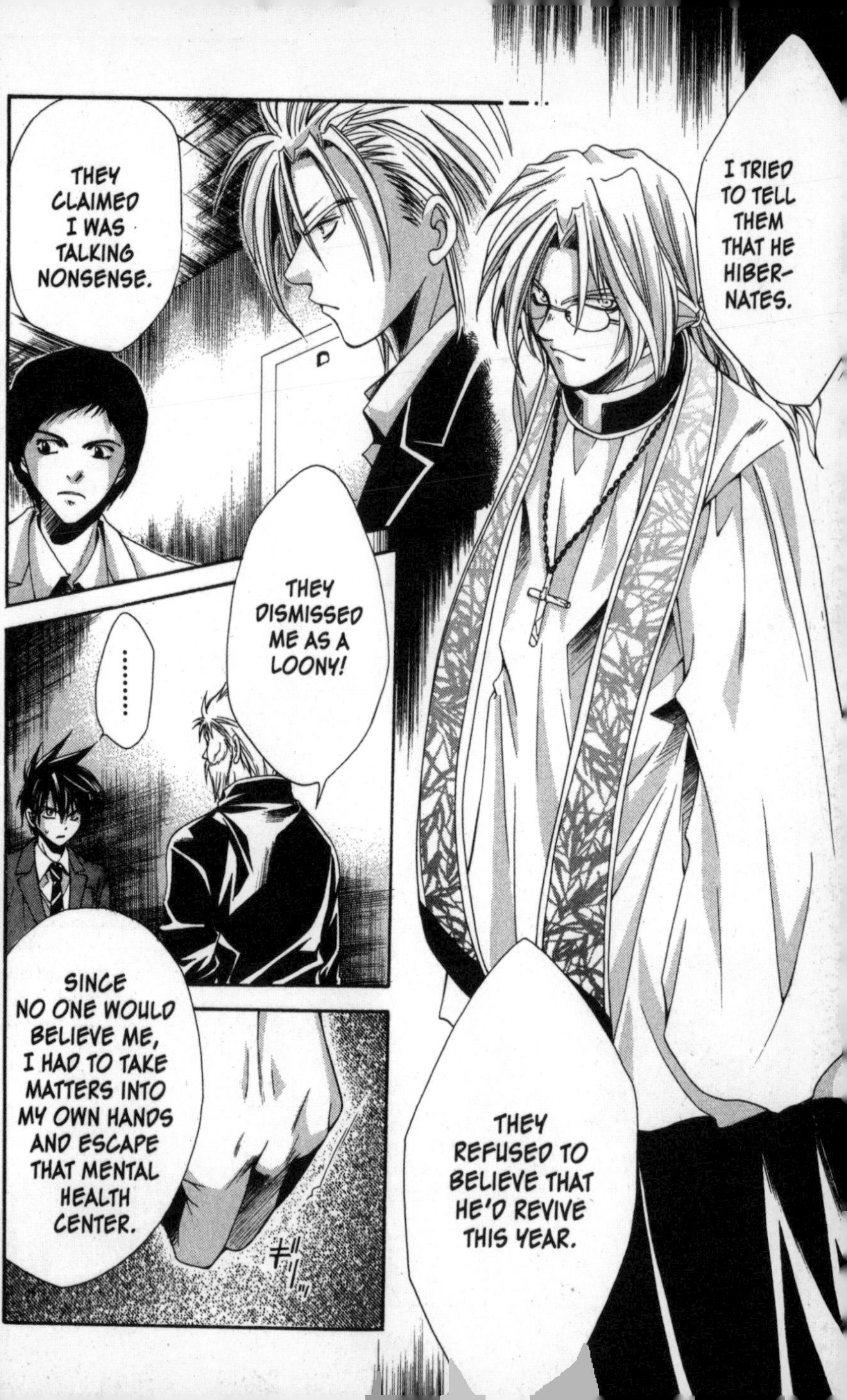
I TRIED TO TELL THEM THAT HE HIBER-NATES.
THEY REFUSED TO BELIEVE THAT HE'D REVIVE THIS YEAR.
THEY CLAIMED I WAS TALKING NONSENSE.
THEY DISMISSED ME AS A LOONY!
....
SINCE NO ONE WOULD BELIEVE ME, I HAD TO TAKE MATTERS INTO MY OWN HANDS AND ESCAPE THAT MENTAL HEALTH CENTER.

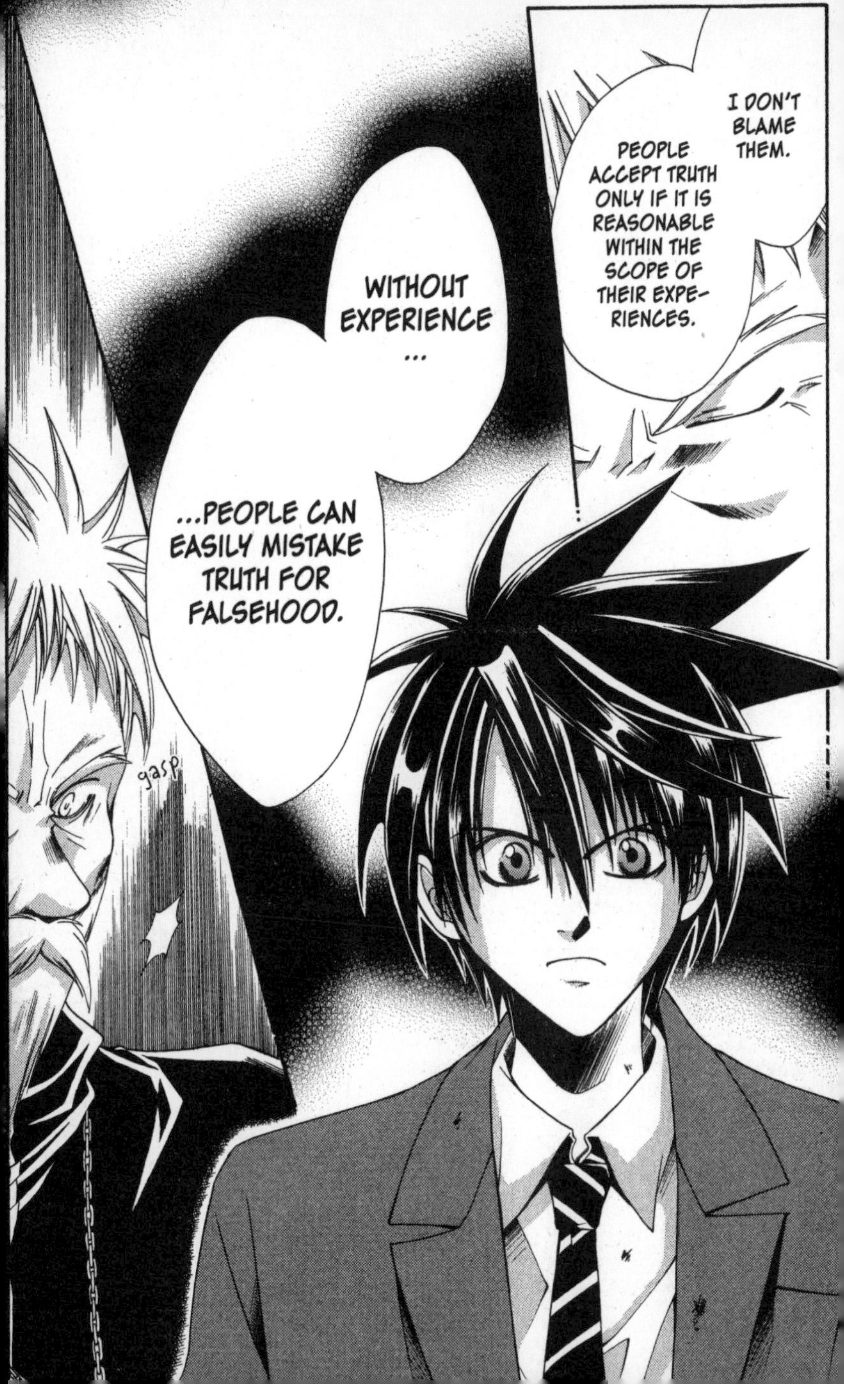
I DON'T BLAME THEM.
PEOPLE ACCEPT TRUTH ONLY IF IT IS REASONABLE WITHIN THE SCOPE OF THEIR EXPE-RIENCES.
WITHOUT EXPERIENCE ...
...PEOPLE CAN EASILY MISTAKE TRUTH FOR FALSEHOOD.
gasp

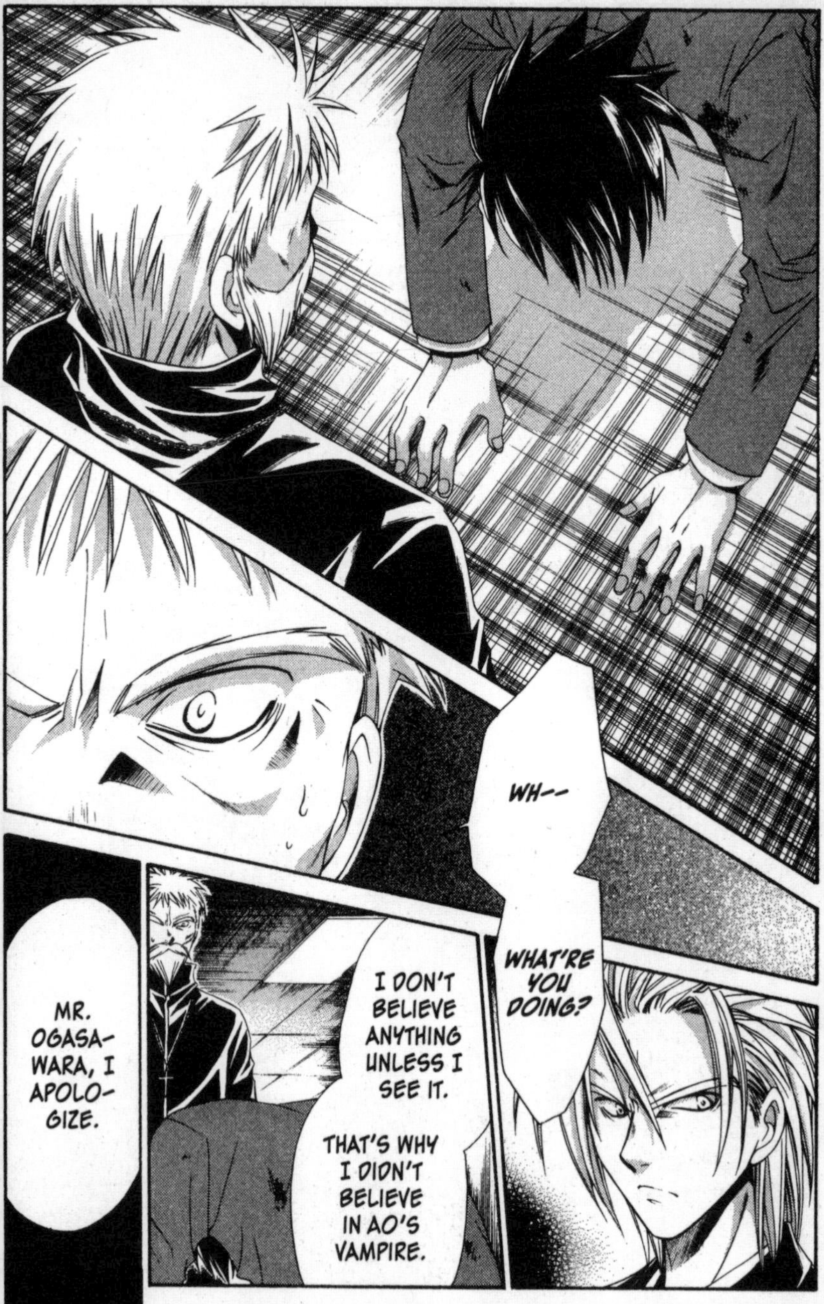
WH--
WHAT'RE YOU DOING?
I DON'T BELIEVE ANYTHING UNLESS I SEE IT.
THAT'S WHY I DIDN'T BELIEVE IN AO'S VAMPIRE.
MR. OGASAWARA, I APOLOGIZE.

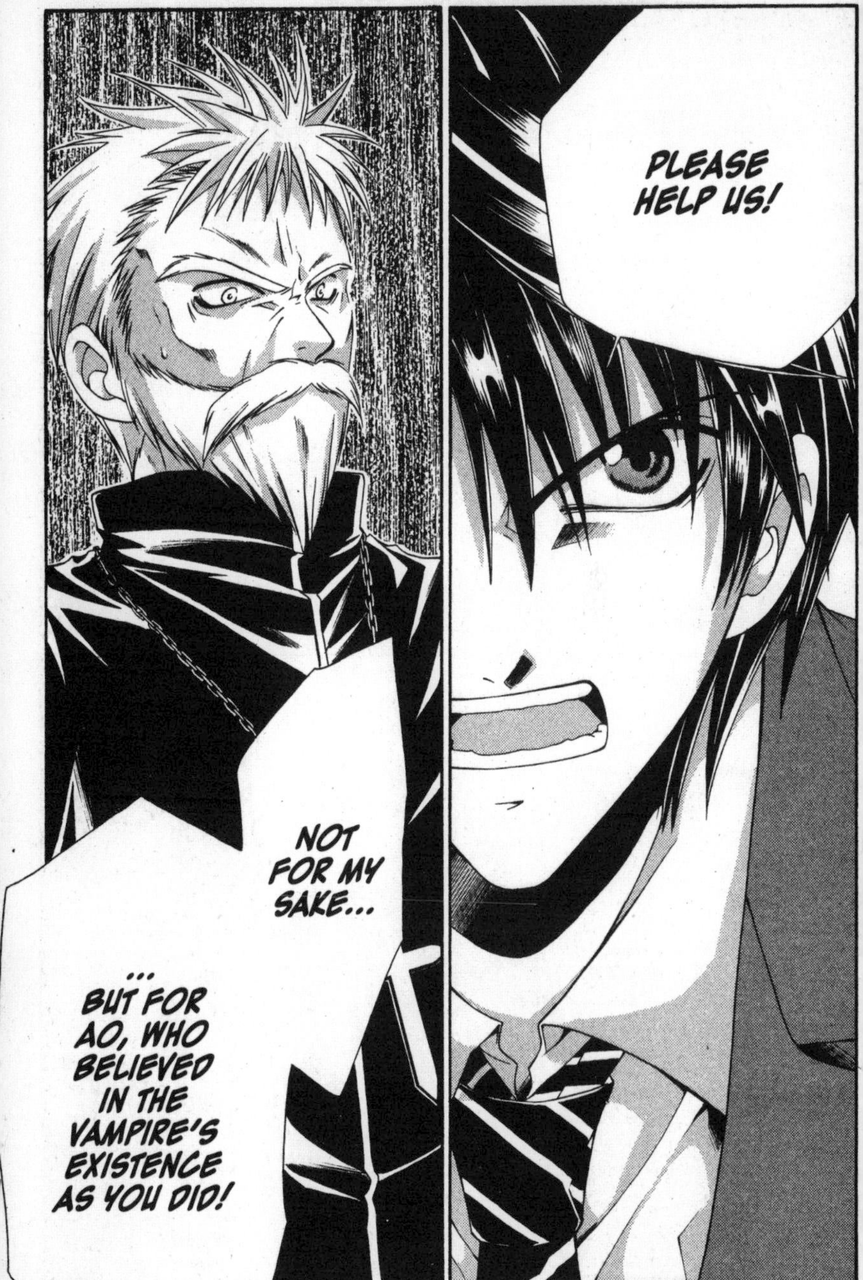
PLEASE HELP US!
NOT FOR MY SAKE...
...BUT FOR AO, WHO BELIEVED IN THE VAMPIRE'S EXISTENCE AS YOU DID!

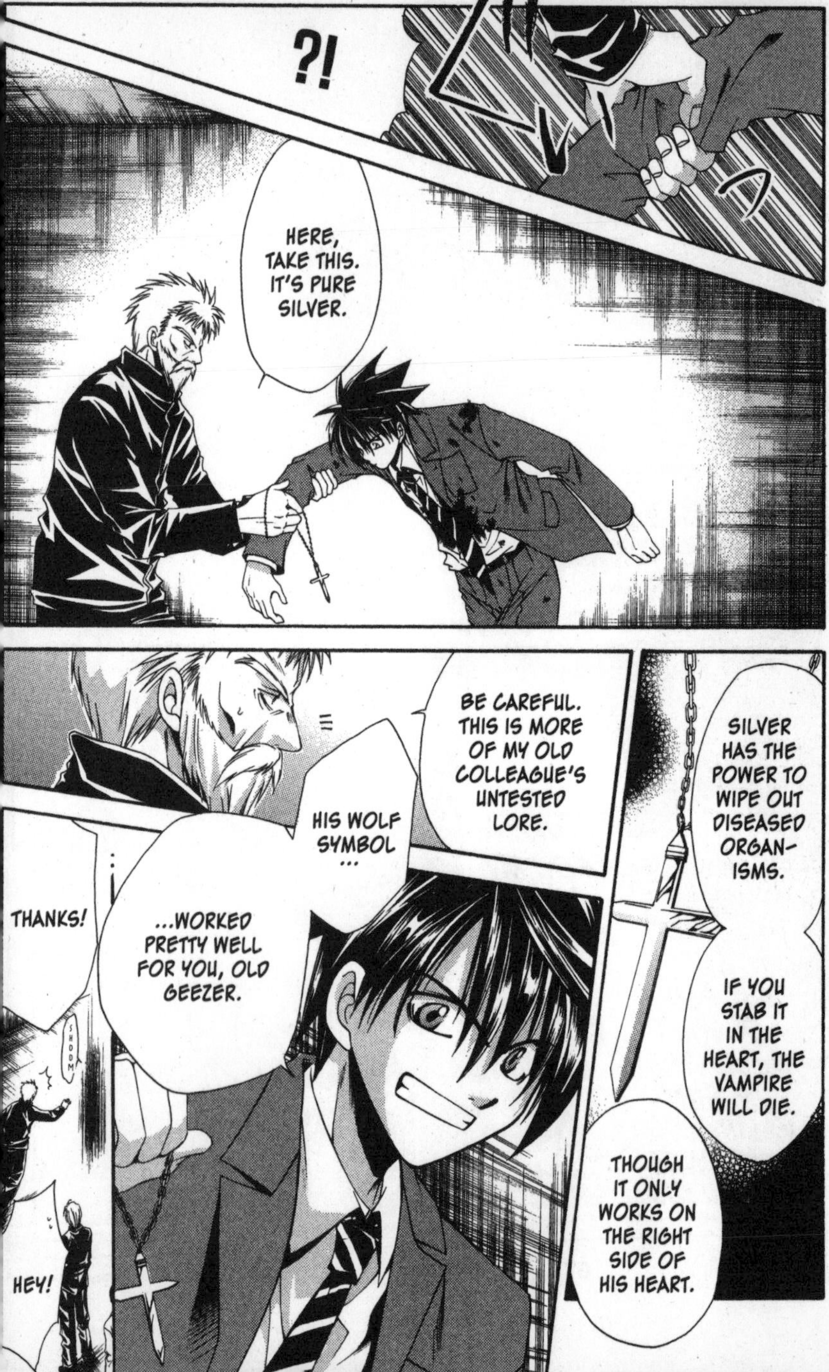
?!
HERE, TAKE THIS. IT'S PURE SILVER.
SILVER HAS THE POWER TO WIPE OUT DISEASED ORGAN-ISMS.
IF YOU STAB IT IN THE HEART, THE VAMPIRE WILL DIE.
THOUGH IT ONLY WORKS ON THE RIGHT SIDE OF HIS HEART.
BE CAREFUL. THIS IS MORE OF MY OLD COLLEAGUE'S UNTESTED LORE.
HIS WOLF SYMBOL...
...WORKED PRETTY WELL FOR YOU, OLD GEEZER.
THANKS!
SHOOM
HEY!

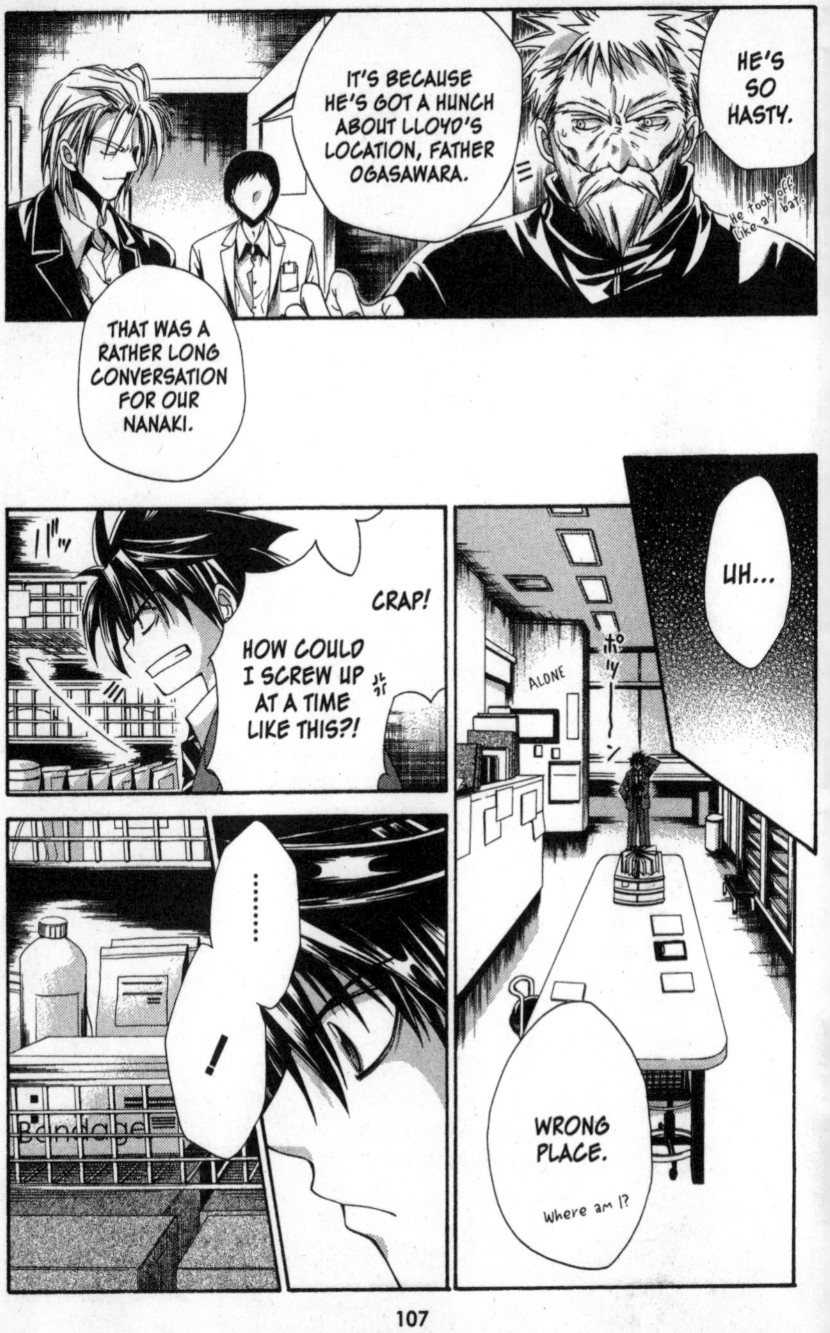
HE'S SO HASTY.
He took off like a bat.
IT'S BECAUSE HE'S GOT A HUNCH ABOUT LLOYD'S LOCATION, FATHER OGASAWARA.
THAT WAS A RATHER LONG CONVERSATION FOR OUR NANAKI.
UH...
WRONG PLACE.
Where am I?
CRAP!
HOW COULD I SCREW UP AT A TIME LIKE THIS?!
......
!
Bandage

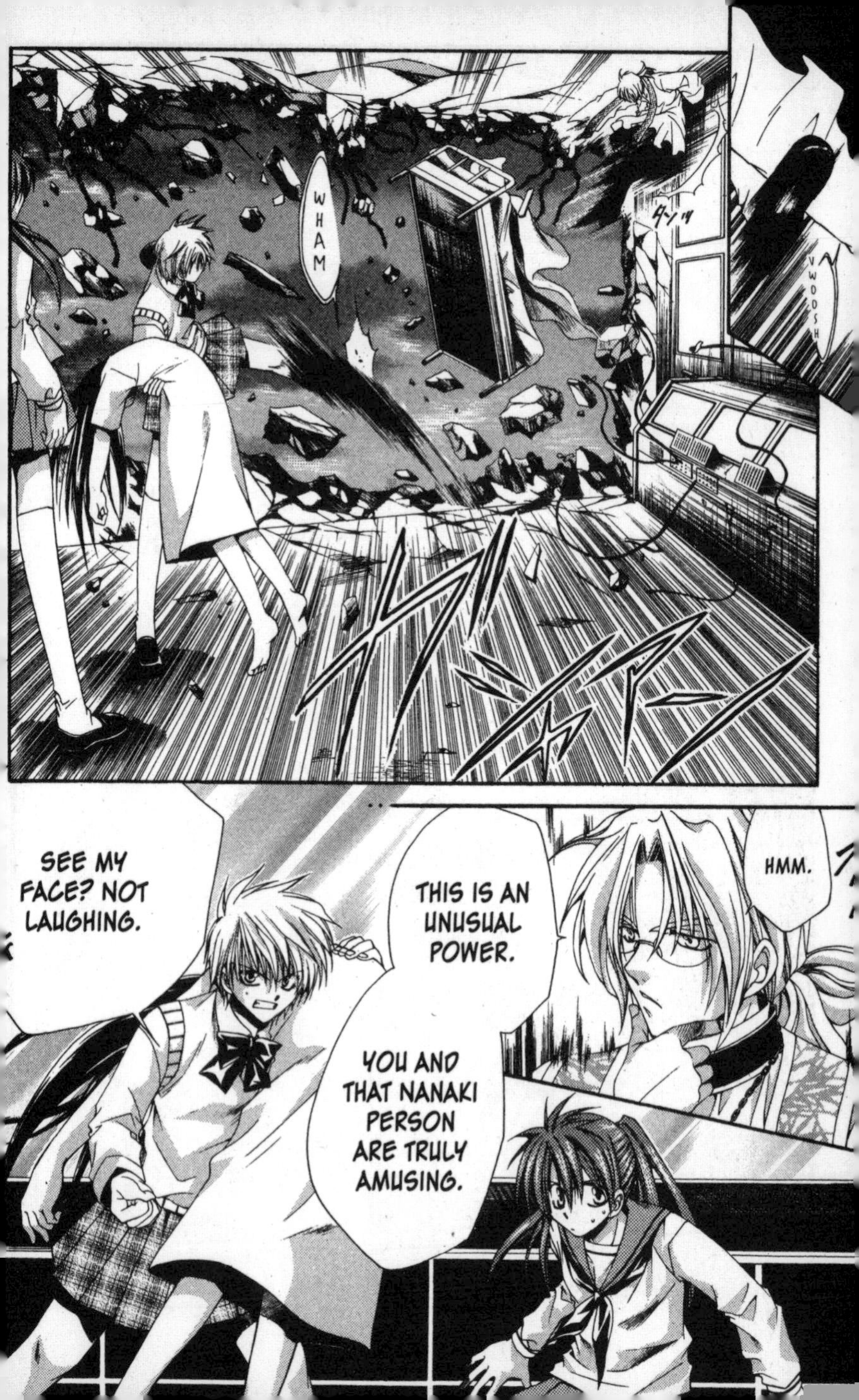
VWOOSH
WHAM
HMM.
THIS IS AN UNUSUAL POWER.
YOU AND THAT NANAKI PERSON ARE TRULY AMUSING.
SEE MY FACE? NOT LAUGHING.

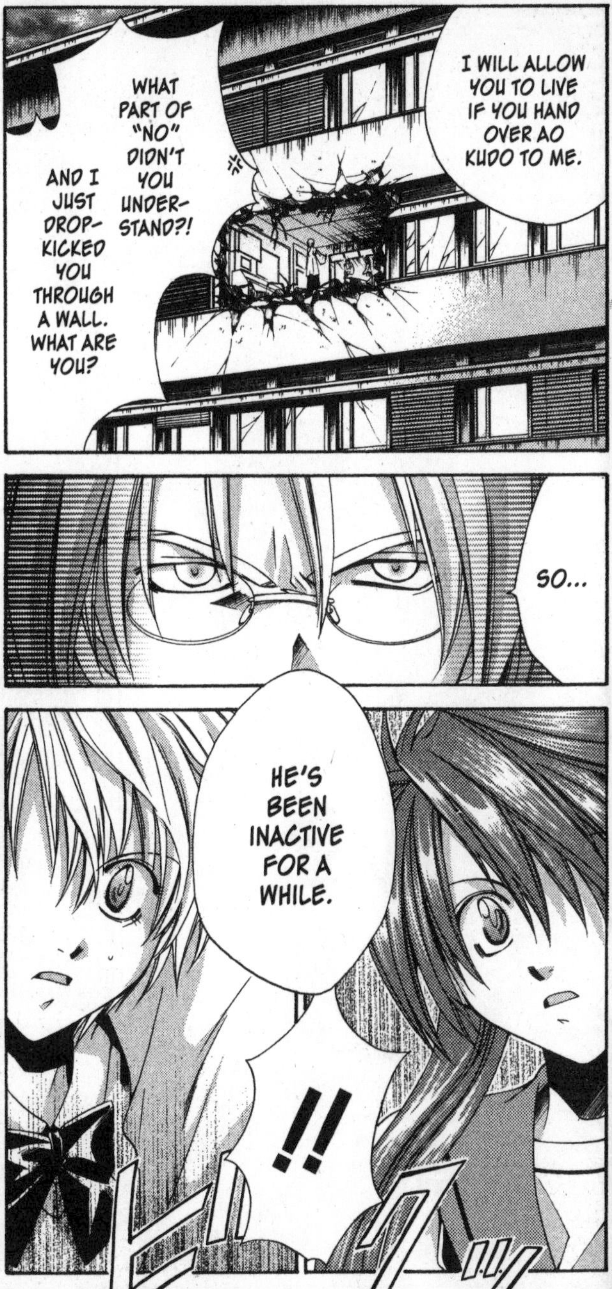
I WILL ALLOW YOU TO LIVE IF YOU HAND OVER AO KUDO TO ME.
WHAT PART OF "NO" DIDN'T YOU UNDER-STAND?!
AND I JUST DROP-KICKED YOU THROUGH A WALL. WHAT ARE YOU?
SO...
HE'S BEEN INACTIVE FOR A WHILE.
!!

About Father Lloyd:
My friends say he is an unusual character for me (lol). I wanted him to be a little different; so for me, this was a positive comment. The only thing I see as really different is his wavy hairstyle, which is uncharacteristic of my style.

I revealed Ao's Reaction to show emotional depth in Nanaki. It takes a major event to affect him, with his irrespon-sible personality. I think there are a surprising number of people like that, so consider Nanaki as their representative (lol)!

By the way, the eye-glasses joke Nanaki used on Father Lloyd came from a certain comedian I'm addicted to and I just had to use it (lol).

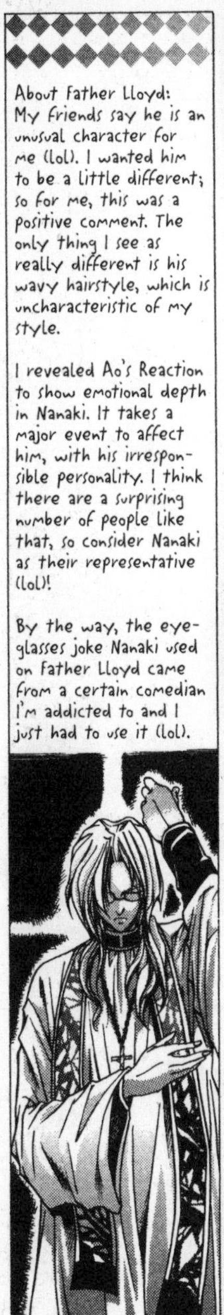

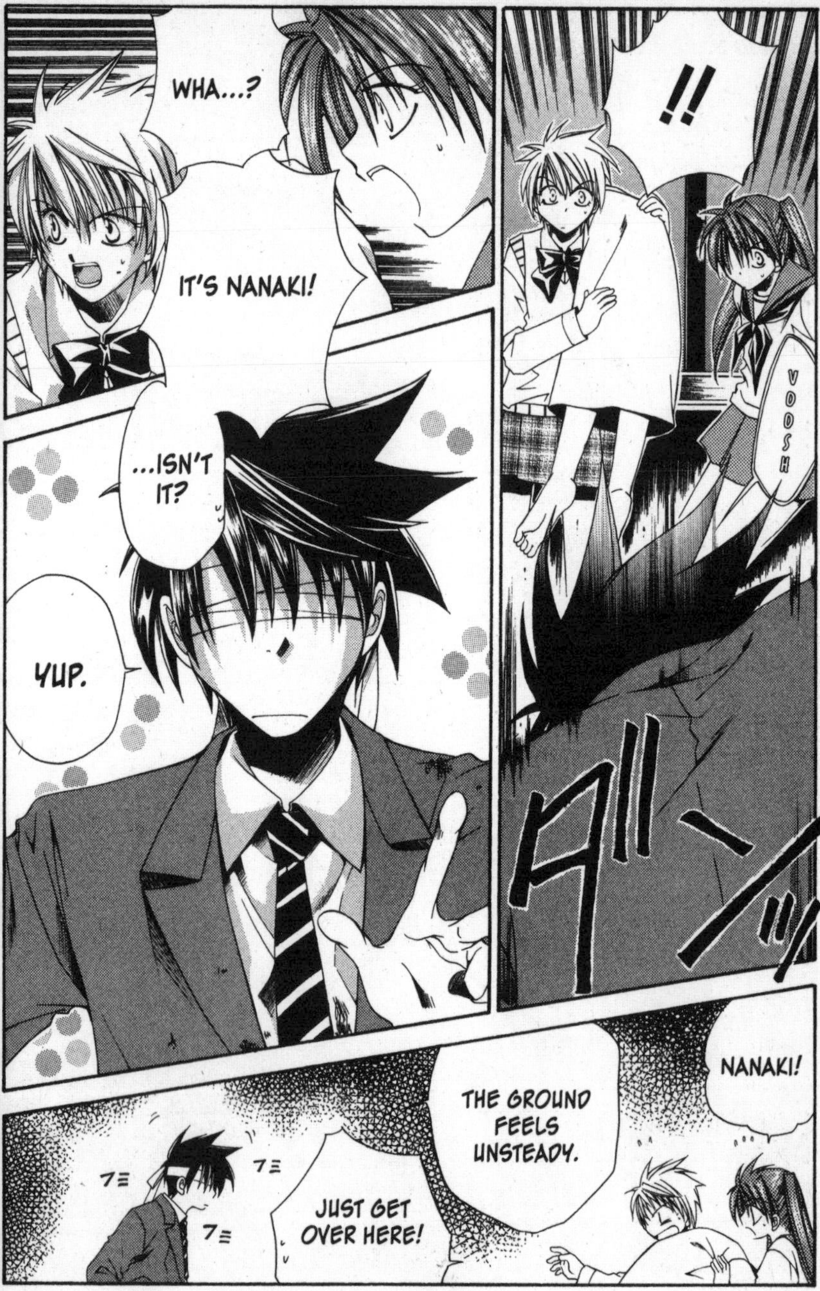
!!
VOOSH
WHA...?
IT'S NANAKI!
...ISN'T IT?
YUP.
NANAKI!
THE GROUND FEELS UNSTEADY.
JUST GET OVER HERE!

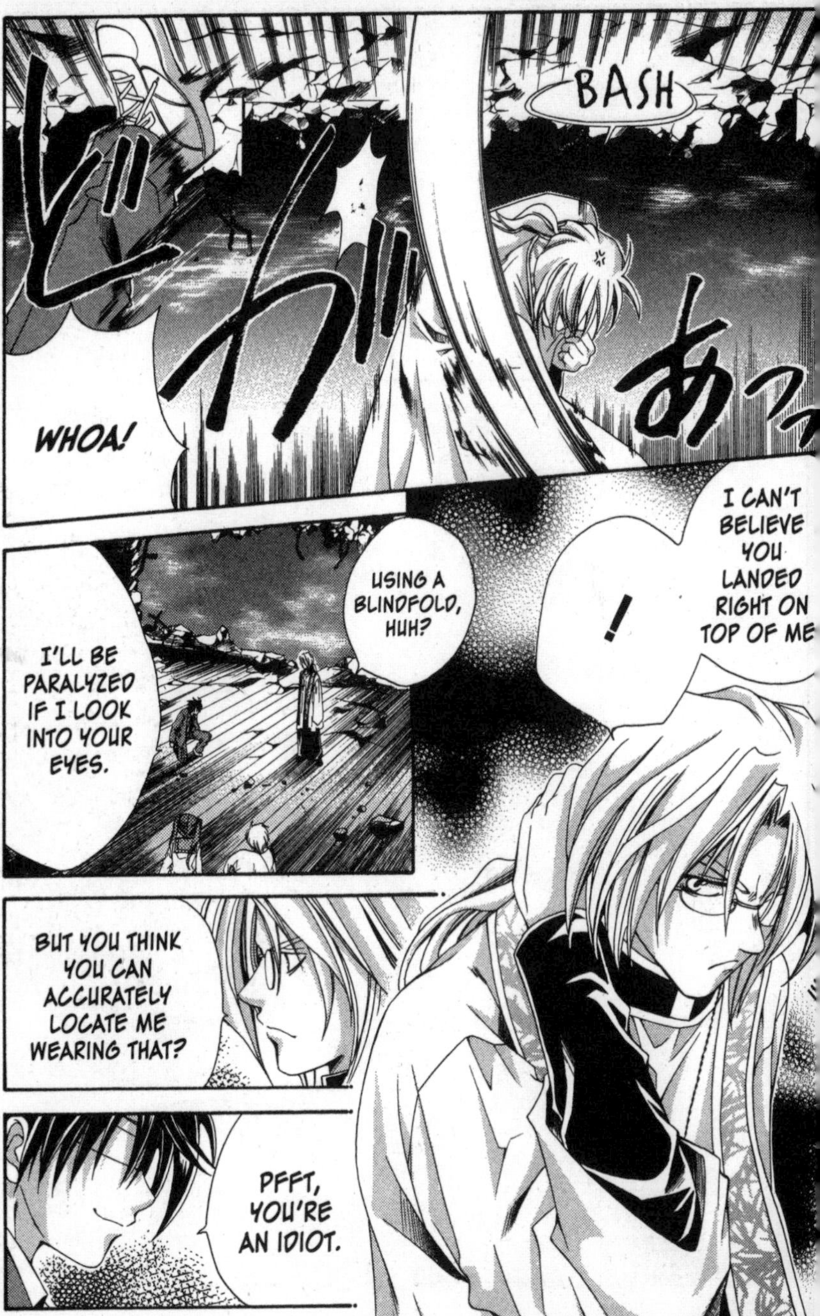
BASH
WHOA!
I CAN'T BELIEVE YOU LANDED RIGHT ON TOP OF ME
!
USING A BLINDFOLD, HUH?
I'LL BE PARALYZED IF I LOOK INTO YOUR EYES.
BUT YOU THINK YOU CAN ACCURATELY LOCATE ME WEARING THAT?
PFFT, YOU'RE AN IDIOT.

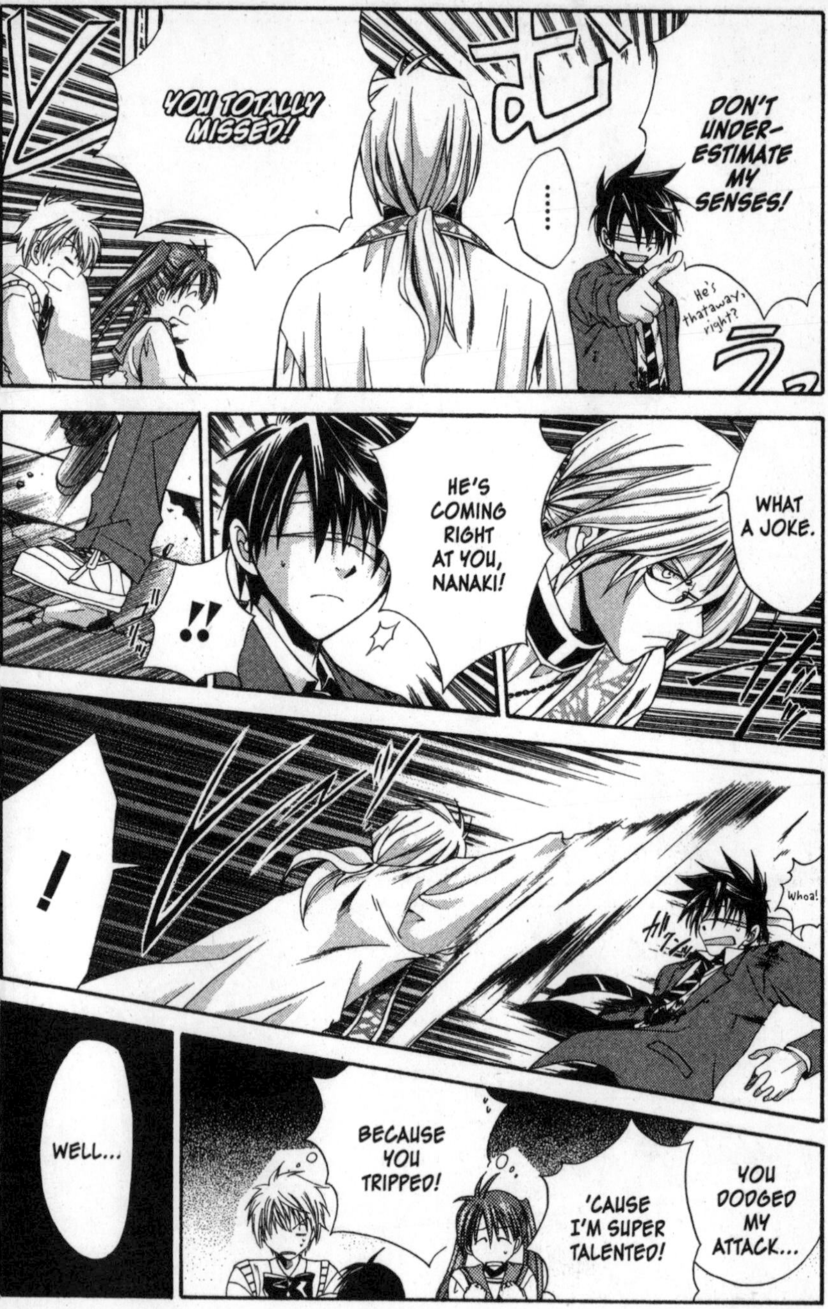
DON'T UNDER-ESTIMATE MY SENSES!
He's thataway, right?
......
YOU TOTALLY MISSED!
WHAT A JOKE.
HE'S COMING RIGHT AT YOU, NANAKI!
!!
Whoa!
!
YOU DODGED MY ATTACK...
'CAUSE I'M SUPER TALENTED!
BECAUSE YOU TRIPPED!
WELL...

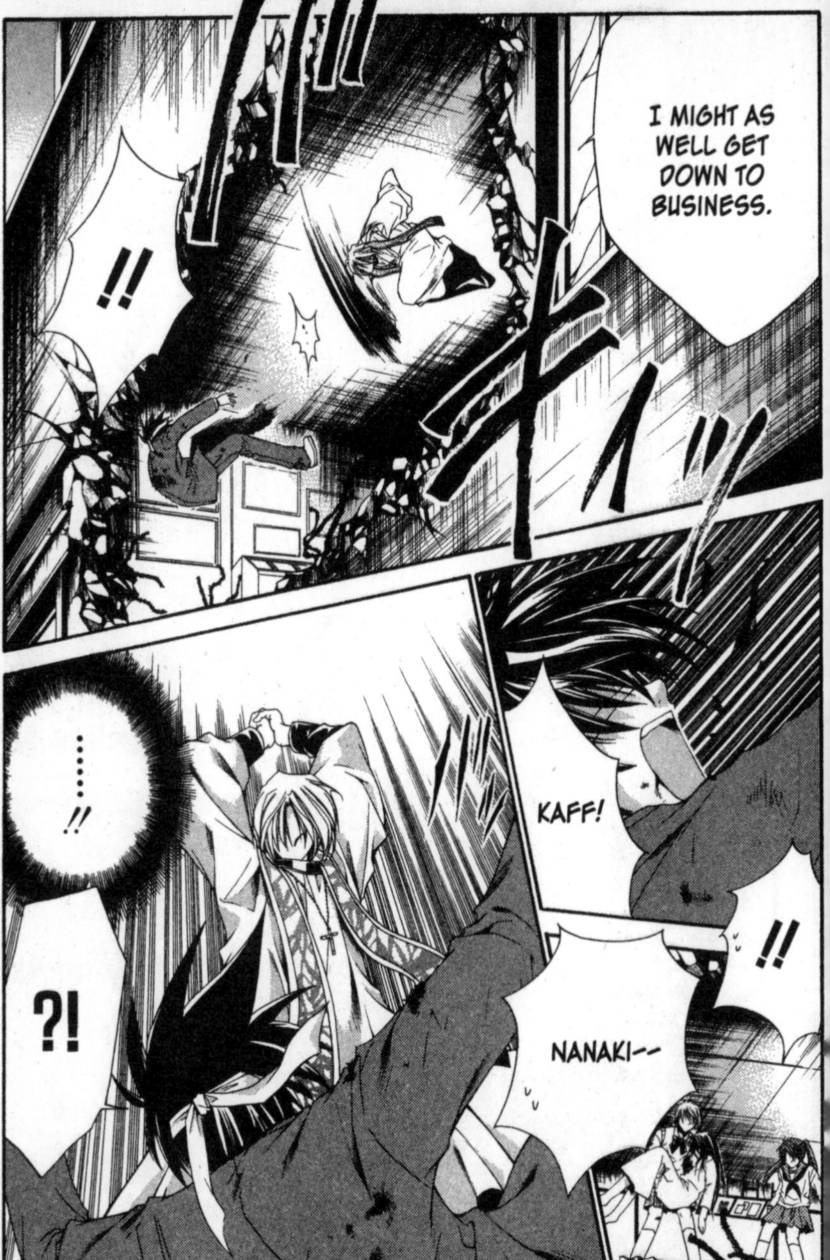
I MIGHT AS WELL GET DOWN TO BUSINESS.
!!
KAFF!
!!
NANAKI--
......!!
?!

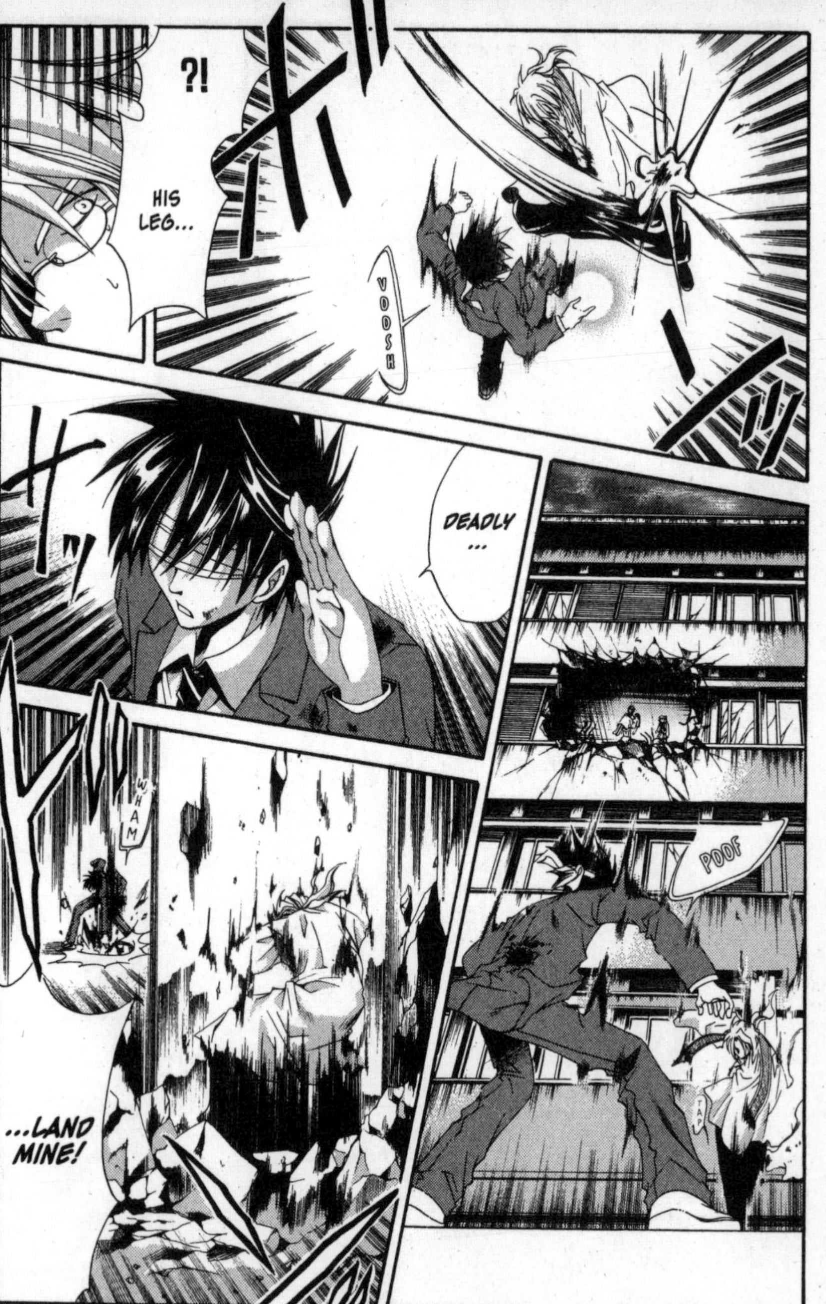
VOOSH
?!
HIS LEG...
DEADLY ...
POOF
TAP
WHAM
...LAND MINE!

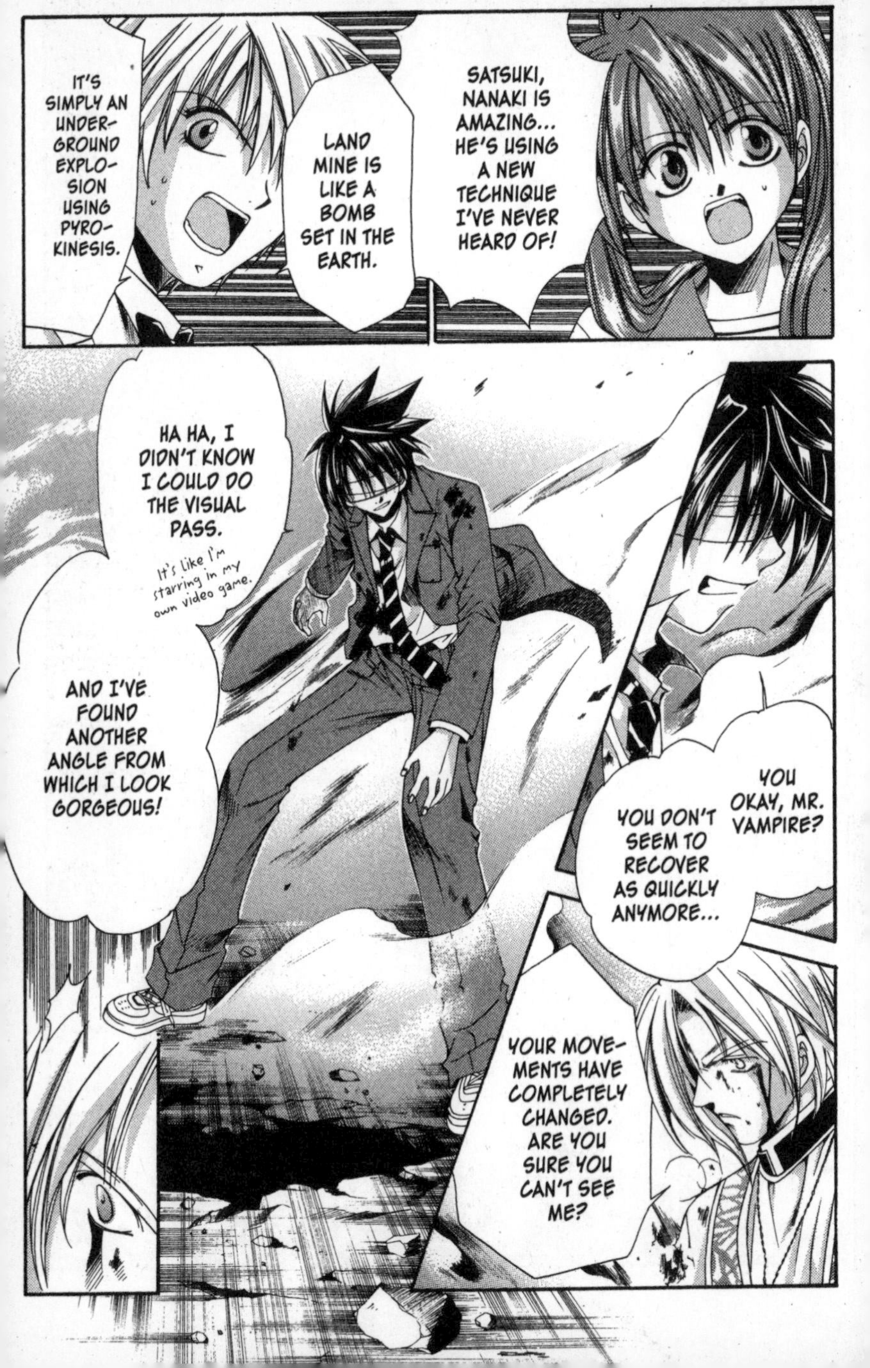
SATSUKI, NANAKI IS AMAZING... HE'S USING A NEW TECHNIQUE I'VE NEVER HEARD OF!
LAND MINE IS LIKE A BOMB SET IN THE EARTH.
IT'S SIMPLY AN UNDER-GROUND EXPLO-SION USING PYRO-KINESIS.
YOU OKAY, MR. VAMPIRE?
YOU DON'T SEEM TO RECOVER AS QUICKLY ANYMORE...
YOUR MOVE-MENTS HAVE COMPLETELY CHANGED. ARE YOU SURE YOU CAN'T SEE ME?
HA HA, I DIDN'T KNOW I COULD DO THE VISUAL PASS.
It's like I'm starring in my own video game.
AND I'VE FOUND ANOTHER ANGLE FROM WHICH I LOOK GORGEOUS!

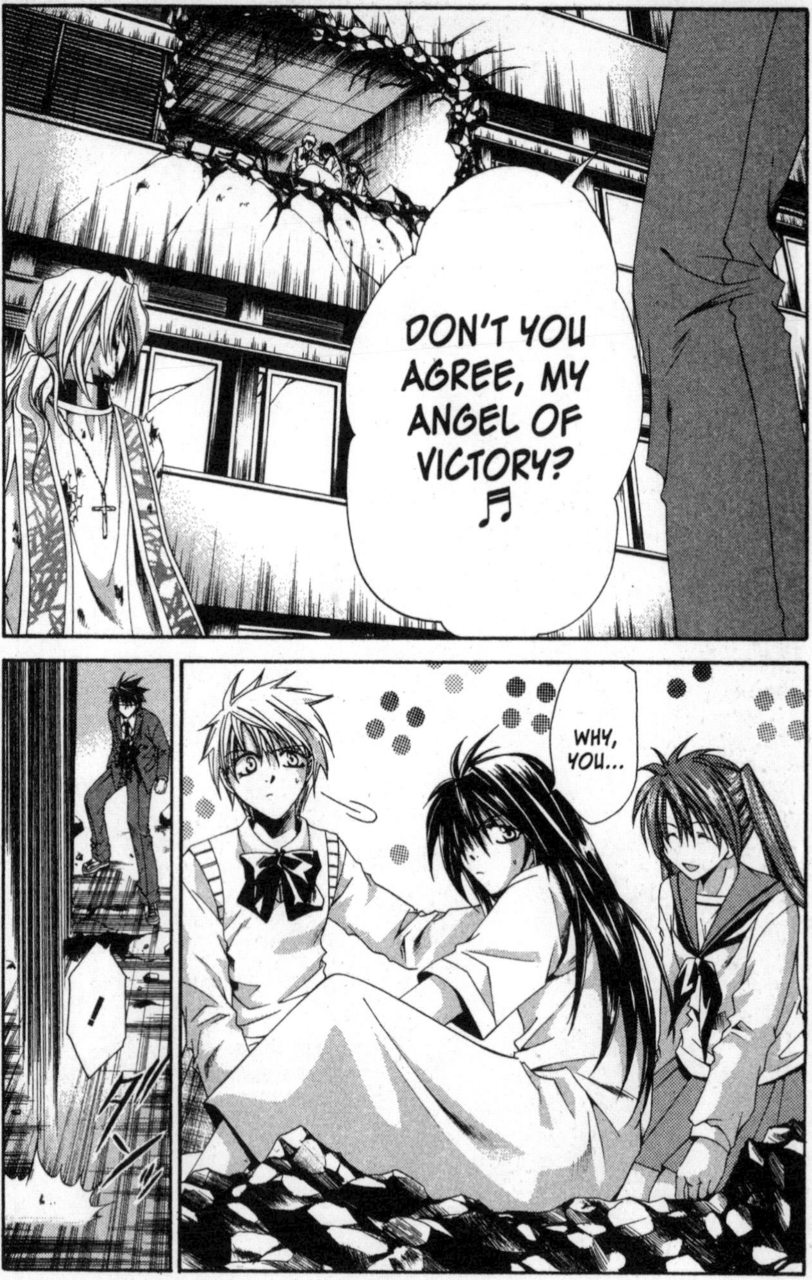
DON'T YOU AGREE, MY ANGEL OF VICTORY? ♫
WHY, YOU...
!

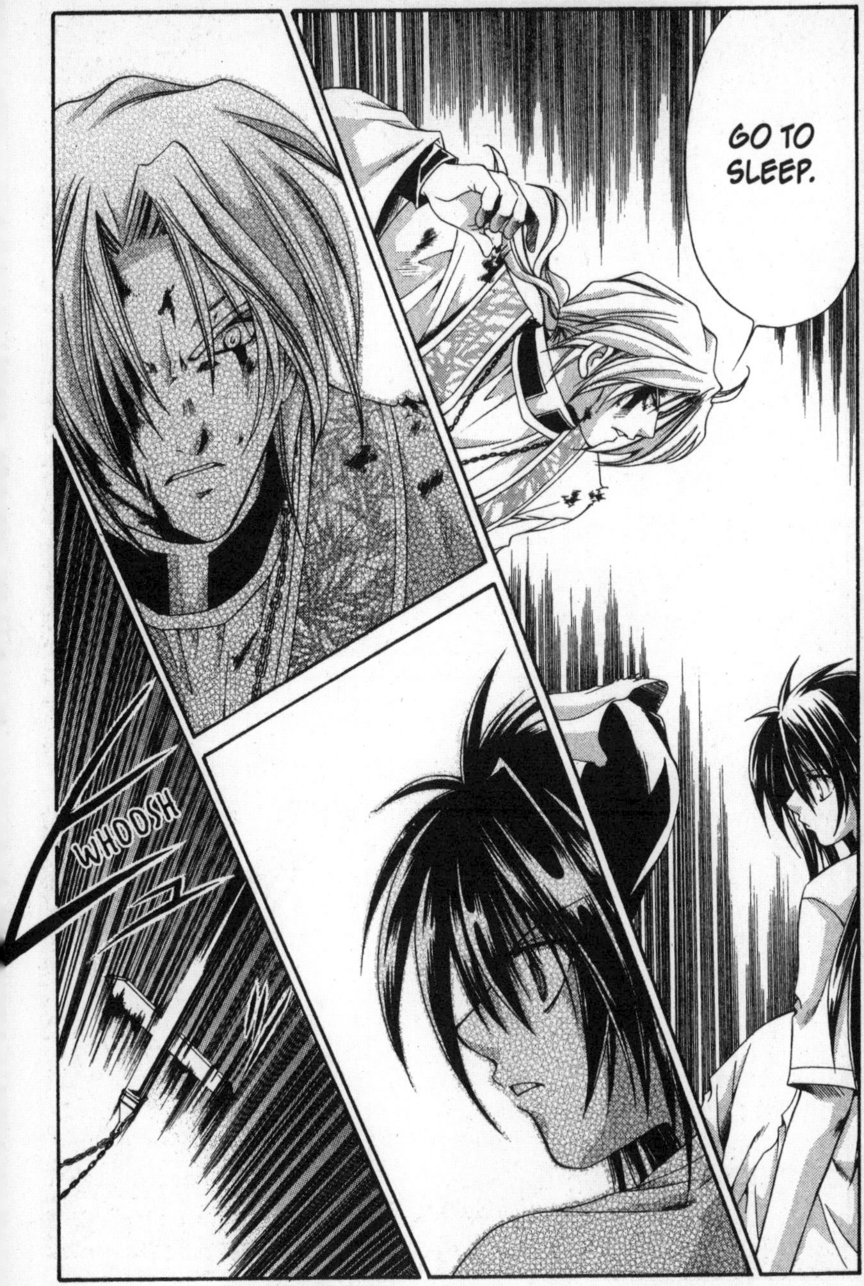
GO TO SLEEP.
WHOOSH

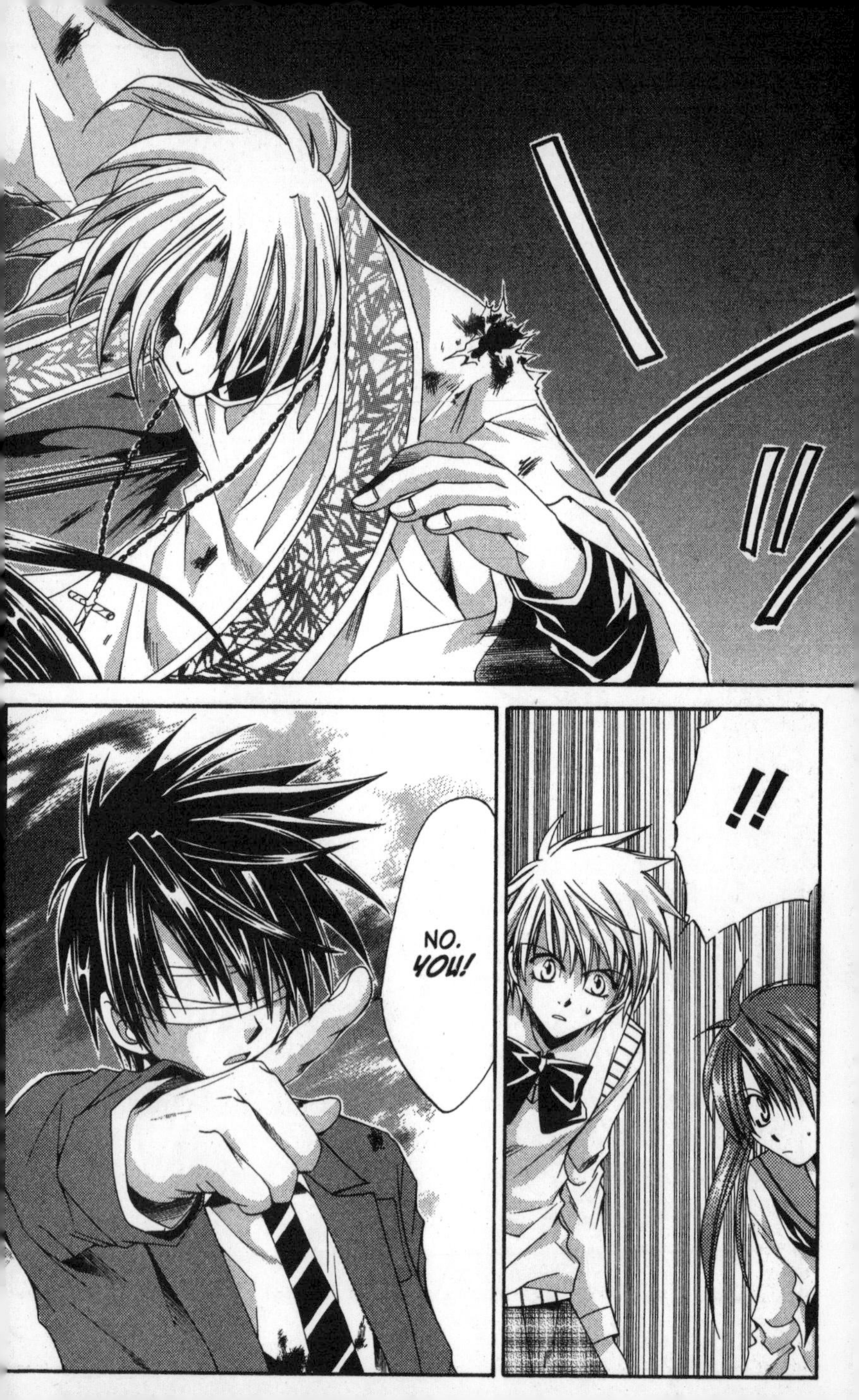
!!
NO. YOU!

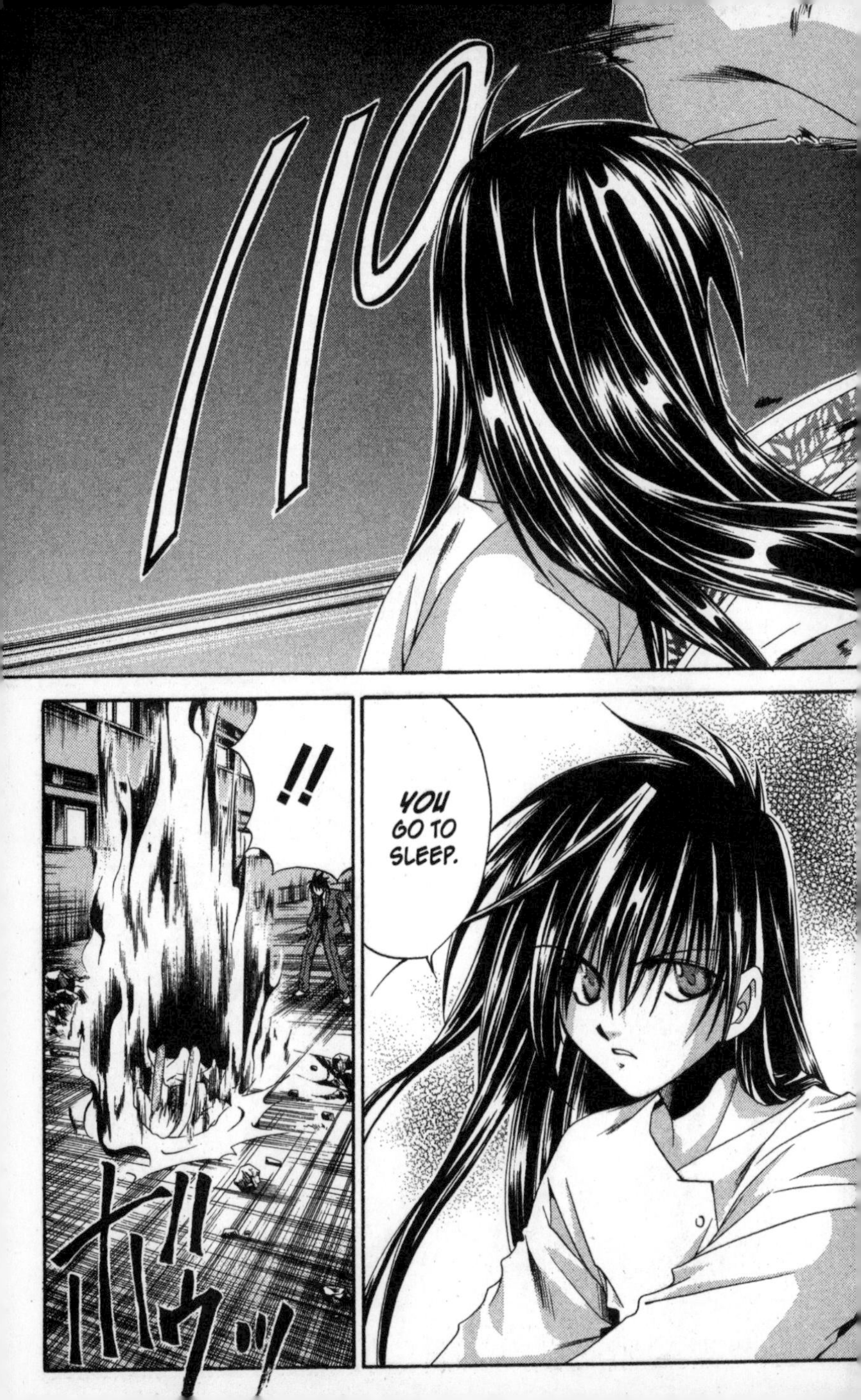
YOU GO TO SLEEP.
!!

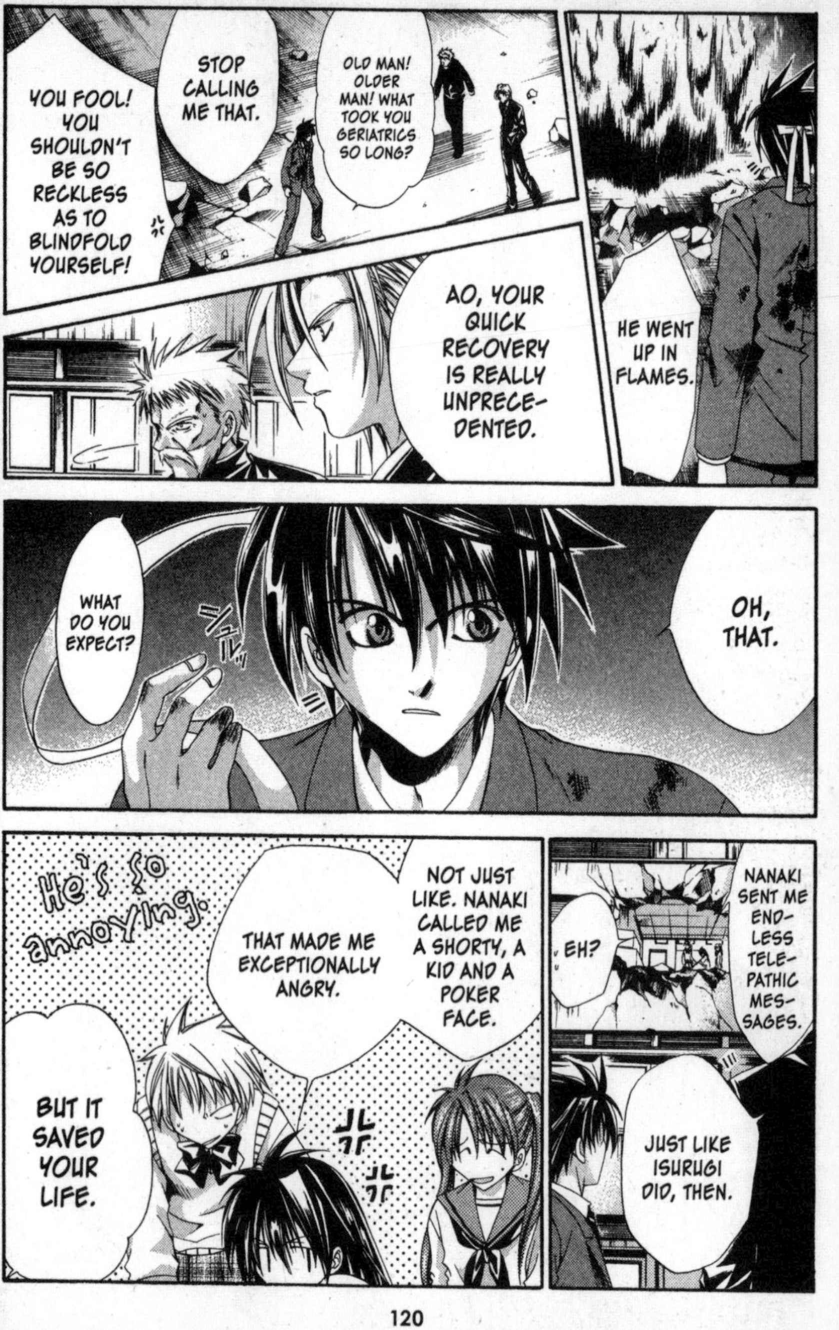
HE WENT UP IN FLAMES.
OLD MAN! OLDER MAN! WHAT TOOK YOU GERIATRICS SO LONG?
STOP CALLING ME THAT.
YOU FOOL! YOU SHOULDN'T BE SO RECKLESS AS TO BLINDFOLD YOURSELF!
AO, YOUR QUICK RECOVERY IS REALLY UNPRECE-DENTED.
OH, THAT.
WHAT DO YOU EXPECT?
NANAKI SENT ME END-LESS TELE-PATHIC MES-SAGES.
EH?
JUST LIKE ISURUGI DID, THEN.
NOT JUST LIKE. NANAKI CALLED ME A SHORTY, A KID AND A POKER FACE.
THAT MADE ME EXCEPTIONALLY ANGRY.
He's so annoying.
BUT IT SAVED YOUR LIFE.

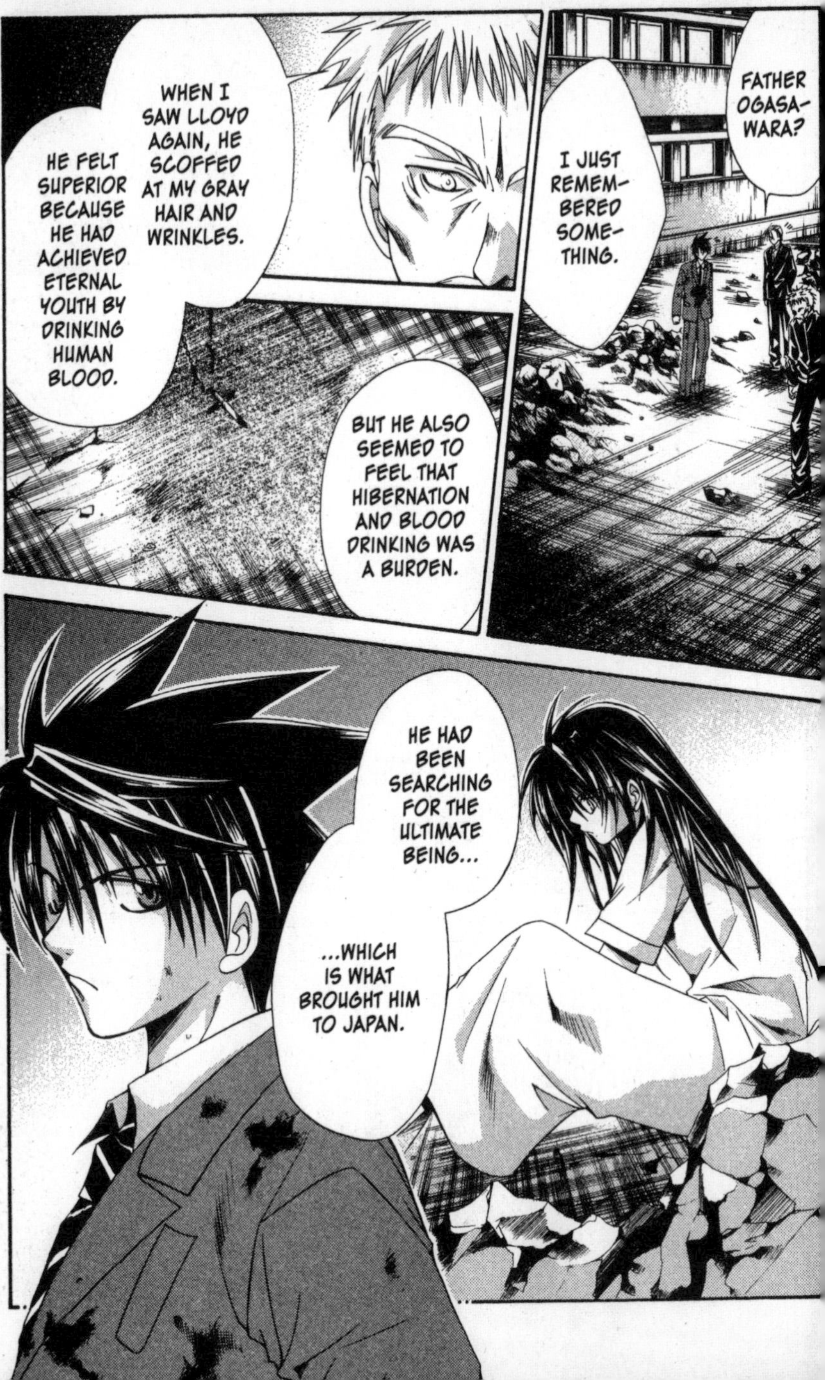
FATHER OGASAWARA?
I JUST REMEMBERED SOMETHING.
WHEN I SAW LLOYD AGAIN, HE SCOFFED AT MY GRAY HAIR AND WRINKLES.
HE FELT SUPERIOR BECAUSE HE HAD ACHIEVED ETERNAL YOUTH BY DRINKING HUMAN BLOOD.
BUT HE ALSO SEEMED TO FEEL THAT HIBERNATION AND BLOOD DRINKING WAS A BURDEN.
HE HAD BEEN SEARCHING FOR THE ULTIMATE BEING...
...WHICH IS WHAT BROUGHT HIM TO JAPAN.

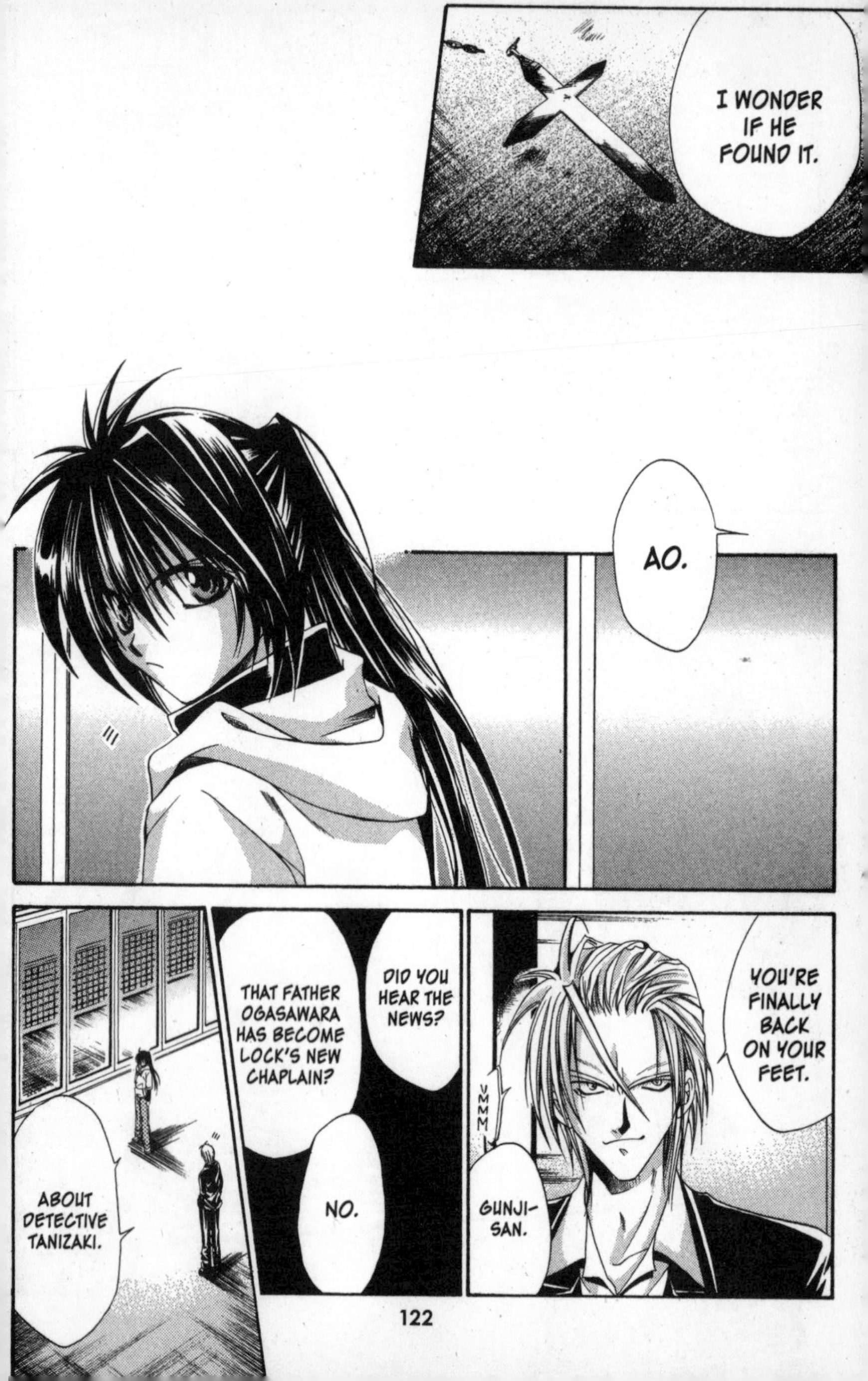
I WONDER IF HE FOUND IT.
AO.
YOU'RE FINALLY BACK ON YOUR FEET.
VMMM
GUNJI-SAN.
DID YOU HEAR THE NEWS?
THAT FATHER OGASAWARA HAS BECOME LOCK'S NEW CHAPLAIN?
NO.
ABOUT DETECTIVE TANIZAKI.

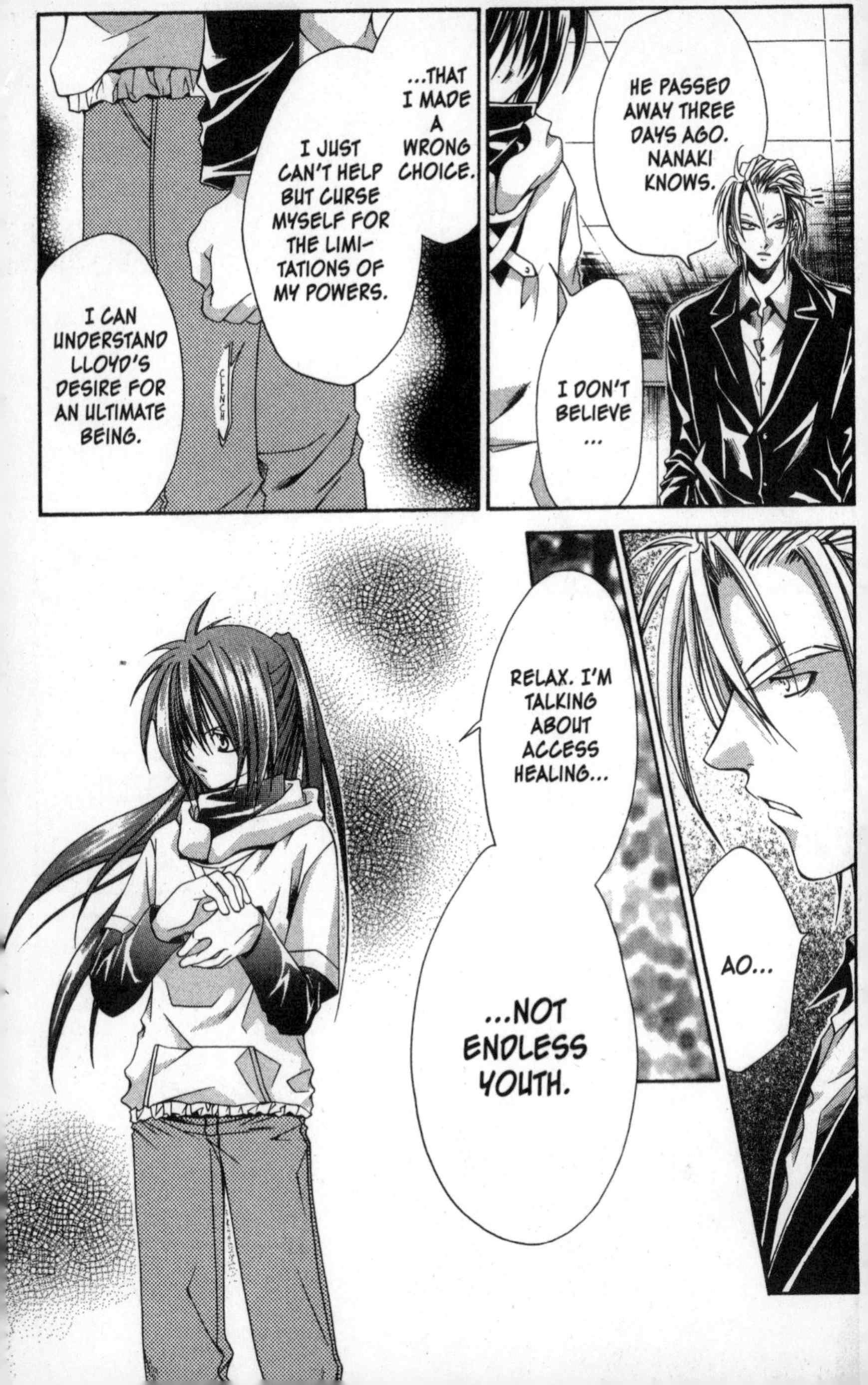
HE PASSED AWAY THREE DAYS AGO. NANAKI KNOWS.
I DON'T BELIEVE ...
...THAT I MADE A WRONG CHOICE.
I JUST CAN'T HELP BUT CURSE MYSELF FOR THE LIMITATIONS OF MY POWERS.
CLENCH
I CAN UNDERSTAND LLOYD'S DESIRE FOR AN ULTIMATE BEING.
RELAX. I'M TALKING ABOUT ACCESS HEALING... ...NOT ENDLESS YOUTH.
AO...

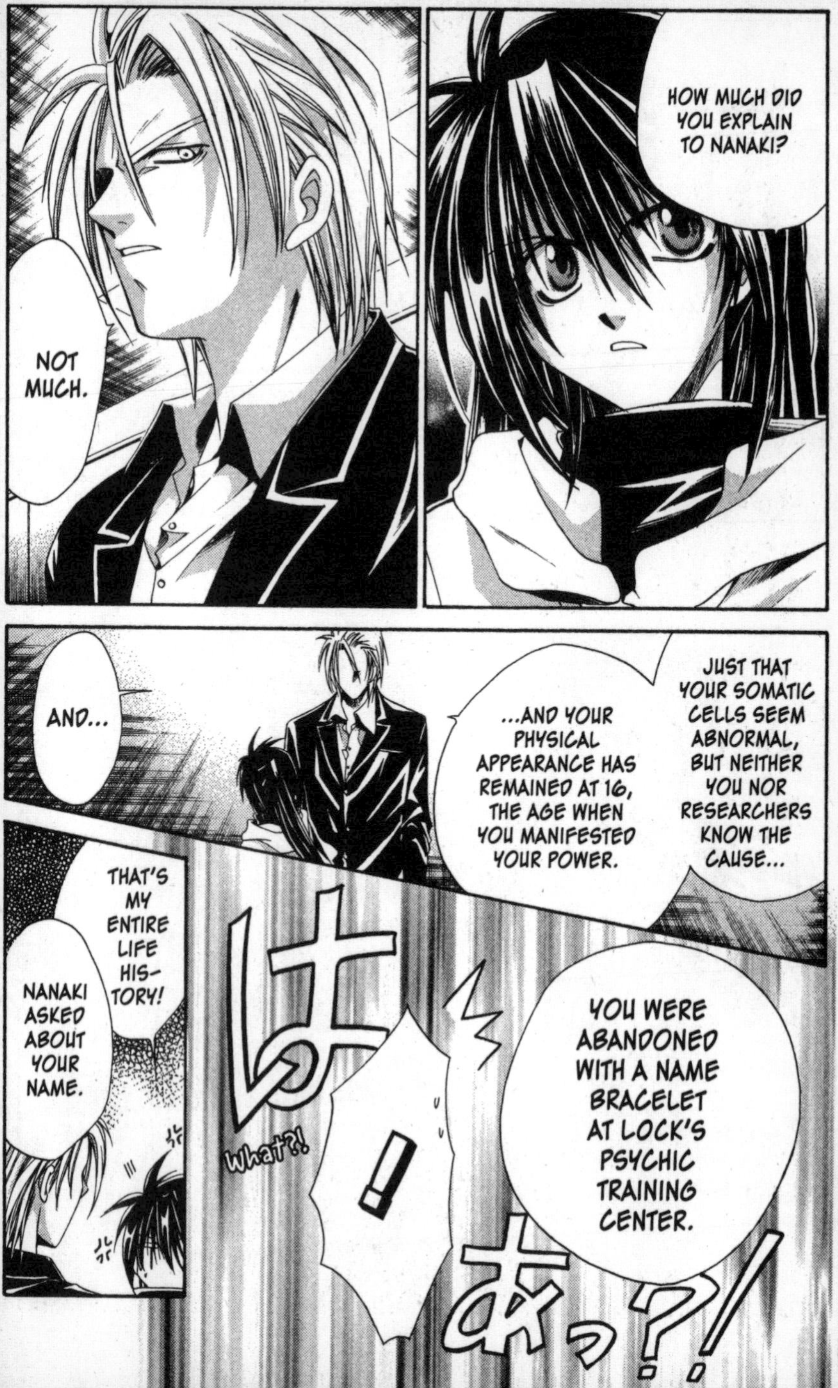
HOW MUCH DID YOU EXPLAIN TO NANAKI?
NOT MUCH.
JUST THAT YOUR SOMATIC CELLS SEEM ABNORMAL, BUT NEITHER YOU NOR RESEARCHERS KNOW THE CAUSE...
...AND YOUR PHYSICAL APPEARANCE HAS REMAINED AT 16, THE AGE WHEN YOU MANIFESTED YOUR POWER.
AND...
YOU WERE ABANDONED WITH A NAME BRACELET AT LOCK'S PSYCHIC TRAINING CENTER.
!
はあっ?!
What?!
THAT'S MY ENTIRE LIFE HISTORY!
NANAKI ASKED ABOUT YOUR NAME.

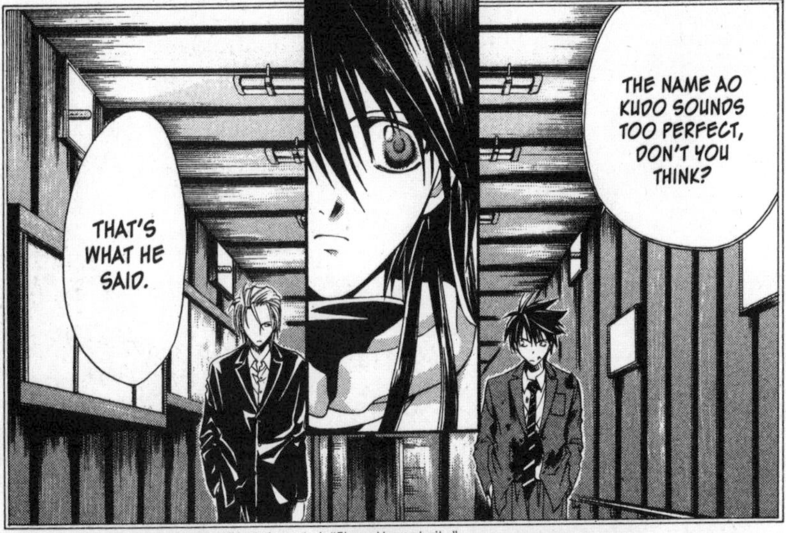
THE NAME AO KUDO SOUNDS TOO PERFECT, DON'T YOU THINK?
THAT'S WHAT HE SAID.

*Note: A possible meaning of the kanji in Ao's name is "Eternal Immaturity."

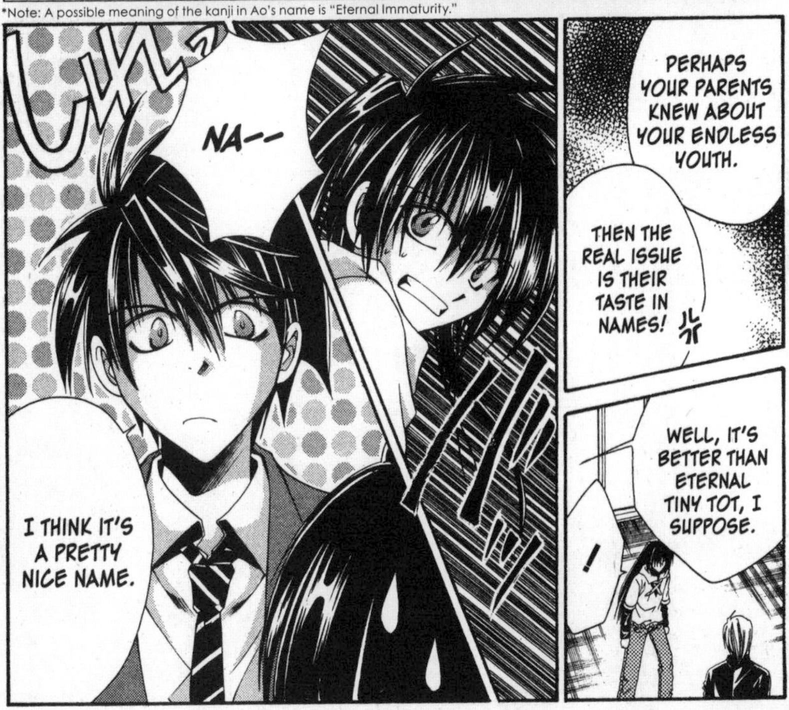
PERHAPS YOUR PARENTS KNEW ABOUT YOUR ENDLESS YOUTH.
THEN THE REAL ISSUE IS THEIR TASTE IN NAMES!
WELL, IT'S BETTER THAN ETERNAL TINY TOT, I SUPPOSE.
!
NA--
I THINK IT'S A PRETTY NICE NAME.

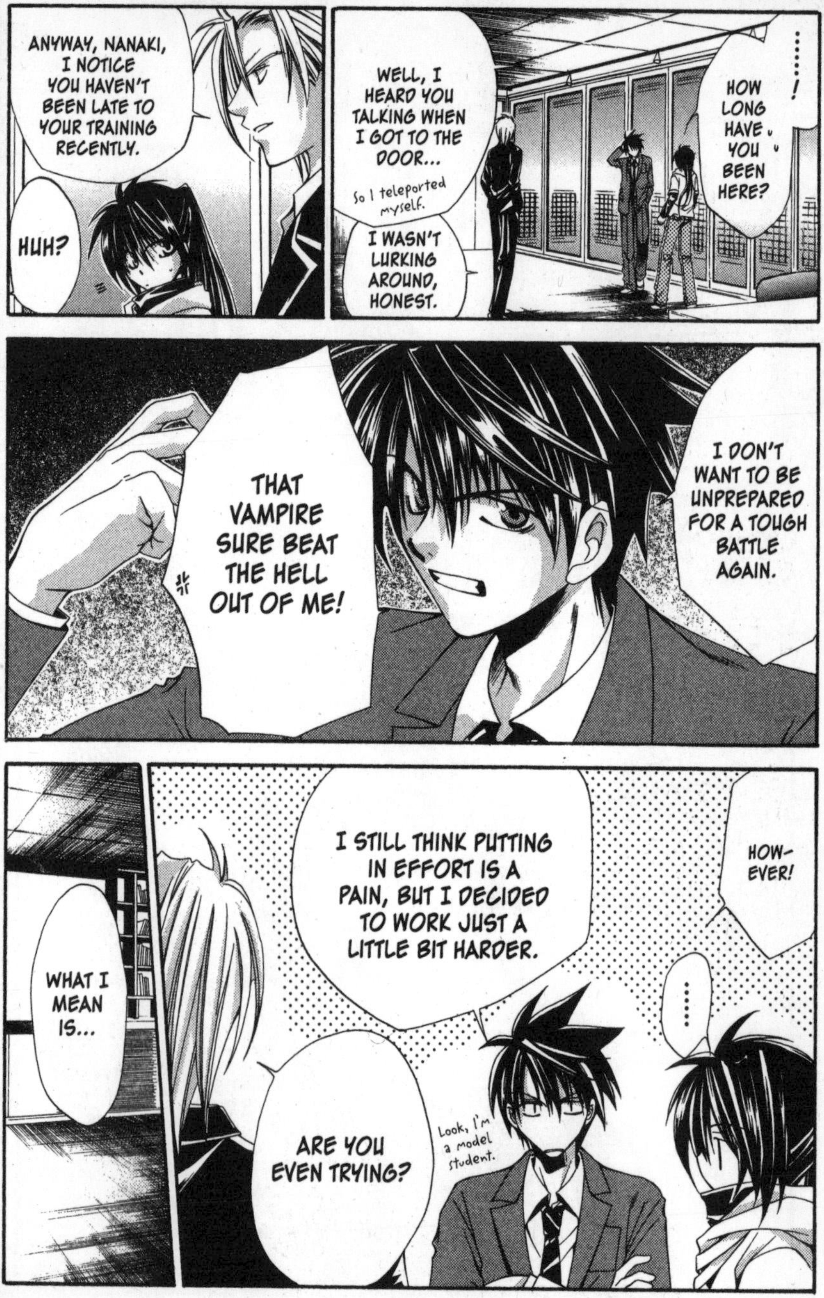
……!
HOW LONG HAVE YOU BEEN HERE?
WELL, I HEARD YOU TALKING WHEN I GOT TO THE DOOR...
So I teleported myself.
I WASN'T LURKING AROUND, HONEST.
ANYWAY, NANAKI, I NOTICE YOU HAVEN'T BEEN LATE TO YOUR TRAINING RECENTLY.
HUH?
I DON'T WANT TO BE UNPREPARED FOR A TOUGH BATTLE AGAIN.
THAT VAMPIRE SURE BEAT THE HELL OUT OF ME!
HOW-EVER!
I STILL THINK PUTTING IN EFFORT IS A PAIN, BUT I DECIDED TO WORK JUST A LITTLE BIT HARDER.
……
Look, I'm a model student.
ARE YOU EVEN TRYING?
WHAT I MEAN IS...

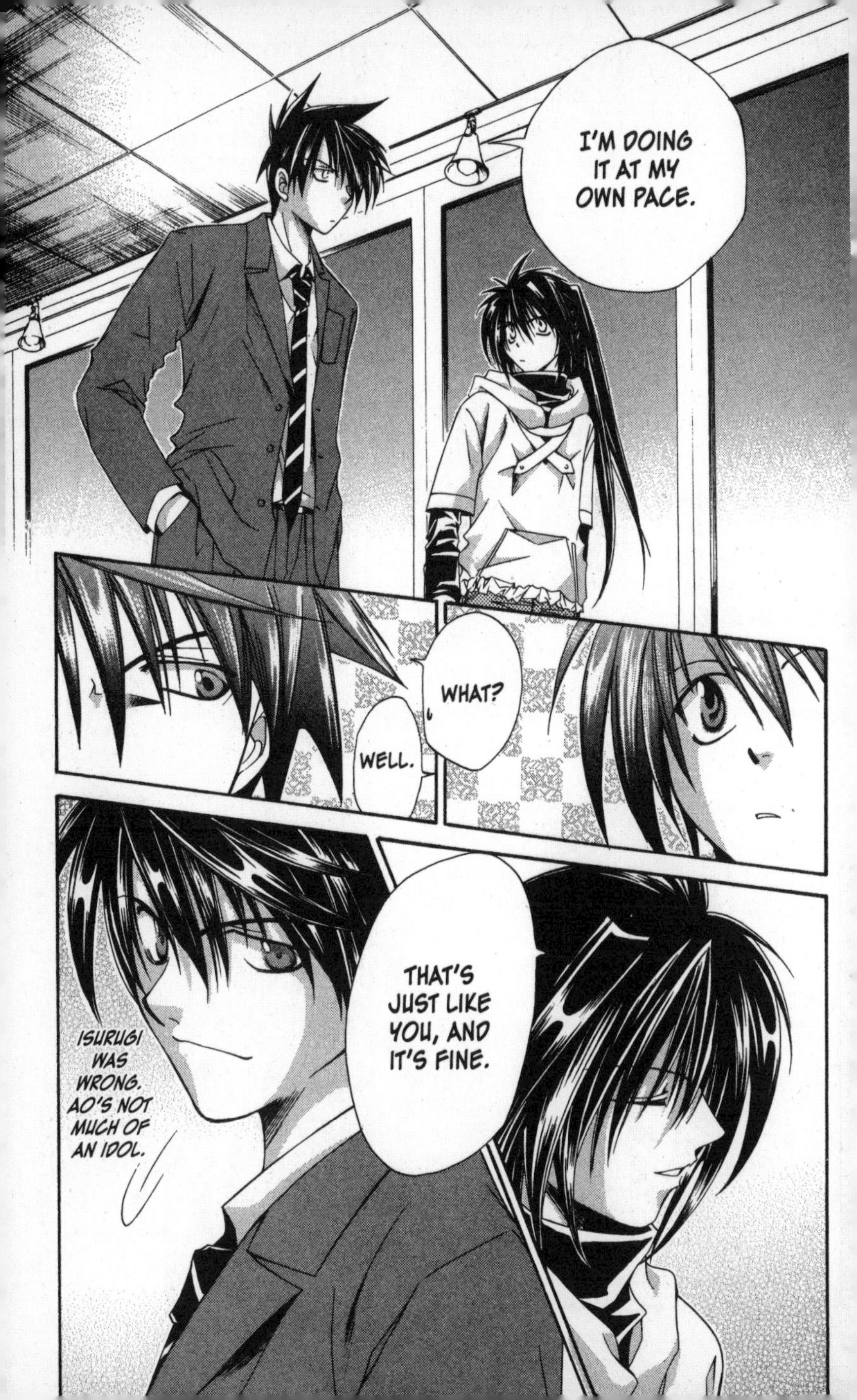
I'M DOING IT AT MY OWN PACE.
WHAT?
WELL.
THAT'S JUST LIKE YOU, AND IT'S FINE.
ISURUGI WAS WRONG. AO'S NOT MUCH OF AN IDOL.

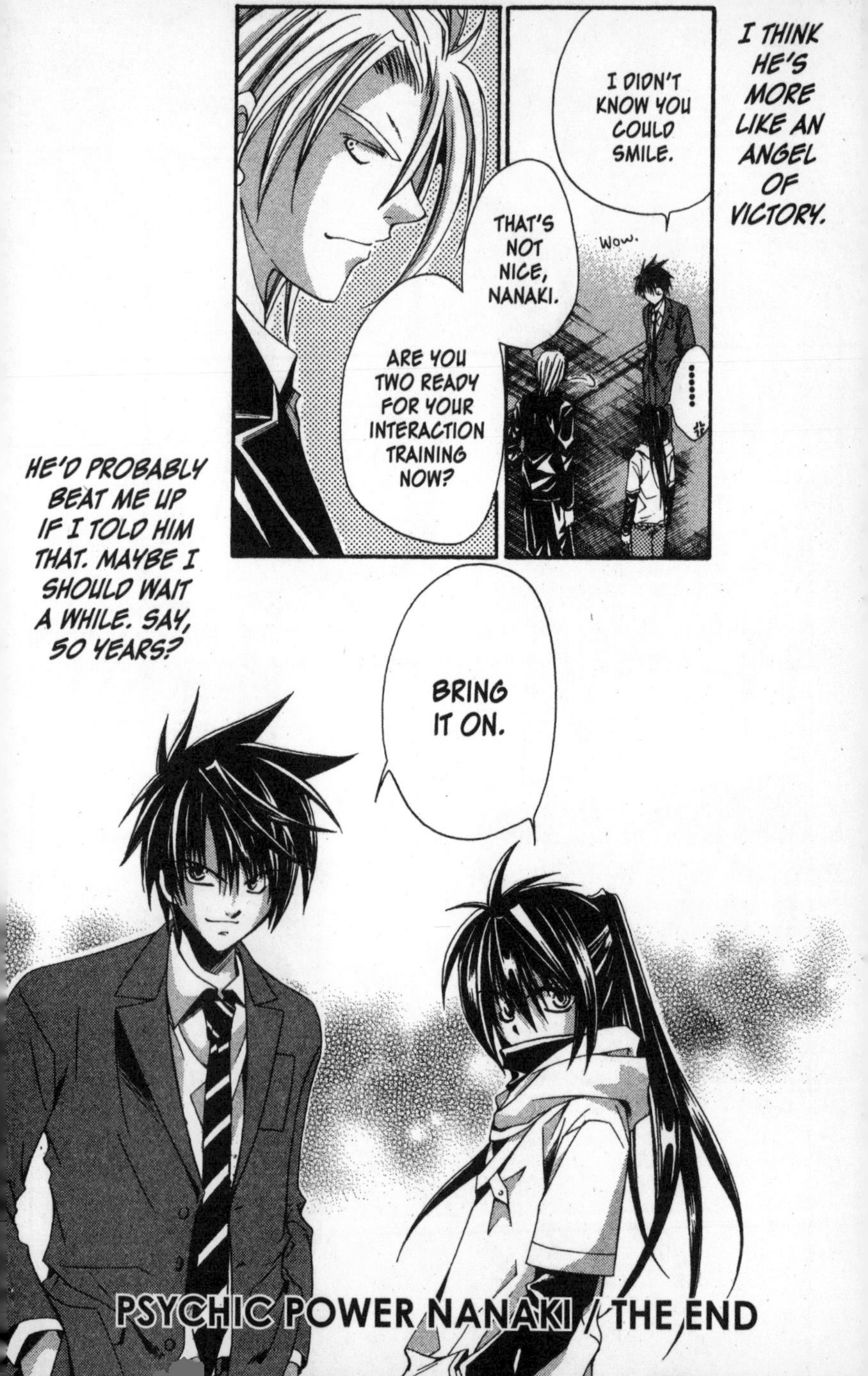
I THINK HE'S MORE LIKE AN ANGEL OF VICTORY.
I DIDN'T KNOW YOU COULD SMILE.
WOW.
......
THAT'S NOT NICE, NANAKI.
ARE YOU TWO READY FOR YOUR INTERACTION TRAINING NOW?
HE'D PROBABLY BEAT ME UP IF I TOLD HIM THAT. MAYBE I SHOULD WAIT A WHILE. SAY, 50 YEARS?
BRING IT ON.
PSYCHIC POWER NANAKI / THE END

LOCK

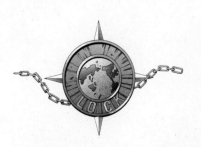

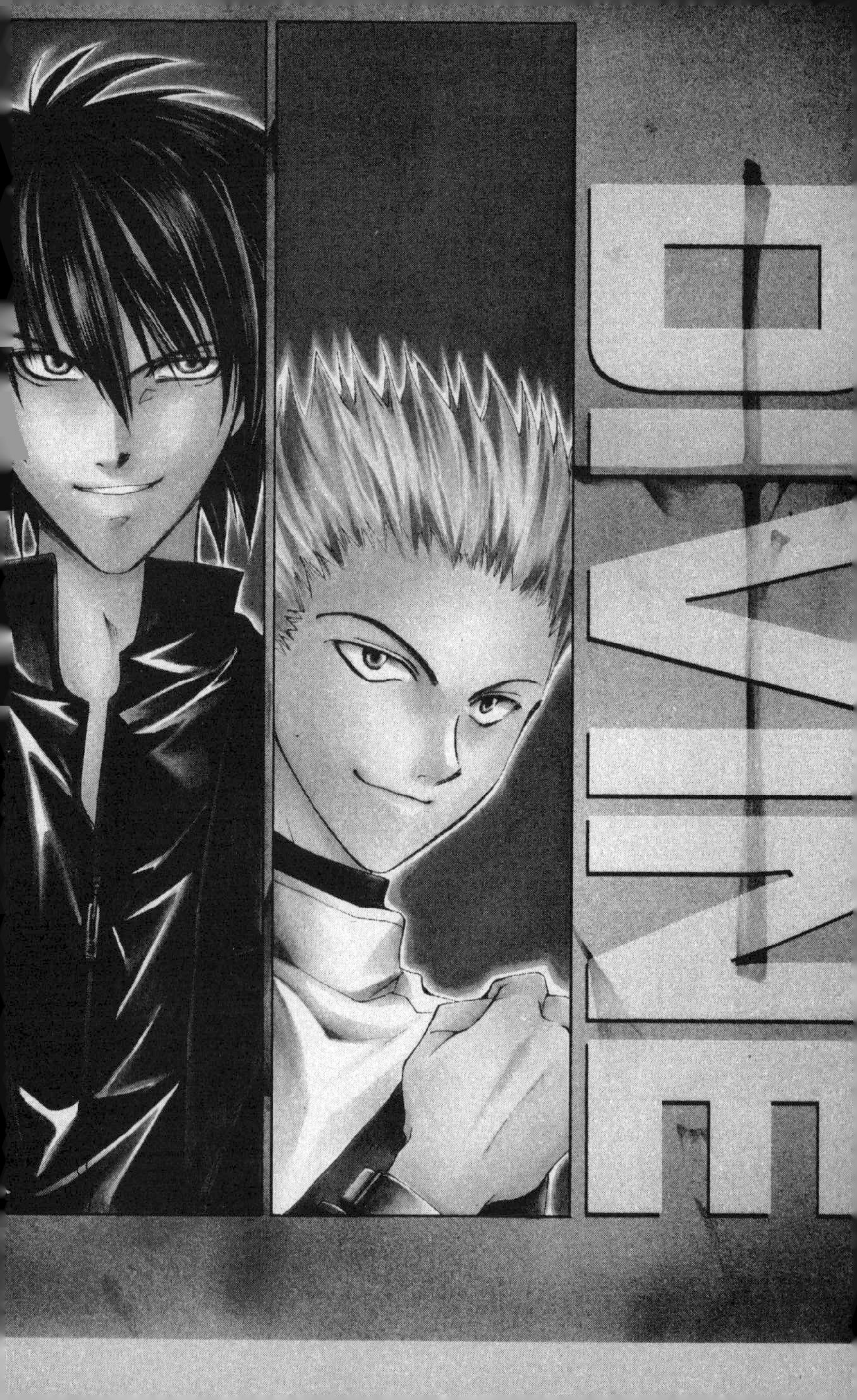
DIVINE

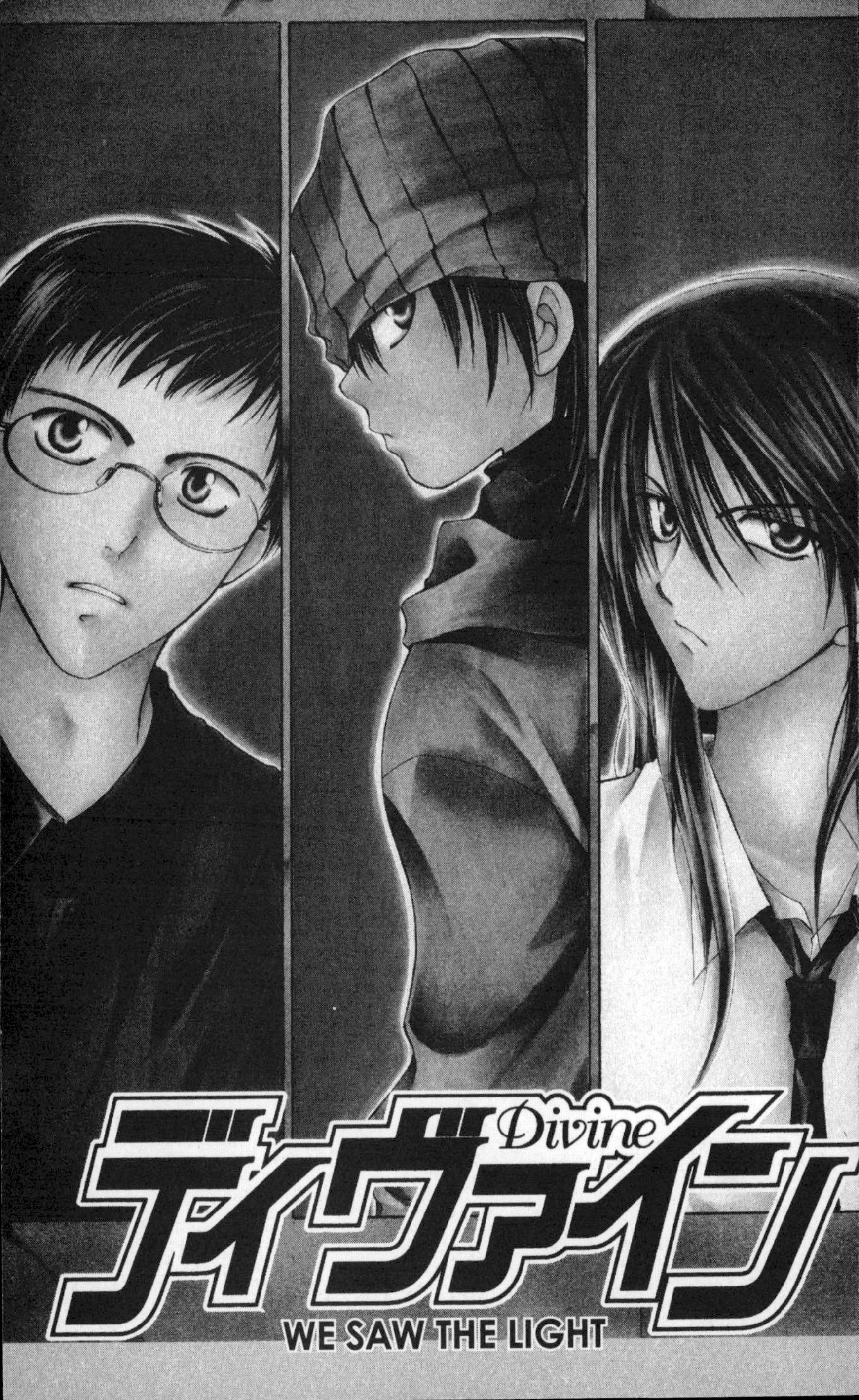

Divine
ディヴァイン
WE SAW THE LIGHT

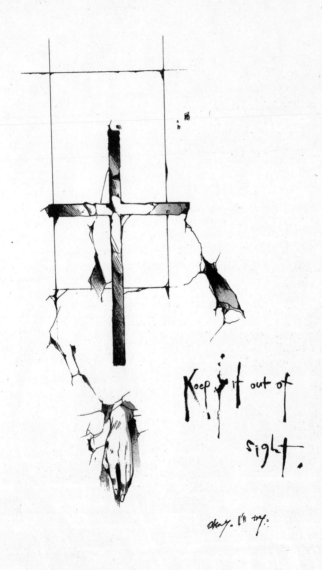

Keep it out of

sight.

okay. I'll try.

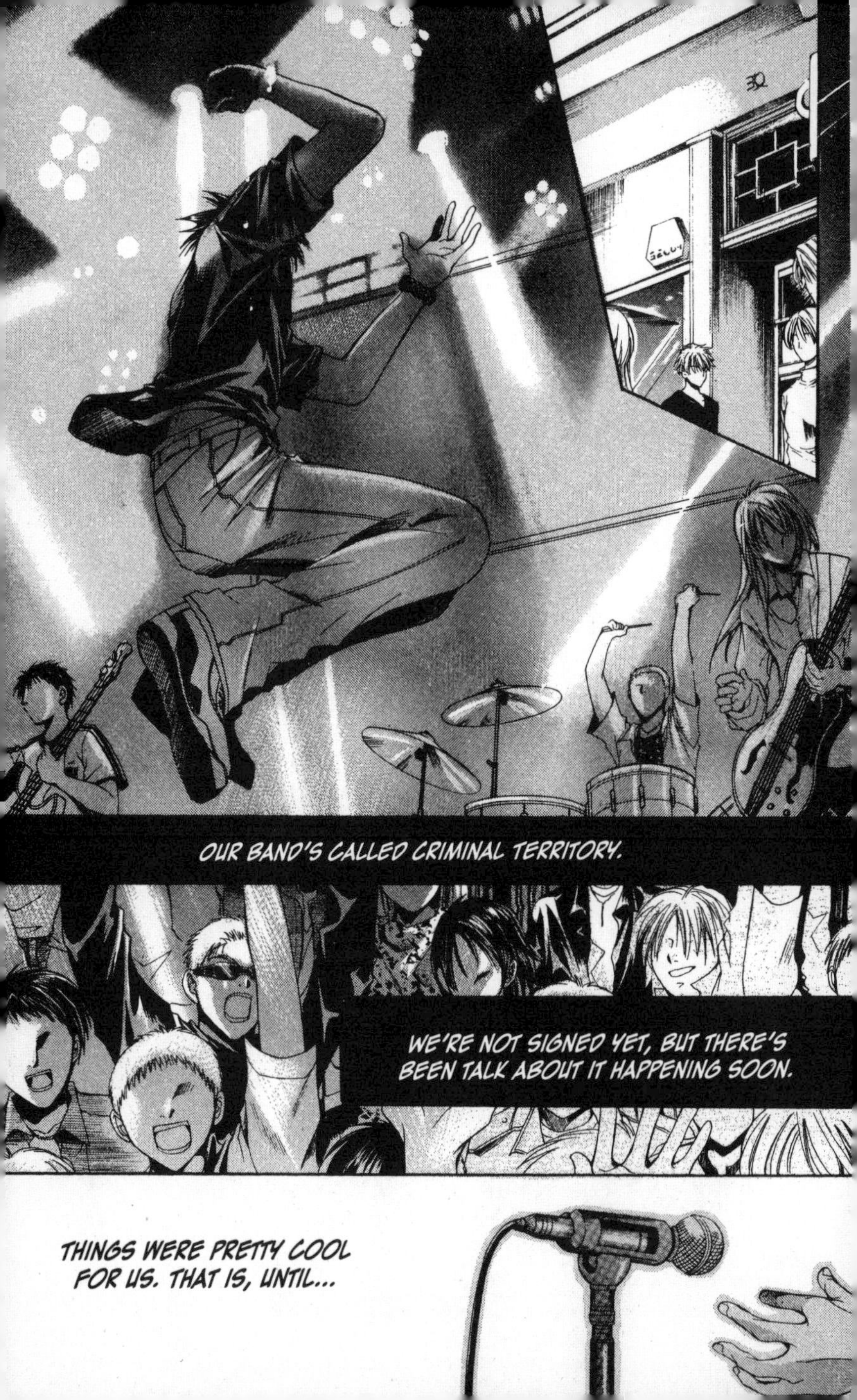
OUR BAND'S CALLED CRIMINAL TERRITORY.
WE'RE NOT SIGNED YET, BUT THERE'S BEEN TALK ABOUT IT HAPPENING SOON.
THINGS WERE PRETTY COOL FOR US. THAT IS, UNTIL...

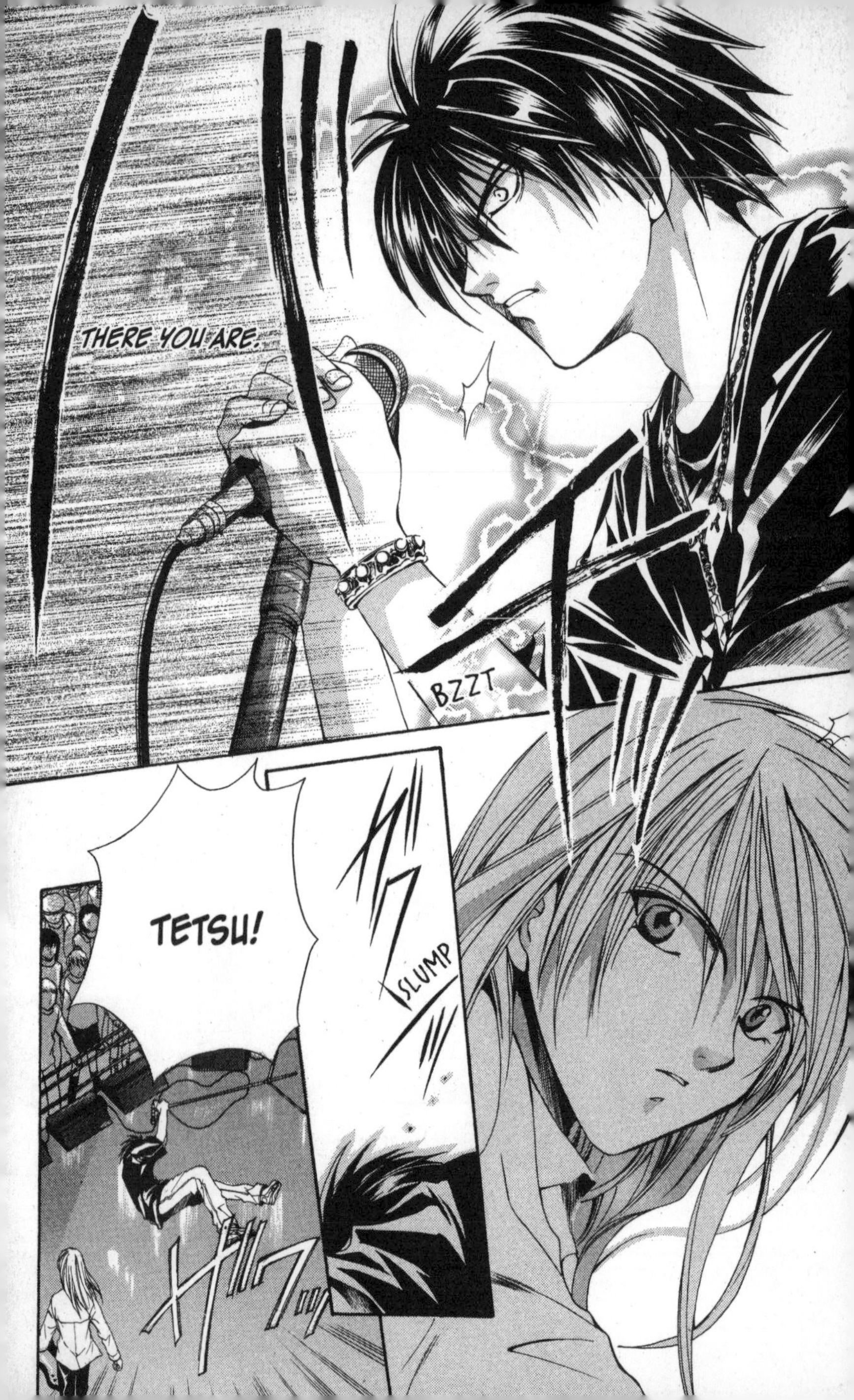
THERE YOU ARE.
BZZT
TETSU!
SLUMP

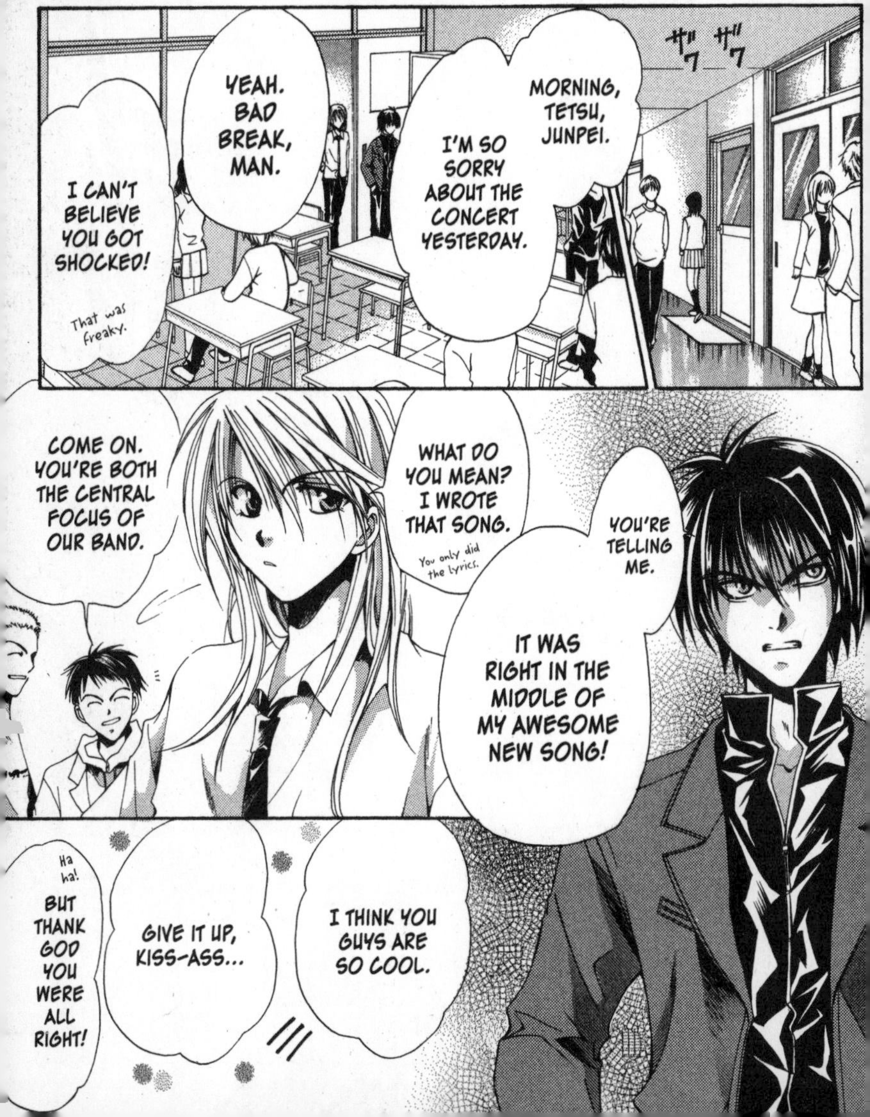
ザワ ザワ
MORNING, TETSU, JUNPEI.
I'M SO SORRY ABOUT THE CONCERT YESTERDAY.
YEAH. BAD BREAK, MAN.
I CAN'T BELIEVE YOU GOT SHOCKED!
That was freaky.
YOU'RE TELLING ME.
IT WAS RIGHT IN THE MIDDLE OF MY AWESOME NEW SONG!
WHAT DO YOU MEAN? I WROTE THAT SONG.
You only did the lyrics.
COME ON. YOU'RE BOTH THE CENTRAL FOCUS OF OUR BAND.
I THINK YOU GUYS ARE SO COOL.
GIVE IT UP, KISS-ASS...
Ha ha!
BUT THANK GOD YOU WERE ALL RIGHT!

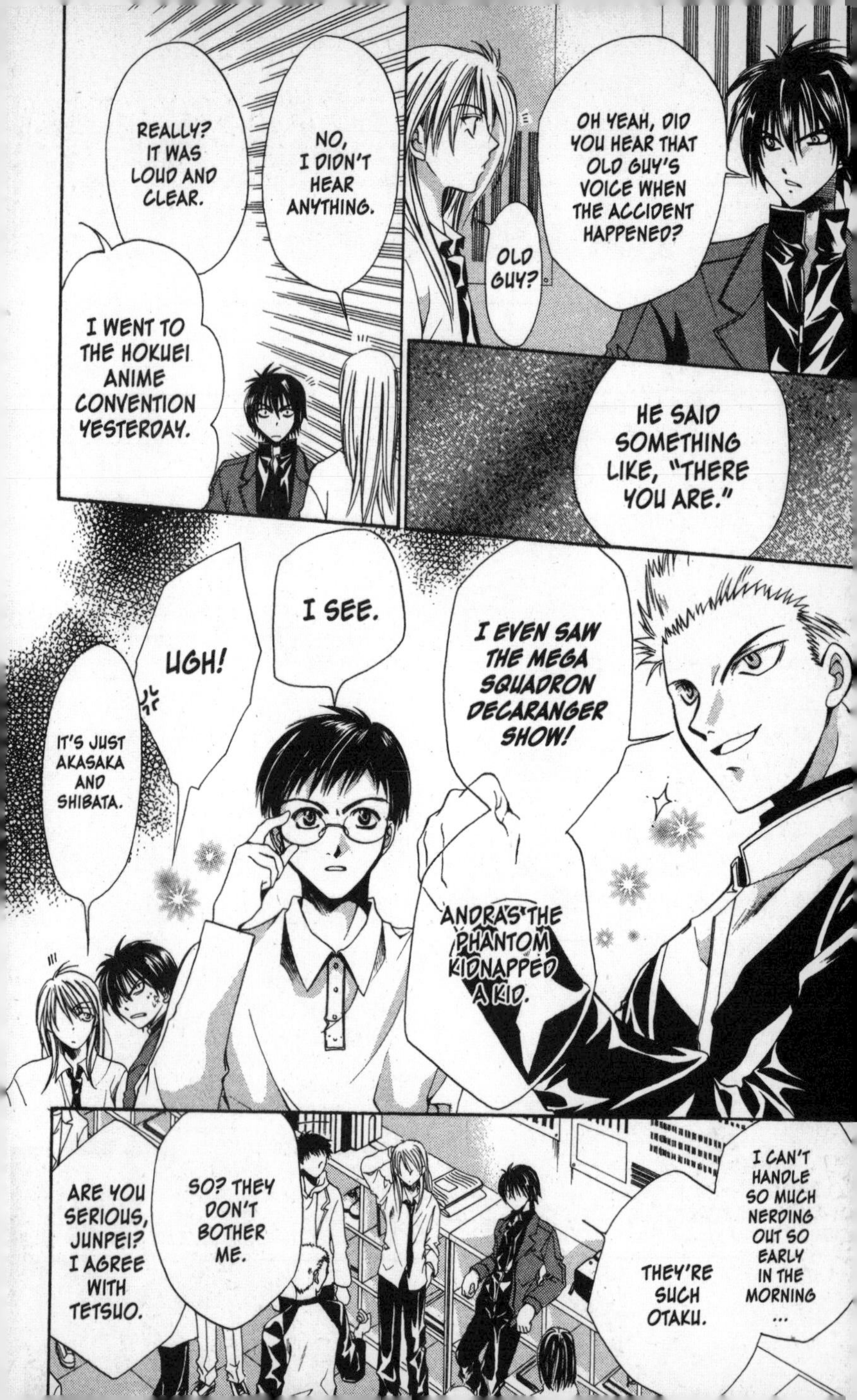
OH YEAH, DID YOU HEAR THAT OLD GUY'S VOICE WHEN THE ACCIDENT HAPPENED?
OLD GUY?
HE SAID SOMETHING LIKE, "THERE YOU ARE."
NO, I DIDN'T HEAR ANYTHING.
REALLY? IT WAS LOUD AND CLEAR.
I WENT TO THE HOKUEI ANIME CONVENTION YESTERDAY.
I EVEN SAW THE MEGA SQUADRON DECARANGER SHOW!
ANDRAS THE PHANTOM KIDNAPPED A KID.
I SEE.
UGH!
IT'S JUST AKASAKA AND SHIBATA.
I CAN'T HANDLE SO MUCH NERDING OUT SO EARLY IN THE MORNING...
THEY'RE SUCH OTAKU.
SO? THEY DON'T BOTHER ME.
ARE YOU SERIOUS, JUNPEI? I AGREE WITH TETSUO.

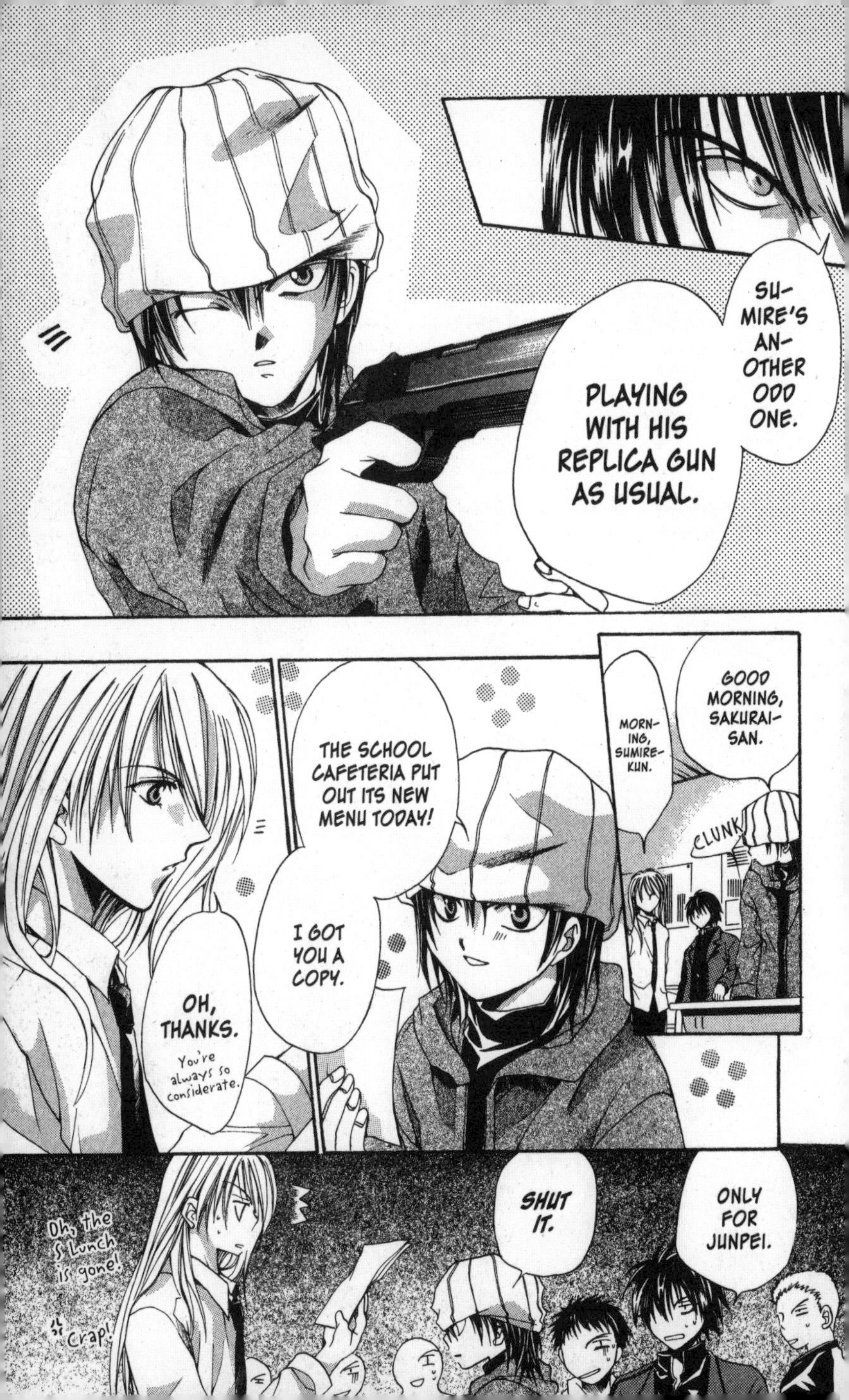

SU-MIRE'S AN-OTHER ODD ONE.
PLAYING WITH HIS REPLICA GUN AS USUAL.
GOOD MORNING, SAKURAI-SAN.
MORN-ING, SUMIRE-KUN.
CLUNK
THE SCHOOL CAFETERIA PUT OUT ITS NEW MENU TODAY!
I GOT YOU A COPY.
OH, THANKS.
You're always so considerate.
ONLY FOR JUNPEI.
SHUT IT.
Oh, the S Lunch is gone!
Crap!

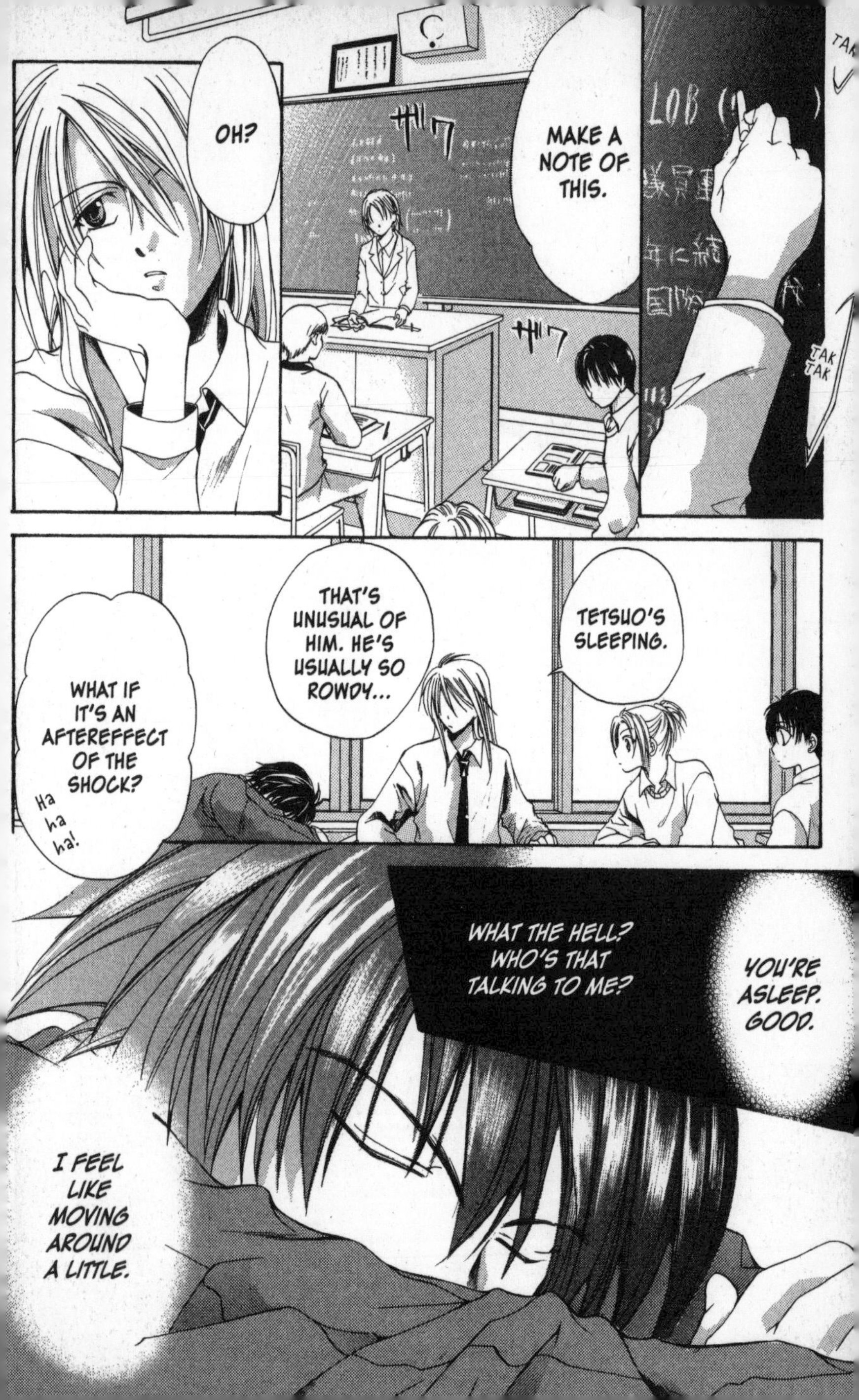
TAK
LOB
MAKE A NOTE OF THIS.
TAK TAK
ザワ
ザワ
OH?
TETSUO'S SLEEPING.
THAT'S UNUSUAL OF HIM. HE'S USUALLY SO ROWDY...
WHAT IF IT'S AN AFTEREFFECT OF THE SHOCK?
Ha ha ha!
YOU'RE ASLEEP. GOOD.
WHAT THE HELL? WHO'S THAT TALKING TO ME?
I FEEL LIKE MOVING AROUND A LITTLE.

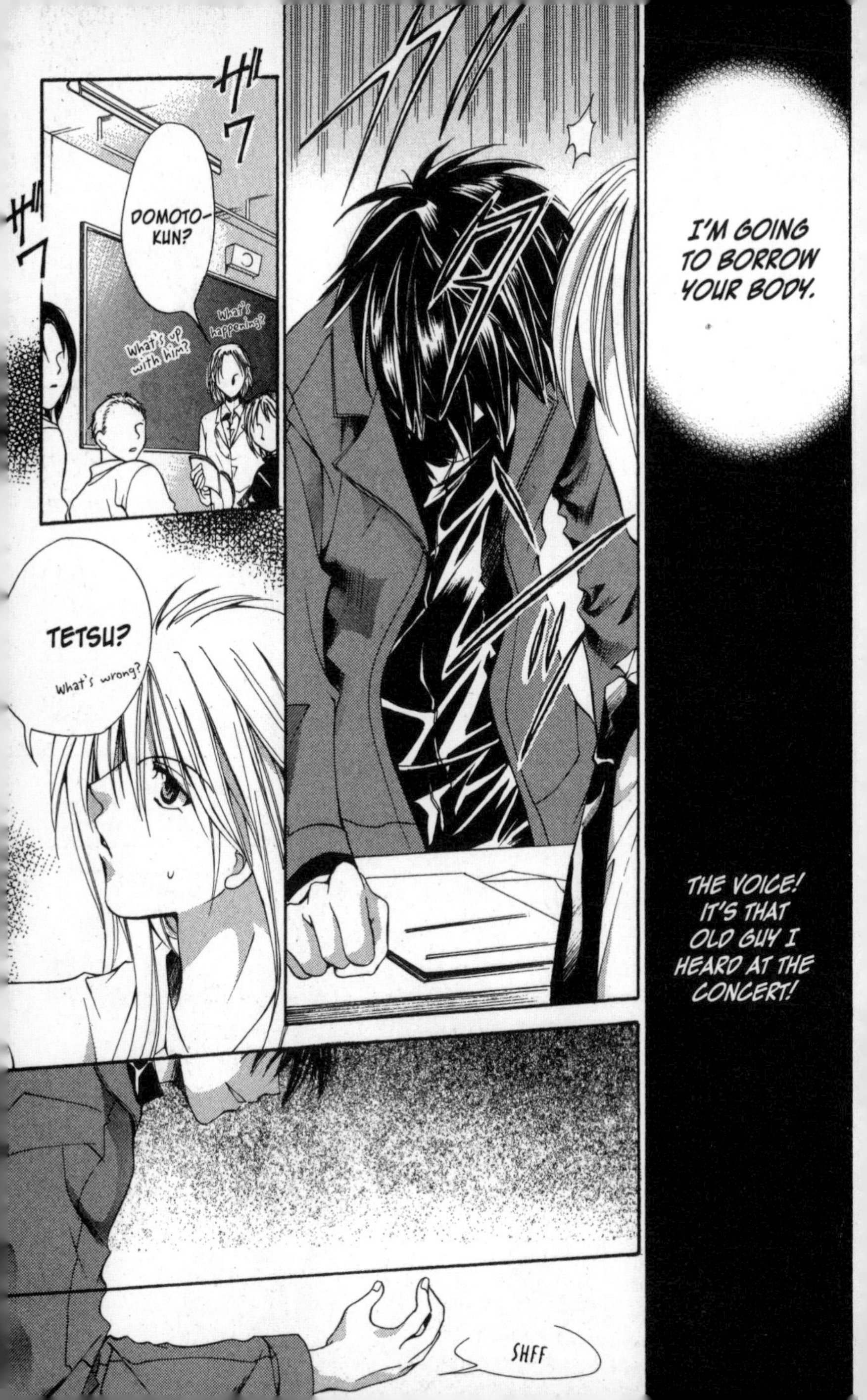
I'M GOING TO BORROW YOUR BODY.
THE VOICE! IT'S THAT OLD GUY I HEARD AT THE CONCERT!
DOMOTO-KUN?
What's happening?
What's up with him?
TETSU?
What's wrong?
SHFF

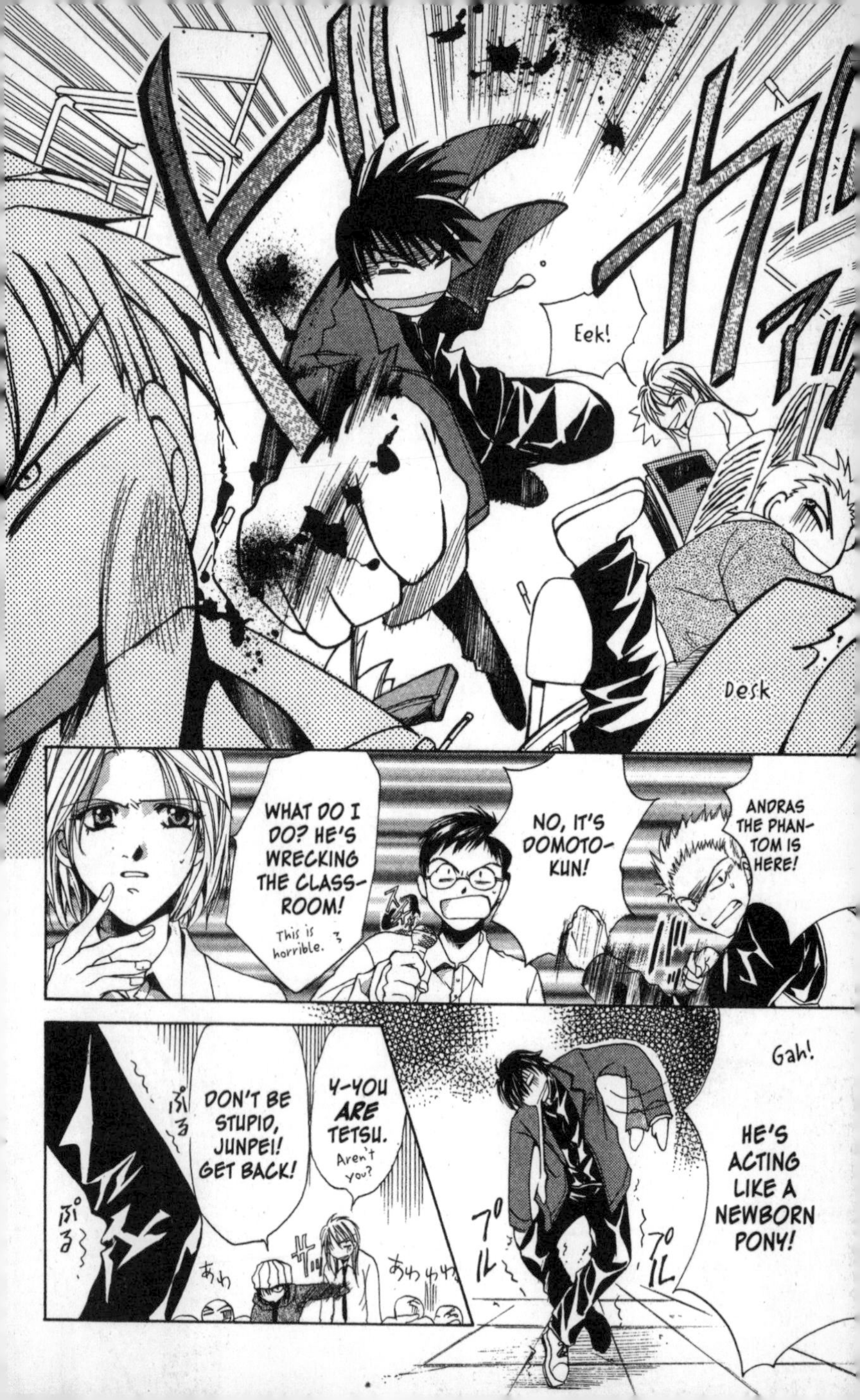
Eek!
Desk
ANDRAS THE PHANTOM IS HERE!
NO, IT'S DOMOTO-KUN!
WHAT DO I DO? HE'S WRECKING THE CLASSROOM!
This is horrible.
Gah!
HE'S ACTING LIKE A NEWBORN PONY!
Y-YOU ARE TETSU.
Aren't you?
DON'T BE STUPID, JUNPEI! GET BACK!

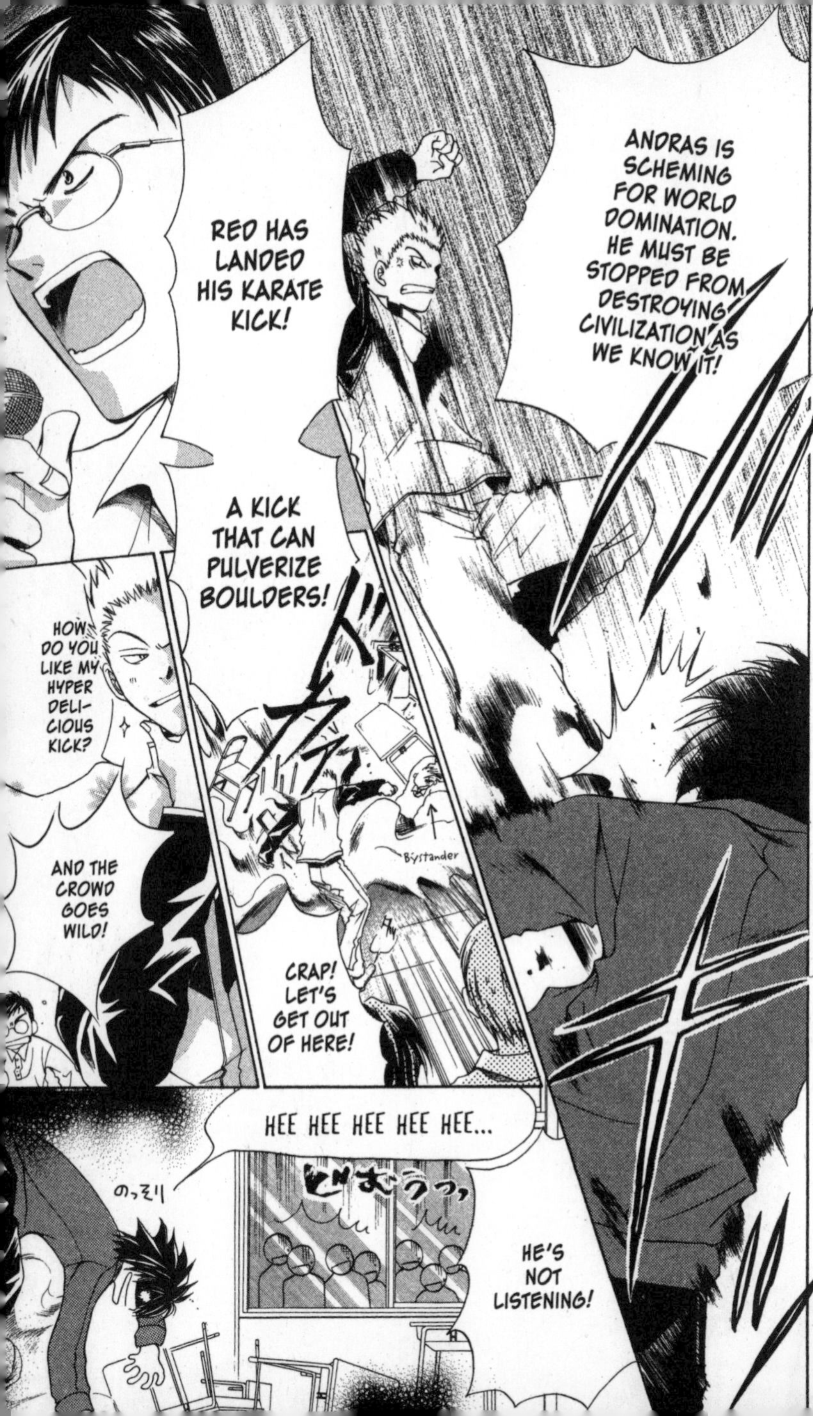
ANDRAS IS SCHEMING FOR WORLD DOMINATION. HE MUST BE STOPPED FROM DESTROYING CIVILIZATION AS WE KNOW IT!
RED HAS LANDED HIS KARATE KICK!
A KICK THAT CAN PULVERIZE BOULDERS!
Bystander
CRAP! LET'S GET OUT OF HERE!
HOW DO YOU LIKE MY HYPER DELICIOUS KICK?
AND THE CROWD GOES WILD!
HE'S NOT LISTENING!
HEE HEE HEE HEE HEE...
のっそり

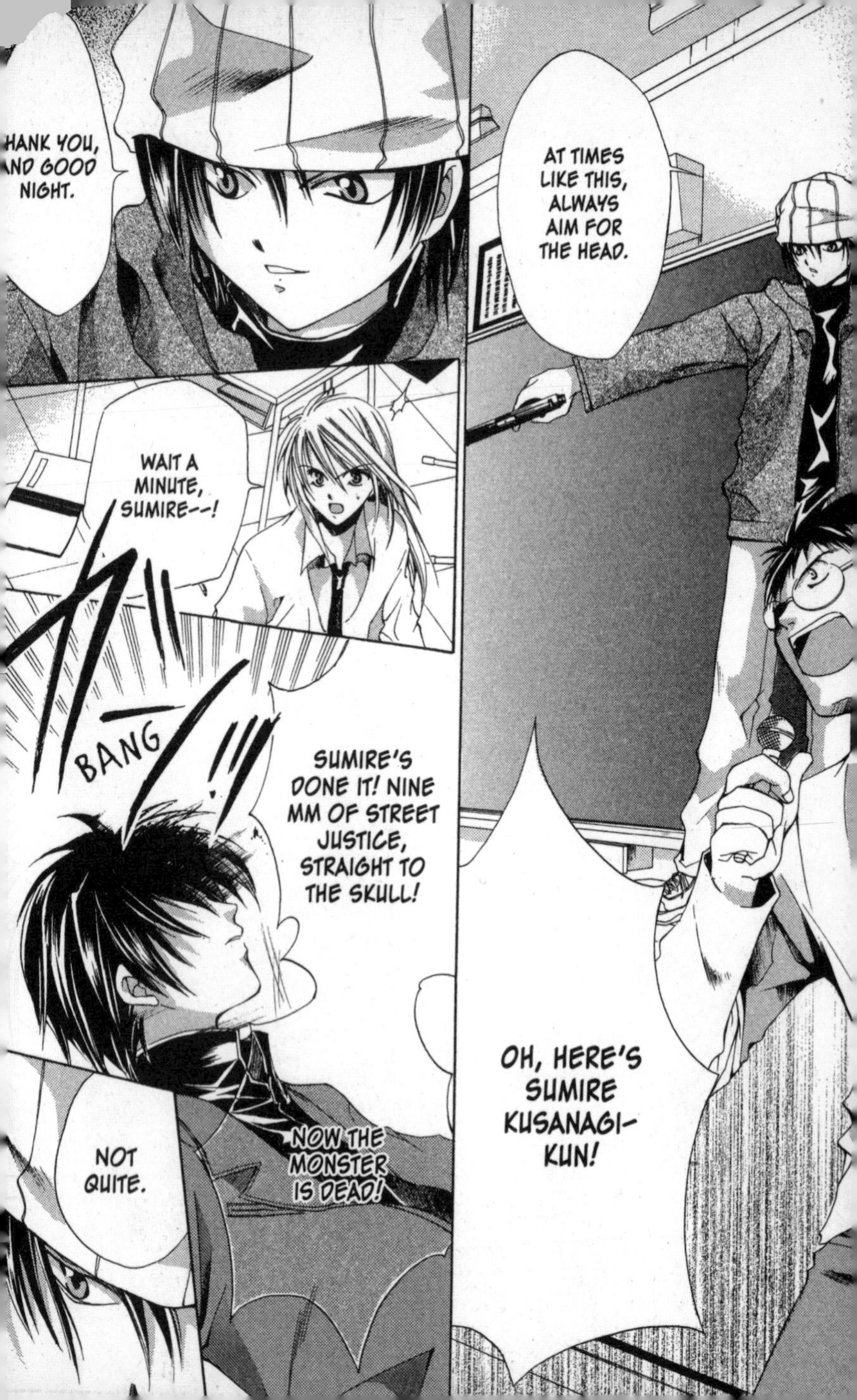
AT TIMES LIKE THIS, ALWAYS AIM FOR THE HEAD.
OH, HERE'S SUMIRE KUSANAGI-KUN!
HANK YOU, ND GOOD NIGHT.
WAIT A MINUTE, SUMIRE--!
BANG
SUMIRE'S DONE IT! NINE MM OF STREET JUSTICE, STRAIGHT TO THE SKULL!
NOW THE MONSTER IS DEAD!
NOT QUITE.

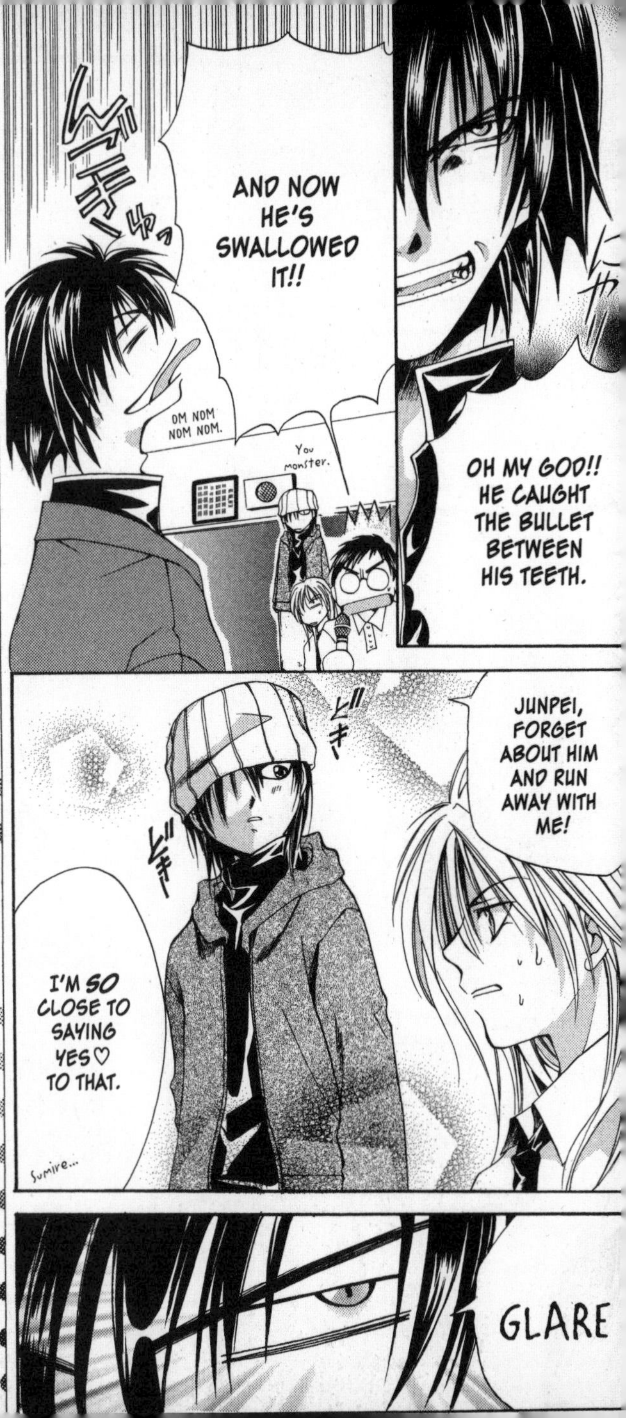
OH MY GOD!! HE CAUGHT THE BULLET BETWEEN HIS TEETH.
AND NOW HE'S SWALLOWED IT!!
OM NOM NOM NOM.
You monster.
JUNPEI, FORGET ABOUT HIM AND RUN AWAY WITH ME!
I'M SO CLOSE TO SAYING YES♡ TO THAT.
Sumire...
GLARE

I never thought Divine would get published in a book.

I created Divine as a gag manga filled with crazy dialogue. It was a story I played around with for fun at the same time that I was coming up with my bonus manga pitches. They were all depressing stories and they all got rejected!

I like all five of the characters because they each have a very strong personality, but Red is especially my favorite. Enjoy him together with Shibaju as a pair (lol).

Personally, I thought Tetsuo and Red were the funniest characters, but I was surprised by my editor's comment on my storyboards.

← NEXT 1/4

※

By the way, there's a special effects TV show called Decaranger. That title was originally my idea, and I didn't take it from them.

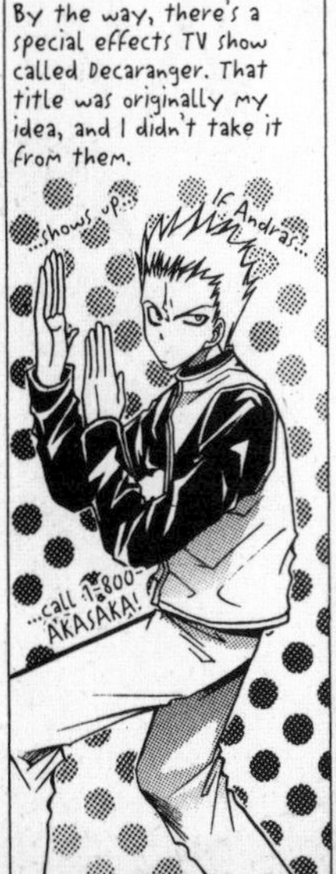
If Andras...
...shows up...
...call 1-800-AKASAKA!

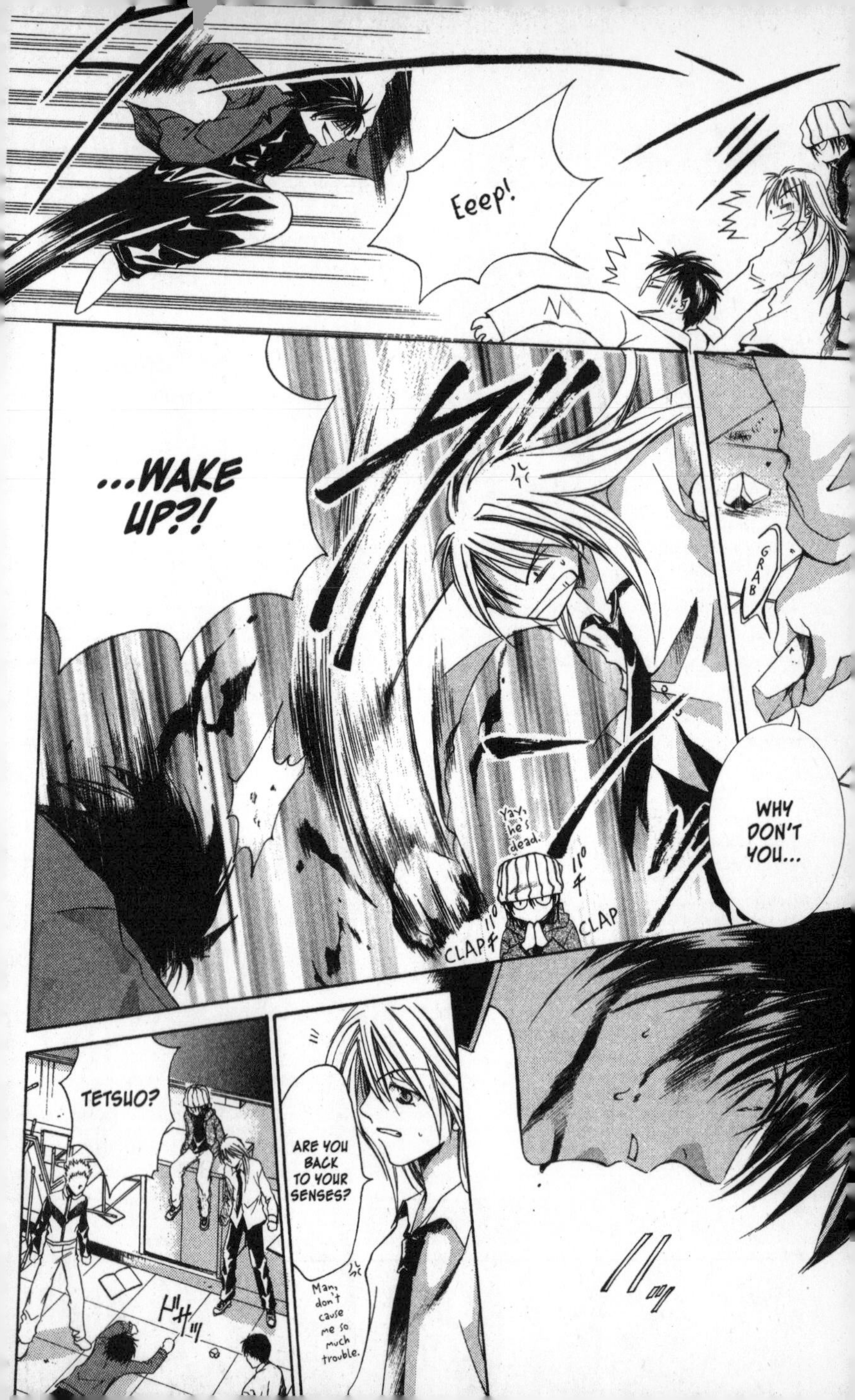

Eeep!
GRAB
WHY DON'T YOU...
...WAKE UP?!
Yay, he's dead.
CLAP
CLAP
ARE YOU BACK TO YOUR SENSES?
Man, don't cause me so much trouble.
TETSUO?

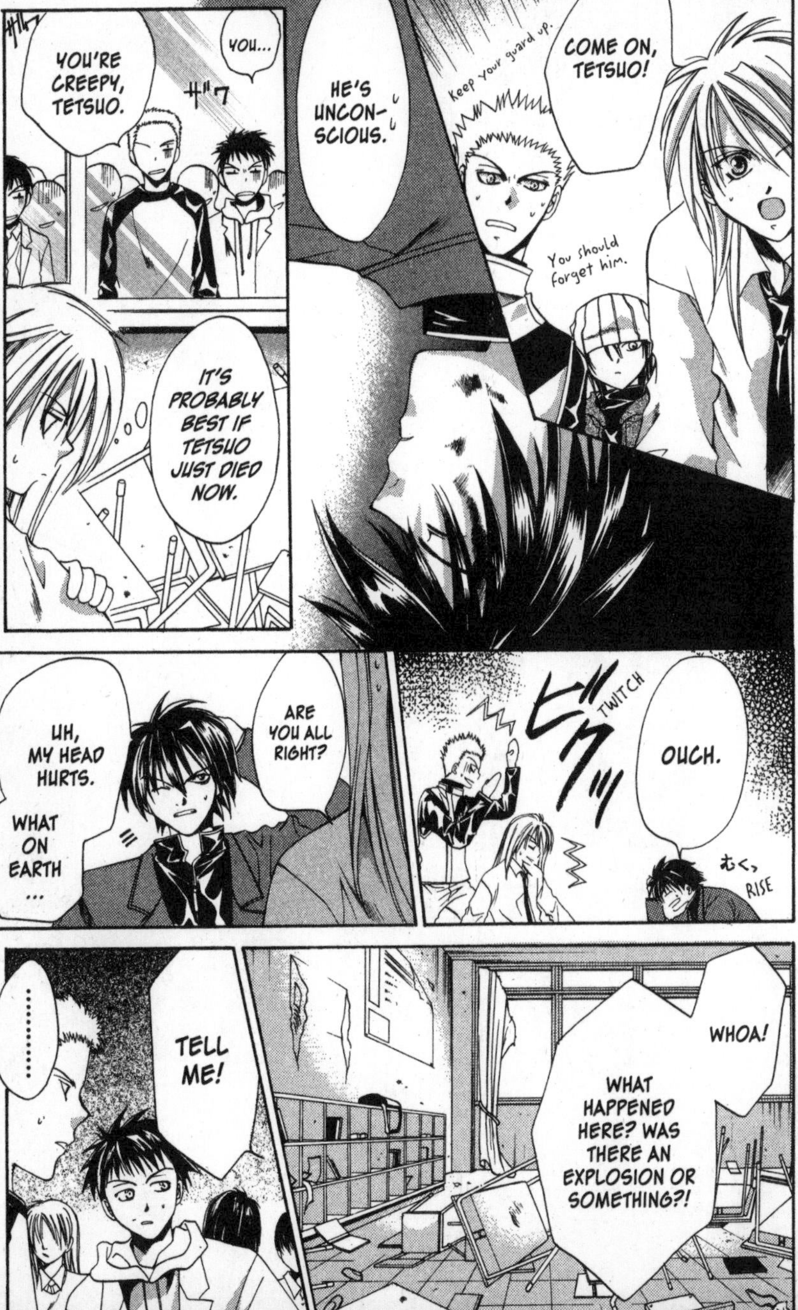
COME ON, TETSUO!
Keep your guard up.
You should forget him.
HE'S UNCONSCIOUS.
YOU...
YOU'RE CREEPY, TETSUO.
IT'S PROBABLY BEST IF TETSUO JUST DIED NOW.
TWITCH
OUCH.
RISE
ARE YOU ALL RIGHT?
UH, MY HEAD HURTS.
WHAT ON EARTH ...
WHOA!
WHAT HAPPENED HERE? WAS THERE AN EXPLOSION OR SOMETHING?!
TELL ME!
....

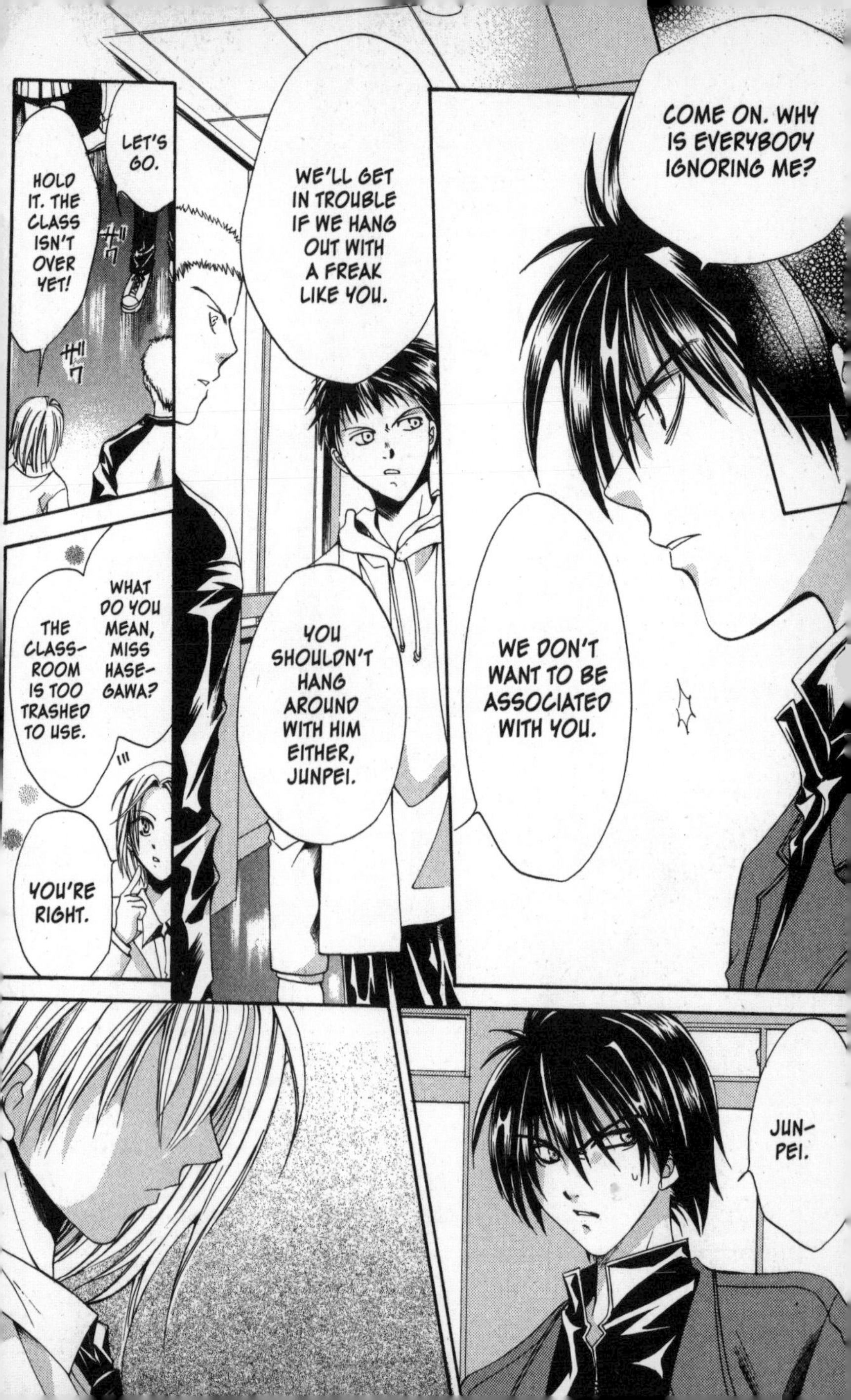
COME ON. WHY IS EVERYBODY IGNORING ME?
WE DON'T WANT TO BE ASSOCIATED WITH YOU.
WE'LL GET IN TROUBLE IF WE HANG OUT WITH A FREAK LIKE YOU.
YOU SHOULDN'T HANG AROUND WITH HIM EITHER, JUNPEI.
LET'S GO.
HOLD IT. THE CLASS ISN'T OVER YET!
WHAT DO YOU MEAN, MISS HASE-GAWA?
THE CLASS-ROOM IS TOO TRASHED TO USE.
YOU'RE RIGHT.
JUN-PEI.

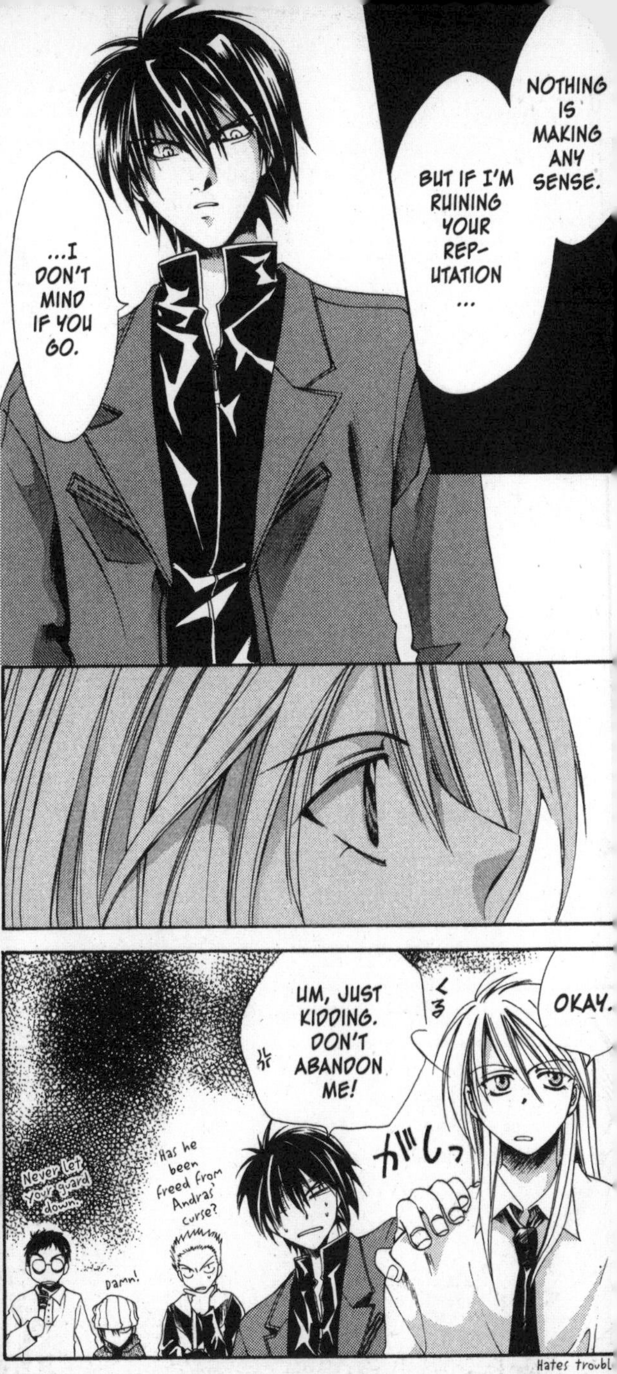
NOTHING IS MAKING ANY SENSE.
BUT IF I'M RUINING YOUR REP-UTATION ...
...I DON'T MIND IF YOU GO.
OKAY.
UM, JUST KIDDING. DON'T ABANDON ME!
Has he been freed from Andras' curse?
Never let your guard down.
Damn!

*Note: Continued from the previous freetalk.

"Sumire is the funniest, isn't he?" wrote my editor after seeing my storyboards.

I couldn't believe it, but when I think about it, that may be true. It's amazing that he's openly showing his adoration for Junpei. Attaboy, Sumire!

Since I wanted to show how cool Tetsuo and Junpei are, I put a major effort in the concert scene at the beginning (lol).

Junpei was supposed to be the only decent character, but Tetsuo was my problem (lol). He goes crazy even in hairy situations so I think I tried to emphasize his gorgeous side to avoid making him seem dumb in cool scenes.

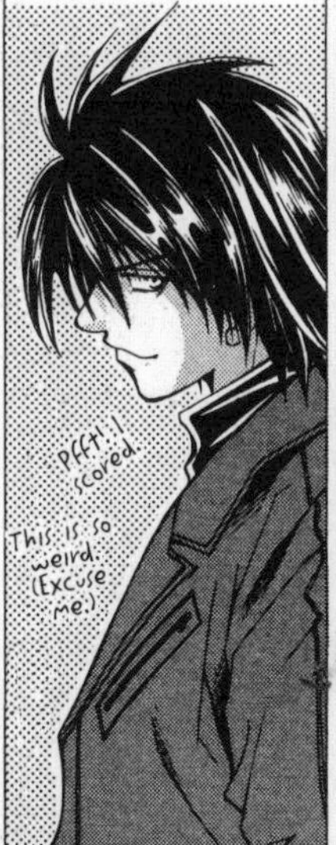
Pfft! I scored.
This is so weird. (Excuse me.)

Hates troubl

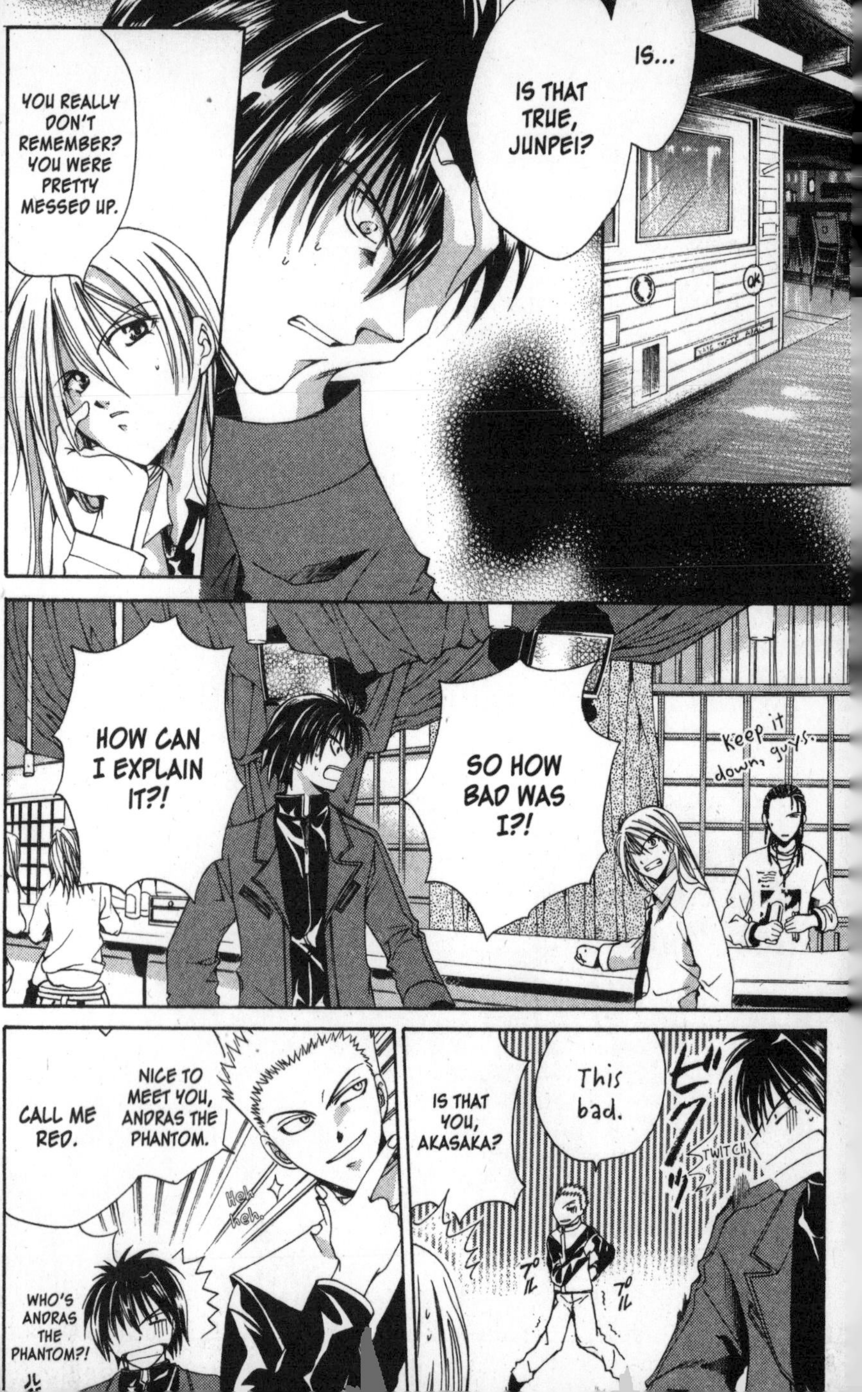
IS...
IS THAT TRUE, JUNPEI?
YOU REALLY DON'T REMEMBER? YOU WERE PRETTY MESSED UP.
Keep it down, guys.
SO HOW BAD WAS I?!
HOW CAN I EXPLAIN IT?!
This bad.
TWITCH
IS THAT YOU, AKASAKA?
NICE TO MEET YOU, ANDRAS THE PHANTOM.
CALL ME RED.
Heh heh.
WHO'S ANDRAS THE PHANTOM?!

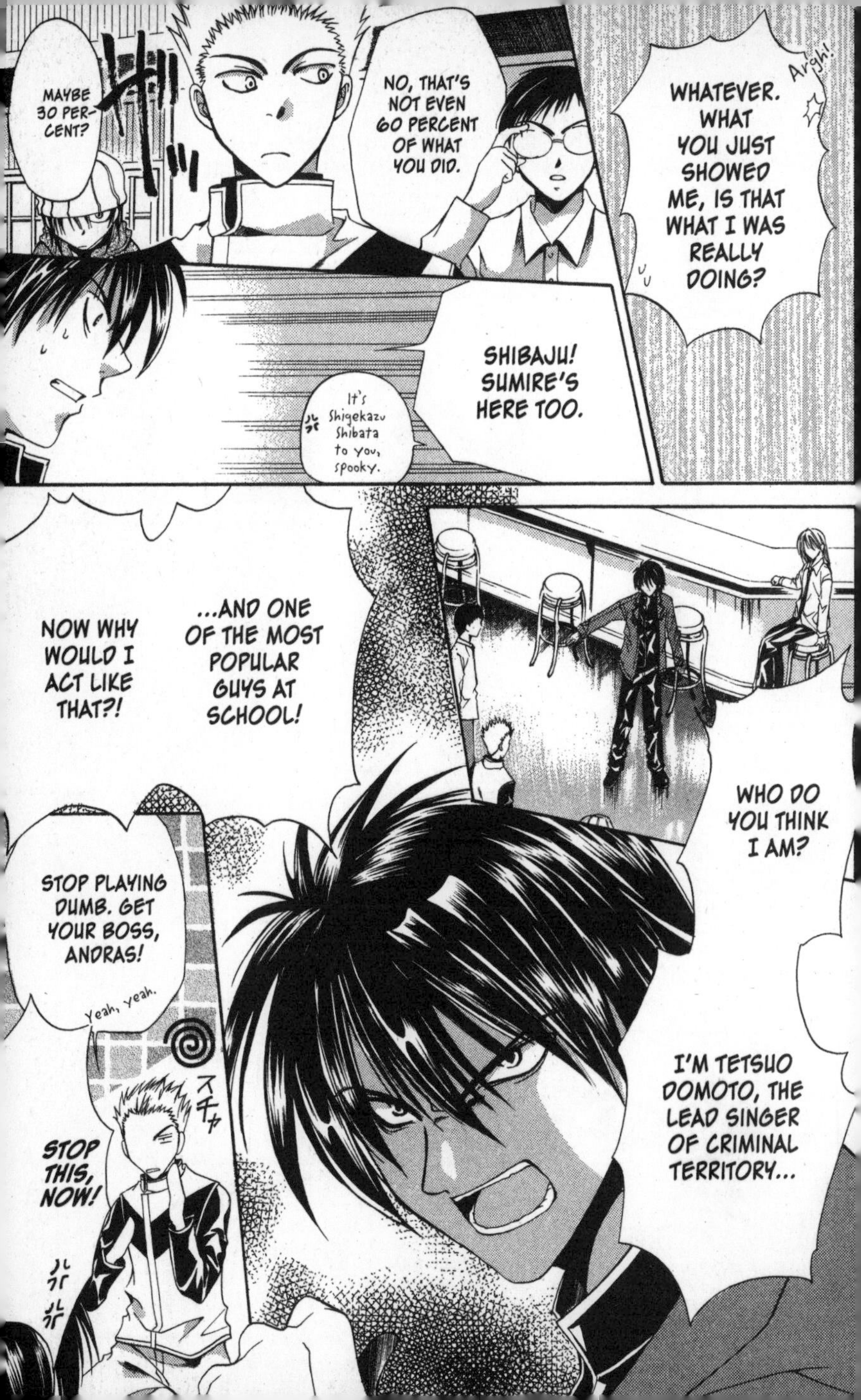
Argh!
WHATEVER. WHAT YOU JUST SHOWED ME, IS THAT WHAT I WAS REALLY DOING?
NO, THAT'S NOT EVEN 60 PERCENT OF WHAT YOU DID.
MAYBE 30 PER-CENT?
SHIBAJU! SUMIRE'S HERE TOO.
It's Shigekazu Shibata to you, spooky.
WHO DO YOU THINK I AM?
I'M TETSUO DOMOTO, THE LEAD SINGER OF CRIMINAL TERRITORY...
...AND ONE OF THE MOST POPULAR GUYS AT SCHOOL!
NOW WHY WOULD I ACT LIKE THAT?!
STOP PLAYING DUMB. GET YOUR BOSS, ANDRAS!
Yeah, yeah.
スチャ
STOP THIS, NOW!

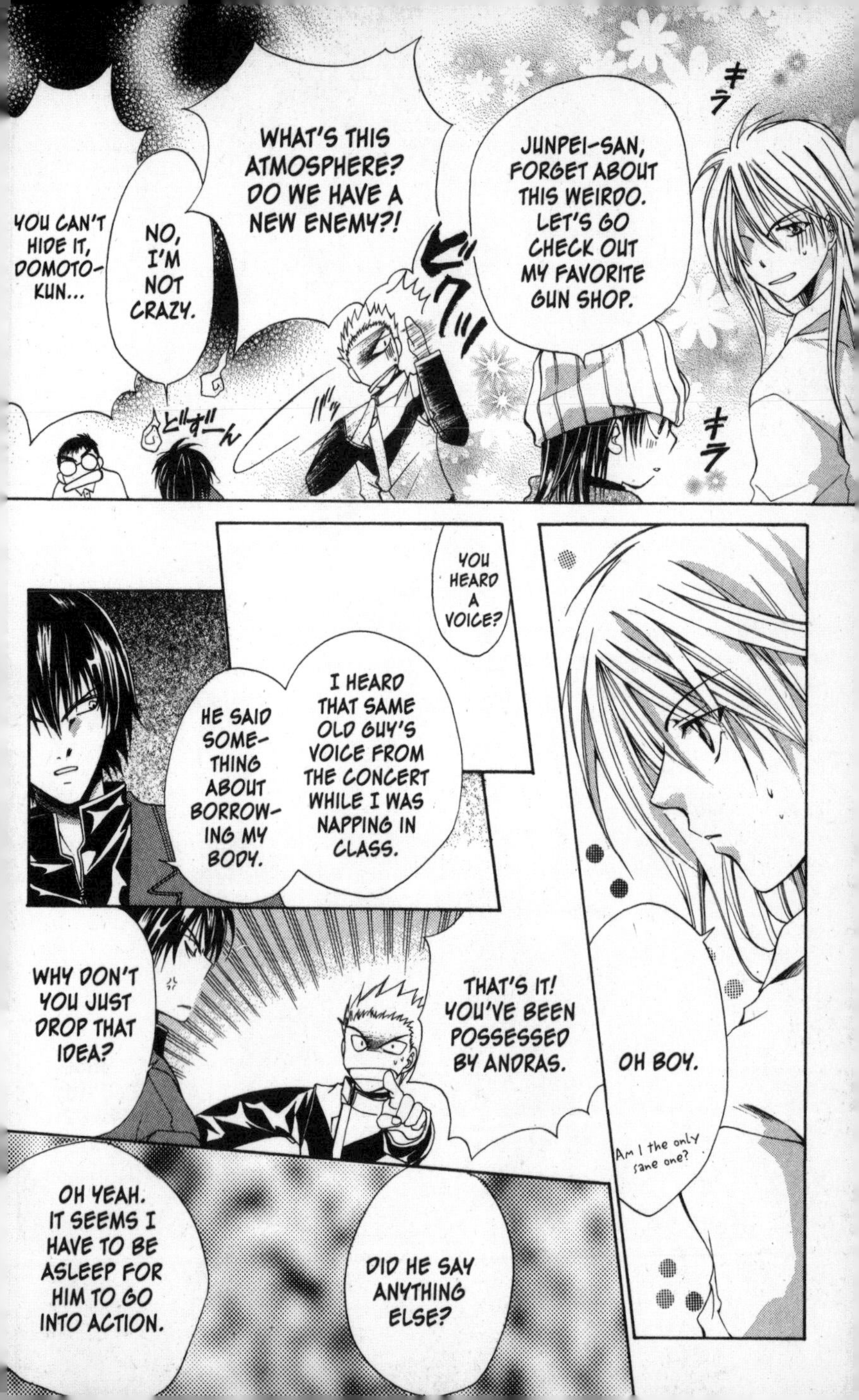
JUNPEI-SAN, FORGET ABOUT THIS WEIRDO. LET'S GO CHECK OUT MY FAVORITE GUN SHOP.
WHAT'S THIS ATMOSPHERE? DO WE HAVE A NEW ENEMY?!
NO, I'M NOT CRAZY.
YOU CAN'T HIDE IT, DOMOTO-KUN...
OH BOY.
Am I the only sane one?
YOU HEARD A VOICE?
I HEARD THAT SAME OLD GUY'S VOICE FROM THE CONCERT WHILE I WAS NAPPING IN CLASS.
HE SAID SOME-THING ABOUT BORROW-ING MY BODY.
THAT'S IT! YOU'VE BEEN POSSESSED BY ANDRAS.
WHY DON'T YOU JUST DROP THAT IDEA?
DID HE SAY ANYTHING ELSE?
OH YEAH. IT SEEMS I HAVE TO BE ASLEEP FOR HIM TO GO INTO ACTION.

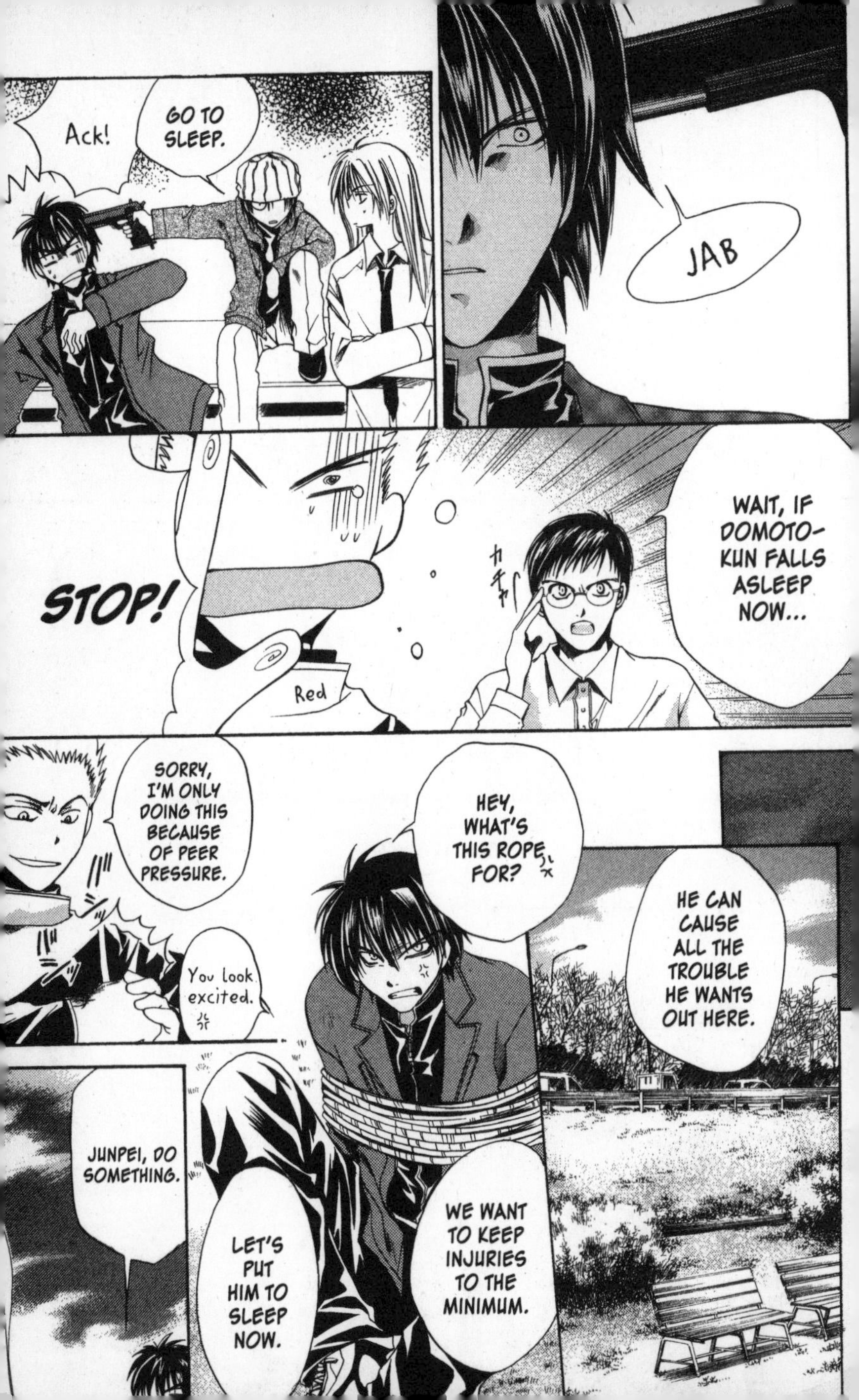
JAB
GO TO SLEEP.
Ack!
WAIT, IF DOMOTO-KUN FALLS ASLEEP NOW...
STOP!
Red
HE CAN CAUSE ALL THE TROUBLE HE WANTS OUT HERE.
HEY, WHAT'S THIS ROPE FOR?
SORRY, I'M ONLY DOING THIS BECAUSE OF PEER PRESSURE.
You look excited.
WE WANT TO KEEP INJURIES TO THE MINIMUM.
LET'S PUT HIM TO SLEEP NOW.
JUNPEI, DO SOMETHING.

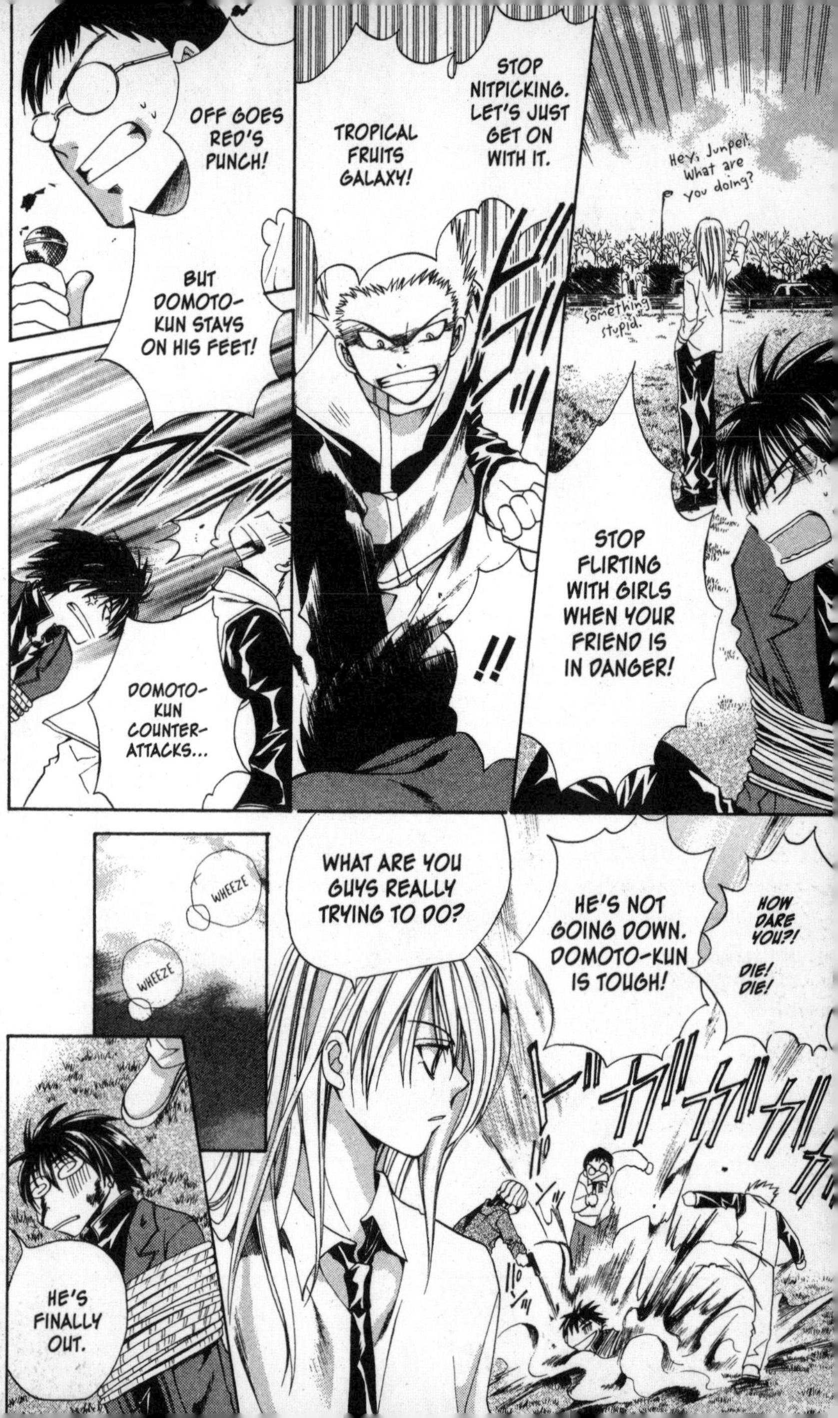
Hey, Junpei. What are you doing?
Something stupid.
STOP FLIRTING WITH GIRLS WHEN YOUR FRIEND IS IN DANGER!
STOP NITPICKING. LET'S JUST GET ON WITH IT.
TROPICAL FRUITS GALAXY!
!!
OFF GOES RED'S PUNCH!
BUT DOMOTO-KUN STAYS ON HIS FEET!
DOMOTO-KUN COUNTER-ATTACKS...
HOW DARE YOU?!
DIE! DIE!
HE'S NOT GOING DOWN. DOMOTO-KUN IS TOUGH!
WHAT ARE YOU GUYS REALLY TRYING TO DO?
WHEEZE
WHEEZE
HE'S FINALLY OUT.

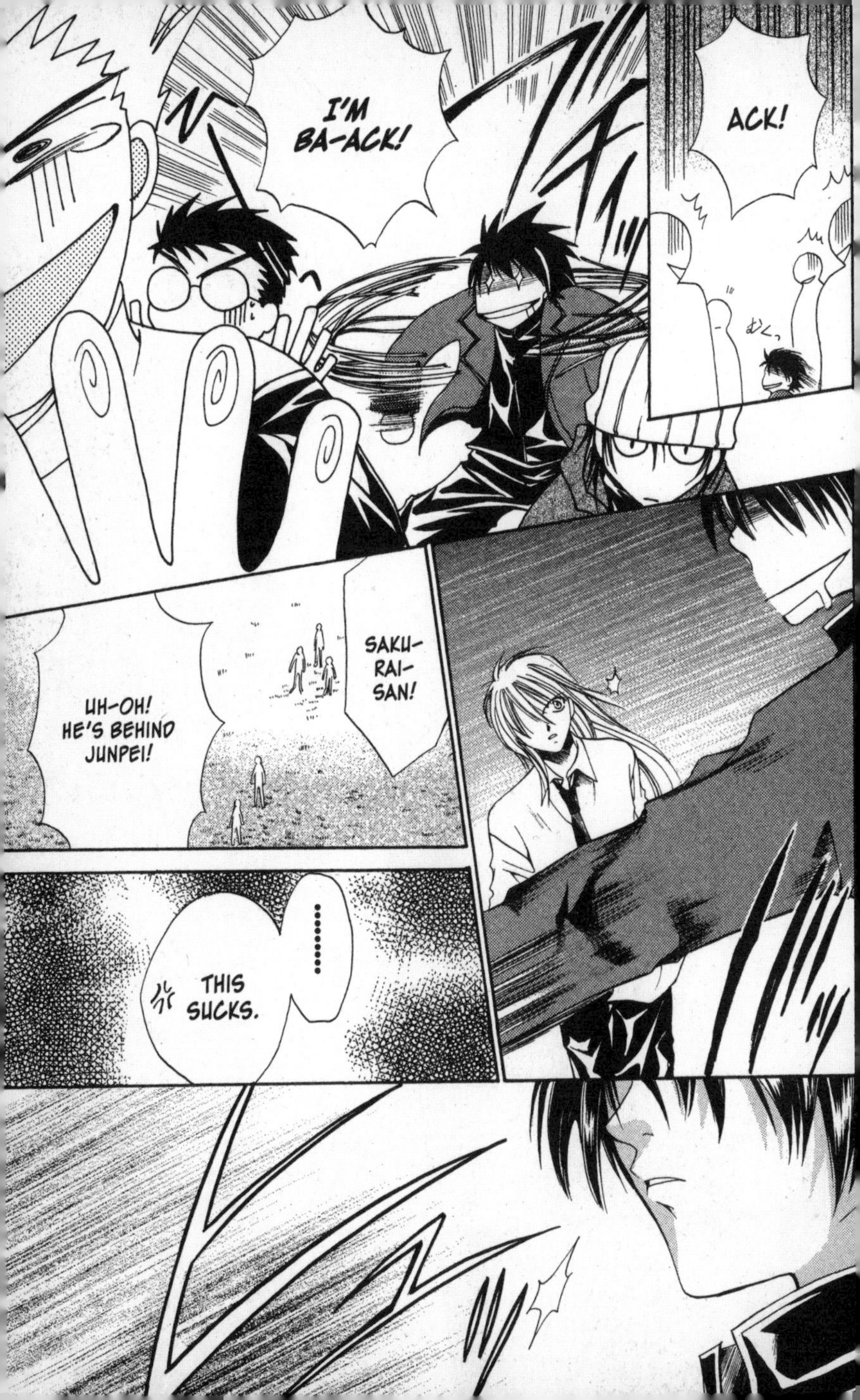
ACK!
むくっ
I'M BA-ACK!
SAKU-RAI-SAN!
UH-OH! HE'S BEHIND JUNPEI!
....
THIS SUCKS.

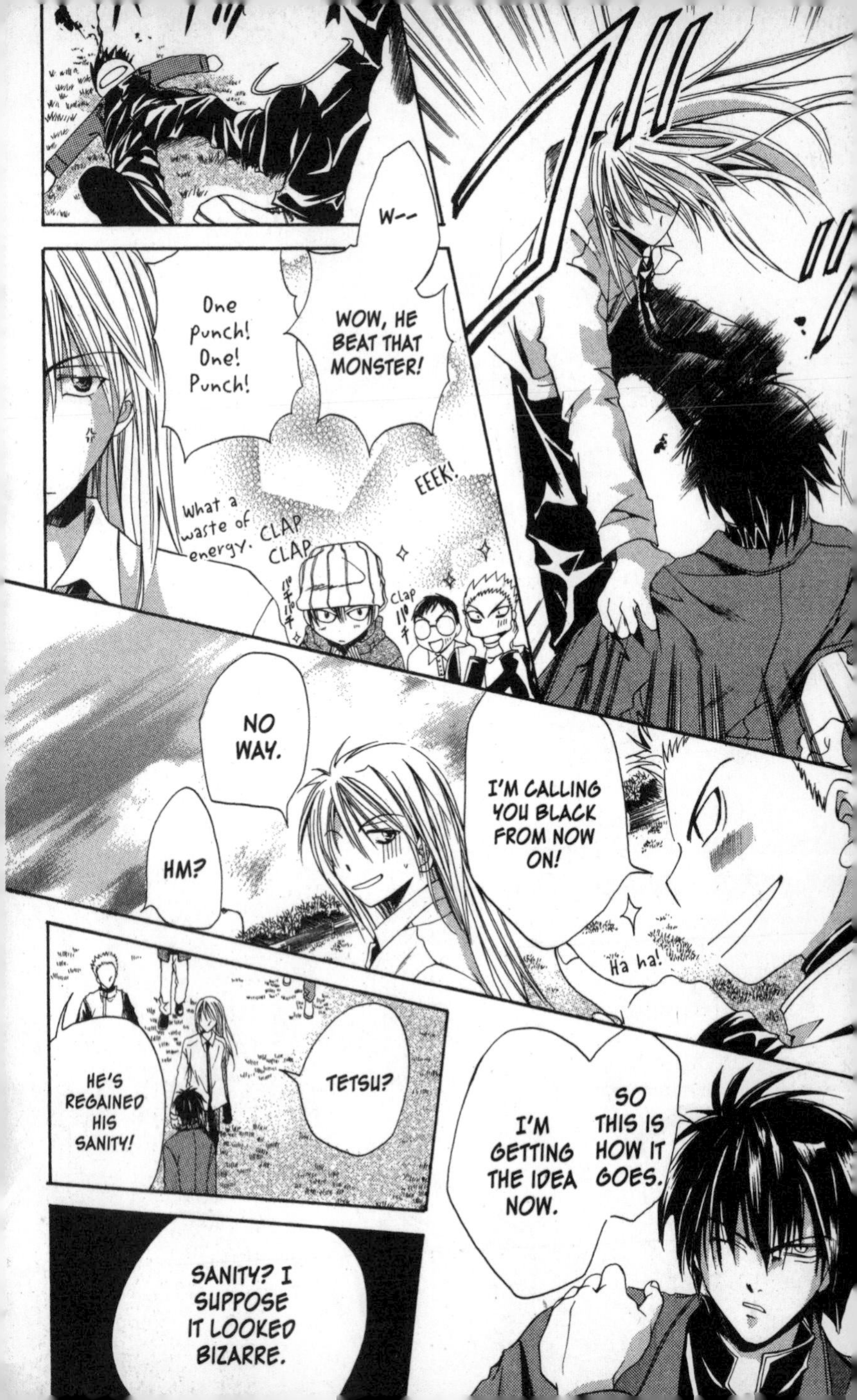
W--
WOW, HE BEAT THAT MONSTER!
One punch! One! Punch!
EEEK!
What a waste of energy.
CLAP CLAP
パチパチ
Clap パチ
I'M CALLING YOU BLACK FROM NOW ON!
Ha ha!
NO WAY.
HM?
SO THIS IS HOW IT GOES.
I'M GETTING THE IDEA NOW.
TETSU?
HE'S REGAINED HIS SANITY!
SANITY? I SUPPOSE IT LOOKED BIZARRE.

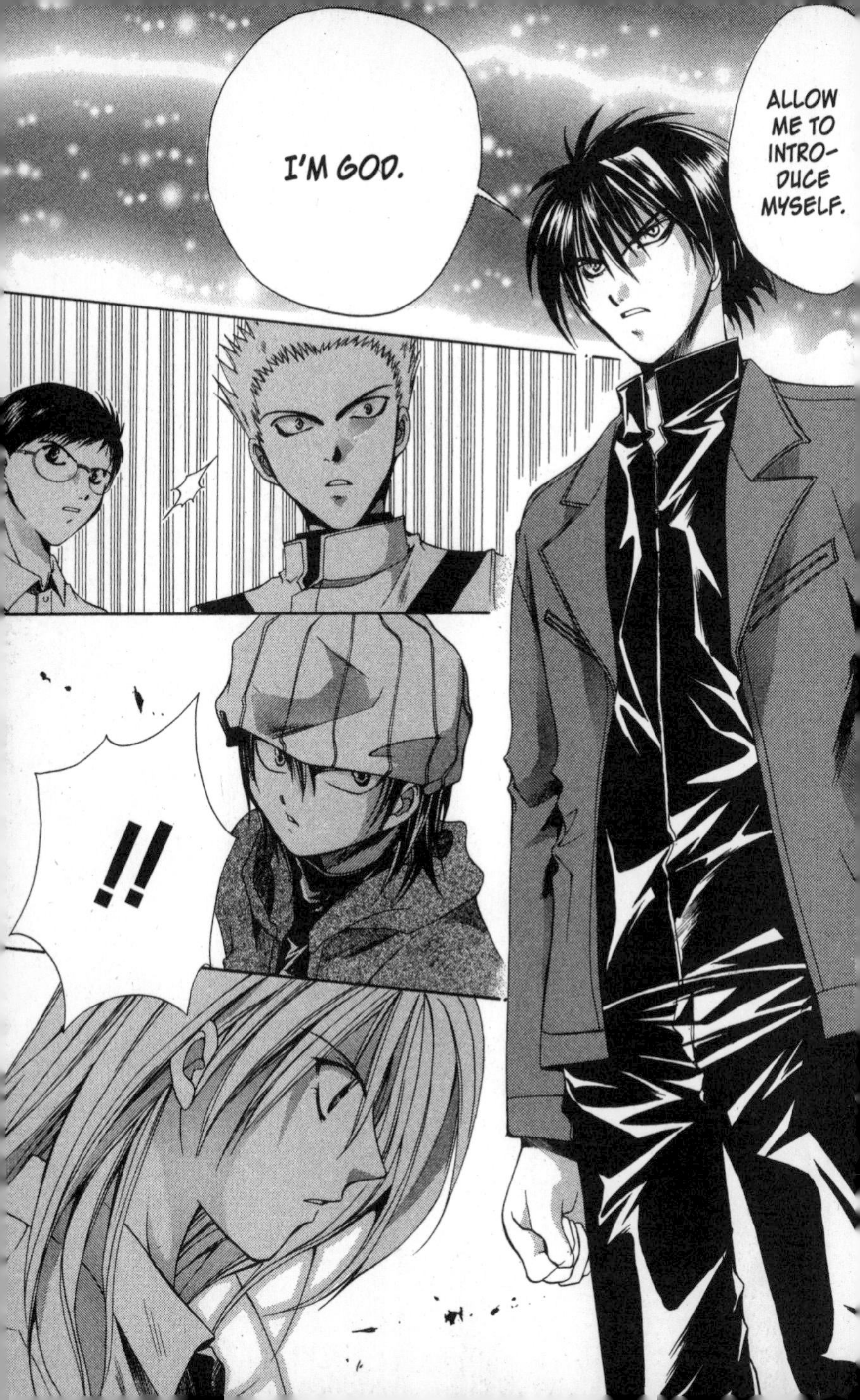
ALLOW ME TO INTRO-DUCE MYSELF.
I'M GOD.
!!

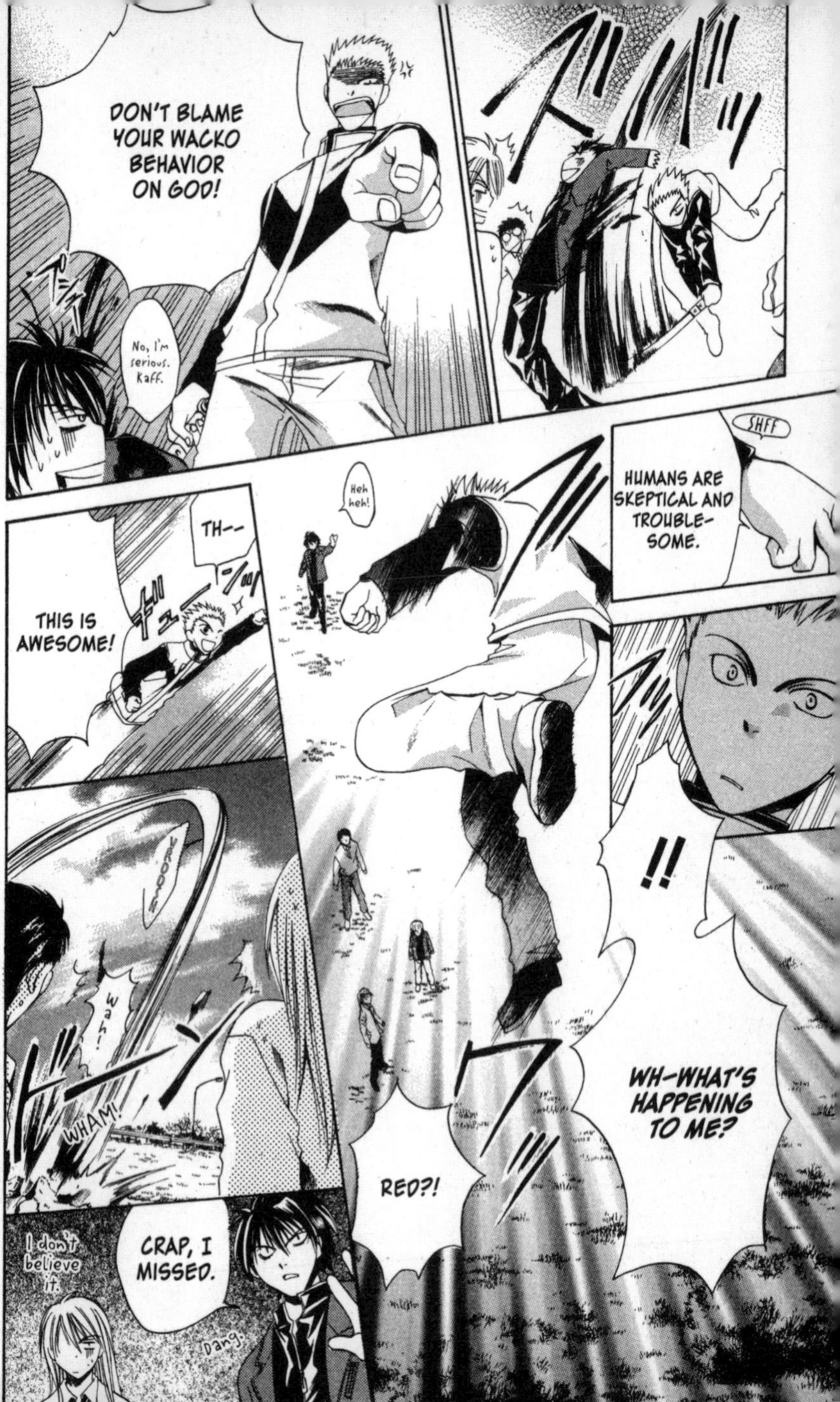
DON'T BLAME YOUR WACKO BEHAVIOR ON GOD!
No, I'm serious. Kaff.
SHFF
HUMANS ARE SKEPTICAL AND TROUBLE-SOME.
Heh heh!
TH--
THIS IS AWESOME!
!!
WH-WHAT'S HAPPENING TO ME?
RED?!
VROOOM
Wah!
WHAM!
CRAP, I MISSED.
I don't believe it.
Dang.

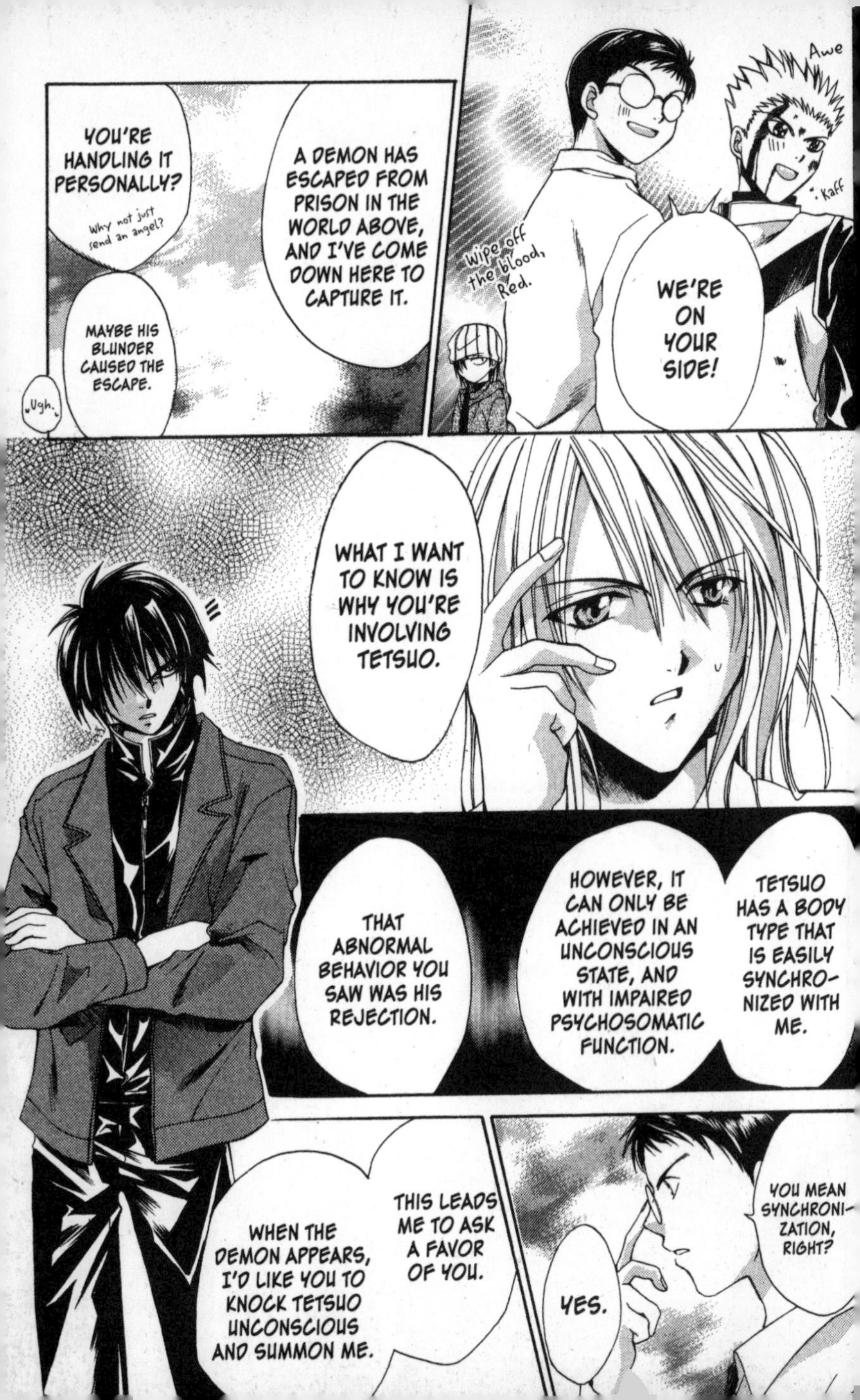
Awe
Kaff
WE'RE ON YOUR SIDE!
Wipe off the blood, Red.
A DEMON HAS ESCAPED FROM PRISON IN THE WORLD ABOVE, AND I'VE COME DOWN HERE TO CAPTURE IT.
YOU'RE HANDLING IT PERSONALLY?
Why not just send an angel?
MAYBE HIS BLUNDER CAUSED THE ESCAPE.
Ugh.
WHAT I WANT TO KNOW IS WHY YOU'RE INVOLVING TETSUO.
TETSUO HAS A BODY TYPE THAT IS EASILY SYNCHRO-NIZED WITH ME.
HOWEVER, IT CAN ONLY BE ACHIEVED IN AN UNCONSCIOUS STATE, AND WITH IMPAIRED PSYCHOSOMATIC FUNCTION.
THAT ABNORMAL BEHAVIOR YOU SAW WAS HIS REJECTION.
YOU MEAN SYNCHRONI-ZATION, RIGHT?
YES.
THIS LEADS ME TO ASK A FAVOR OF YOU.
WHEN THE DEMON APPEARS, I'D LIKE YOU TO KNOCK TETSUO UNCONSCIOUS AND SUMMON ME.

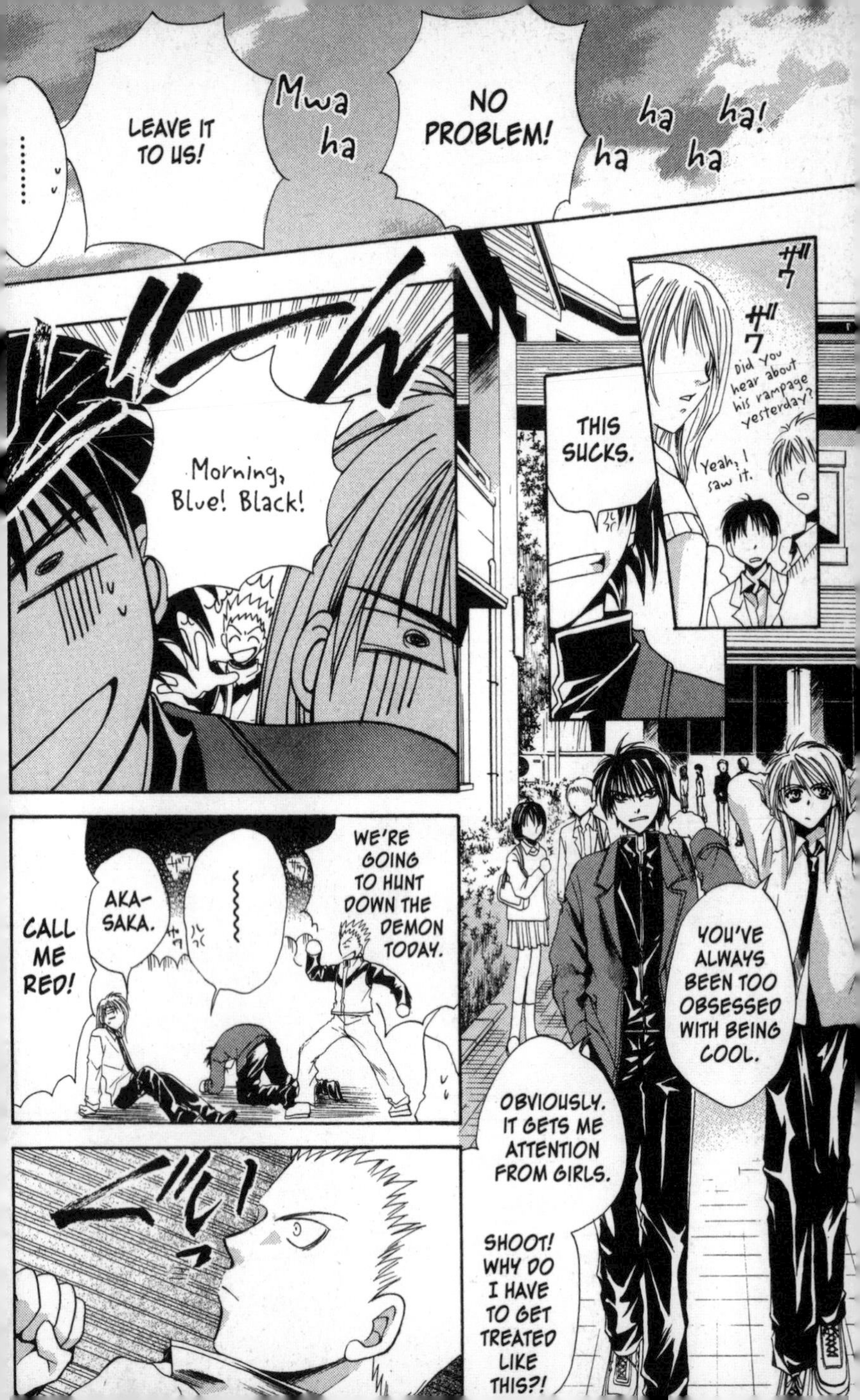

ha ha ha ha!
NO PROBLEM!
Mwa ha
LEAVE IT TO US!
......
Did you hear about his rampage yesterday?
Yeah, I saw it.
THIS SUCKS.
Morning, Blue! Black!
YOU'VE ALWAYS BEEN TOO OBSESSED WITH BEING COOL.
OBVIOUSLY. IT GETS ME ATTENTION FROM GIRLS.
SHOOT! WHY DO I HAVE TO GET TREATED LIKE THIS?!
WE'RE GOING TO HUNT DOWN THE DEMON TODAY.
AKA-SAKA.
CALL ME RED!

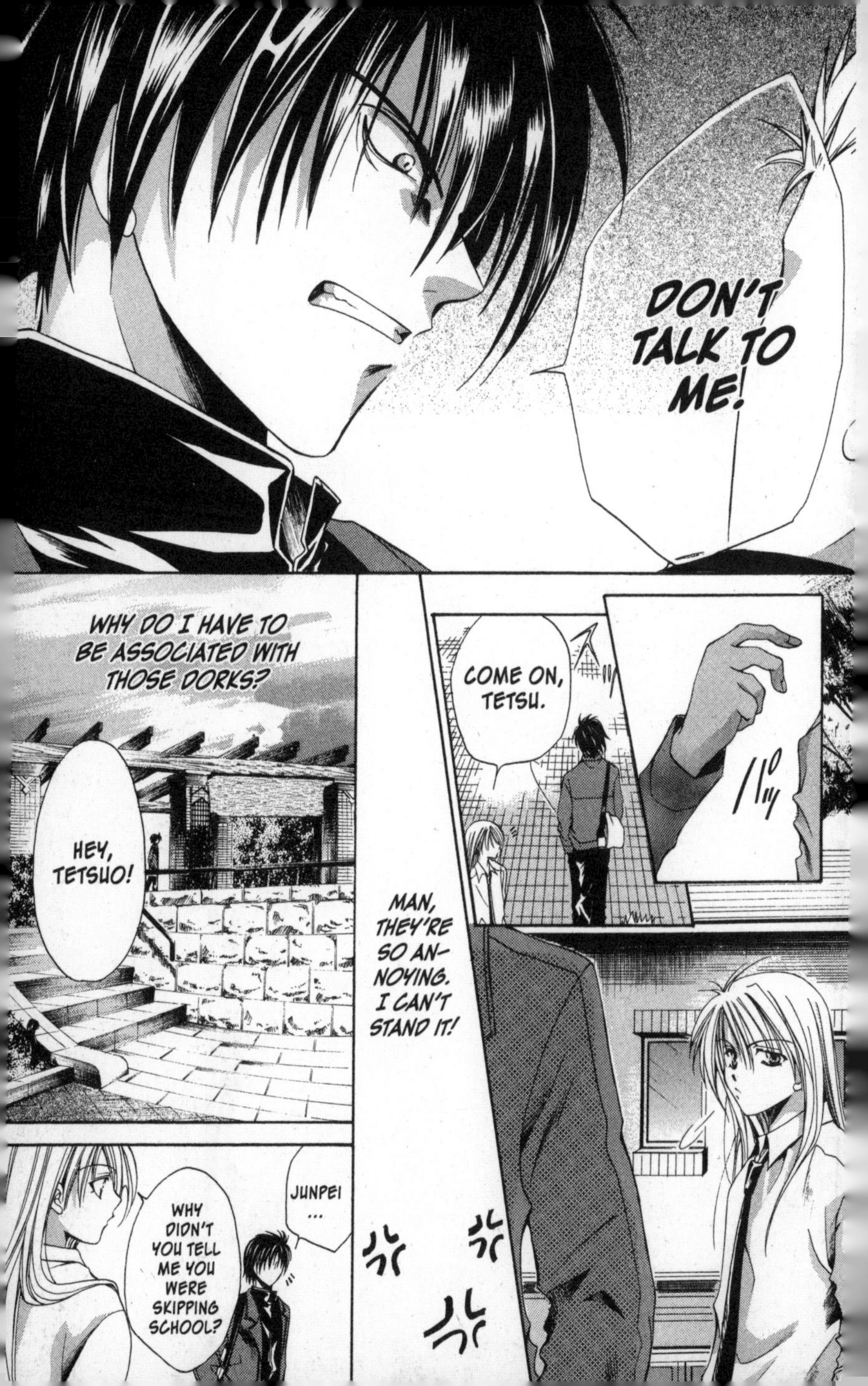
DON'T TALK TO ME!
COME ON, TETSU.
MAN, THEY'RE SO AN- NOYING. I CAN'T STAND IT!
WHY DO I HAVE TO BE ASSOCIATED WITH THOSE DORKS?
HEY, TETSUO!
JUNPEI ...
WHY DIDN'T YOU TELL ME YOU WERE SKIPPING SCHOOL?

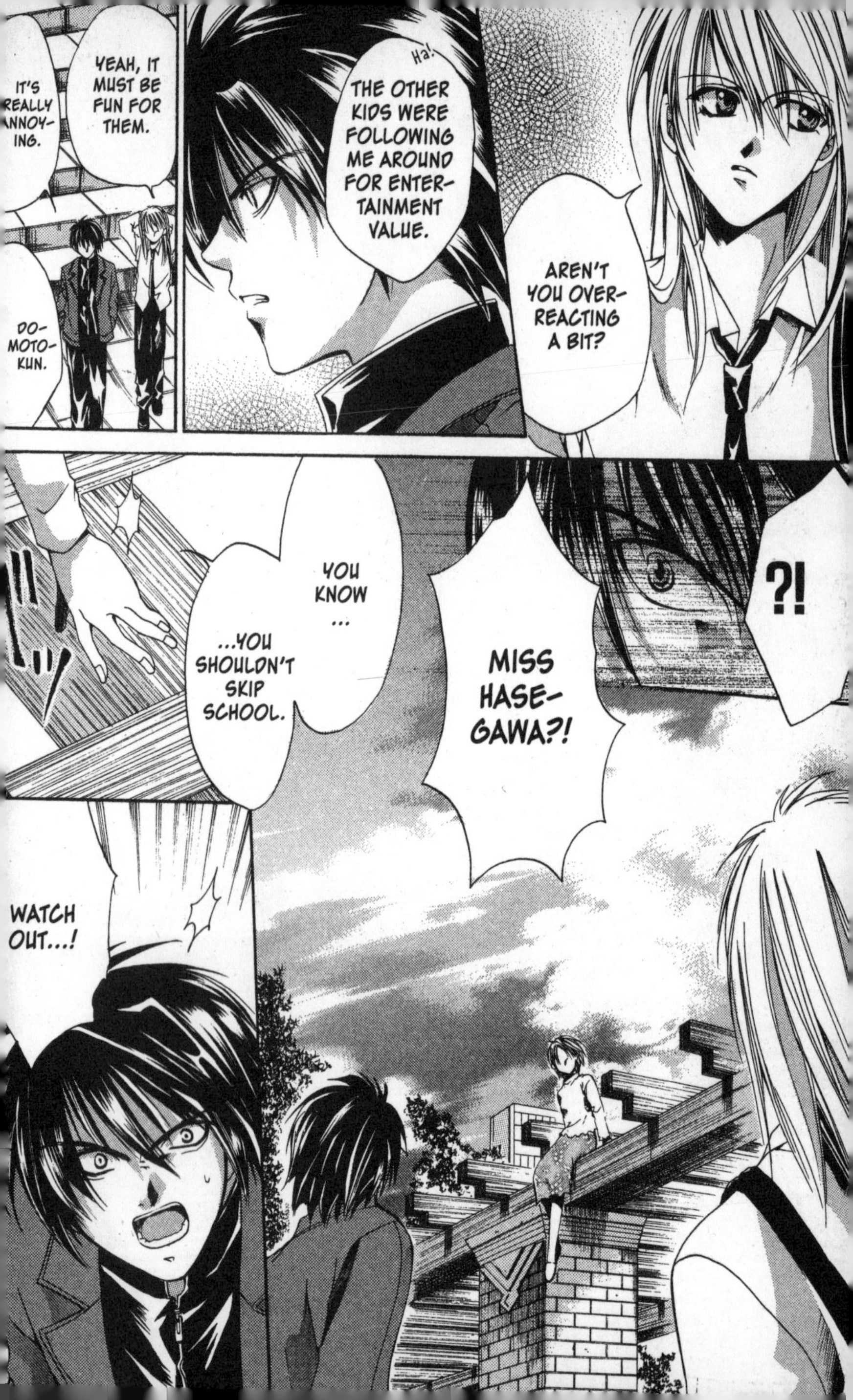
AREN'T YOU OVER-REACTING A BIT?
HA! THE OTHER KIDS WERE FOLLOWING ME AROUND FOR ENTER-TAINMENT VALUE.
YEAH, IT MUST BE FUN FOR THEM.
IT'S REALLY ANNOY-ING.
DO-MOTO-KUN.
?!
YOU KNOW ...
...YOU SHOULDN'T SKIP SCHOOL.
MISS HASE-GAWA?!
WATCH OUT...!

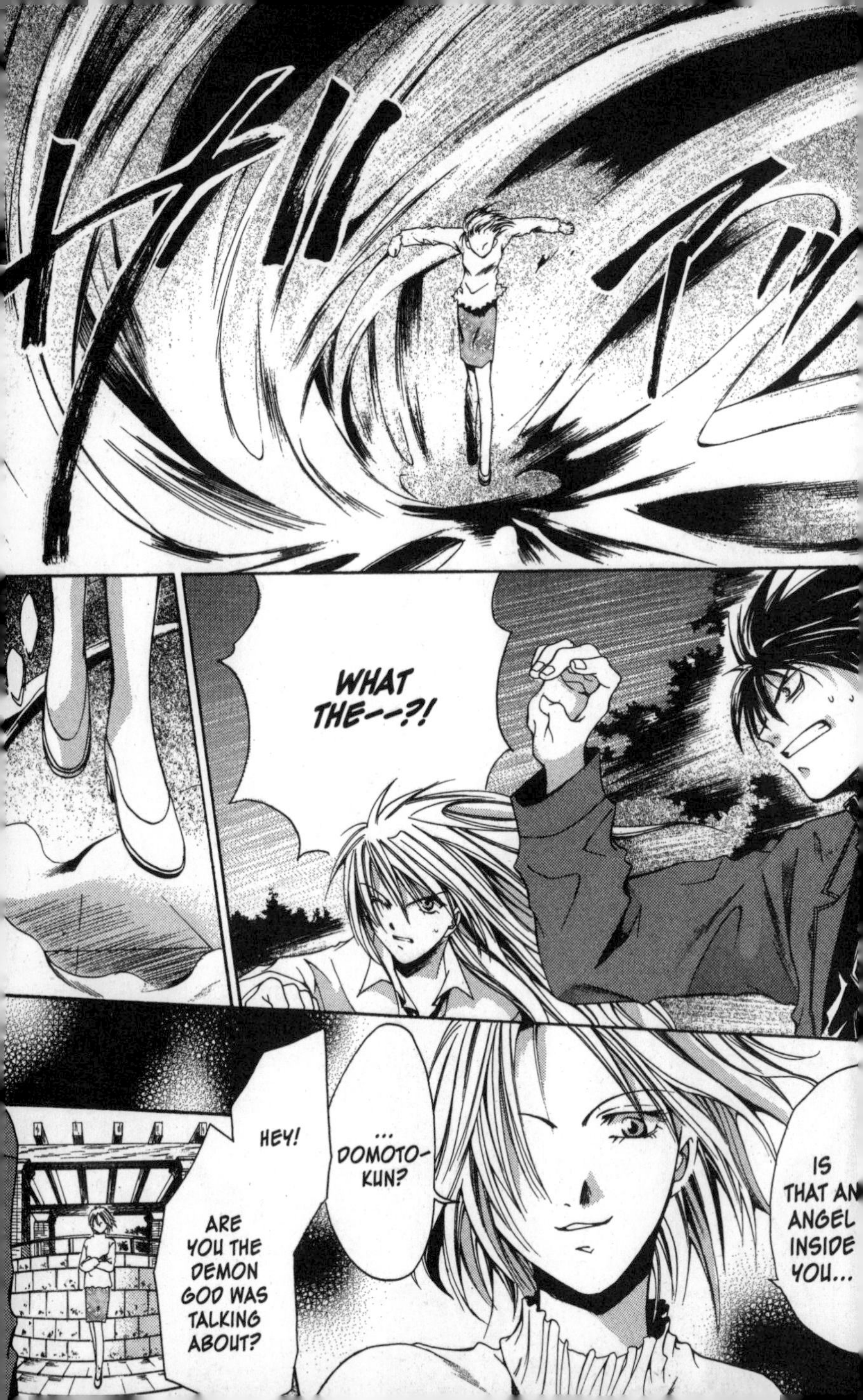
WHAT THE--?!
IS THAT AN ANGEL INSIDE YOU...
... DOMOTO-KUN?
HEY!
ARE YOU THE DEMON GOD WAS TALKING ABOUT?

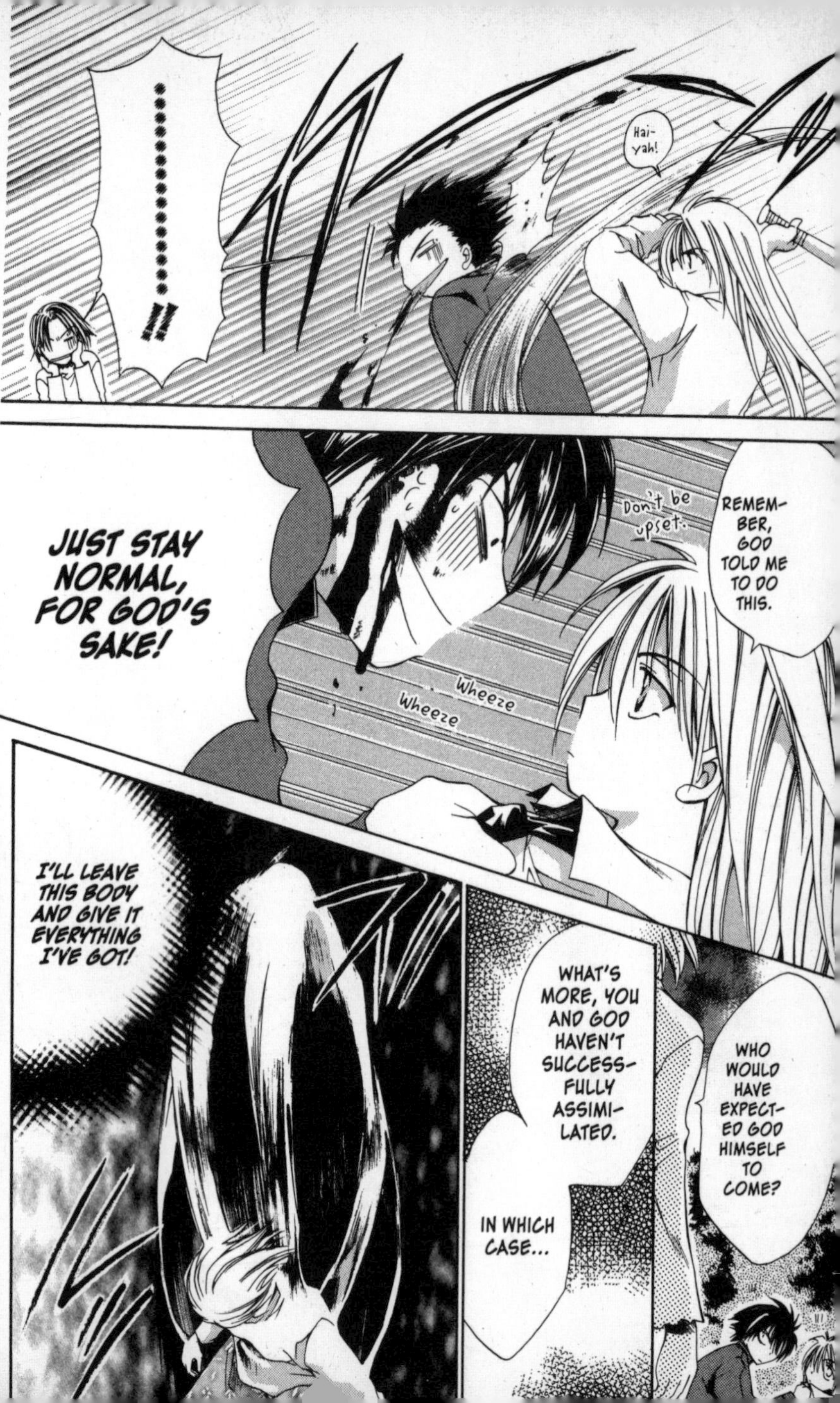
Hai-yah!
...............!!
REMEMBER, GOD TOLD ME TO DO THIS.
Don't be upset.
Wheeze
Wheeze
JUST STAY NORMAL, FOR GOD'S SAKE!
WHO WOULD HAVE EXPECTED GOD HIMSELF TO COME?
WHAT'S MORE, YOU AND GOD HAVEN'T SUCCESSFULLY ASSIMILATED.
IN WHICH CASE...
!!
I'LL LEAVE THIS BODY AND GIVE IT EVERYTHING I'VE GOT!

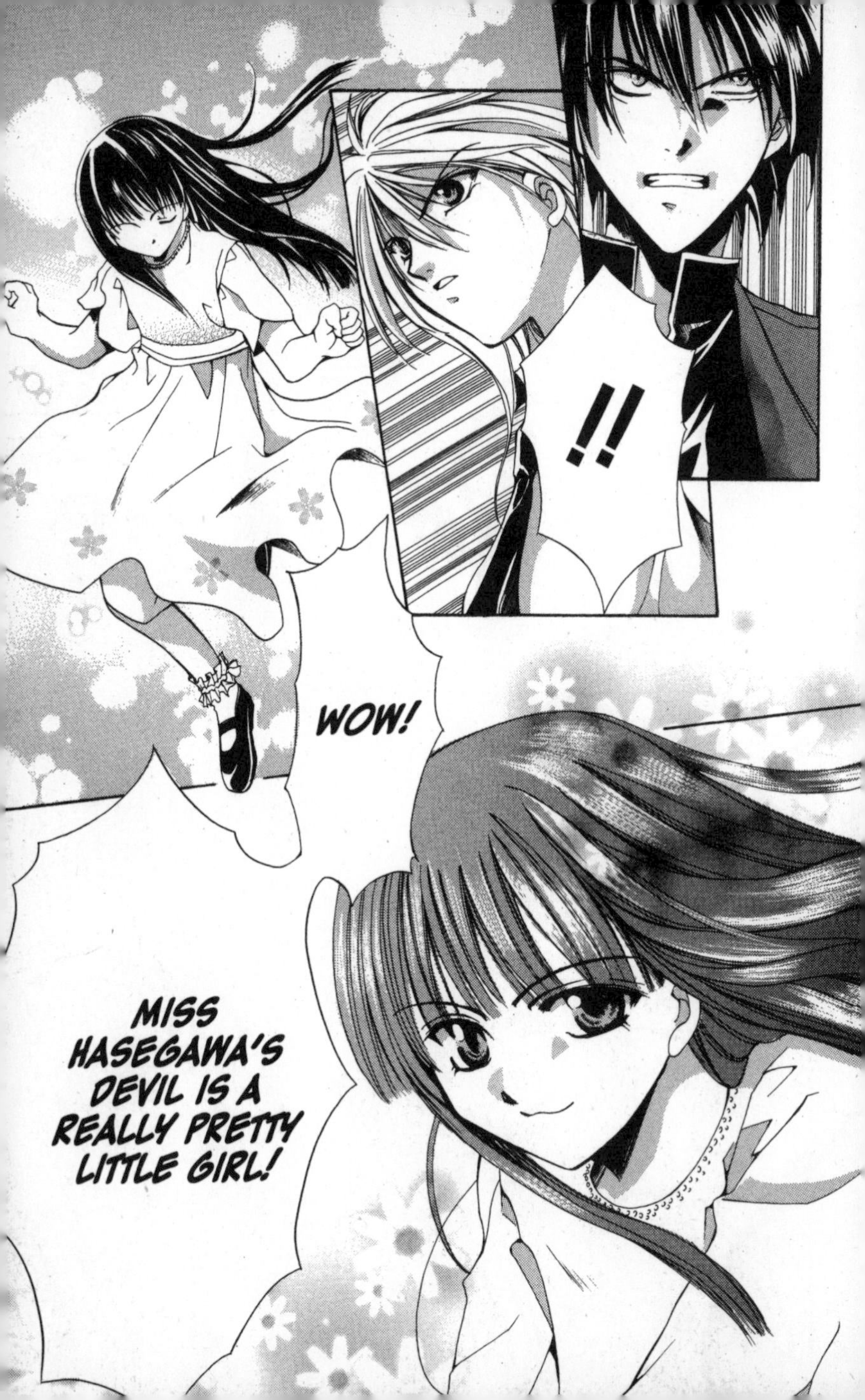
!!
WOW!
MISS HASEGAWA'S DEVIL IS A REALLY PRETTY LITTLE GIRL!

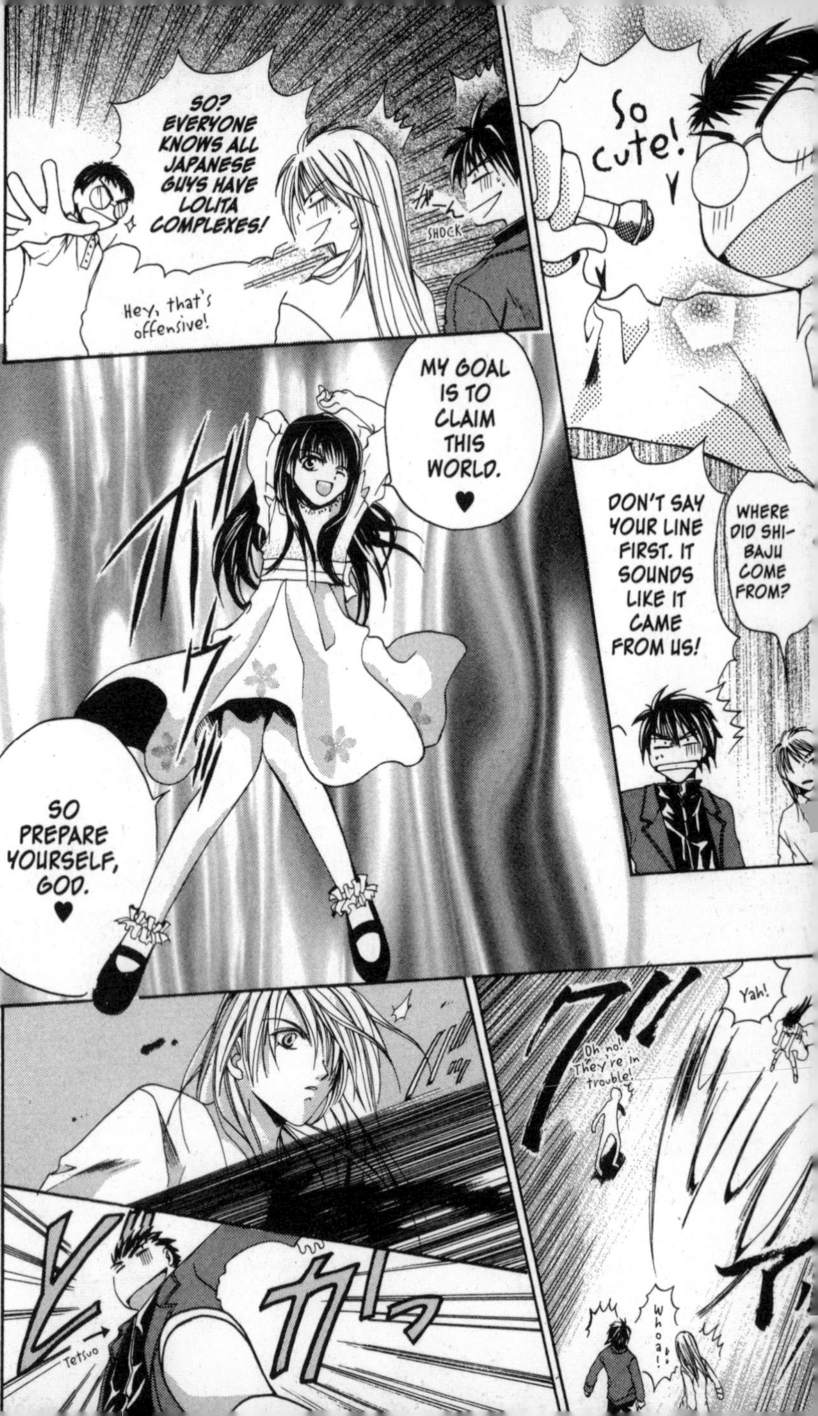
So cute!
SO? EVERYONE KNOWS ALL JAPANESE GUYS HAVE LOLITA COMPLEXES!
SHOCK
Hey, that's offensive!
MY GOAL IS TO CLAIM THIS WORLD. ♥
SO PREPARE YOURSELF, GOD. ♥
DON'T SAY YOUR LINE FIRST. IT SOUNDS LIKE IT CAME FROM US!
WHERE DID SHI-BAJU COME FROM?
Yah!
Oh no! They're in trouble!
Whoa!
Tetsuo

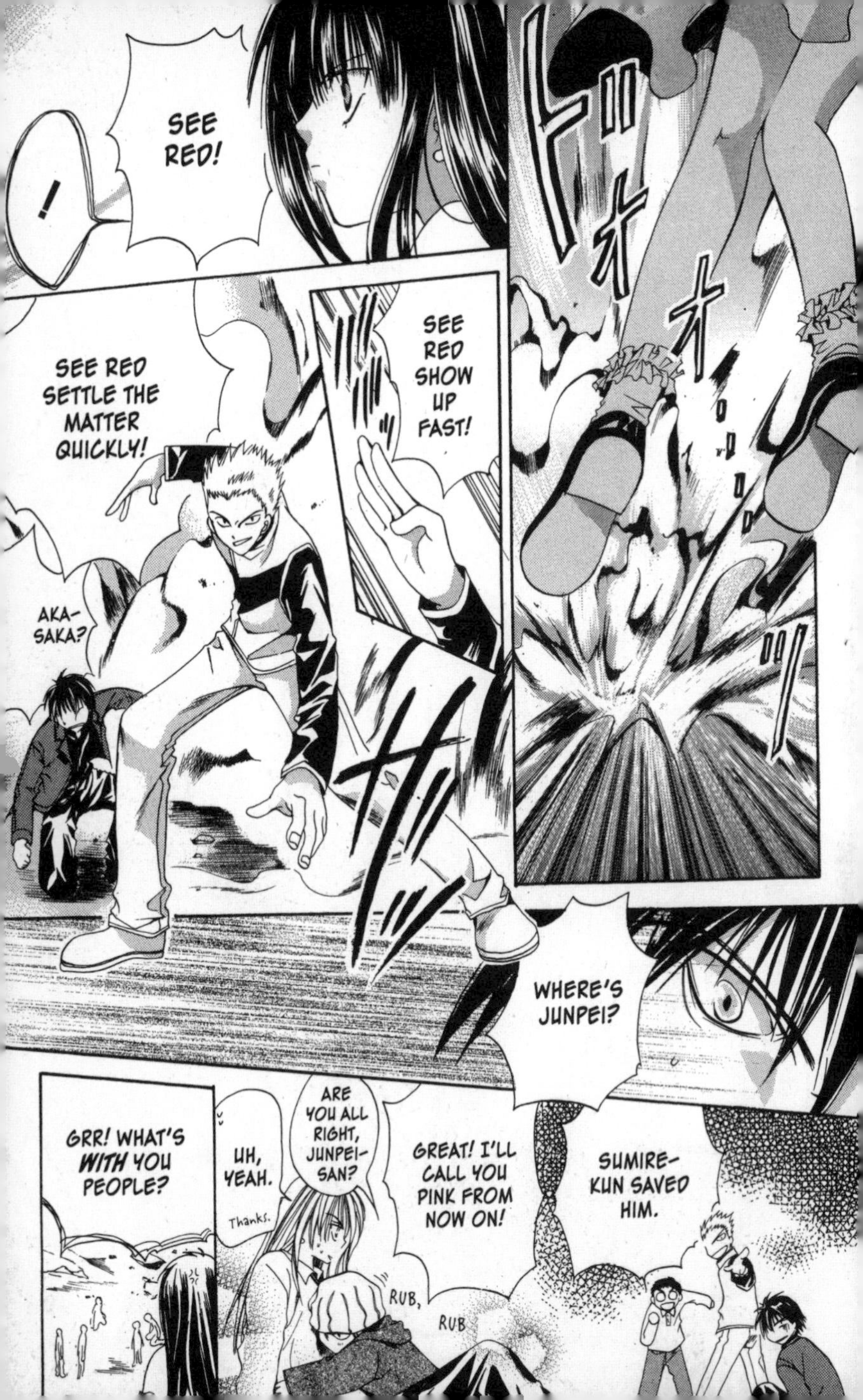
SEE RED!
!
SEE RED SHOW UP FAST!
SEE RED SETTLE THE MATTER QUICKLY!
AKA-SAKA?
WHERE'S JUNPEI?
SUMIRE-KUN SAVED HIM.
GREAT! I'LL CALL YOU PINK FROM NOW ON!
RUB,
RUB
ARE YOU ALL RIGHT, JUNPEI-SAN?
UH, YEAH.
Thanks.
GRR! WHAT'S WITH YOU PEOPLE?

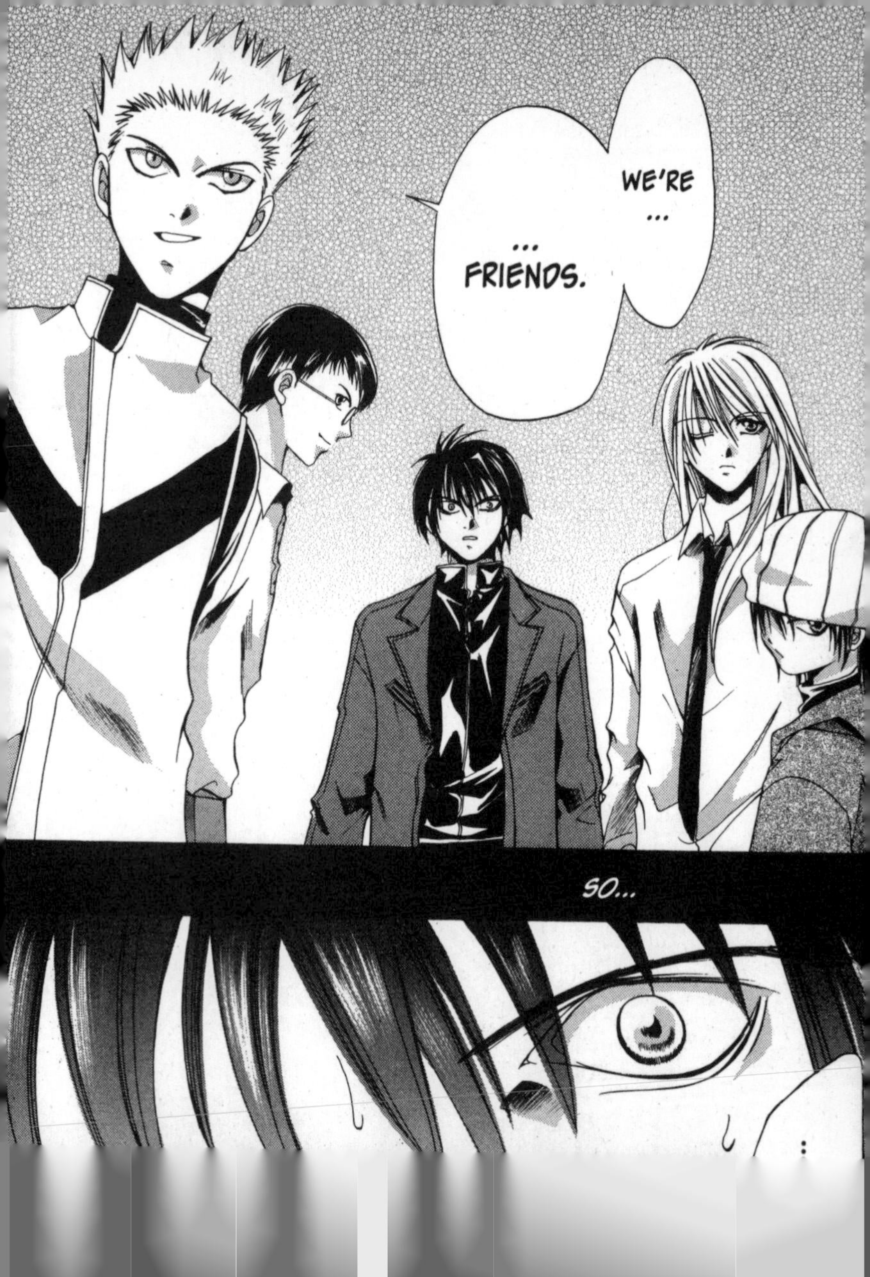
WE'RE ...
... FRIENDS.
SO...

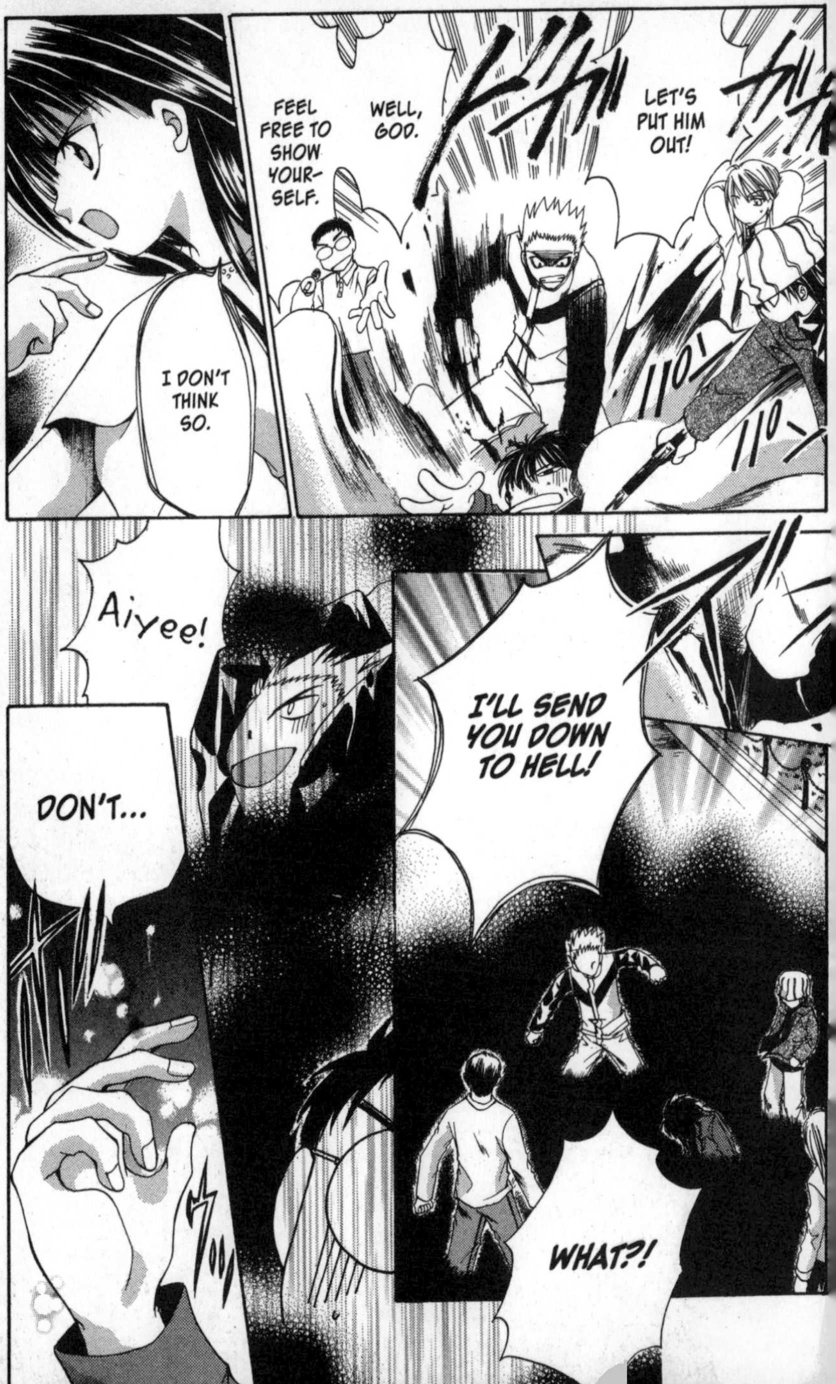
LET'S PUT HIM OUT!
WELL, GOD.
FEEL FREE TO SHOW YOUR-SELF.
I DON'T THINK SO.
I'LL SEND YOU DOWN TO HELL!
WHAT?!
Aiyee!
DON'T...

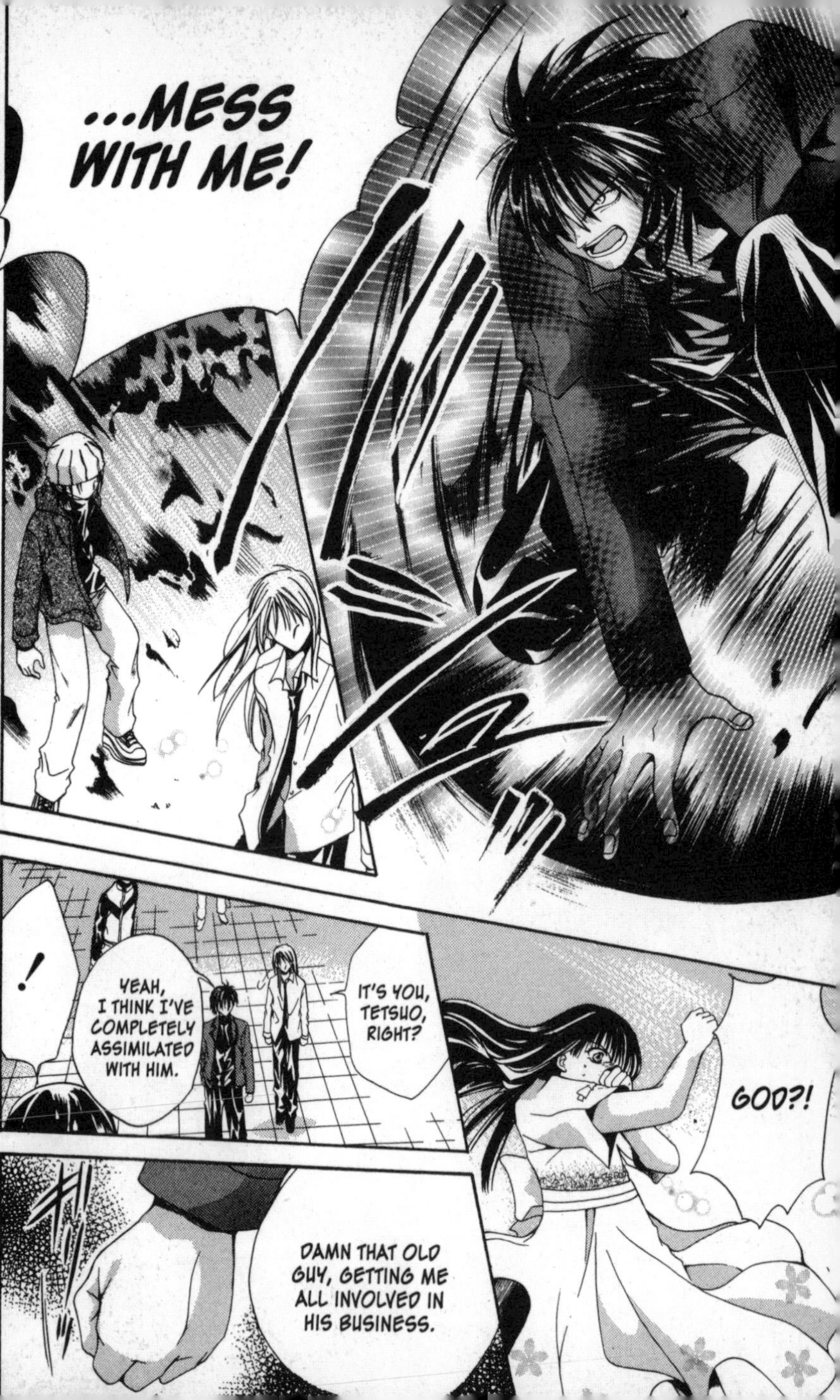
...MESS WITH ME!
GOD?!
IT'S YOU, TETSUO, RIGHT?
YEAH, I THINK I'VE COMPLETELY ASSIMILATED WITH HIM.
!
DAMN THAT OLD GUY, GETTING ME ALL INVOLVED IN HIS BUSINESS.

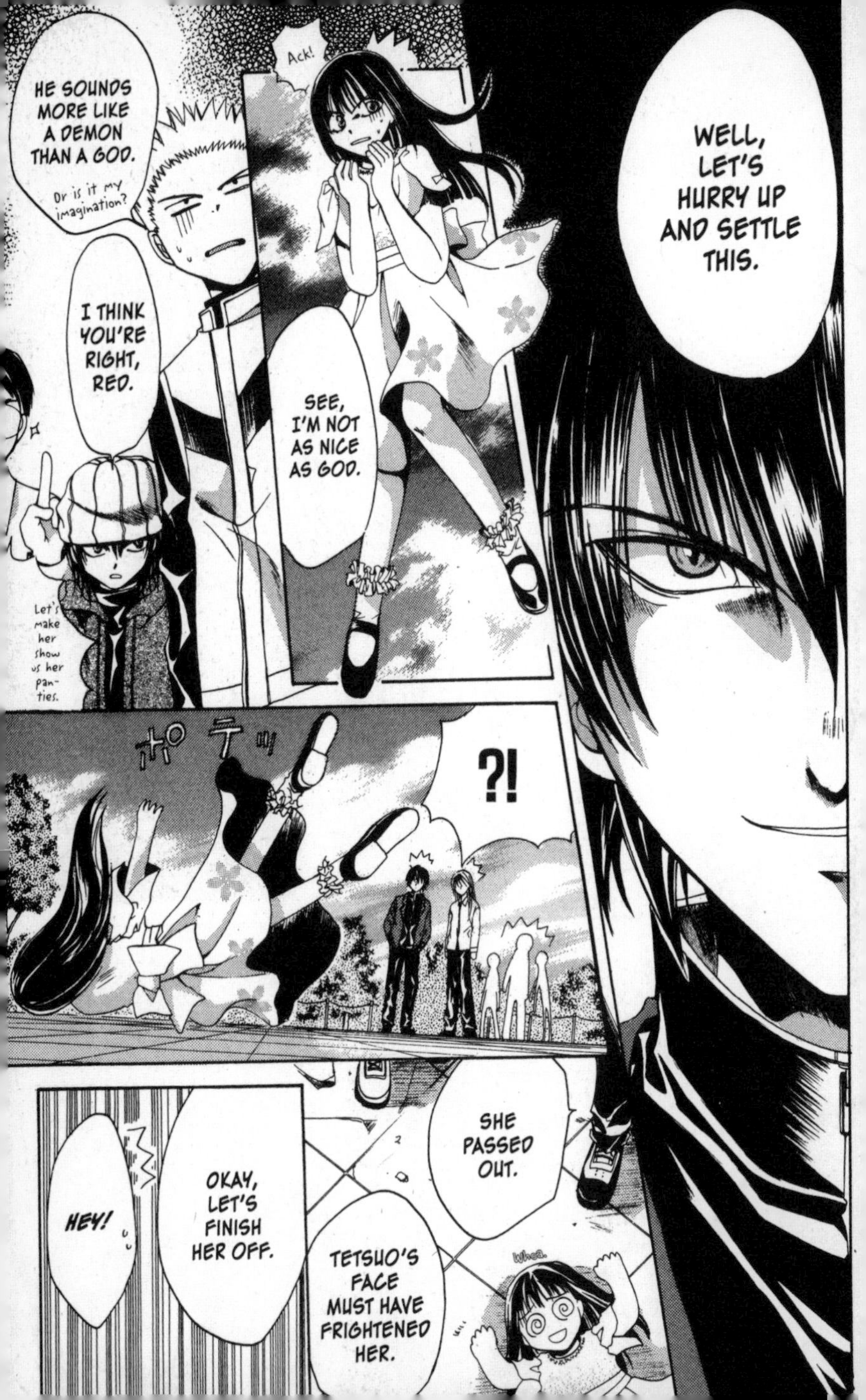
WELL, LET'S HURRY UP AND SETTLE THIS.
Ack!
SEE, I'M NOT AS NICE AS GOD.
HE SOUNDS MORE LIKE A DEMON THAN A GOD.
Or is it my imagination?
I THINK YOU'RE RIGHT, RED.
Let's make her show us her panties.
?!
SHE PASSED OUT.
TETSUO'S FACE MUST HAVE FRIGHTENED HER.
Whoa.
OKAY, LET'S FINISH HER OFF.
HEY!

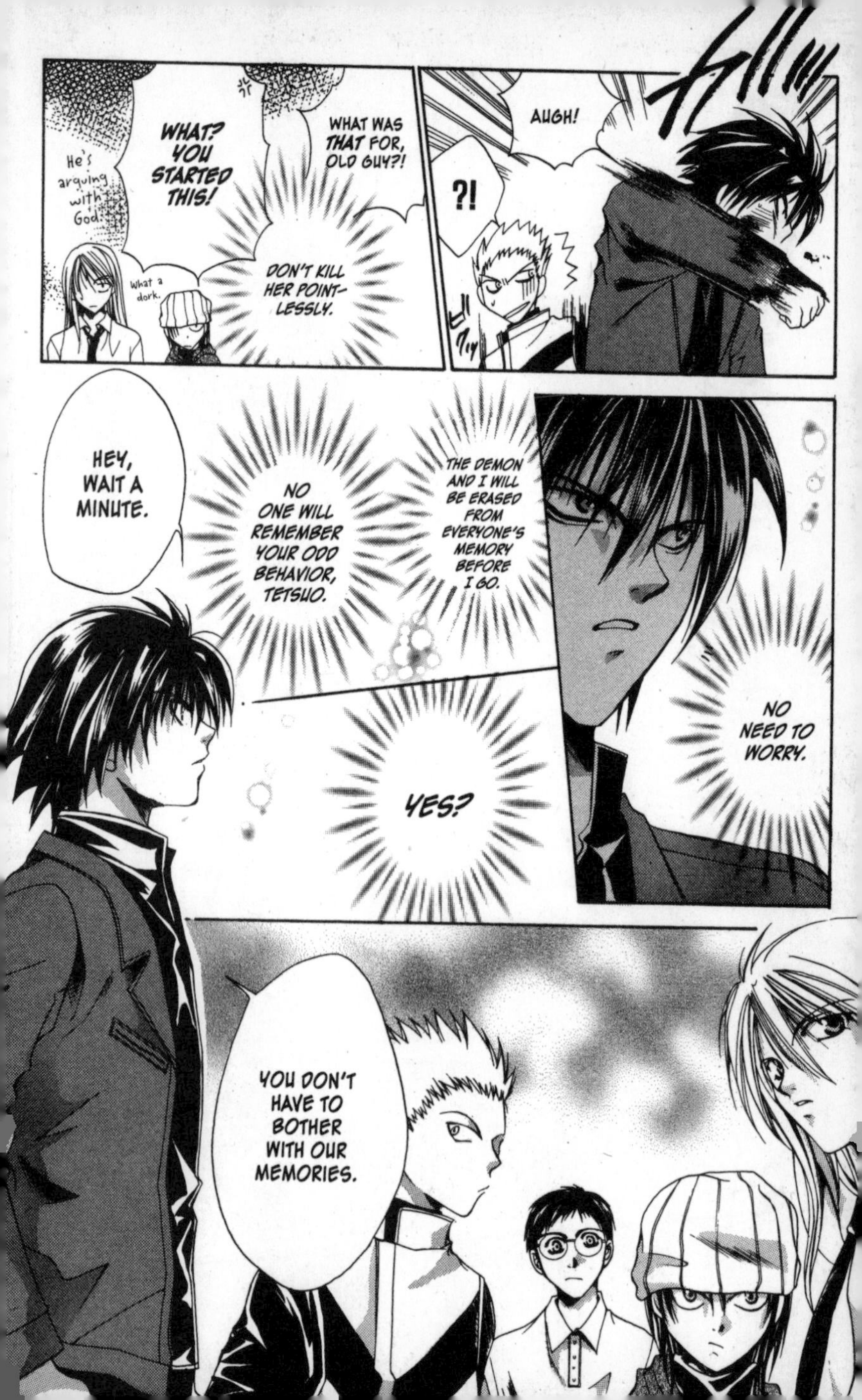
AUGH!
?!
WHAT WAS THAT FOR, OLD GUY?!
DON'T KILL HER POINTLESSLY.
WHAT? YOU STARTED THIS!
He's arguing with God.
What a dork.
NO NEED TO WORRY.
THE DEMON AND I WILL BE ERASED FROM EVERYONE'S MEMORY BEFORE I GO.
NO ONE WILL REMEMBER YOUR ODD BEHAVIOR, TETSUO.
HEY, WAIT A MINUTE.
YES?
YOU DON'T HAVE TO BOTHER WITH OUR MEMORIES.

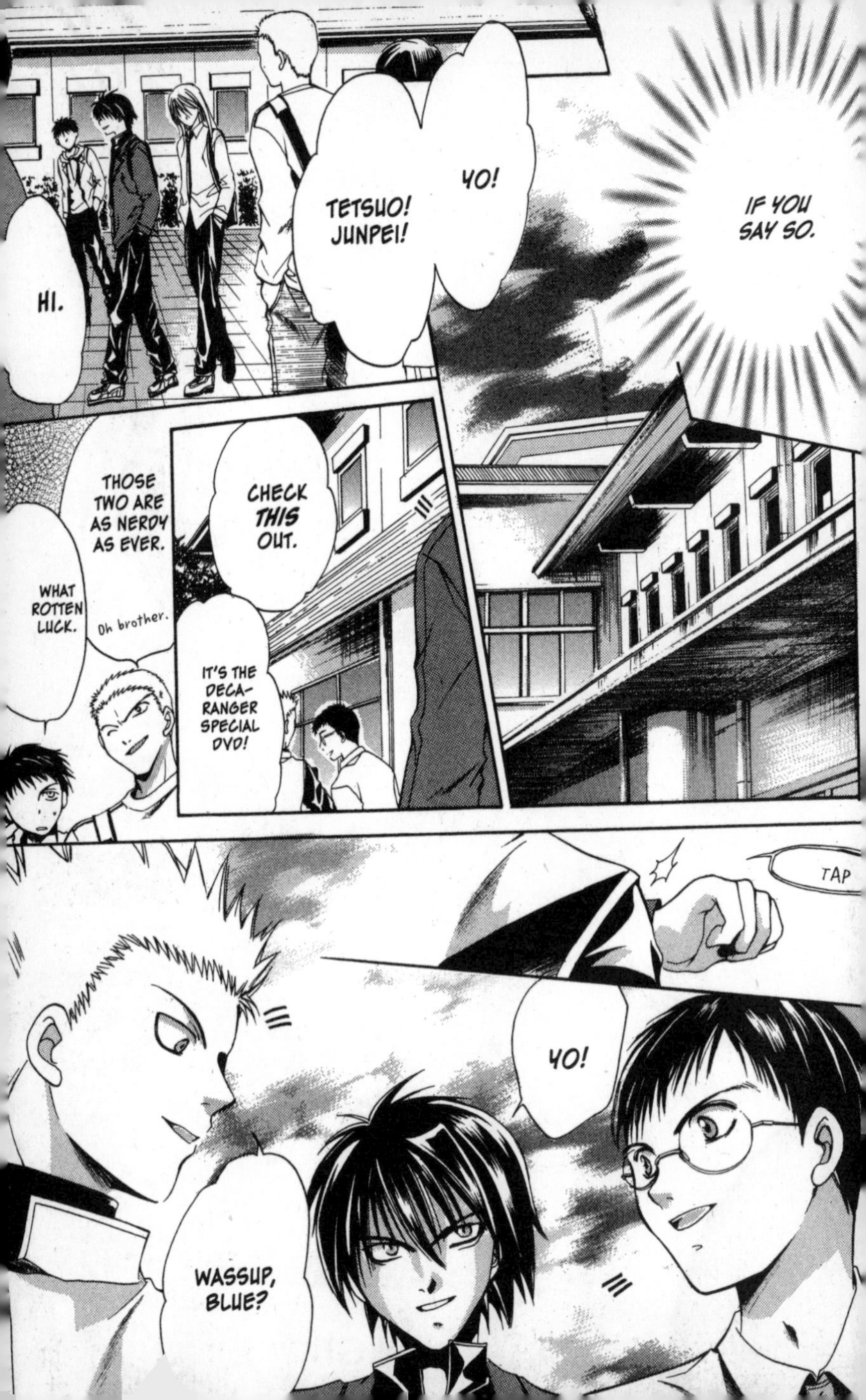
IF YOU SAY SO.
YO!
TETSUO! JUNPEI!
HI.
CHECK THIS OUT.
IT'S THE DECA-RANGER SPECIAL DVD!
THOSE TWO ARE AS NERDY AS EVER.
Oh brother.
WHAT ROTTEN LUCK.
TAP
YO!
WASSUP, BLUE?

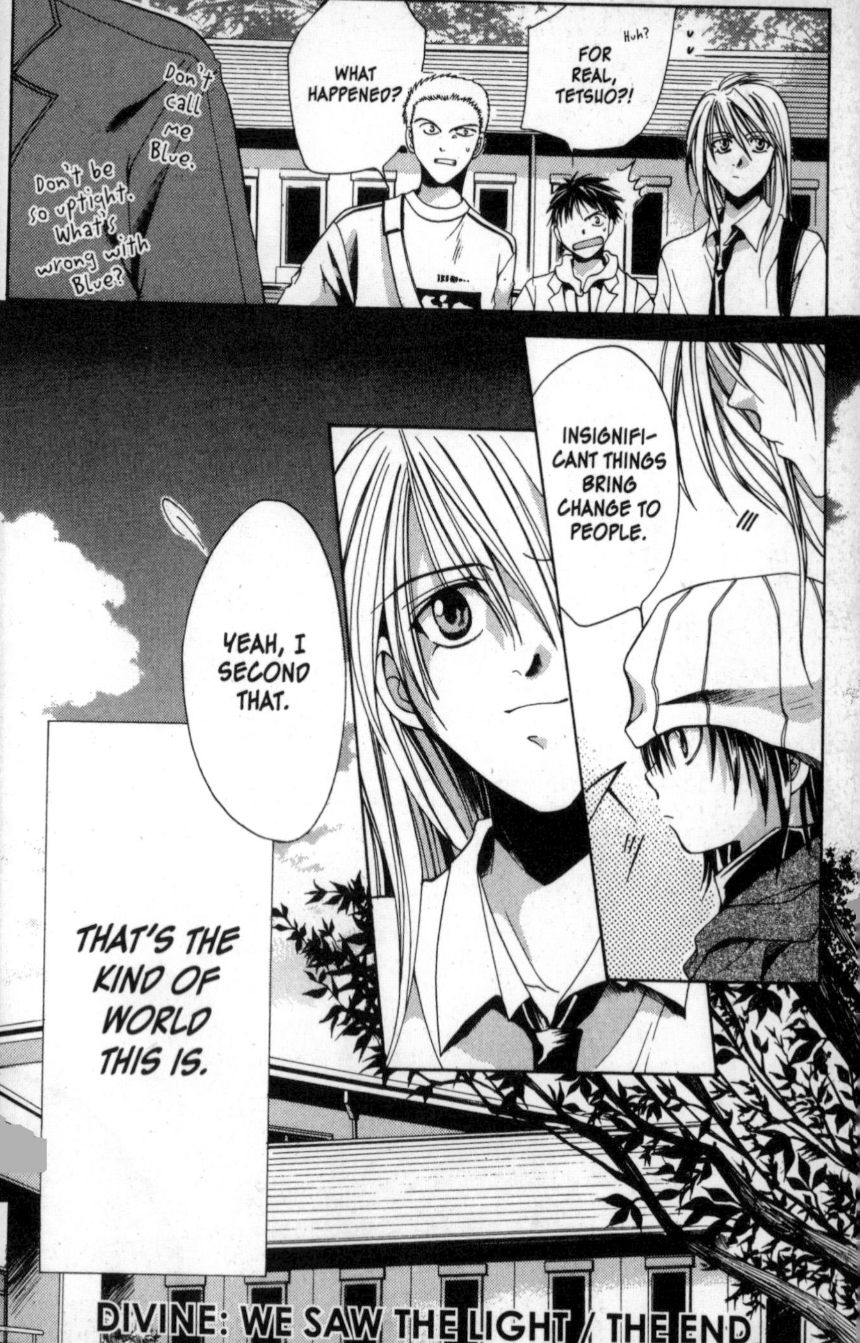
Huh?
FOR REAL, TETSUO?!
WHAT HAPPENED?
Don't call me Blue.
Don't be so uptight. What's wrong with Blue?
INSIGNIFICANT THINGS BRING CHANGE TO PEOPLE.
YEAH, I SECOND THAT.
THAT'S THE KIND OF WORLD THIS IS.
DIVINE: WE SAW THE LIGHT / THE END

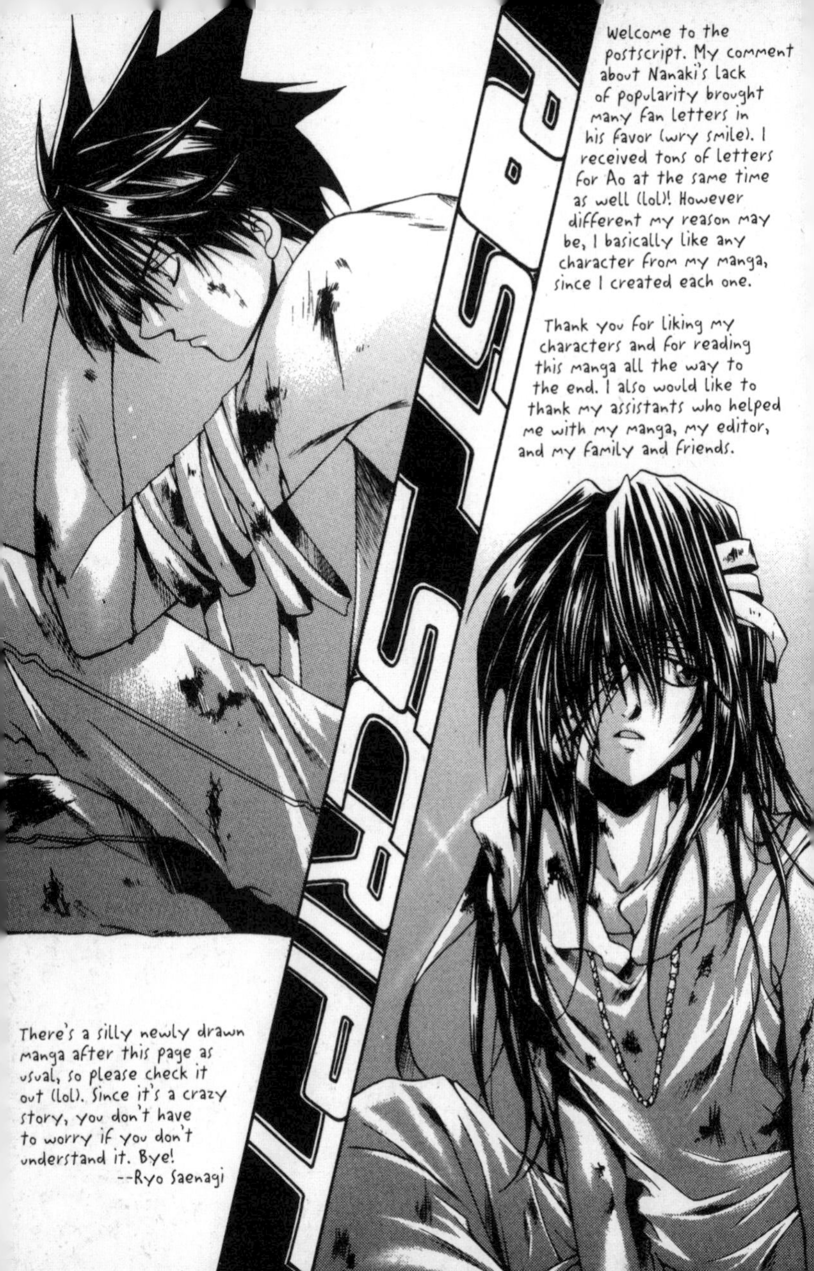
POSTSCRIPT

Welcome to the postscript. My comment about Nanaki's lack of popularity brought many fan letters in his favor (wry smile). I received tons of letters for Ao at the same time as well (lol)! However different my reason may be, I basically like any character from my manga, since I created each one.

Thank you for liking my characters and for reading this manga all the way to the end. I also would like to thank my assistants who helped me with my manga, my editor, and my family and friends.

There's a silly newly drawn manga after this page as usual, so please check it out (lol). Since it's a crazy story, you don't have to worry if you don't understand it. Bye!

--Ryo Saenagi

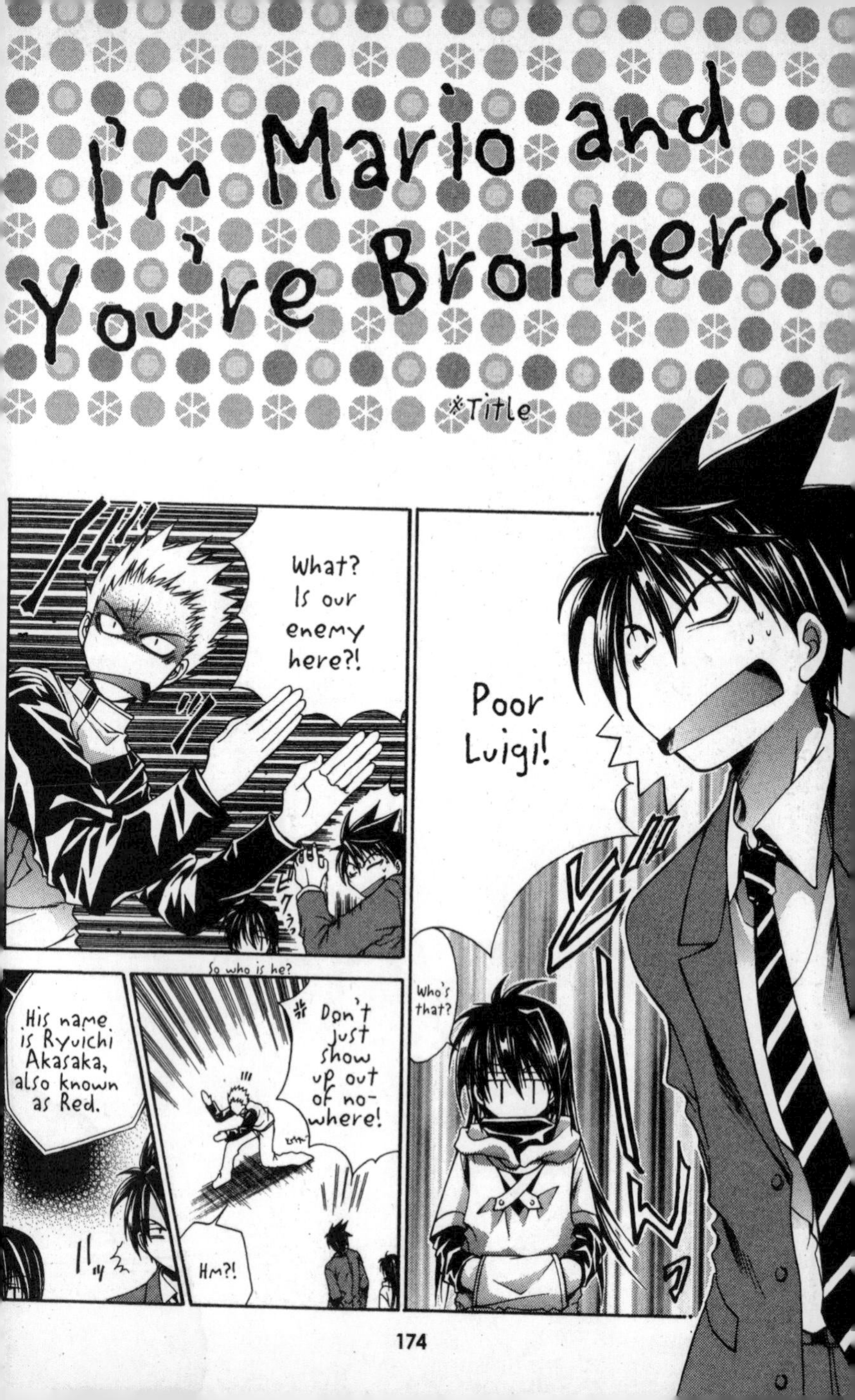
I'm Mario and You're Brothers!
※Title
Poor Luigi!
Who's that?
What? Is our enemy here?!
So who is he?
Don't just show up out of nowhere!
Hm?!
His name is Ryuichi Akasaka, also known as Red.

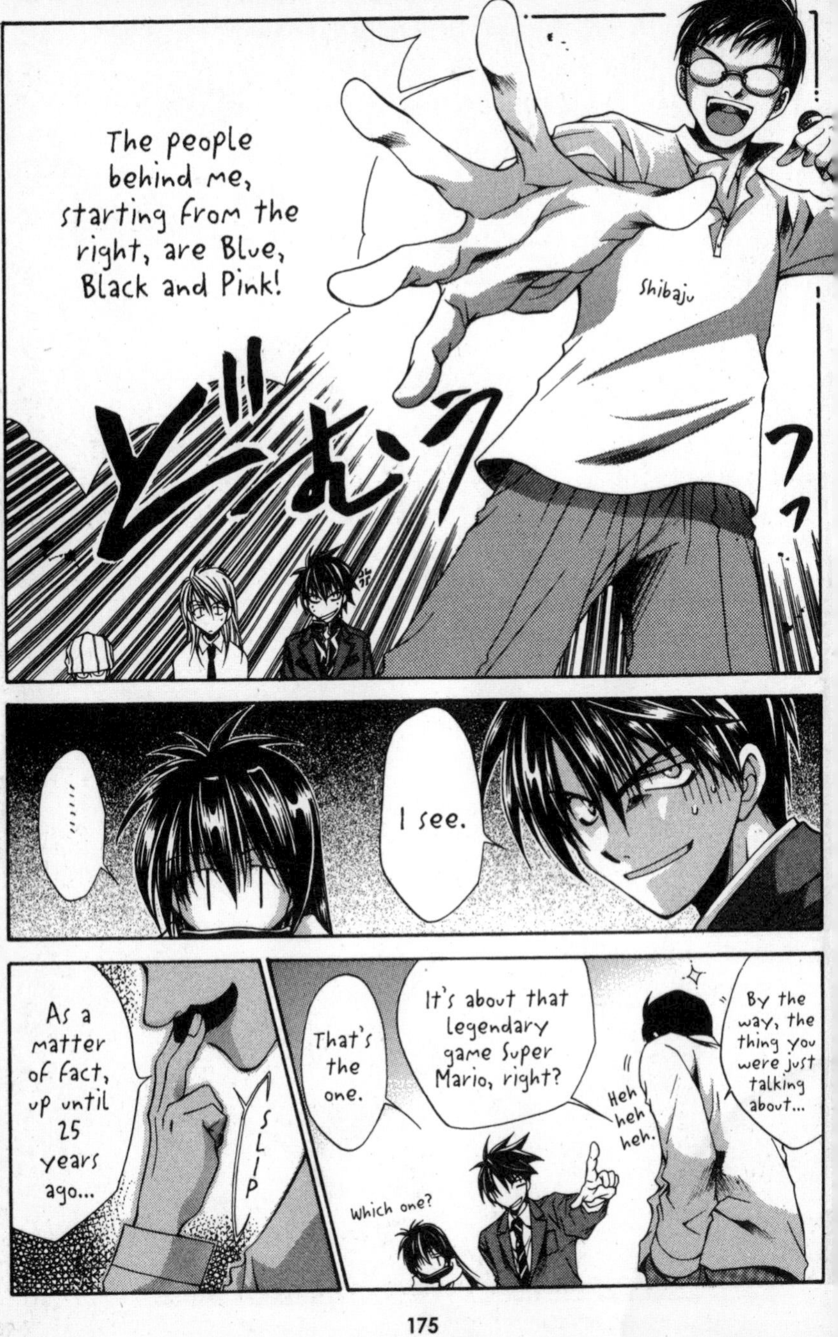
The people behind me, starting from the right, are Blue, Black and Pink!
Shibaju
I see.
......
By the way, the thing you were just talking about...
Heh heh heh.
It's about that legendary game Super Mario, right?
That's the one.
Which one?
SLIP
As a matter of fact, up until 25 years ago...

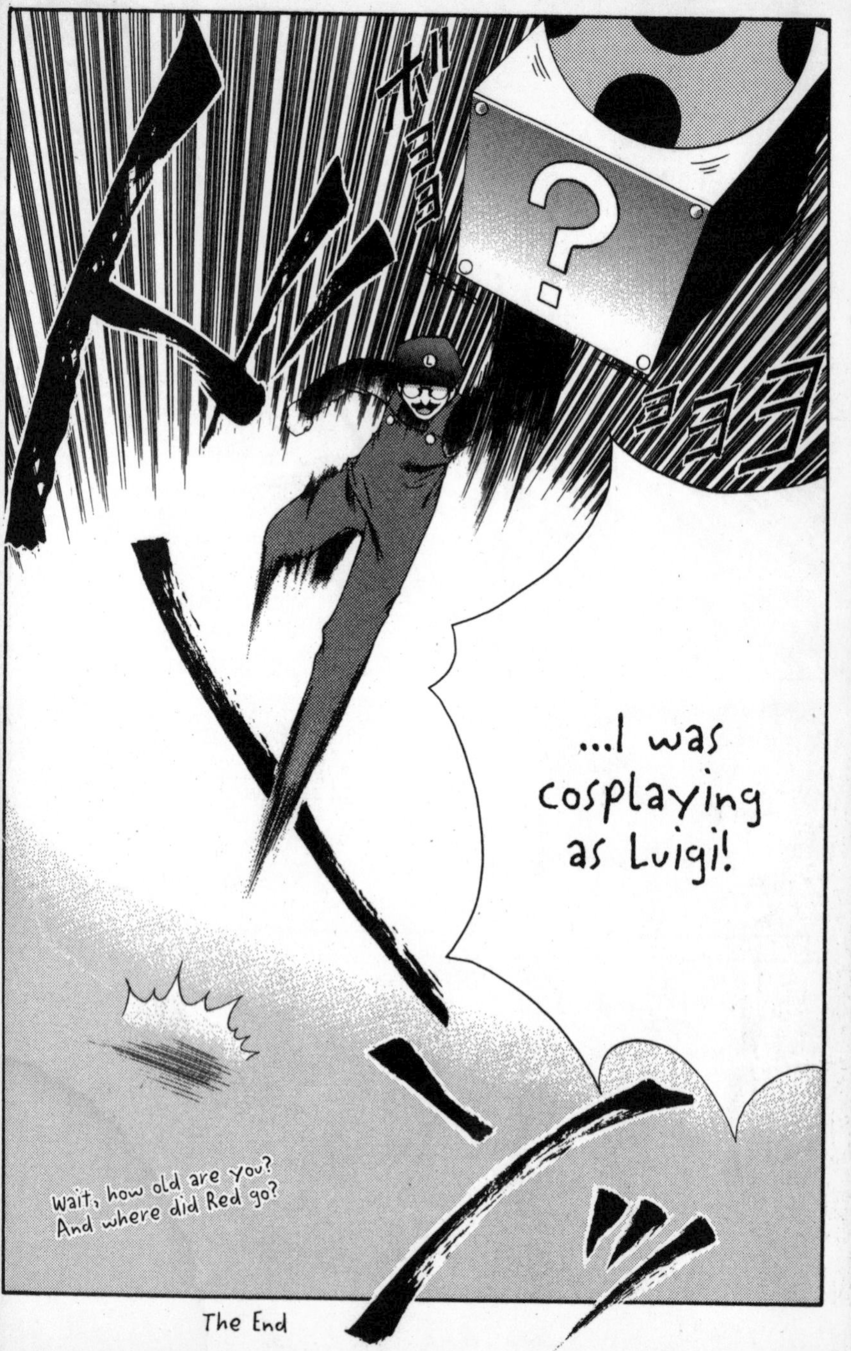
...I was cosplaying as Luigi!
Wait, how old are you? And where did Red go?

The End

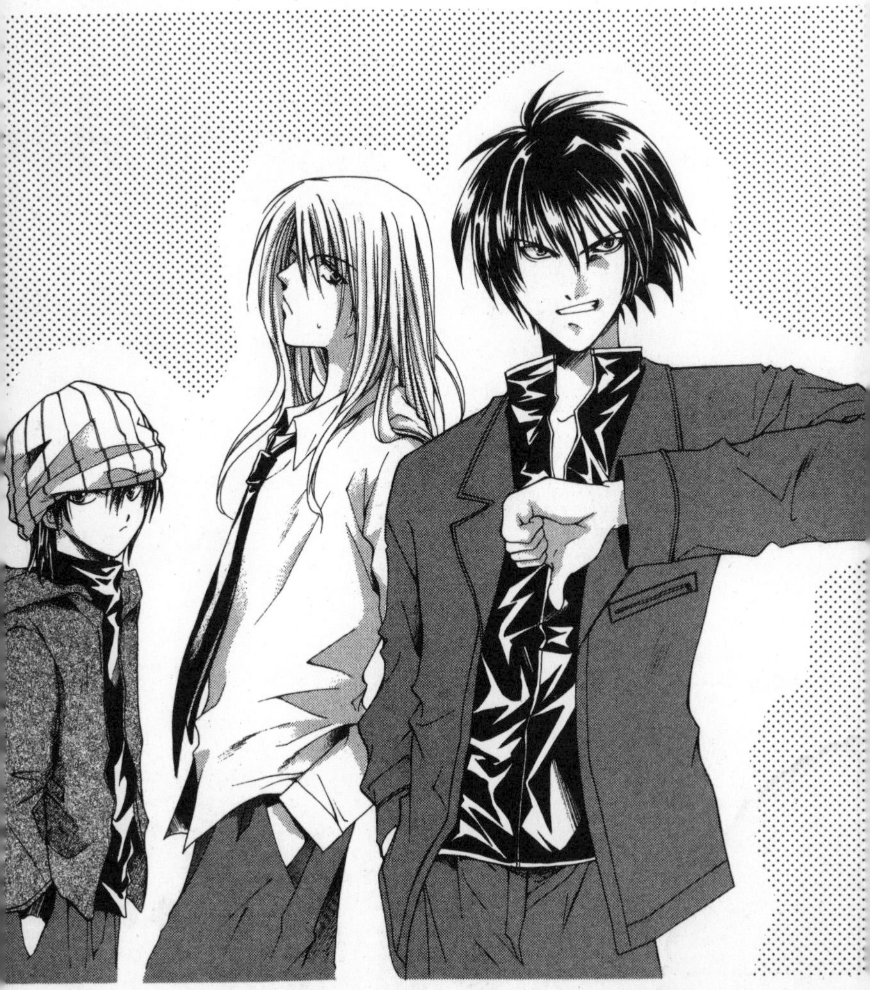

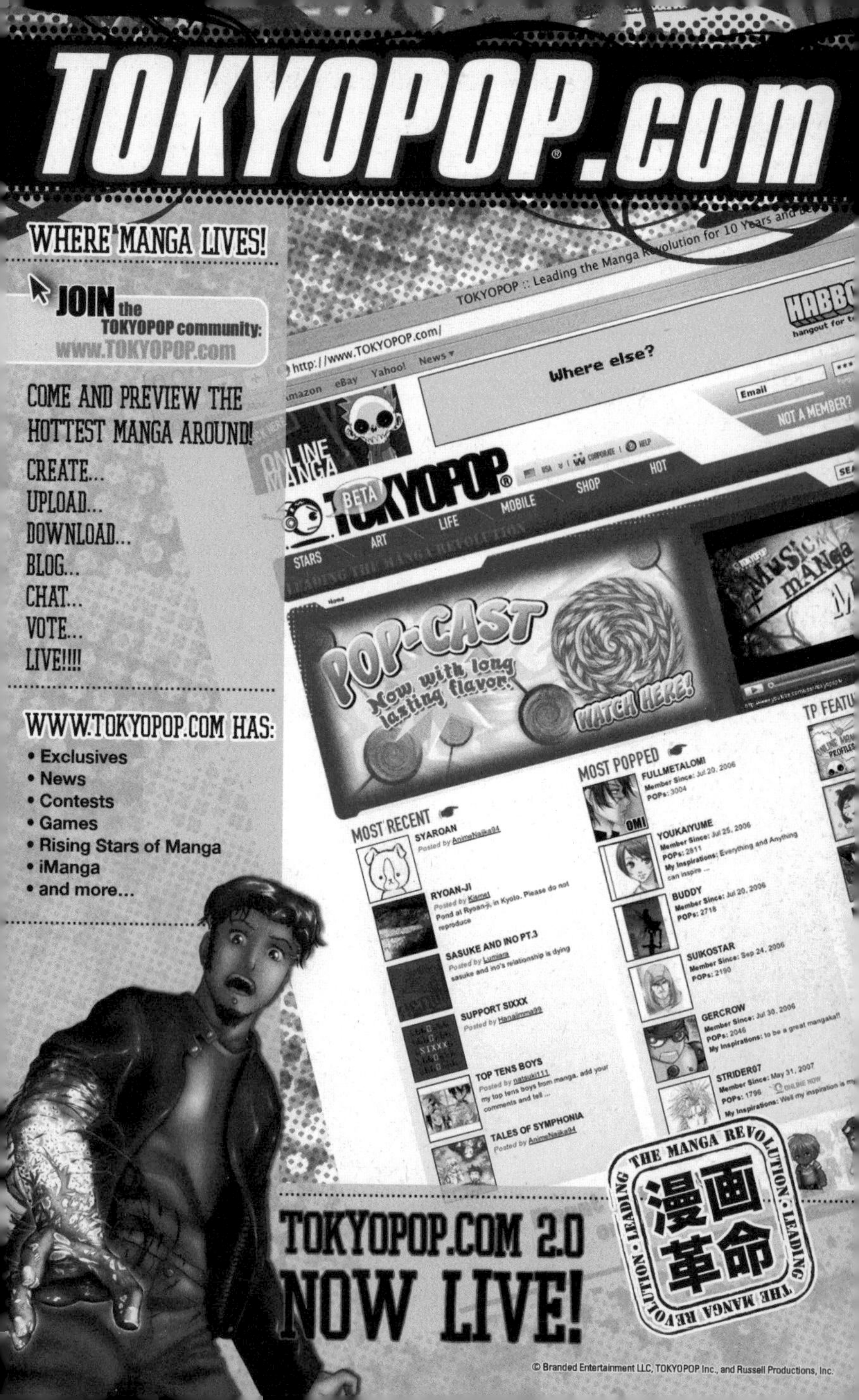
TOKYOPOP®.com
WHERE MANGA LIVES!
JOIN the TOKYOPOP community: www.TOKYOPOP.com
COME AND PREVIEW THE HOTTEST MANGA AROUND!
CREATE...
UPLOAD...
DOWNLOAD...
BLOG...
CHAT...
VOTE...
LIVE!!!!
WWW.TOKYOPOP.COM HAS:
• Exclusives
• News
• Contests
• Games
• Rising Stars of Manga
• iManga
• and more...
TOKYOPOP :: Leading the Manga Revolution for 10 Years and Beyond
http://www.TOKYOPOP.com/
Where else?
TOKYOPOP®
STARS
ART
LIFE
MOBILE
SHOP
HOT
POP-CAST
Now with long lasting flavor
WATCH HERE!
MOST RECENT
MOST POPPED
TOKYOPOP.COM 2.0
NOW LIVE!
THE MANGA REVOLUTION · LEADING THE MANGA REVOLUTION · LEADING
漫画革命
© Branded Entertainment LLC, TOKYOPOP Inc., and Russell Productions, Inc.

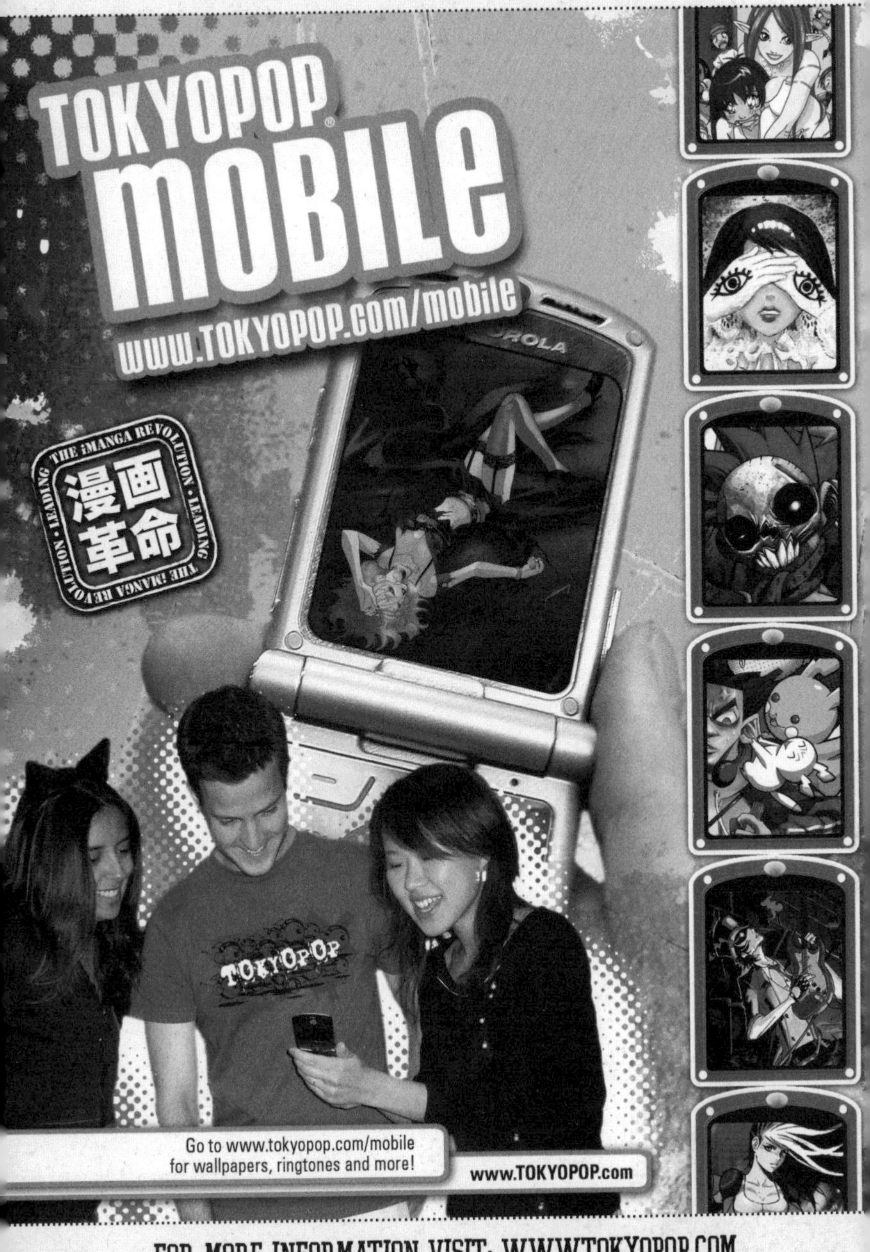
TOKYOPOP®
MOBILE
www.TOKYOPOP.com/mobile
THE iMANGA REVOLUTION · LEADING THE iMANGA REVOLUTION · LEADING
漫画
革命
Go to www.tokyopop.com/mobile
for wallpapers, ringtones and more!
www.TOKYOPOP.com

FOR MORE INFORMATION VISIT: WWW.TOKYOPOP.COM

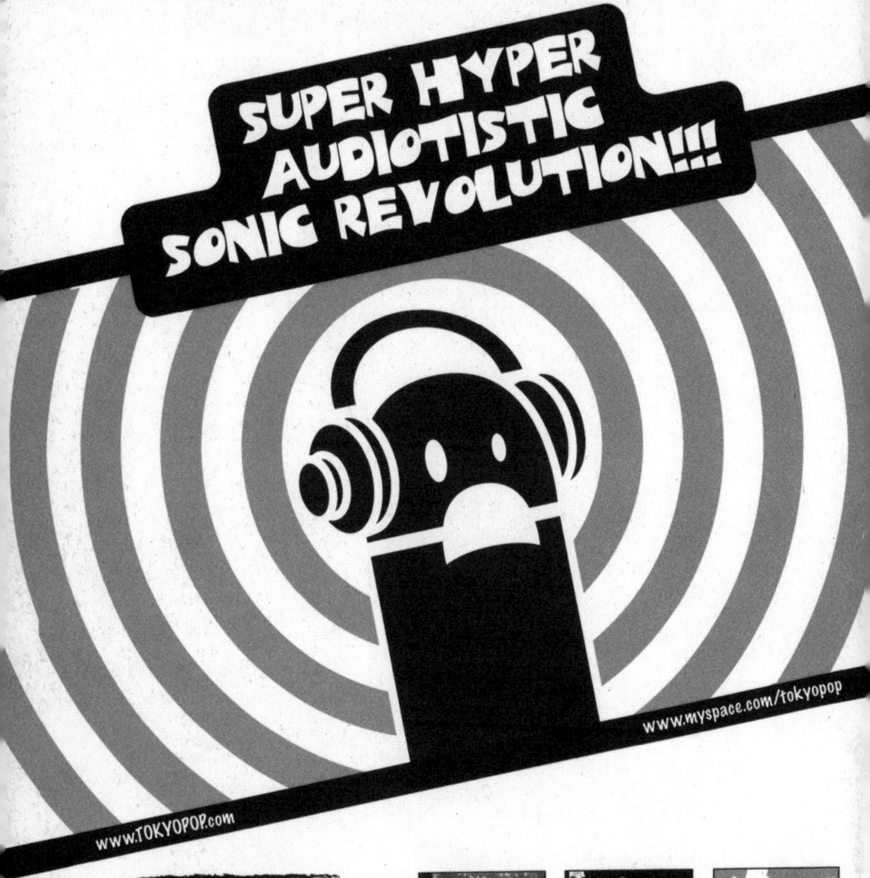
SUPER HYPER
AUDIOTISTIC
SONIC REVOLUTION!!!
www.myspace.com/tokyopop
www.TOKYOPOP.com

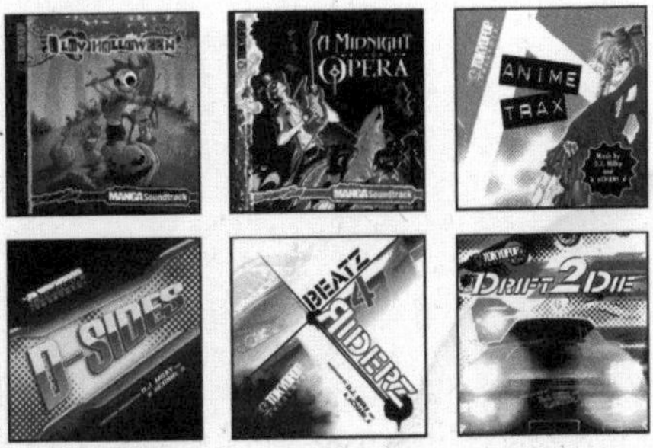
A MIDNIGHT OPERA
MANGA Soundtrack
ANIME TRAX
D-SIDES
BEATZ 4 RIDERZ
DRIFT 2 DIE

that I'm not like other people...

Dear Diary,
I'm starting to feel

When a young girl moves to the forgotten town of Bizenghast, she uncovers a terrifying collection of lost souls that leads her to the brink of insanity. One thing becomes painfully clear: The residents of Bizenghast are just dying to come home.

ART SUBJECT TO CHANGE © Mary Alice LeGrow and TOKYOPOP Inc.

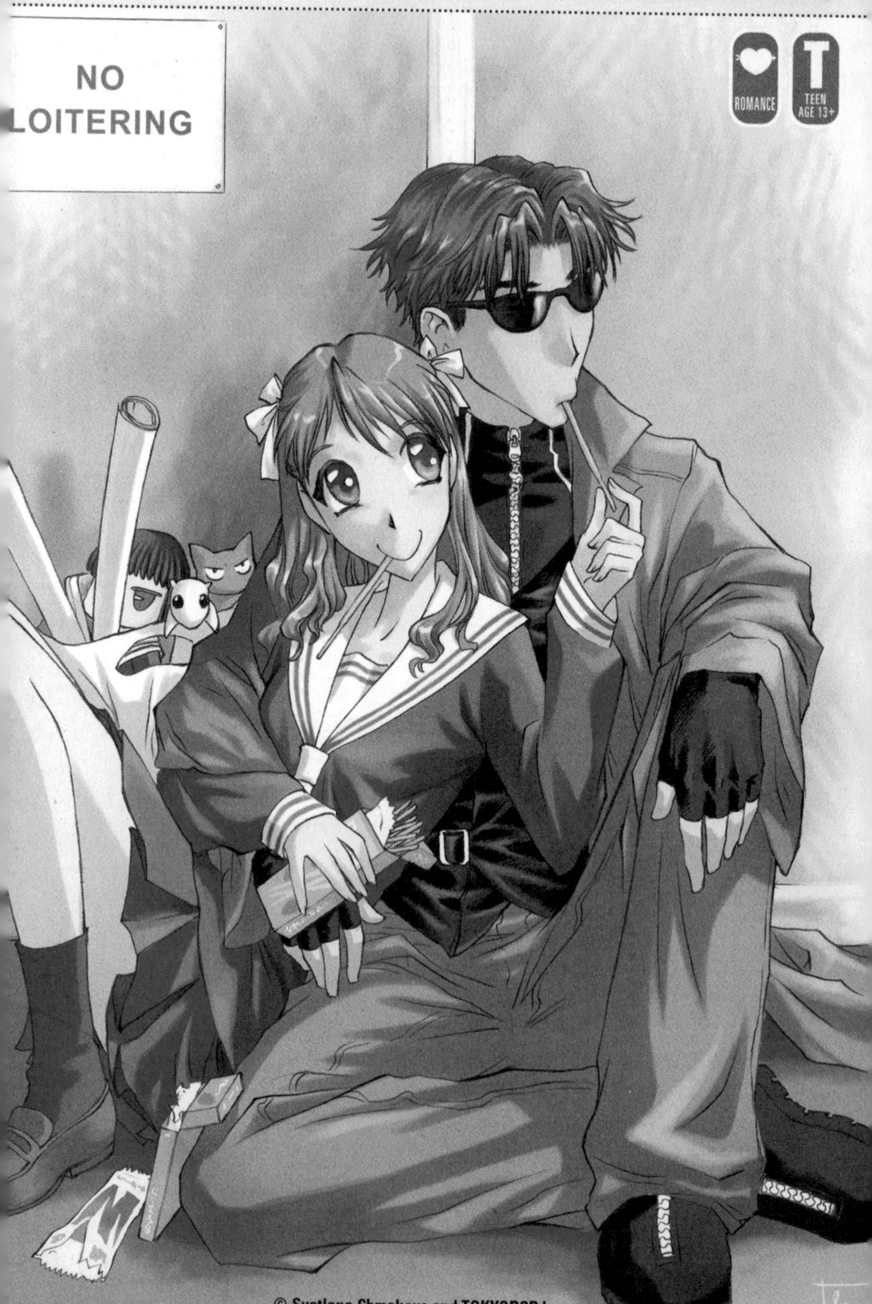
NO
LOITERING
ROMANCE
T
TEEN
AGE 13+

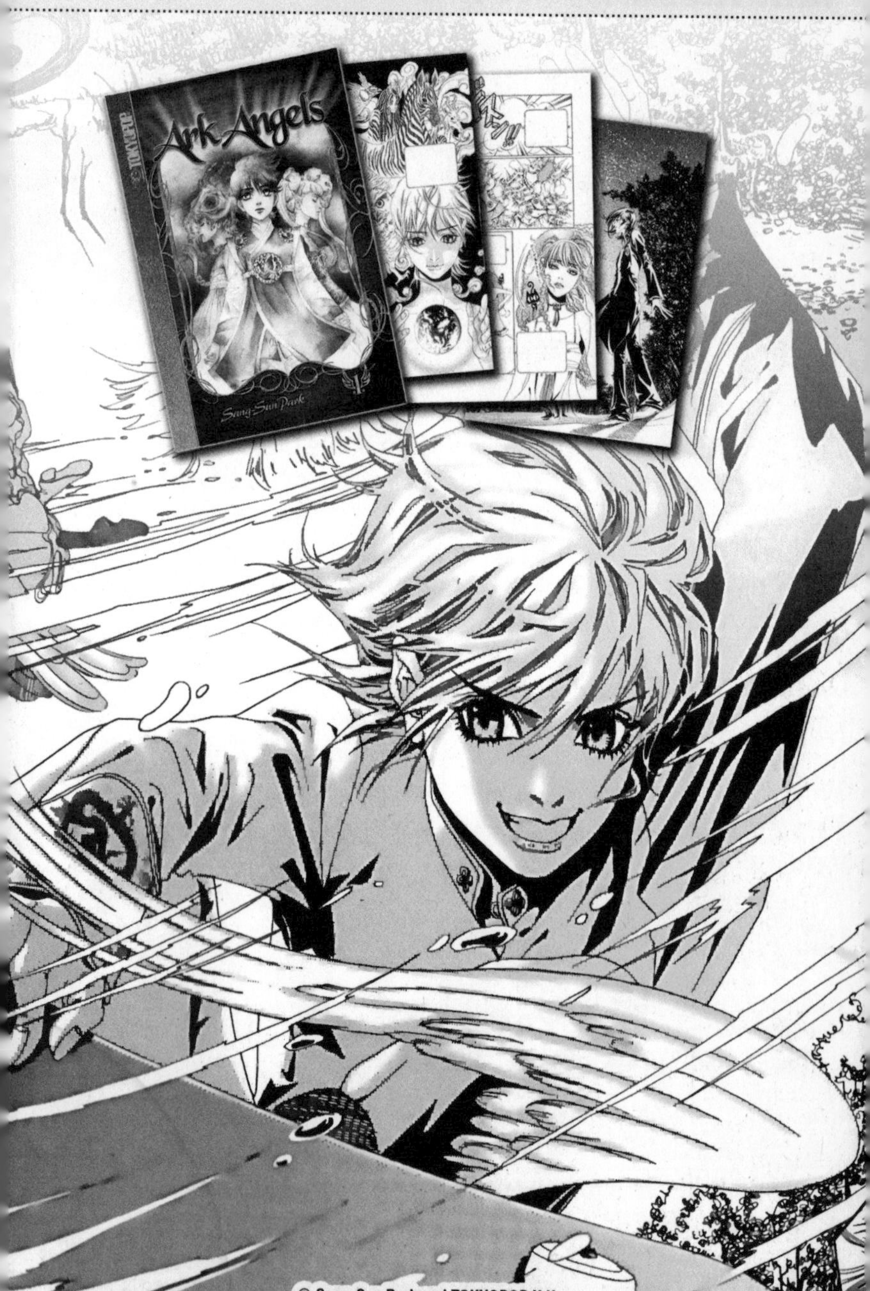
TOKYOPOP
Ark Angels
1
Sang-Sun Park

Ark Angels ™

Girls just wanna have fun— while saving the world.

From a small lake nestled in a secluded forest far from the edge of town, something strange has emerged: Three young girls— Shem, Hamu and Japheth—who are sisters from another world. Equipped with magical powers, they are charged with saving all the creatures of Earth from extinction. However, there is someone or something sinister trying to stop them. And on top of trying to save our world, these sisters have to live like normal human girls: They go to school, work at a flower shop, hang out with friends and even fall in love!

FROM THE CREATOR OF THE TAROT CAFÉ!

T
TEEN
AGE 13+

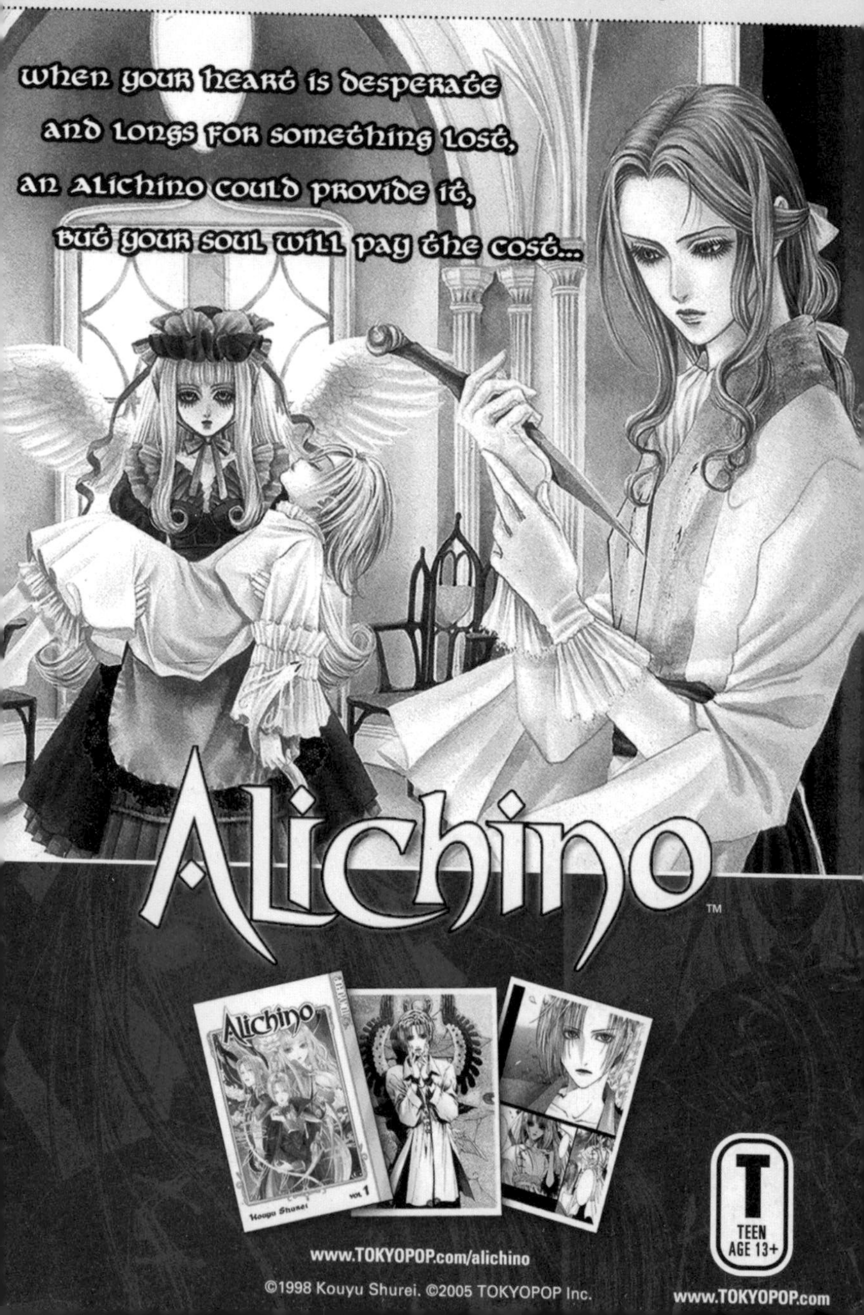
When your heart is desperate
and longs for something lost,
an Alichino could provide it,
but your soul will pay the cost...
Alichino™
Alichino
Kouyu Shurei
VOL 1
T
TEEN
AGE 13+
www.TOKYOPOP.com/alichino
©1998 Kouyu Shurei. ©2005 TOKYOPOP Inc.
www.TOKYOPOP.com

STOP!

This is the back of the book.
You wouldn't want to spoil a great ending!

This book is printed "manga-style," in the authentic Japanese right-to-left format. Since none of the artwork has been flipped or altered, readers get to experience the story just as the creator intended. You've been asking for it, so TOKYOPOP® delivered: authentic, hot-off-the-press, and far more fun!

DIRECTIONS

If this is your first time reading manga-style, here's a quick guide to help you understand how it works.

It's easy... just start in the top right panel and follow the numbers. Have fun, and look for more 100% authentic manga from TOKYOPOP®!

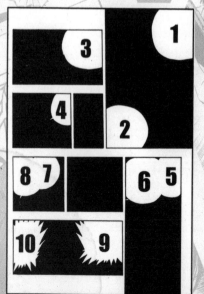